# FALCON DAGGER

## CHRONICLE III

Azalea Dabill

Dynamos Press
Coeur D' Alene, Idaho

azaleadabill@yahoo.com
Azalea Dabill/Dynamos Press, LLC
Coeur D' Alene, Idaho
www.azaleadabill.com



Book Layout ©2015 BookDesignTemplates.com, Crimson 6x9, Cover Designer Derek Murphy of Creativindie, Editing and Marketing Alena Orrison and Emily Moore of Spirited Ink LLP



Keywords: Fantasy historical romance, alternate history military fiction, good fantasy series, Martial art fantasy, boys christian adventure books, christian adventure for girls, Korean fiction books, Noblebright young adult fantasy, Exotic lands Brittania, Korea, Arabia, Clean YA fantasy, Multicultural travel, Fight for right, Friendship Fiction, God, Christian Supernatural thread, Found family, Tales of courage, Noble sacrifice, Strong heroine or strong hero, Save the kingdom, Clean Christian novel, Non-magical book series, Martial art and self-defense, TaeKwonDo books, Teen and young adult good read, PG-13 violence and G romance. Fantasy literature for children and young adults, Good vs. Evil, Family friendly.

LCCN: 2024926917, Falcon Dagger Chronicle III/ Azalea Dabill. -- 1st ed.
ISBN 978-1-943034-22-2

# Contents

Preface .......... 1
Kingdom's Fall~Prologue .......... 5
Old Danger .......... 9
Sword Call .......... 21
Brother Band .......... 33
Rival Unbound .......... 43
Deep Deceit .......... 55
Torch Point .......... 73
Dark Deed .......... 83
Poisonous Fruit .......... 93
Bitter Witness .......... 105
New Traitor .......... 117
Broken Oath .......... 133
Infernal Weapon .......... 147
Brigand Betwixt .......... 159
Brother Found .......... 173
Final Foe .......... 187
Falcon Dagger~Prologue .......... 201
Falcon Dagger .......... 203
Rival's Oath .......... 217
Friend and Foe .......... 227
Counter and Coil .......... 241
Court's Call .......... 257
Gambit's End .......... 269

Harry and Hunt....283
Armsman's Trial....299
Letter and Land....311
Armsman's Trust....325
Pierce and Protect....335
Treachery's Truth....347
Breath and Bone....359
Cieri's Daughter~Rival....373
Cieri's Daughter~Revolt....395
The Warrior - 1....411
The Path - 2....425
Other Books 1....445
Other Books 2....447
Other Books 2.5....448
Falcon's Ode....449
Fantastic Journey....450
Story Chat....451
Readers....453
Glossary....454
About the Author....463
Acknowledgements....464

## What Readers Say

IV

Recommended for YA readers and fans of tales of romance and adventure with strong female characters and inspirational messages. It gave a feel of ancient or early Medieval Britain but in a Historical Fantasy setting...

What's not to love! – English Lady

This book takes place around 800 A.D., spans continents from the British Isles to Korea, and is full of war and adventure and human nature. ... I like how the main character in all of the sections has to make hard choices, but also learns from them, and in the end, draws closer to God. – Ami

It definitely has the feel of another time with a focus on faith, loyalty, and honor... While this book is not normally in the genres I typically lean toward, I did appreciate all the details that made the story world epic in scope, and that the good characters were truly good. – Christina

Action, adventure and intrigue in the medieval times. An enjoyable conclusion to the Falcon Chronicles. – Marlene Rempel

This is an amazing chronicle based in the Middle Ages! It is always twisting and turning! I would recommend to anyone who likes adventure or historical fiction! – Candace

V

*To George, Melissa, and their children Elizabeth, Matthew, Hannah, and Sarah.*

*This book is dedicated to you.*

VI

## The Falcon Chronicles

Falcon Heart Chronicle I

Falcon Flight Chronicle II

Falcon Dagger Chronicle III

Lance and Qull - A Novella

Falcon's Ode - Poetry Companion

**Suggested Reading Order**

*Falcon Dagger* Two Prequels

*Falcon Heart* A Novel

*Falcon Flight* A Novel

*Lance and Quill* A Novella

*Falcon Dagger* Two Novels (and Two Prequels)

*Fantastic Journey: The Soul of Speculative Fiction and Fantasy Adventure*

VII

# Preface

This clean Noblebright fantasy series is a work of fiction and is not meant to be a historically accurate account. Rather, the Falcon Chronicle is a historical fantasy of what may have been somewhere, sometime in early Britannia, Araby, and Asia in the Land of the Morning Calm.

Years ago, I began to write the account of the Chronicle. This story collection titled *Falcon Dagger Chronicle III* contains *Kingdom's Fall, Falcon Dagger, Cieri's Daughter,* and *Path of the Warrior.*

*Kingdom's Fall* ties into *Falcon Flight,* setting the stage for *Falcon Dagger* the last novel in the series. *Cieri's Daughter* is a prequel that introduces Kyrin and her first victory and the seeds of early conflict in Britannia. I included the prequel *Path of the Warrior* at the end of this story collection in honor of my Grandmaster, Tae Hong Choi. It is also in honor of Grandmaster Vince Church, my martial arts Master in Ji Do Kwan Tae Kwon Do. I deeply respect and honor them both, though they have passed from this world.

I miss Master Church very much. He was a kind, wise, and godly man in many ways who taught me far more than kicking and punching. He taught me how to live with tenacious courage. And who is not in need of courage in this life?

My interest in the Korean martial art throughout this book series began under Master Church, who later became a Grandmaster. My fascination with martial art naturally extended to the Korean Choson culture, especially in that time around the Silla dynasty when Subak, or early Tae Kwon Do, is thought to have begun.

I gained most of my formal knowledge of early Korea and its written history of martial skill, or Mu-sool, from *5,000 Years of Korean Martial Arts,* by R. Barry Harmon, and *A Killing Art,* by Alex Gillis. The Korean names in the story came primarily from Sherrilyn Kenyon's *Character Naming Sourcebook,* second edition. I did extensive research on the other lands in the series as well, including Arabia, the surrounding area, and Britain.

I used the English naming system in my first books to avoid confusing readers who, like myself, are unfamiliar with the Korean naming system, where the surname comes before the given name. I also took poetic liberties.

But in the present revision of *Path of the Warrior* as part of this companion book, *Falcon Dagger Chronicle III,* I wish to express my deep respect for the Korean people by using the name order they are familiar with in this tale, set in the land that birthed Ryu Tae-shin.

I have transcribed Alaina Ilen's notes on Tae-shin, who was exiled for a crime he did not commit but kept his honor and saved his people. After he was enslaved, he came to be known as Tae Chisun, given that name by his captor before he won his freedom.

Please forgive any mistakes, which are my own. I hope you enjoy this portrayal of the honor, beauty, and courage of different cultures and countries, including the Choson culture and the people of the Land of the Morning Calm.

*Pil-sung!* Certain victory through courage, strength, and indomitable spirit.

Azalea Dabill
November 30, 2024

Crossover - Find the Eternal, the Adventure

# Kingdom's Fall~Prologue

*Familiar human frailties—a lie, betrayal, and oath-breaking.*

*It began with a small lie, as men call it. That a man can craft his own destiny. Planted by lords pursuing wealth and power by unlawful means, the destructive seed grew in the fertile belief that no oath among men is worth an alliance that heralds betterment. It bloomed in the betrayal of a brother's hope.*

*So the lie waxed by sinuous, deadly, hidden ways to bring about a kingdom's fall.*

*Until one man refused the lie.*

*—Alaina Ilen, consort and scribe to Prince Faisal Ben Salin.*

Thain Mornoth stared out from a stone embrasure of his uncle's stronghold, a forgotten horn of mead in his hand. Banished from the king's court, was he?

The wooden shutters were flung back to their furthest extent, letting a paling sun and a wandering, chilly breeze in the window, carrying the sweet musk of fallen oak leaves. Winter was near, near as the Humber River rippling over its unseen bed with its dark dankness coiling in the back of his throat.

There were other paths than the king's favor that the house of Mornoth could pursue. It would lead to acknowledgement of their worth by the northlords, from the ancient north Wall of the Eagles to the Humber River, their southern border. That brown snake of water roughly divided Lord Dain Cieri, leader of the northlords, from his uncle's southern stronghold of Alkborough.

Their only northern ally, Lord Nidfael Keffer, ruled his lands and Keffold stronghold a four-day ride northeast. Thain frowned. If only he was free to take counsel with Nidfael. He could help gain support for the house of Mornoth in the north. The rest of the southlords who claimed Britannia's lands from the Humber to the far south already saw the grandness of their vision.

At the sound of steps, he turned, coughing in annoyance at the mead that spilled over his hand. His brow rose. Ah, a messenger from the bishop of Richmond. "Yes?" The mud coating the man's boots witnessed his five-day ride south from Richmond by fast horse.

"Greetings, my lord, from Bishop Caddaric." The envoy bowed, his voice soft, his movements fluid and precise. "My master bids me reply: though Lord Dain Cieri is of old northern blood, he yet holds the king's ear."

Thain glared at the bishop's voice in the flesh. "Tell me something I don't know, fool!" He spun in a whisper of silk and leather toward the window. Churchmen *were* fools, the lot of them, good for nothing but writing lies and honing whispers. This one was likely a shadow of the cloister. But he must tread cautiously. The church also hired those who would get their hands dirty in its service. He whirled back and growled, "Far more irritating, that cursed upstart thwarted my uncle's counsel before the entire court."

The envoy hesitated.

Thain glanced at the bits of half-dry mud dropped on the floor of newly spread rushes with a baleful eye, then pointedly at the slender envoy. "When Lord Fenwer's puling whelp died, he left Fenwyrd stronghold lord-less. Despite our protest, at the king's own request, Lord Dain Cieri took up Fenwyrd, though it lies on the coast far from his lands and far closer to ours! Now, instead of seven northlords, there are six. Yet the cursed sixth rules two strongholds and speaks with their might behind him."

The envoy bowed again. An unadorned black velvet tunic hung dull and dark across his gaunt shoulders and over his slightly rounded belly, reminding Thain of a crow, fat from slaughter. A slaughter doubtless bought with the bishop's intrigues. Yes, Thain rather thought the man might be one of the church's crows. But here all the power was his.

At last, the man broke his gaze, his mouth insolent. "You may not know *this,* my lord. Whether his people ride the mountains and vales of Cierheld or train about Fenwrd's forests and cliffs, Lord Dain Cieri's strongholds near run themselves. His armsmen are unsurpassed. None get by the net of their vigilance. Their power is spreading, despite my master's efforts. Only three days up the coast from your hold, I gathered news from an armsman outside Fenwrd's walls. He was touchy and suspicious as a winter-starved cat." Sweat glistened faintly on his pale, thin face. "Lord Dain Cieri's ambition will feed our kingdom to the dogs, my lord."

Thain lifted his horn for a sip of mead, bitter as ill-made ale, and stared at the envoy. The machinations of the bishop's cunning mind would serve the house of Mornoth well until it was time for Caddaric to pay the pied piper. But the bishop's crow was not the bishop himself.

It would not do to speak too plainly. Thain drained his cup to the dregs, and his blood quickened. "Tell me, for the eminence of your master, Bishop Caddaric, what is the name of the man in Bolton Abbey who cries that Cierheld's first daughter is a heretic? It would be well to counsel with him."

If only the king had listened. The house of Mornoth would raise Northumbria to heights of untold wealth and learning, and with it, all of Britannia. Thain lifted his head. The king would listen in the end. He would see to it. The house of Mornoth must rise.

1

# 

*I will guard my ways... ~ Psalms 39:1*

Already the kingdom was weakening. With a dark scowl, Brother Rolf hunted bright fall leaves off the church stoop. He swept fiercely. The wooden broom handle nestled in his grip, heavy as his old spear shaft. If a leader did not rise from the Northumbrian mists, glittering fieldstones like to the granite beneath his feet would soon mark the last resting places of his people.

The entry-stone stretched two lengths into the walled court under the warmth of the new sun peering over the walls of Bolton Abbey. Beneath the edge of his black habit, the chill pierced his bare toes. A shiver raised Rolf's freckled skin where his thick wool sleeves did not protect him. He moved faster, chasing an errant oak leaf red as his hair, vibrant as the dew spangled dawn.

Brigands harried the northern holds beyond the Humber River, as he did the leaves. With few to stay them while the king lay ill, the raiders had grown ever bolder. The king's regent, who took his place hands of days ago, was weak. Even Lord Dain Cieri of Cierheld stronghold, who led the northlords from within his walls of uncommon stone, did not have enough armsmen to guard every hold between the Humber and the ancient Roman

Eagles' North Wall. The brigands melted like frost when chased yet seemed always to know where to strike. And with talk growing in the north against the southlords, the unrest in Britannia might mean more than brigands. It might mean war.

His breath shot in a thin cloud above the lower step. Early light streamed past the open gate two spear-throws distant. Turning, Rolf swept a last leaf of yellow ash from the side door with a vicious stroke.

Though the brigands had not yet come near Bolton Abbey, it was their nature to hunt the vulnerable. Unlike some church holdings, his brothers of the abbey had little in the way of riches. Their dedicated church utensils were not of gold, but bronze. Abbot Alton would not keep gold when their people in Bolton village were hungry. Rolf smiled a little. Then his scowl crept back. He was slipping indeed, not to have suggested to Abbot Alton the looming possibility of attack.

The thud of small hooves in the morning stillness and the soft, heavy step of a man against the dirt of the courtyard rang loud at his back. With a swift, level stroke of his broom, Rolf spun.

A man leading a donkey evaded the broom that lashed for his head and swung in return. The blur of a long weapon sliced in at Rolf from the left. Heart in his throat, he sprang back to the edge of the step, bringing the broom across his body in both hands to soften the blow. Blade struck wood with a dull thud. Rolf blinked.

The weapon did not bite. Leather sheathed the sword. And the giant beyond it...

His breath of relief became a growl. Knocking the sheathed blade to the side, Rolf dove down the steps and thrust his broom handle straight forward. The donkey reared. Standing beside it, the large, black-haired man wrapped one arm about the donkey's grey neck and twisted his upper body to let Rolf's attack slide past.

"Cease, little brother!"

Familiar dark eyes twinkled above a bristling black beard and a misshapen nose. That pot of a dented helm and the big feet in leather boots caressing the earth—Rolf knew them both. A merry laugh rolled from the man's chest, shaking the expanse of black hair beneath his gaping tunic.

"Ye've not lost all yer' skill."

Rolf glared at him, and the man whisked the sheathed blade around to rest at his throat with a pointed smile. Rolf squinted down at the weapon. The plain hilt marked his erstwhile blade. It was his no longer.

He'd found a place in Bolton Abbey when he fled the Wall in horror of his heart's own blackness. He stiffened and pushed his long-buried shame and the end of the sheathed sword away together. A grin tugged at his mouth. With a long stride, he reached to clap the man on the shoulder.

"Lester! Have the painted people driven you from the Wall at last? You were to put that blade to good use."

"Ach, no. The painted people 'ave been quiet as sleepin' babes. We've been recalled, an' are lookin' for those as could use a strong arm and a loyal hand what knows 'is weapons."

With a wrinkle of his brow, Rolf leaned on the broom. "Recalled? You say 'we.' Have some of the others come?"

"Oh, aye, we're all 'ere." Lester gestured with a large arm.

From within the shadows of the gate, three men rode to a stop behind him. Two more moved quietly from between the guesthouse and the tower opposite, and the rest trotted through the outer gate. One man strode on foot behind.

Rolf had noticed none of them. A tingle ran up his spine. It was his entire old tensquad. Hooded and cloaked in dull shades of wool for cold travel, they all bore blades. A longbow graced Kilden's rangy figure as he neared, and he tugged the chest strap to settle his quiver. Rolf's gaze flicked to Lester's spears, tied to his donkey's offside in their leather case. Then to Lester, who cradled Rolf's old blade in his arm as gently as a babe.

There lay his bane and his temptation. The blade called to him, though he'd sworn before his Lord above not to touch the iron again with intent to wield it. Rolf jerked his scowl back to his men. Why had they come to the abbey? Yet his squad leaders had not forgotten his training to approach a target from various sides. Lester doubtless sent scouts to foray, who saw him kneeling within the church. The squad must have come through the unguarded gate from the west road, thinking it high sport to stalk a brother. They would have kept to the shadows along the wall, pressing close to the transept tower across the yard, which overshadowed the guesthouse.

Rolf took a firmer grip on his broom, jaw tight. They had been in full view of Brother Niel, who had charge of the inner gate. But Niel had been distracted from gate-duty by a few winks in the welcome sun to make up for early prayers. After all, there was a bell just outside the out-wall to summon him. With a rueful shake of his head, Rolf wiped a damp hand on his robe. If his squad had been brigands, they could have taken him and Niel both. Brother Niel would have had a rude awakening, and the abbey would have been overrun.

He said, "I am now but a brother of stable and garden and prayer." Let them make of that what they would. He had naught more to do with the sword. And the blade had naught to do with him. He was Brother Rolf now, no longer Rolf Caedmon, the warrior.

Lester grinned, and there were a few chuckles among the dismounting men.

Kilden, grizzled and lean, nudged his beast forward a step. The archer's green gaze was sharp, knowing Rolf's watchful habit had slipped, as Kilden had always known when he failed in past days. He dismounted without a word.

With Kilden and his squad, Rolf had protected Engleland against the painted tribes at the Wall. Rolf frowned. His third had always been slow to speak, but never silent. He cleared his throat and glanced from Kilden to Lester. "You ought to have stopped at Cierheld stronghold, up the dale before the north pass, instead of our humble abbey." He waited, then continued quietly, "Even though Father Ulf says the northlords' welcome of Lady Kyrin as first daughter of Cierheld portends ill."

"How so?" Lester rumbled, taking the bait with a grin.

"Our dean swears Lady Kyrin Cieri wields an unearthly knowledge of the warrior's arts. He mutters of witchcraft," Rolf said soberly.

Kilden cocked his head, a deceptively gentle smile lurking about his mouth. His hand strayed to the dagger on his right hip. Kilden always had hated judgement leveled against another without due course of right and reasonable proof. Still, they said nothing of the reason for their coming.

Rolf swallowed. "Be that as it may, Abbot Alton would bid me give you good welcome this noon, though how much longer, I do not know. We've naught but turnip soup. Hungry mouths from the strongholds have taken refuge here. Young and old seek what scraps they can find in Bolton village this moment." He raised his hands in a helpless shrug and struggled to keep the sudden bitterness from his voice. "By order of Father Ulf, our dean under Prior Dickon. But we can feed *you* this day. Too many holds and crops have burned near about, and there is little to spare. The brigands hound us sore." His hands tightened.

He looked round at them, almost defiantly. Only moments ago, he'd knelt in brief peace in front of the altar, drenched in the quiet morning glory that streamed through the east windows. Then he had risen to face his duty, as unaware of his approaching danger as a babe. For his squad brought danger.

Mayhap Kilden and Lester merely rode to guard a southern stronghold nearer to the Humber and stopped on the way to see how their brother fared. But Lester spoke of strength and loyal hands, and brought the blade that Rolf wished never to lay eyes on again. No, something deeper was at work. If only his brothers *could* help them, but it was impossible.

"Oh, aye. That explains the hungry crowd in tha' village. We pushed on."

Rolf gave Lester a small smile. "Our Lord above commands charity."

They stared at him without a word, the men exchanging quiet glances. Why had they truly come? Rolf set his broom against his shoulder. "The holds are in need of strong and loyal hands, as you say. You will be welcome."

Kilden nodded at last. He said mildly, "The forest and the hills hereabout give rich cover for brigands."

Rolf glared at him. If Kilden hid his purpose from an old companion, at least he could speak his mind. "It is more than brigands that harry my soul. There is a pattern to what is happening, a pattern I cannot touch." He also could talk around the bush where prey had gone to ground. He forced his voice to lighten. "The talk of ill portents started when Cierheld's first daughter, Kyrin, returned from slavery in Araby."

Lester grunted, brow creasing. "Be she a brigand?"

The listening men leaned in.

"No." Rolf almost choked on a laugh. Trust Lester to chase one thought until it died of exhaustion.

Kilden watched him close. "There's the matter from the Wall that is 'na finished."

Rolf stiffened. Kilden spoke true. The matter at the Wall was not finished. Not in his heart and not in God's. He had failed his test of leadership that day. Was this why they had come? But his sword could not touch him here. He gave a careless shrug and crossed his arms. He could be just as hard to pin down as Kilden if it came to it. "I am a warrior no more, though I mean to try Kyrin's skill at staves someday."

"Who?" Lester scratched at the black hair straggling from under his helmet.

"Kyrin, the first daughter of Lord Cieri of Cierheld."

A spark lit in Kilden's eye. "Why?"

Rolf pointed outside the gate, beyond the road, and let surprise creep into his tone. "Do you hear nothing at the Wall? Like you, she came out of the woods. But she came disguised and bearing weapons. She wields a blade like no man in Engleland, and she is trained in skills I have never seen. With naught but a staff, she took down a bunch of ale-heads harassing a poor woman, and one of them with an axe. He often cuts our winter wood. Father Ulf extended the abbey's favor to him, despite his ale-sopped state. A bit of a troublemaker, Thorgil is." Rolf shot a sidelong look at Lester. "The man is built rather like you. And considering my oath against wielding sharp iron, she seems a fit opponent."

Lester's brows rose, and Kilden's eyes narrowed. Rolf eyed them, hiding his amusement. "Surely you know of Cierheld's doings? Men talk of little else."

"You say this Father Ulf did nothing to uphold the laws of the abbey in regard to drunkenness, and this woman and her attacker?" Kilden watched him.

"Our dean is rather a law unto himself when our good Abbot Alton is absent." Rolf winced and turned quickly toward the cloister.

Around Father Ulf, strife sprang up like weeds, as often as not. He moved toward the inner gate to escape a hemmed-in feeling. His tongue had grown more than loose enough.

"But that is of little matter. Forget my ill-spoken words. Come, let us talk within, over a hot drink."

Kilden assented, a bare inclination of his head, and the others followed as one. Kilden had trained them well. Rolf swallowed a thickness in his throat. He'd felt the same when he fled the year before, in his twenty-second summer. Had he learned nothing in his time at the abbey?

The outer abbey wall stretched east and west on either side of the north gate the squad had entered by. Lester tapping one large finger against Rolf's sheathed blade. He examined the open court about them and glanced back at another wall cutting across from the church to meet the outer. The two walls enclosed the east garden behind the church.

Was he calculating how easily they could get *out?* Rolf frowned. His old brothers were uneasy indeed. The court was empty but for themselves, as Rolf led them away from the church and garden toward the inner gate beyond the guesthouse and tower.

Then Lester's gaze fastened on the rampart ahead. The stripped tree trunks of the inner gate rose twice the height of a man, bristling in a row of sharpened points at the top. His bushy brows drew in. "Your abbot has no inner walk along the wall-top, no loopholes? Spear casters and bowmen would 'ave need of such."

Rolf said sharply, "I've not become a heedless babe, though study overshadows my warrior days. We do not live as chickens in a yard, with no care for the hawk. There is yet one lord in

Northumbria who will not tolerate such blindness, even in the church. That man is Dain Cieri. Our abbot consulted him about the defenses. And if you must know, Brother Niel guards this oaken gate to our inner courts in times of trouble. I'll back none against Niel! Not when he's awake."

Every eye was on him. Rolf seized the moment. "Most abbeys are not made to withstand siege, but at Bolton there is more than meets the eye. Even your piercing sight, Kilden. Those steep pitched inner roofs have more purposes than shedding snow. There are other defenses, designed to be hidden from without." He smiled wryly.

Lester brightened. "Ah, ye must show me." Always interested in a new way to defend or attack, he was.

Kilden's gaze on Rolf was as deep and heavy as moss-covered granite. He knew his ploy to distract. Rolf swallowed. His old third need not look at him so. He would speak with him about what happened at the Wall privately.

Rolf offered Lester a smile. "Certainly, you shall see them. Abbot Alton would wish your advice on expanding our protections if he were here. But surely you would break your fast?"

His squad brothers were over-interested in the abbey's defenses. Did they know something he did not? But the defenses were the duties of armsmen and Abbot Alton. A duty as dim as the mist of his past to him. His allegiance now was to his brothers of the abbey. He must *not* accompany his old squad about the grounds, no matter he wished they might ask.

Kilden said, "Food and a bit of hot drink, that would be welcome. But this Lord Dain Cieri of Cierheld, I would know more of him when your duty permits." His voice was dry.

Rolf drove down his yearning. That, he could do. Mayhap he would learn something useful to the abbot in his talk with Kilden, not least their reason for disturbing the abbey's peace.

"We'll talk more at table, of course, but thoughts in our abbey differ widely about the stronghold of Dain Cieri. You may well have heard his first daughter bears an earring of black stone."

Lester growled, "Did you not take her confession once?"

Rolf stopped short, and the men halted. It was bait and switch. "Where did you hear *that?*"

"Oh, I ken I hear a *bit* 'ere an' there." Lester smiled, an innocent grin spreading across his wide face.

His old squad was enough to drive a sane man mad. Rolf grimaced, contemplating the sky as if pleading for patience. "If you heard so much, you'll know Father Ulf believes her earring is some foreign sigil of the evil eye."

"A black jewel I hear—"

Rolf cut him off firmly. "I have not seen its like before, or any lady like to her. But she is *not* evil."

When forced, she'd chosen him for her confession. It had seemed to rankle Father Ulf. Something stood between them, that he could speak so easily of his own niece in the same breath as witchcraft and heresy. The first daughter of Cieri claimed she needed no confessor but her Lord.

Lester closed his mouth, and Rolf smiled at him sweetly. "Since Father Ulf is only our dean, and *not* our abbot, those of house Cieri remain welcome here. But, of far more import to us, Lady Kyrin Cieri also brought the abbey a copy of the Vulgate. Her sister of hearth and salt translated it from the Araby tongue—"

Lester broke in with heavy irony. "An' Father Ulf reveres the holy writ, does 'e now?"

Rolf looked at him sharply. "*I* do. As does the good dean, though he checks to make sure the copy is pure." Rolf jerked his chin toward the church behind them. "It lies on the altar within.

Our Lord's word never goes amiss when evil seeks to rise in the world."

Lester fairly crowed. "An' so evil cannot hide! An' he calls forth those who would wield truth against it. Such as us." He shared a glance with Kilden. They both looked at Rolf.

Kilden said slowly, "Yes, a leader in truth we must have, for we would not strike amiss. We fight when we know evil's face."

Rolf's neck heated, then chilled. He shook his head. 'When we know evil's face.' The words held a strange weight. Something dark as his own thoughts drove them.

2

# Sword Call

*If you come... to betray me. ~ 1 Chronicles 12:17*

"Aye, you have the right of it, bro—" He let out a desperate breath and swallowed back the *brother* that almost tumbled out. *The face of evil.* That was the key to find the wrongness in Northumbria.

But he walked with another band of brothers, now. Brothers who served their Lord within these peaceful walls. Kilden would not thank him for naming him among them. Rolf's throat tightened. He'd been a hypocrite in his last battle at the Wall, when he failed to keep the honor of his blade and his men. Like the false actions of too many other holy men who denied the very word in their mouths.

Suddenly fierce, Rolf clapped his broom against his shoulder and cupped his hands to his mouth. "Niel! Niel! Open the gate, brother! Guests await!"

There was a startled grunt above, then rapid steps, and a clunk of metal on wood. The gate of the inner rampart that protected the heart of the abbey swung open silently. Niel at least kept the hinges well-greased. Rolf motioned the squad forward. He'd no call to be so short with Niel.

As he guided his beast through the gate, Kilden turned to Rolf. "I hear Lord Dain of Cierheld and his armsmen foray after the brigands as they ken."

Rolf huffed out a breath. What was his squad second's interest in the brigands? "Oh aye, though it's little enough use. They never find them. Some loose-tongue in his cups noised it around that those of Cierheld sought the leader of the brigands. They disappear like our morning frost." He shrugged.

Lester mused from behind, "An' so the leader of the band was never brought to answer at the king's seat. They must 'ave a ring of mouths to speak and ears to listen, if they 'ave such a gift of escape."

As the gate shut behind them, the song of an unseen robin rose on the warming air within the cloister near the fountain on their left.

Rolf lifted his hands. "I cede! The wrong ears hear far too much, it seems."

Kilden slowed. "It explains Lord Dain taking refuge behind his walls. Mayhap he seeks the mouth and ears sure to be hiding in his hold."

Rolf shook his head. It did *not* explain Cierheld's silence on the matter of the raids. Early light streamed through patches of cold ground-mist between the cloister pillars beside him and the stables just to the right of the paved walk beneath their feet. Damp leather boots whispered about him on the stony way. It led to the refectory, dormitory, and infirmary further down from the cloister on his left, while the gardens and kitchens adjoined the stables. The darkness of night was almost gone. Until now, the abbey had never looked as if every shadow held a vague threat. He shivered, cold through.

Kilden said softly, "Whether he walks in truth or no, every man must use his strength, his weapons, and everything he commands on behalf of those he leads. Or he will not lead long." He strode toward the stables, tugging his donkey.

Lester sniffed agreement and followed.

*Whether he walks in truth or not, he will not lead long.* Rolf's heart quickened. Did his squad brother refer to him, or Dugar? As squad leader at the Wall, he had not minded his men's good-natured belittling of his sword skills. Until another replaced him.

Squad leader Dugar Isen, had driven him to his last fateful battle. "Ha! *Armsman?* Rather call yourself *armless.* How you made squad leader I know not! A man must lead in every weapon. Spear skill makes up for nothing. You'll never amount to a warrior worthy to shield our people. Even if you manage to blood that blade instead of fall on it!"

Dugar's scorn had been clinging fire. Rolf dropped his gaze. If he had blooded the blade or fallen on it, this moment he would be dead or a confirmed murderer. In neither case would he be tortured by his old ways and old brothers. But he could not forget.

He looked up. "Where is Dugar?" The man would never miss an opportunity to remind him from whence he had fallen. Dugar must have let his old brothers approach to feel out the waters, to assure they were not turned away.

Lester opened his mouth, but Rolf was already searching. Dugar must lurk among the men, mayhap at his back. But only the squad gripped the leads of their mounts in frost-bitten hands, most looking back at him courteously. None were Dugar. Hollow-eyed, they appeared quite ready for food and drink.

Except for the man Rolf had noted hanging behind the rest. Facing away, he reached for his donkey's saddlebag. One hand tugged his hood forward. Rolf clenched the worn oak of his broom.

Had Dugar been demoted by squad consensus? Or forced down in rank, or judged unworthy, that he did not wish to face him? His nostrils flared. Vindication would be sweet.

Head down, Dugar approached, still not quite facing Rolf. Kilden jerked his head. The rest of the squad edged their mounts aside, leaving an aisle between them.

Rolf's throat closed, his heart cold with anger. Things he saw, he remembered. It was his curse. If Lester and Kilden were that loyal to him, to see Dugar's hard words settled, he owed them much. If his squad also meant to see the grace of forgiveness between them, it would be well. He would face Dugar. Then he could walk in truth before all men. His heart rose. He was to be a scribe of truth; he could at least walk in it. Rolf fought to slow his breathing. It would end now, one way or the other.

Lester spat noisily and wrapped his donkey's lead tighter around his arm. He dropped the point of Rolf's sheathed blade to the tip of one boot. "Work for our blades 'as been right thin on account of that brigand, curse 'is hide. We thought we'd come an' beg a bit of bread." He turned sharply toward Dugar. "Come 'ere, hasten on. As Kilden says, our Rolf won't eat ye, though he's near enough a brother, an' they can get uncommon hungry, 'specially on turnips. An' *my* stomach's near gnawing me backbone." Lester slapped the hooded man's shoulder as he neared and pulled him to face Rolf, rumbling, "This one's a right part of our band now, isna' that right, lads?"

With a disapproving sigh, Kilden interrupted. "This is Seldon, Rolf. Dugar is not with us."

Rolf drew a sudden breath. His ears hummed. There was something familiar about those straightening shoulders, that lifting head, just visible under the hood.

He remembered that figure, head bent after their last furious clash of blades at the North Wall, which ended with his opponent on his knees. That dirty young body had been near bare under blue woad, but for a helmet. And staring at the ground, he'd drawn a last gulp of air with a shuddering breath, forcing back the fear of Rolf's blade that eagerly hugged his neck. He looked up and faced his death. White hot with defiance, his strong-boned face was as like to Rolf's as a brother. Under Rolf's stony gaze, his eyes had blazed granite to storm-grey as Rolf knocked his helmet away.

It was his nemesis in the flesh, his deep red hair less matted, now. Rolf shut his gaping mouth with a snap.

Seldon shuddered, every line of him rigid.

The anger from the Wall slammed back, chilling Rolf's veins. And the fear. What did his men name him? They would call him a warrior who lost his courage, or a murderer with blood cold as a snake's. Sweat sprang out on Rolf's body.

Seldon, his name was. Those eyes gleamed, watching him. Did he come to bring him to account? There would be a scar on his neck, under the cloak. A scar of murderous intent.

Rolf shivered. He sought only the strength to face his demons, to forget his shame. How dare they bring his failure here? He turned his glare on Lester and growled, "You know I sent word—"

"That ye meant to join the church, to avoid murder. We didna' believe it. But we meant no 'arm!" Lester protested. By his expression, Lester half believed it now.

Rolf's eyes stung. He dared not shut them to quit this evil happening. Would his shame never die? If they had seen his heart at the Wall, Kilden and Lester would forsake even his name. Rolf breathed through his nose. He would conquer the icy rage; he would walk in honor. He was redeemed, even if he had fallen once. He was protected by his oath.

Seldon shoved back his hood. His hair waved to his shoulders with the rich gleam of dying embers, and he lifted his chin in the old defiant gesture.

Almost Rolf smiled. The whelp was a little shorter than his lanky frame, but broader through the shoulder. Seldon's eyes were not as keen as his. Abbot Alton always said his stare gleamed cold as blue sea ice when he was angered.

Kilden smiled, a humorous quirk across his thin face, and broke in, "Why, you're wonderin' how we found 'em? Truth is, he came to us. Lester had naught to do with it. Seldon was huntin' you, Rolf."

Rolf moved forward. Though uncannily alike in face, there were differences enough between them, and deeper than bone. His own flame-red hair just tickled the tops of his ears, shorn as a novitiate's. Though Seldon looked his brother by blood, the whelp could have come with no good purpose.

Rolf looked swiftly between Kilden and Seldon. If his squad second had been teaching Seldon the blade...but the whelp bore no weapon but the eating dagger in his belt. Whatever evil it was, he must thwart Seldon's purpose.

Kilden said hastily, "Don't mistake me. He wasn't huntin' you for harm, Rolf. He wanted, well, he says he admires your sword arm."

Rolf twitched. He threw an incredulous glance at Seldon. "You'll see none of that. I never had much skill with a blade. That's your province, Kilden. A spear, now, that I once cast well. Since last spring, I deem even that has rusted away." He spun his broom neatly. They must not see his shadowed soul. "If it happened to be the staff young Seldon looked to learn, I suppose I could beat *this* somewhat into his hide. As a brother, I use broom and shovel enough to keep my hand in practice, at least enough for a whelp." Rolf smiled thinly, his gaze on Seldon.

Seldon said nothing, but his eyes narrowed and red crept up his neck. Lester was grinning. Kilden watched without expression. The others looked on carefully.

Rolf's mouth twisted. Best lay out the matter plain, so there could be no mistake. "That is not my sword, Lester. Never more. I am our Lord's man now."

"I would learn the sword from you." Seldon's voice was stiff, young.

Stubborn whelp. The broom anchored Rolf's trembling hands and gave space for his harsh breath. His spear had taken lives enough in defense of right; that did not pain him. But he went out that last morn in a hellish anger, to prove by burning cold murder that he could wield a blade as well as Dugar.

But Dugar was not here. His nemesis was. Rolf could hardly get the words out, every muscle drawn tight as a bow. "My weapons are laid down before our Lord on account of him." Fixing his gaze on Seldon, who stood straighter, if that were possible, Rolf said sternly, "I will not wield steel or iron. So, what is it to be, whelp? Why have you truly come?" He turned to the squad. "You cannot think I will leave here and go with you."

The others looked at him in surprise. His heart sank. Was that why Lester carried his blade? They could *not* ask him to leave with them.

Lester cleared his throat. "We came fer' yer skill in more than blades, Rolf, if ye truly wilna' take yer own. We're in sore need of ye, and that's God's truth. Seldon doesna' replace ye as a ten, though his tongue does fly quicker than yers. You've led us through tryin' times before." He grinned briefly. "None of us can fill the hole ye left. Ye kept us together, despite yer ill sword work. Ye made us more than we thought, somehow. If ye go before us, we fight to good purpose. Others would 'ave us split to the winds. Indeed, folk hereabouts is right distrustful. Though if ye ask me, they'd be better watchin' them men of the bishop of Richmond's. Sword or no, we would stay with ye." His face wrinkled, and his brown eyes looked pained.

Rolf stared at him, heart thundering. "Tempt me not, as you love me. I cannot touch the iron and trust myself. As for coming here, better that Cierheld stronghold welcomes your strong hands and loyal hearts, even the whelp's."

Seldon stepped forward, close to Rolf as a breath. "I am no whelp! My name is Seldon. And your men," he looked uncertainly at Kilden, "they deserve more." He stared into Rolf's eyes. "When you fought me, you had a fire within. A fire I would follow."

Rolf stared back. "That man is dead, never to live more on this earth. It is well he died."

Rolf felt his smile breaking before them all, sharp and jagged. *I near murdered you, for jealousy of another.* His squad would join Cierheld's armsmen. It was the only way. There, Seldon would not trouble him. Cierheld had armsmasters in plenty to train the whelp. His defeat at the Wall at Rolf's hands would fade from his mind, with any thoughts of revenge or evil purpose. Mayhap he would find a use for his voice. The squad would find useful employment. They would forgive him.

Seldon looked at him, incredulous. "You waste yourself on moldy books and passing out bread when you could be securing grain for many, defending their lives far better with steel? You cannot be the man we were told to find." Seldon searched his face. "No. I will not believe we have come all this way for nothing!"

"Indeed, no, I think not. Rolf cast us out? I do not believe it." Kilden shook his head. His voice sank to a drawl. "The bishop now, after he held audience with Lord Ludwin Mornoth's man, he took squad leader Dugar. For his own use, he said. He refused the rest of us. The bishop sent us without letter of introduction, saying you were introduction enough, on our behalf. Can we not take counsel with you, Rolf, and your abbot? You can teach Seldon without wielding a blade yourself, you know."

Shock jolted Rolf as he met Kilden's calm gaze. Dugar had deserted them for the bishop's retinue? And his old squad had been *sent* to Bolton Abbey at a southern lord's behest? And most astounding, Kilden suggested *he* train a recruit in the sword?

Kilden was not finished. "There's somethin' odd about the bishop's word, coming so soon after the arrival of the messenger of that southern lord. I forget his name. He was a forgettable man." He snapped his fingers. "Ah, it was a Lord Ludwin Mornoth, I believe."

No matter his rank, Kilden *never* forgot a name important to their affairs. At the Wall, Rolf had trusted him implicitly with supplies, scout training, and order among the men, for his squad second was sharp, quiet, and deadly as an owl. A warrior among the best. He was now evidently acting as first squad leader. He used Seldon's words to draw them about to follow in some hunt after a matter to do with the bishop, like hounds coursing a hart.

Yet despite Kilden's odd pretense, Dugar Isen was his squad's business. Lord Mornoth's affairs, certainly the bishop's, were not the concern of the abbey, or of one named Brother Rolf. Rolf stared at him, unblinking. Kilden never excused one who proved unfaithful. Especially a man like Dugar. Or a man such as himself, if Kilden counted *him* a traitor. But Kilden would not speak so much if he believed so little of him. If he could perceive Kilden's game, might they both catch what they wanted?

Rolf nodded. "So then, we'll take counsel over soup, as you say." He was curious despite himself. Had his men come to Bolton Abbey on the bishop's word alone, or had they come for him, or for another reason altogether?

An edge in his voice, Seldon broke in, "Why counsel over soup? Is there aught to hide from us that you refuse to instruct me? Is that broom too weak a weapon to defend yourself, or less, too weak to ward your brothers? It is truly no blade. Can you not prove yourself with one?"

Rolf spat, "I said no iron, and I'm not in the habit of breaking my word!" He would defend his own how he could, with stave, with quill or, if need arose in the future, his bare hands. His voice dropped. "As to instructing you in the way of the quarter-staff, I must know who you are. Seldon, you name yourself. Yet you are no painted man. You do not speak as one from beyond the Wall. Despite the blue woad!" The last words pierced like a shard of ice.

Seldon's mouth was mulish. His throat bobbed. "I'm for learning the sword, that is all."

"Well, I'm fer' table." With a grunt, Lester handed off his donkey and Rolf's sword to Seldon.

How expertly his squad second turned the whelp's purpose aside. Rolf scowled. In the best tradition of the squad, the youngest in skill always served the elder. Lester gave him the means to deflect his anger, the blade, and the whelp at once.

Rolf held up his hands. "We are men of peace. I but keep the stables and oft the garden. I am a man under God's hand, under oath, as we all are in this place of learning. There is no need of weapons at the moment." Let them know strife was not welcome in God's house, nor undermining of authority, nor of oaths. Here, learning was prized. "Let us eat, then we will speak of weapons-play."

There was a mutter behind Rolf, "Then we'll learn more than the whelp asked for." Seldon glowered past him at the speaker. The man ducked his head.

Seldon sniffed and wiped his nose against the cold. "God can save by one hand or by many. By a blade or without. As *we* ought to know."

Anger burned through Rolf. God spared Seldon from his edge, true enough. Yet the thin white scar on the whelp's neck attested to the bitter truth that yet lay between them. He shoved his ire back and inclined his head. "We do know."

"Do you, *Brother* Rolf?" Seldon dropped his hands, brushing Rolf's sheathed sword against his thighs. "Best take your blade from me. If you can. Or are you full of talk alone?"

There was only one way to convince him. Rolf crouched slightly. Kilden waved the others back, and barefoot as he was, Rolf was right glad the court was dirt. His voice was soft. "That blade is not mine. But you are right. God may work beyond what we ask or think. I say again, who are you?"

"Best answer him, lad," Lester said.

"I told you, and you do not hear! So can you take it?" Seldon gripped the sheath in his hand, white-knuckled, belligerent, his red face working to curious effect beneath his glowing hair.

He hid something in that expression of desperate defiance. Rolf's broom rested easy in his fingers. "Between master and pupil, defiance and learning are opposed at their root. You and I know the fear of the killing ground, and the fear of God, who allows the stroke or turns it aside. I need to know *you,* if you seek my teaching. Mayhap you seek revenge?"

Lester shifted his burly weight. Likely ready to stop his former squad leader if he forgot all bonds of place and oath. Rolf's mouth flattened. That was one thing Father Ulf had taught him. How to contain the cold heat of rage with purpose.

3

# Brother Band

*A brother offended is harder to be won than a strong city. ~ Proverbs 18:19*

His face impassive, Rolf swung.

Seldon sprang aside and backed toward the stable, seeking to block Rolf's swift blows with the sheathed blade he held. Rolf pursued, stabbing with a veritable flurry of the broom twigs and handle for his face, belly, legs, then back to his throat, never making hard contact. "Who seeks Bolton Abbey? Why do *you* seek me?"

Seldon tripped, fell against the stable wall, and scrabbled back toward the gate. Rolf slid forward, his staff tip plunging for the whelp's throat.

As he halted just short, Seldon blurted, panting, "I am Seldon. I know no other name. The tribes found me when I was quite young. I ran during the battle, and I...you did not kill me. That's why I came."

Thin-strung logic, that. But Seldon spoke of running, and nothing of murder. Had he not seen Rolf's intent that day? Or he mistook it for battle rage. Rolf stood over him, broom cocked, shaft pointed at Seldon's chest as a spear. If he thumped him, it would serve the irritating whelp right.

But there was a hint of pleading in those grey eyes. As there had not been when Seldon faced death that day. Humiliation was a bitter brew. And his blade...Rolf sighed and stepped back to glare at Kilden. "Teach him not to back into corners—" Too late, a blur of motion near his feet warned him.

The sheathed sword cracked across Rolf's ankles. His breath hissed between his teeth. Seldon vaulted to his feet, on him in a fury.

Borne to the ground, Rolf rolled and lost the broom, struggling to fend blows from hilt and fist. He grappled for the sword. Seldon twisted aside. Then Rolf had the leather in his grip. Each strained to wrest the weapon from the other, hands braced, arms shaking, straining. Rising to their feet, they were near equal in strength. But not in cunning.

Sharp and hard, Rolf pulled the prize toward his chest. Then released the blade. He dove after Seldon's backward stagger with a forward roll and came up on his feet to lift his broom cross-body. He threw it lengthwise at Seldon's face.

Seldon's hands opened instinctively as he reached up to fend it away. And he dropped the sword. Realizing it, he jerked down after the blade, then fumbled back for the broom. He caught neither.

Before the broom dropped below chest height Rolf seized it from the air. He pinned Seldon against the rampart. Ramming the broom handle hard across his chest, he slid it up to his throat.

Gulping for breath, Rolf said as evenly as he could, "Instruct him never to drop his weapon." The whelp's brow furrowed. Rolf said, "You're a mite off balance if you seek to swing a blade well."

Seldon's throat jerked. Despite his burning face, he gritted out, "It's why I seek...why I ask you to teach me." He lifted his shoulders in the smallest shrug. "Even if it is only staves." His gaze dropped at last. "I would not be so unprotected again, as I was."

"You mean, as you are now." Rolf's clipped voice brought a lift of Seldon's chin and an angry surge against restraint. "Until you take learning wherever you can, from whomever you can."

"Kilden does teach..." Seldon pressed his mouth tight and said no more.

Eye to eye, they glared, breathing hard. At last, Seldon swallowed and winced, turning his head aside from the pain of the wood. The fight was gone out of him. For the moment. Even so, a brother could not have one underfoot who fed his flesh with the fuel of desire to have a true spear in hand again. Old memory of true aimed casts and laughter and brotherhood pulled at him. Surely it was only the blade that he had betrayed himself with. But his oath was his oath.

Rolf snorted and straightened with a wince of his own. His back hurt. It had been overlong since he'd used a combat roll. Why did Seldon ask him for training in the sword? He never was a swordmaster. None came to him for training in the blade even when he was squad leader. He'd been learning with Kilden himself, then. Now he was not a brother at arms, but a brother of the abbey. He sought to master the wood instead of steel, and his own heart.

Rolf propped the broom against the rampart, then dusted dirt from his habit. He glanced at Seldon, who rubbed his throat, watching him with a baleful glare.

Rolf said mildly, "Not quite so eager now? Training with Lord Dain Cieri will serve you better. Cierheld's armsmasters are known the length and breadth of Northumbria for their weapons' skills. And the daughter of Cieri, well, if you ever meet her, remember it. I promise you will not soon forget." The whelp could do worse.

Suddenly lighthearted, Rolf retrieved his sheathed blade from the ground and tossed it to Seldon. The weight of steel and worn leather felt unbalanced, as it left his hand, the hilt flashing in the sun. It was well. His only weapon associated with iron would be the quill and its iron-gall ink, if Father Ulf did not keep him from the scribe table.

Seldon caught the blade neatly, his mouth a thin, white line. Rolf shrugged. Let him learn what he could from his first and last lesson with the blade. Yet another thing to take up with Kilden over soup.

Rolf gestured toward the refectory. "Now we have proper brotherly greetings out of the way. Abbot Alton will be pleased to speak with you when he returns. We will take counsel, though lords and bishops are best left for discussion within other walls. I warn you; any gossip is ambrosia to my brothers. They may hound you for news of outside doings." Kilden should catch the veiled warning.

"Is that so?" Lester stroked his beard with a huge hand. "Time was, ye were part of those doings. I would take it 'ard if ye thought of us as outside now."

Rolf looked at him, quick and sharp. "I did not mean so. You also are my brothers." His thought was silent. *You always will be.* His gaze fell on Seldon, and his mouth tightened. He turned for his broom and strode toward the stables.

They followed, their mounts' hooves clopping across the packed earth of the yard. Rolf's sword rested again in Lester's hand as he fell in beside him. Rolf's back prickled. That blade had felt so heavy. Was he simply weak, as Dugar once said? His ribs ached, and a line of fire across one toe burned where Seldon had stepped on it. But ferret-lean Kilden and Lester, his loyal giant, flanked him, guarding him and the squad as they ever had. A warm feeling of familiarity crept around him.

"You've taken to talking right priest-like. You aren't become a brother yet, are you?" Kilden asked, eyeing him.

Rolf ran one hand over his hair, without tonsure, wondering if he felt proud or uneasy. "Thanks to our gracious abbot, I bear the name brother without the oath of office until I gain the knowledge I need to pass from novice." He cleared his throat and said dryly, "I fear I will remain an unworthy novice in Father Ulf's book until the judgement."

"That's good, then."

Good? He could not call it so. He had a scribe's place to secure, and an inner stronghold of ice-black anger to overcome. Rolf glared at Seldon. Yet none of it was the whelp's fault. Rolf quickened his pace to forestall the questions he saw growing on Lester's tongue.

"Is it well, brother?" Niel's careful tenor carried from the rampart behind. He would have seen Seldon's challenge, and the result. Rolf lifted his broom and waggled it without turning. "Glory to God!" he called. The watchword was the only key to peaceful entry. If Lester and his squad had been brigands, he would be facing his Lord's glory this moment.

"Three in One," came the reply.

Rolf raised the broom again in acknowledgement. That was Niel's voice, and Prior Dickon's. The abbey was not entirely weak; it had a staunch guard in Niel and his brothers. By nature, Niel was not a suspicious man, but the cloister and the heart of the abbey was his charge. There was doubtless a brother or two by his side, hidden above, with rocks and hot water from the kitchen to hand. Another sat his mount at the stable gate, ready to ride for Cierheld with the alarm, though far too late if there had been real peril. Kilden might remedy that unreadiness and strengthen their defenses.

Defense. It was why Abbot Alton had ordered the transept tower built opposite the church instead of on the usual south arm—to give advance warning, and to distract unwelcome visitors while preparation was made inside.

Things could have gone worse. Seldon might have beaten him before them all, proving every scrap of manhood lost to him. Or Dugar could have come and found a way to stick a blade in him. Dugar was a master at backing men into corners with weapons and words after rendering a man's companions helpless to assist. But his men had not believed Dugar, not about him. Rolf rubbed his face, his hand aching. That must be comfort enough.

The squad was a motley group amid sharp scents of leather, damp morning, and tired animals. Almost they could be returning from battle together. But Lester and Kilden were his no longer. As for Seldon, the whelp never had been his man. And Seldon came for more than sword skill. Rolf knew it in his bones.

Lester stopped in the stable doorway as the rest moved inside and glanced at him. He rumbled, "So brother, ye'd rather that twiggy stick in yer hand than a blade? At least the spear spit yer enemies at a distance through the gizzard, afore they knew ye was huntin' 'em."

Rolf said nothing, merely tightened his grip.

Lester's gaze roamed down the row of arched entrances stretching away. The orderly cloister opposite, then the refectory, and dormitory. The infirmary lay at the end, opposite the garden Rolf so often tended, rife with smells of wet earth, lavender, and mint. Stalks of Dickon's tall, fuzzy knitbone leaned inquiring spear-shaped leaves past the end wall of the stables. Rolf turned back to the comforting warmth of horses within, the acrid smell of dung, and low welcoming whickers in the stalls. Kilden's donkey answered the stable occupants with a deafening bray. It echoed between the walls, and Rolf chuckled.

Kilden's mouth flattened in embarrassment, and Lester let loose a lady-like snort of high laughter. There were a few smothered noises among the men, then the dam broke. The squad roared.

Lester slapped Seldon's shoulder, rocking him a step, tears in his eyes, while Kilden frowned. They laughed harder, and Rolf's delight rose among them.

"Aye! That's it, brother. Ye need to smile more!" Lester grinned. "Then yer enemies wilna' care if ye come with sword, stick, or stave. They may make a brother of ye!"

Rolf stared at him. *Make a brother of ye.* Knitbone mended flesh and bone, but not deeper wounds of spirit. The great heart that drove Lester's powerful arms had taught Rolf as a green squad leader to cast his spear well. But Father Ulf had scant warmth for anything to do with Rolf. He said he would never make a brother. Rolf's smile died. How he would go back if he could do it honorably.

Seldon caught his glance, his grey gaze wary and sober.

Rolf turned abruptly to gesture at the horses, who peered curiously from their stalls. "We have some of the best mounts in Bolton. Lord Dain keeps spare mounts for his messengers here. We're not short of fodder. See your beasts settled."

Lester did not move. He growled, "I didna' mean tha' amiss. Ye are a worthy brother, indeed. It was a jest."

"I know it." Rolf laughed as much as he was able. It was a jest that held more truth than he wished. At times, he felt a true brother to none, despite his calling.

"I know what ye'd ask." Lester stepped closer. "Promoted Dugar was, to lead the bishop's men. Then word came we were to be leavin'. We dinna' know why. But you are rid of him, as are we, and all to the best."

"The bishop would not hire you, so near winter?"

Rolf leaned against the stable door, warmed by a shaft of sun, while Kilden and the rest moved to wipe down, water, and feed the beasts. His sore back felt good against the wood that arched over his head in solidity. In the cloister across the way, pillars enclosed a large court, its walls cradling cool, trimmed grass with wide and welcoming arms. The fountain gurgled merrily behind. It was restful.

"The bishop said we were na' needed along the Wall or on his lands, but back home they were beggin' for the likes of us. An' we've had naught but doors slammed in our faces along the way and close-like talks with every village reeve, or 'is men, urgin' us to move on."

Not his concern, but still. "That was ill-done by the bishop, brother. What a price we pay, fallen men with shadowed hearts, on a cursed earth." Rolf frowned sadly at his hands. They still stung from the struggle with Seldon. His strong, lean fingers were marred with the indelible pale marks of weapon scars. Why must the peace he had gained be taken from him?

Lester's brow rose. "There is hope of better."

"Regent Codi Golding is presently ill, and there is no other to take his place, as there is none worthy of our late king's throne." Bitterness swirled cold and hungry in him, or it might be that his belly still roiled from the whelp's vigorous blow. "Our land suffers under the leader of the brigands. It seems none will stay them. For how long?"

"I know not. Until heaven pleases to raise us up a deliverer." Lester's brown eyes were still and dark as a peat mere, depths unplumbed beneath a reflecting surface. He carried a kind of hunger himself as he looked at Rolf. Expectancy tightened the cool air, hemming them in.

Rolf stared into that hunger, wordless. His squad sought a leader and a deliverer? Surely they could not mean him. Injustice in anyone, squad leader or bishop, crawled under his skin, as it ever had. But *he* could not save them. Had he not a moment's peace? All the lives in the abbey rested on his shoulders at times.

Rolf said softly, "You mean we will be saved when the king's regent secures his seat." The regent was too biddable, even by the church.

Lester let out a breath, and his shoulders sagged. After a moment he grinned, with a tight lift of his great shoulders. "Ye cannot blame a brother fer' tryin'."

Rolf laughed with a wry shake of his head, and the last of his anger retreated. All men were driven by things they did not wholly understand, not least their own hearts. He held back the urge to clap Lester's shoulder again.

As he dumped his saddle on an empty stall wall, Kilden lifted his head, sniffing. "Ah! Is that sharpness I smell turnip soup? And baking bread? You're a prince among brothers, my brother!"

Rolf grinned. "That's Brother Mial, in the refectory. His haven, well, he truly makes it into a small heaven for others. I trust you will be pleasantly surprised." He smiled around at them, and gestured them all out, toward Brother Mial's refectory. Thinking was better done with food in the belly.

Kilden lengthened his stride, eager as ever for the table. Seldon walked in his wake. Rolf eyed his brown-cloaked back. Nemesis or no, the whelp must not distract him from the needs of the abbey. If Seldon kept his place, and Lester and Kilden saw to it he did no ill, it would be well enough. The men must find a place for the winter. No church was safe, with the brigands hunting. And with temptation before him, he must think on what to do. He and Seldon bore so near the same face, but for the Benedictine robe and their shades of hair. Brother Dickon said near every man had a look-a-like somewhere in the world.

Rolf had probably seen more of warfare. Yet who could say what Seldon had seen among the painted people? Mayhap war upon war, even human sacrifice. It was said they gave some to the bogs, and some in other ways, to their demons. He would learn what he needed of Seldon.

The whelp watched him so carefully. Did he seek kin of a sort, a band of brothers, and Rolf because the squad seemed incomplete without him, as Lester said? How good was the whelp with weapons? In the challenge, he had not drawn the blade or his dagger, even when he was losing. What had Kilden taught him? Regardless, Lady Kyrin's armsmen would teach him a thing or two more. Doubtless Seldon and his men would fare well enough with Lord Cieri's mercenaries.

Lester said aside to Rolf as he turned in to follow Kilden, "Ye're thinking again, brother. We shall see. When a leader *must* come, he comes. It may be the king's regent."

Rolf watched them go. "Yes, we shall see," he said quietly.

Northumbria was falling, not to enemies without, but within. A weak regent, and his oath barred him from wielding all but the quill and the staff. But his men were true; he would stake his blood on it.

Mayhap they could help push back the brigands for a time, if the abbot agreed. He would suggest the abbot, his squad, and Lord Cieri confer about the raiding band. Seldon...well, any brother could deal with a whelp he had already beaten twice. Surely.

4

# Rival Unbound

*Many are the plans in a man's heart. ~ Proverbs 19:21*

A shadow crossed Father Ulf's desk, where he sat in the scriptorium, and he frowned. "What is it, Rolf?" he snapped, and looked up from the illuminated manuscript of the Vulgate under his quill, hand poised. "Ah, my pardon, my lord. How may I serve?"

Lord Ludwin Mornoth's long moustache twitched below his mane of gold-bright hair. His smile was wry. One strong hand rested casually on his sword hilt. "In any hunt, 'tis wise to look before you leap, father."

"You would know, my lord, I am certain."

Lord Mornoth's teeth were white. "I know to walk softly. And some hunts warrant more caution yet."

Father Ulf sat back. "Do they?"

Lord Mornoth leaned over the desk, briefly towering over Father Ulf. His shoulders strained his blue tunic. "Do not seek to pull the wool over *my* eyes, monk!" He stepped back, and his smile returned. "You know what I speak of. The jesting cap of Lord Dain Cieri's fool does not become you. In more ways than one, would you not say?" The words bore heavy irony.

Father Ulf set his quill carefully in its pot. In the undercurrents between Cierheld and the other strongholds around Bolton, an unseen battle raged. At this critical point, with Lord Cieri wounded, Cierheld was vulnerable. A discerning mind must craft the net that would take such a fearsome prize as a stronghold, and more, win the souls within. What man could find a better tool than another with the power to do all his will? If he could make him willing.

Father Ulf felt a shiver of excitement. He took in the empty scriptorium with studied weariness and cocked an eye at Lord Mornoth. "It is true. I have been in the position of Lord Dain Cieri's fool more often than I would wish. May our Lord forgive him."

"His Lady Willa would not have wished it so. When she left this earth, Lord Dain Cieri cast you, his own brother-in-law, out of Cierheld."

Father Ulf's mouth flattened, and he glared at Lord Mornoth. He had no right to take Willa's name in his mouth. *Willa, my fairest sister dedicated to our Lord, until you turned away for the sake of a man, deserting even me. And then Dain turned his back.*

"My pardon." Lord Mornoth waved a lazy hand. "But you must grant it was then that your fortunes changed. No more a respected priest of Cierheld stronghold. Even now your brothers in your abbey do not see the danger that Cierheld courts, refusing your services and your wisdom. Especially after the inauspicious return of their first daughter."

Father Ulf brought his hands together, studying Ludwin Mornoth over the tips of his fingers. "You are right. Heresy has small beginnings among men. A woman's wiles, allied with evil, can make heresy grow like the plague. Prior Dickon cannot see it, still less our good abbot. The abbot believes the lord of Cierheld but a trifle stubborn in his ideas, harmless so long as he guards the border to our north. This, despite the jet earring of the evil eye his daughter carries. Alton believes it is what Lord Cieri says, a mark of her slavery in Araby. Her father hates to speak of her trials." Father Ulf's mouth soured.

Lord Mornoth tilted his head, sardonic. "Or is it that Lord Cieri's men and patronage muddy the vision of your abbot's eye?"

Ulf frowned. "You may not speak evil of a ruler of your people."

"No, I did not say so." Ludwin lifted his shoulders and spread his arms in an expansive gesture. "Rather, it is a regrettable mistake to ignore heresy—a costly mistake that a wiser head would rectify."

"As you say, I do what I can as dean." Father Ulf folded his hands in front of his brown robe, the linen creasing across his lean middle.

Lord Mornoth laid both hands on the desk and leaned forward. "Therefore, if you rose in the church of our Lord by most fortunate circumstance, I could trust you to ferret out the last scrap of evil? Wherever it hid?"

"Such is my duty, my lord." Father Ulf's breath quickened. He wrinkled his nose at the smell of last night's wine on Lord Mornoth's breath. "Heresy may not be allowed. It must be cleansed to the last taint. Even if I command it from my cell, walled in from the world where I hope for peace as an anchorite. There I will always seek power from above for those with the wisdom to ask for it."

"Ahhh." Mornoth smoothed his moustache, stroking the ends neatly into his beard. "Would you grace my table at the next full moon? I know the road is rather long, but I would strive to make it worth your discomfort. Since, as you say, I may not see your face once you are walled away. So, seeking wisdom from above, I find that my stronghold has need of your service. There we may speak further of these dangers you see, and of the wise course."

Father Ulf let his inner smile touch his mouth. "I thank you for your kind words, my lord. I will come."

§

Brother Rolf removed the bridle from the red dun and hung it on the wall, humming. "Well, sister," he said, "our good Father Ulf has been out for a dawn ride. What tales you could tell. You may yet speak. Did he go to solitary prayer, or was he after something else under the trees? Most morns he's a keen one for his quill, but he declares me more fit to tend you. Not that I mind you, sweet sister. Better this than study his most obscure work. Though I miss my own quill and ink."

Rolf sighed. But for his Lord's gentleness and Abbot Alton's acceptance, he might have given up long since on becoming a scribe. But it *was* his place in Bolton Abbey, though the way was hard. "Serving here in more than the choir is challenging. Father Ulf does not care I serve as best I can. You hold more charity than...never mind." Rolf's jaw tensed. "I must find my way between his scorn and my quill. It is true, I blot the page at times. What man does not? I only blotted the fifth page of his most ragged translation. Now I may not touch any of his work. Is that just?" He scowled.

The mare lipped Rolf's hair, and with a little laugh, he gave her a carrot. "Father Ulf declares it a waste to give you a root that men might eat. But if I give you one of mine, no ill is done."

Rolf lifted the heavy wooden saddle from her back and groaned. He settled it quickly on its rack. His arms still ached from the tussle with Seldon. The sword had never been kind to him. He ought to thank the whelp, for he was humbled, which was the aim of every heart in God's house.

Rolf leaned forward. "Yes, I am humbled, and we'll tighten our belts later this leaf-fall, but Father Ulf has not been reduced to carrot tops. He will thank you for keeping this from his trencher." He gave her the rest of the carrot. The mare snorted agreement, and Rolf grinned.

Then he sobered. His squad had come, and the whelp, while the danger to Britannia was deepening. If Seldon was indeed from beyond the Wall by capture, had he come to search out their weaknesses? But Bolton was too far south to be reached by a foray from the Wall.

Rolf said to the mare's ear, "You trust me, do you not? At the Wall, my squad knew our lives depended on faithful beasts like you, worthy of trust. As my life depended on their skill and courage. They were on the border far longer than I. Have you seen the north?" He eyed the mare pensively. "You'd have need of a brave heart to face the painted people." He grabbed the hay fork. "Instead of brave, I became jealous of Dugar, bitter as a vat of oak tannin."

"Bitter you *were.* I dare hope you are not now, brother."

Rolf spun.

Seldon stepped from the shadows. His mouth twitched into a half smile. "It sounds as if Brother Rolf, so deft with spear and staff, may have a less than fair hand at scribing."

Rolf shot back, "And you have less manners than my sister here. If you are the newest man of the squad, why do you lurk in the corner?"

Seldon watched the hay fork warily. "I did not come to listen out of turn, Brother Rolf. I but came to see if you might teach me a little of the staff." His face was red again. "Father Ulf gave me leave to ask," he finished, his rich, clear voice awkward.

Rolf forked hay into the mare's box with swift stabs. "I pick up the staff when I can, whelp. As you can see, I am not free now." He said more evenly, "There is another who wields a staff far better than I. You ought to see the first daughter of Cierheld. The limber ash seems to know her thought. It's as if they speak to each other, the wood and her will. Even Father Ulf cannot deny her skill." He fished another carrot top from his tunic and rubbed the dun's nose as she crunched.

"So you have said." Seldon ran a hand through his hair, looking frustrated. "None can deny a staff bout is good for body and soul. It lets out evil humours, and it harms none."

"I agree. There's no wrong in the exercise, or blood on the wood. Naught beyond a few barked knuckles. The abbot thinks it rather child's play." Rolf smiled at Seldon. Then his smile disappeared. "But you know what stands between us. A bout with staves is well enough, but from the oak to the iron is a short leap. I will not spar when there are none here but you and I." The mare nudged Rolf's side. He scratched her forelock.

"You do not trust me?" Seldon said between his teeth. "I have told you nothing false."

Yet he had not told them all. Rolf shook his head. "As the Book says, my flesh is weak. I pray for strength. I also prayed for our abbot's safety from the brigands before he left." He muttered for the dun's ear, "From Bolton to Richmond is a long road, even for your sister, Mairne, carrying our Abbot Alton." He stroked the mare's neck, then looked up at Seldon. "I would not break my word, by accident or design."

Seldon's forehead wrinkled.

Rolf crossed his arms while the horse lipped at his sleeve. "You must understand, Father Ulf despises my staff. He says there is no use for it, and I come too late to the quill, as I did to the blade." He cast the hay fork against the wall. The tines stuck in the earth and the wood handle thumped to rest. He looked after it, chest heaving. "Small time do I have for my staff now. Or the quill."

Seldon watched him. Rolf huffed out a quivering breath. Who was he trying to fool? Denied his staff and his quill, it did naught but throw wood onto the blaze of hunger for his familiar spear and the ways he once knew.

Seldon's voice came soft, amazed. "You deeply love them, don't you."

"Aye." Rolf sighed explosively. "Oh, not the killing. But the protecting; the good saved; the solid wood, never treacherous; the well-thrown cast. I like to do things well." He looked at him, pleading for understanding. "It is one of God's pleasures. I would have liked to learn the sword also." He shrugged. "Now I work hard at the quill instead. Though my scribing often pleases me not, I am learning. I love books. And my brothers." He had not meant to say so much. It was Rolf's turn to redden.

"I also would learn, and seek to mend my balance," Seldon offered.

Rolf's tension eased. "Yet I dare not teach you without another to witness. I must keep my oath."

Seldon hesitated, then nodded.

Rolf said, "Someday Father Ulf will see my hand is steady on a page with his iron-gall ink. It blackens my fingers, but it is a far fairer stain than blood. Especially *your* blood." He laughed abruptly. "It is a far easier stain to wash from men's minds than what Father Ulf calls heresy, the stain the first daughter of Cierheld stronghold bears."

"You talk much of her." Seldon crossed his arms. "I would meet this first daughter."

"You will." Rolf shut his mouth. He nattered on as if Seldon were his brother in truth, instead of a man whose intentions he was not sure of.

There was a scuff of feet without, and Niel burst through the door, slight, dark-haired, and grinning. "There you are, brother! Father Ulf is off to the southlands. He needs a good mount, he says, one sure-footed for the road." Pausing for breath, Niel nodded a greeting to Seldon.

"We'll see to it." Rolf motioned Seldon after him and took the bridle from its hook and moved down the aisle between the stalls. Seldon grabbed the saddle from its rack and followed.

Father Ulf stepped inside the doorway. "Rolf! I have need of the grey for abbey business. Be quick about it! If you can." With a grumbling snort, he glanced at Seldon, his old eyes bright under his white hair.

"Yes, father." Rolf moved quickly, despite his stiff back.

The grey had the last stall, the farthest from the door and thievery. If only the chill fire in him had no harsh words to feed on, it would die. How he strove to keep his oaths to his Lord, and to the abbey. If only Father Ulf would see it. But it might take a seven-day of penance for his heart to see Father Ulf aright again. Seldon answered a curt question from Father Ulf that Rolf could not quite hear.

He opened the stall door. Seldon puzzled him. The whelp could have sprung at him from hiding and avenged his most recent defeat. He had not. And he did not seem angry. That was most troubling of all.

The grey nibbled at Rolf's ear when he bent to check his back legs, and Rolf shoved his head away. A murmur came to him down the aisle, interrupted by the slam of a hoof on wood from the grey, as impatient as Father Ulf.

Rolf poked his head out of the stall. "If you would bring the saddle, Seldon."

The whelp said something, with a quick bow to Father Ulf, and hurried toward Rolf, stirrups thumping his calves. He tripped and near deposited the saddle in Rolf's arms. Shying, the grey jolted back with a snort.

Annoyance filled Rolf. "Walk softly, softly about them, whelp. It appears you've no hand, or rather feet, for stable work. But we'll train you."

"Oh, he's trainable, with a scribe's hand far fairer than yours." Father Ulf had followed. His smile did not reach his eyes. Rolf stared sharply at Seldon. What kind of man lived with the painted people and knew how to scribe?

Seldon looked at him and swallowed. "I learned from a captive. One like your brothers, who taught me to be of use to the village leader." He shrugged. "He wished me to spot spies."

"And did you?"

"I thank God there were none to catch."

Ulf shouldered in. "His hands are clean enough. As yours never will be."

Rolf remembered Seldon under his blade, and his own deadly anger. Seldon surely fought for something greater than pride. He had been about to die under the stroke of one gripped by desire for his utter annihilation. He had betrayed every man in that act, and himself. Whelmed by that black knowledge, Rolf dropped his sword. He had heaved the contents of his stomach over a nearby bush, but it had not rid him of the cold knowledge inside, or the smell of hot blood.

Rolf shivered as he stared through the memory at Father Ulf. Then he straightened. Had he not taken the oath to control his evil tendency? "Father Ulf, I will serve you. I will learn the quill."

Smooth as oil, Father Ulf said, "You serve well in your place. That place is not at my scribe table."

Rolf began, "The abbot will stand surety for—"

Ulf sighed. "I will give you one season, and we will see if your skill improves. It may be best it does not, as you seem to love the beasts, and they you."

Rolf blinked. Though it was true he worked well with them, there was more for him to do than tend the abbey beasts. He must learn the craft of scribing and be of some use in the world. Be of use and be allowed to read more of the books. And the great Book, in particular. He would go mad within these walls if he were not allowed to see out of them, especially in spirit. If Father Ulf did not see his need, he would consult with the one who knew the hearts of all men.

Father Ulf wore a satisfied look. "All remark on it, even the abbot. They have never served us so well or been so content."

Seldon's mouth was flat. He said slowly, "A quill can destroy an enemy as much, or more so, than a blade, with right words for the moment. They strike the heart. And a stave can do better than both of them. It can come unexpected. The element of surprise is a weapon in itself."

What was he remembering? Rolf watched Father Ulf's interested gaze turn to Seldon. "Do you hold to that?"

"I do." Seldon drew himself up. "A quill never drew a man's lifeblood, as I hope to do, yet it can turn multitudes."

Rolf drew a breath.

Father Ulf grunted and swung into the saddle. He turned to Seldon. "See that you are in my scribe's chair when I return. A great work awaits us."

"Yes, father." Seldon bowed his head.

Rolf clenched his hands. "All things will be as you say, under Prior Dickon, father," he called, as one of his brothers opened the gate. Then he sprang after Father Ulf, "Wait!" He trotted, keeping pace. "Prior Dickon requested you bear a message to Lord Ludwin Mornoth. He asks him to take pity on the poor souls within our walls. If some of Bolton Abbey's hungry mouths may go to Lord Mornoth's stronghold, or if Mornoth sends supplies, he would do much good."

Father Ulf's thin face went rigid. There were beads of moisture on his high forehead beneath his white hair. "You forget, brother, our good abbot left me to care for these people while he consults with the bishop of Richmond." He spun the grey and kicked him toward the abbey gate, calling back, "The people are not your care, and Prior Dickon must not be distracted by common matters. If the moment is meet, I will ask."

Rolf shouted a protest, but Father Ulf disappeared through the gate. Seldon opened his mouth and closed it again, grim.

The moment would never be right. Rolf gritted his teeth. Many in the abbey looked to him. His brothers often came for advice, so as not to bother Father Ulf. And Ulf knew it well.

The people were Rolf's care, as they were every brother's concern under the hand of Prior Dickon, the abbot's able administrator. Brother Niel faithfully reported to Brother Rolf as head of the stable. They both did to Father Ulf as dean. But all of the brothers were responsible to Prior Dickon, and he to Abbot Alton. It was the prior who had charge over all with breath in the abbot's absence. That was the burr under Father Ulf's saddle.

Rolf strode back to the stable. With a freezing glance at Seldon, he picked up the hay fork and attacked a pile of dung. Anyone with an eye to how a horse spoke with ears and tail could take Rolf's place, giving him more time to practice scribing. But he feared Father Ulf would not see, no matter the season. Seldon would take his place there also, at the scribe table. His nemesis, indeed.

5

# Deep Deceit

*Men loved the darkness rather than the light... ~ John 3:19*

Rolf fought the blackness of jealousy inside him. He would take up the quill again this even'. His concentration on the scratch of the nib over parchment always made him forget, for a time. Not that Father Ulf would let him near his precious parchments, let alone the translation of the Book of the Vulgate. As he granted to Seldon, with barely a trial. A 'fair hand,' had he called it? Rolf dug the fork deep. He felt he might explode in icy shards, piercing all living things near him. He almost wished it.

"This is truly a place of learning, of far more than scribe-work." Seldon scuffed at the stable floor with one boot, diffident. "I would yet learn staves from you."

He was well spoken for a painted one, and that voice—. Reaching after an evasive horse-apple with the fork, Rolf thawed enough to grant him a few words. "The great Vulgate is worth reading. His Book is precious. It changes a man."

Seldon looked at him, brow raised. Somehow, he looked older in that moment, his gaze a hawk's.

Rolf straightened. "I *can* read quite well, though my hand is awkward. That's God's truth."

He always felt different when he came away from the snatches he could read from the Vulgate. He found himself praising his Lord's goodness with David, or pondering how to oust the darkness in himself, or watching anew the warmth of Prior Dickon's smile. The prior was a man worthy of his position.

"I see." Seldon stared at the stable floor, a crease between his eyes.

Watching him, Rolf wondered if he saw Father Ulf's duplicity, and how much he saw of his own heart. "The translation of the Vulgate was meant for the people." He gestured beyond the door. "For those Father Ulf said are not my care, as well as for you and I. The Book rests in the church those rare moments when Ulf does not require it on his desk for copying back into Latin, word for word. None of the words were polluted as Lady Kyrin's sister rendered them in the common tongue, not that *I* expected it to be so. Father Ulf has not found a wrongly translated word yet."

"I caught a glimpse of the Book when I met Father Ulf in the church this morn. The illustrations are quite striking."

"He has a painstaking hand."

Father Ulf took joy in his craftsmanship, if he gave him his due. And he but wished to do the same, for the glory of the One who made all things. That, he thought, was the end of his jealousy. At the moment, he could do little except wait and pray. But what of it? None could stop him from serving his Lord. Patience would bring fruit, though his Lord promised suffering as well, and that usually first. Rolf smiled crookedly to himself. As in the squad, discipline near always came first. On the abbot's return, he would ask Abbot Alton if he might find some small task worthy of his quill.

Seldon cleared his throat and leaned over a stall next to the grey's empty one. He looked at the young black gelding there.

"This you have done right well. He has a sleek coat and a bright eye. Niel says the abbey's beasts are well over the thrush infecting them, due to your care."

"True." Rolf looked at Seldon gratefully. Even Father Ulf could not say otherwise. The black gelding paced, and Rolf put aside the hayfork and laid a hand on his restless back. There *would* be more for him in the abbey than working in the garden and stable. Then someday he might be able to look on a spear without the desire to heft it.

Seldon said, "Do you know, men say whatever power resides in the dark ring Kyrin Cieri bears in her ear is broken by her necklace of the fish, the sign of the Christ. Father Ulf talks of her evil eye and witchy ways, but *that* sigil is no small thing. Hal Loring is a worthy warrior from all I hear, and she defeated him, and then made him a friend." His gaze was searching, a small frown between his eyes.

"No, that sigil is no small thing. Though the sign of the fish holds no power in itself," Rolf added. "Even the sign of the cross. All power resides in the one it signifies; the power is his."

Seldon cocked his head slightly. "You believe not in the power of relics and sigils, or talismans? Strange, for one of the church."

The black stretched out his neck and nibbled at Rolf's hood. Rolf pulled his worn habit from the horse's teeth, and his mouth tightened.

He would test Seldon's seeming support and his mettle. "Don't tell Father Ulf I said so. Not that a sigil is the same thing as a relic. They hold different kinds of power to sway men, and what power they bear is never their own. A sigil's power lies in the meaning it carries. I have seen several that carry deep and high meaning. On the other hand, many believe a relic's power comes from our creator, though nowhere in his Word does he speak of relics as we do, such as a splinter of the true cross. He *does* tell us he has used inanimate things such as Elisha's staff with the widow's son. Note that Elisha's servant bore his staff and laid it on the child's face without result. No power resided in the wood itself." He gave Seldon a wry glance. "It takes a person of will to wield the wood to a desired end, as every staff fighter knows. He healed as he willed. He also gives us the power to will evil or good. As for talismans, now those are oft supposed to hold power as in a vessel. Talismans do have to do with power—unlawful power. Power that men use outside his will. There lies the danger. Here." He handed Seldon the last carrot top he'd tucked inside his tunic. "There'll be no more of those till spring, barring a miracle. See you make the most of it."

"But what of the daughter of Cieri and the talisman of the evil eye she bears? Does it have the power to corrupt? Will you cross staves with her?"

The whelp's questions ran one upon another. "Oh, aye. I doubt not I will have a try at staves with her." Rolf stared into the gelding's fathomless eye as it nuzzled after Seldon's carrot top and rubbed its nose. "All I saw in her is a heart that follows hard after our Lord. Her claim to his forgiveness seemed more certain than mine. Yet what does that signify in the end but our Lord's mercy?"

"You avoid me, brother. I wonder about this evil sigil of power Father Ulf speaks of."

No one could accuse the whelp of being slow. He was persistent. Rolf's mouth quirked. "As to that, whether you think it from a sigil's meaning or a talisman, power is not a thing to speak of lightly. Where does it come from? That is always the question; is it lawful or unlawful?

"That earring is a sign of her old bondage. It is no sigil of darkness. She does not consort with unlawful power. She follows our Lord's word. And where God dwells, he seals that soul. In her hands, the earring is a jewel of jet only."

"And if another took it? Answer me that."

Rolf shook his head. "I am not sure. If another sought unlawful power in it, demonic power may very well come to associate with such an object. As to whether it would come to dwell inside the jewel, I do not know." He paused. "I do know God made all things, and to some men, and to demons, he allows evil power, for a time." How had the whelp drawn him to speak deeper than he did with any other, despite who he was to him?

Seldon looked skeptical and Rolf said, "Well enough. When Kilden and the others return from the village, we will talk more about your training with the staff. I will teach you naught else," he warned. "Abbot Alton should return soon, then we'll settle the matter. But rest well this even'. On the morrow we'll ride for the beeches. The conkers should be near ready. Abbot Alton is partial to his beech nuts, so says Prior Dickon."

Seldon inclined his head with a disgruntled smile. "I suppose they will be welcome this winter."

"Aye, they will be. Come, Brother Mial is at his work again."

Rolf shut the stable door on the matters tangled behind them and strode with Seldon toward the refectory and the smell of hearty meat pasties the wind brought. It had been too long since he'd bitten into one of Brother Mial's hot pies. It threatened to be spring before he tasted another. This winter would see every bit of meat stretched as far as it would go—and that meant pottage stew in small bowls. Seldon would show his colors soon enough.

Beside Rolf, Seldon sniffed the air inside the spotless refectory in appreciation. Tables stretched end to end down the long room, crowded with men, women, and children in worn tunics and hose, for the most part. Some were barefoot as the monks scattered among them. Mial strode across from the kitchen and served them himself, as large as if he always tasted his own cooking. He hefted the steaming kettle in his arm, with a thick cloth about it, and Seldon chatted with him as he dipped out a bowl of thin soup to go with the small pie for each of them. At least it was hot.

"My thanks, Mial."

The cook dipped his round head, blonde hair tonsured close. He smiled, fair cheeks ruddy as apples. "It is my pleasure, brother. I hear Father Ulf is to speak for us?" He lowered his voice. "Of our need in the abbey."

There were spies about, in the church and elsewhere. And many ears here. Rolf stared at his wooden bowl and the carved spoon beside it. "I pray so, but there is more involved than simply asking." There was also indebtedness for a favor given. Rarely was a gift from any lord simply that, a gift.

"Ah," Mial raised a finger knowingly. "The regent's hands are yet tied by the vying council factions between the northlords and the south. But have you heard ought else?"

Rolf considered. He must be wary, but the anger between the north and southland lords was common enough knowledge, and he could see no harm in Seldon hearing of a possible accord. "Aye, Lord Ludwin Mornoth requested Father Ulf's presence on a matter of import to the church, Prior Dickon says. He may succeed on our behalf."

He hoped Ulf laid importance on forging peace and goodwill. Meanwhile, the odd bits of parchment he'd had no use for would serve Rolf's quill and ink well, between his prayers from Lauds to Prime. When the parchment ran out, he'd use bark from the forest. He looked around at the crowded tables amid a clacking of spoons in bowls.

"For the sake of all of us, I hope so."

Mial studied him. "As do I."

Further down the table, a babe began to cry, and Brother Mial hurried off to serve more of his eager flock. Seldon and Rolf ate quickly. Stepping outside, his stomach warm and full for the moment, licking the last spicy venison gravy from his fingers, Brother Rolf led the way toward the church.

Seldon kept pace. "So the regent's hands are bound," he said slowly. "What do you think? Of the south, I mean. Kilden says they are right blind, or too lazy to act for any but themselves. And Lester says he cannot think a good regent, even weak as he is, would be so powerless he cannot help our people in their hour of need. But what of the king to come?"

Those were dangerous waters. Best to curb his tongue. Rolf set his jaw. "There is one thing we can do. Come."

He would kneel and pray to the one with the power of grace for the needs of kings and men, even for one like himself. But first, he lifted the last of his pasty toward the sky in solemn salute. "Though I am but a lowly brother, I will see to it, as my Maker absolves me, that every brother, man, and woman has that Book on the altar of Bolton Abbey before their eyes. For it is God's goodness to men." Kyrin had brought it, and he had promised to see it done.

"And?" Seldon asked, watching him. "Does not Father Ulf say its pages are not for common minds?"

Rolf passed through the inner gate, biting his tongue as his leather shoes thumped the earth harder. To his surprise, his voice remained mild. "Does not the Psalmist say, 'Thy word is a lamp to my feet, and a light to my path?'" He turned from Seldon to look at the sky. "Is it not your own word, Lord?"

"Ah. True," Seldon said. "We do need light in both realms, but food also. A generous gift of grain or coin would go far toward redeeming Lord Ludwin Mornoth in my eyes."

"Though he is a southlord, with that I agree."

A strangled laugh pulled them around. Leaning against the wall before the outside gate, a boy stared at them, a pie in his hand. He piped shrilly, "Don't ya know anythin'? The southlord lives across the river. The Humber and is' trade-way lies between us. We'll get nothin'! Alkborough's too far. An' as for readen' any word, I'm na good at learning."

Learning. Rolf and Seldon looked at each other. Rolf grinned. "Oh, I might learn to kiss the lord's fingers if he saw fit to spare us grain, and you might learn to read."

Seldon called, "I will learn the sword!"

The boy tilted his head, curious, and Rolf saluted him, touching hand to breast and brow, with a last outward flick of his fingers in the old armsman's gesture of respect. Father Ulf was not there to reprimand him.

Seldon added softly to himself, "You are as much 'common' as I, boy. You'll find the Book a comfort when you least think it. You are both eternal."

Rolf shook his head, irritated. How much could the whelp know of the Book? The boy gave back Rolf's salute and ran around the corner of the wall. Laughter rose. Yet Seldon spoke true. True of the Book, and of the boy.

§

Fish and eel, fen and reed, Father Ulf knew the smell of the river that came to him, even without the line of greenery that wended below the Alkborough hills. Around him, Lord Mornoth's escort of armsmen picked up the pace. Alkborough stronghold loomed at the hillcrest. The gatekeeper opened quickly for his lord's guest. Ulf's smile at the gatekeeper faded.

Brother Rolf ought to take note of such promptness, without needless questions for his betters. But then, that young armsman-turned-monk was full of ill-grace, always forging his own way, even with his quill. Father Ulf sniffed. His underling's stroke was far too bold—in life, as in his scribing. He would never make a monk. Ulf pursed his lips. He would make Rolf see his unworthiness, or he might simply let him discover it at Seldon's hands. Failure always sank deeper into a heart left to its own devices, to its own dark mirror. Seldon showed much more promise as a scribe and was likely a fit tool for more.

"Sir." His escort saluted.

Silently, Father Ulf inclined his head in acceptance of their service rendered, and Mornoth's men turned toward the stables.

"Ah, well come, well come, father!"

The cry brought his head around. Lord Ludwin Mornoth shoved the double-leaved oaken door of Alkborough hall wide with his own hand, and motioned Ulf inside with an expansive gesture. It was a grand invitation to a great house. The hall entrance was framed with imposing peeled logs of planed facings, the walls of stone and wood, with wide stone steps leading upward.

Father Ulf dismounted, leaving his horse with a stable boy, and walked up the steps. The tart sweet of late berry pie and other delicacies that had not graced his tongue for far too long tickled his nose.

"Ah, I dare believe you have an excellent cook."

"We try, good father, we try." Mornoth motioned him within to a chair at the great table looming in the middle of the hall.

To the right of Lord Mornoth's ornately carved oaken seat, a rather round man with hair the colour of damp straw slouched in another chair, the high back of intricately woven willow. Ah. Lord Nidfaol Koffor, of Koffold stronghold and Pately Bridge. A young man sat a couple of chairs down from him.

"This is my brother's son, Thain. He is present to learn. He studies often with Lord Nidfael Keffer. You make speak as freely before my nephew as myself."

Thain rose to bow, his dark hair and eyes neither handsome nor ugly.

Lord Mornoth drew out a chair for Father Ulf, ignoring Keffer's raised brow. Father Ulf nodded as if it were usual for his host to seat him and arranged his robe regally. He made his smile warm.

"I am at your service, my lords." As they would be at his. He glanced about. It seemed their circle was complete. No one stood around the walls, with tongues to prattle of their business. It was well.

"We have heard, good father, that you pursue a most holy task. One the regent regards, but others do not. Not all minds think alike."

Father Ulf's eyes narrowed. Lord Nifael Keffer spoke of what some might call treachery. "Do you mean the scribe school our Britannia has need of, and those who oppose it? Or the copy of the Vulgate that I seek to prove worthy of the church?"

Nidfael's voice soothed. "I mean that, and more, Father Ulf. No task undertaken by our mother church is unholy."

"Nor unrewarded." Lord Mornoth leaned forward in his chair, intent as a cat, his eyes glittering.

Father Ulf took a studied sip of wine from the heavy goblet beside his two-pronged fork and wide plate, swirling the fragrant red liquid. "Our window to act is narrower than the crenels of Lord Cieri's gate."

Lord Keffer turned a triumphant smile on his host, then said to Ulf, "How so, father?"

"My abbot even now rides for Richmond, leaving me the titular head of Bolton Abbey in his absence, for hungry mouths have come to us for charity. Our Lord Bergrin Jorn of Jornhold is poorer than a church-mouse. He cannot feed those in his own hold, let alone assist Bolton. I doubt the abbot will be gone more than a seven-day. That is our moment." He looked from one to the other pointedly. "My lords, it comes to my ears that Lord Bergrin Jorn was reduced, in great part due to your efforts."

Nidfael bristled. "If you refer, father, to the Lady Myrna Jorn, I held her a short while in my stronghold as my lord requested, until we..." He looked uneasily at Lord Mornoth. "We were most foully tricked out of her bride-price by that upstart of a witch, Kyrin Cieri. As to the rest of Jorn's fortunes," he spread his hands, "the fault is not ours."

Father Ulf raised a brow. No more "good Father Ulf." At least they had no love for Cieri and were not averse to bringing down a northlord like Lord Jorn. It was as well to be plain with them, or at least to have them think so.

"As you say, my lords," he said smoothly. "The brigand and his band are busy, as is the witchling, and so we must be. Since you ask, I propose that you, my Lord Keffer, may well watch the roads between your stronghold and Alkborough for treachery, and my Lord Mornoth may do well to gather his loyal men for the good of our land."

"And you?" Mornoth asked, his beard golden in the light.

Thain said nothing, merely leaned back and listened.

Father Ulf smiled. "It is only meet to guard our interests until the abbot returns. I also will attend to my proper business, that of heaven on behalf of men, with all our business in between."

Mornoth rubbed his chin, a slight quirk at the corners of his mouth. "Does this 'on behalf of men' include justice done to heretics and a strong bond between the church and the lords of north and south? If such is the case, you need not trouble yourself about the brigand, father. When the north has been dealt with, the house of Mornoth will see that he does not interfere further."

Father Ulf smiled inside. There was a tie between Lord Mornoth and the leader of the brigands, as he'd thought. Such a bond, and his knowledge of it, might prove useful. He must search out its depth.

He raised his voice. "But certainly, my lord. As for this 'strong bond' you speak of, I would not presume to order that which you know better than I." He inclined his head. "Men and arms and the southlords belong in hands strong enough to wield them, under a lord with enough wit to foil the brigands." *Under one in the north, wise enough to yield to a higher power. One such as I.*

Keffer's smile soured.

Lord Mornoth's grin widened and he lifted his horn of ale in salute. "And then for you, perhaps, acknowledgement as the worthy father, mayhap even bishop to be, who brought a new translation of the Vulgate into the world. Who established a scribe school worthy to house it and drew men to uphold the rightful glory of the church."

Father Ulf straightened in his chair. He was copying another's translation. But that was not important—only that others saw the illustrations' bright beauty. None could doubt his was the illustrating hand. Before his inner eye, the bright colors he'd penned in the last days dimmed.

He shoved his discomfort aside. It was only the dark vision of all he had yet to set right that shadowed those pages. Nothing more. Perhaps Bolton would gain a bishop as Abbot Alton aged.

"If it is our Lord's will, my Lord Mornoth." Father Ulf bowed his head. Lord Dain Cieri would rue the day he took his sister's hand and led her to heresy and to death.

Nidfael glowered. Mornoth said, "So be it." He turned to Keffer. "Even you must see it, Nidfael. A new age is begun." He poured more drink all around with a good-natured flourish. "To prosperity and peace!"

Nidfael said grudgingly, "Yes, of a certainty. But there will be war first." He shifted in his chair and brushed crumbs from his green tunic. "This Kyrin Cieri, Cierheld's first daughter. They say she is a fighter of strange ability who carries the evil eye." His blue gaze on Father Ulf was level with challenge.

"A wrinkle in the order of things that will be cared for in its proper hour." Father Ulf shrugged. "Mayhap you will take part in that since you hold the next closest dale to Bolton. Though I am sure there will be a certain amount of fighting before Cierheld will be molded to the proper order of the new kingdom. A kingdom where witches are not suffered gladly."

Ludwin beckoned. A servant approached, lowered a steaming leg of venison between them on a platter, and retreated. The mouth-watering scent wafting about Father Ulf. He cocked a brow as Ludwin Mornoth continued, rising to carve the joint.

"The servants have gone; now we can get down to the meat. Never will any man say I cannot serve those who serve me." His eyes sparkled. Thain smiled faintly in amusement.

"To strong arms, sharper blades, and our enemies' fall!" Lord Keffer smiled, his teeth bared in anticipation of hunger satisfied.

Father Ulf slid his plate forward, returned Nidfael's smile, and said, "To the fall of the enemies of the church! I willingly drink to that." As a weapon of righteousness in his hands, they would accomplish much.

"To a renewed kingdom." Mornoth nodded and dumped Ulf's portion of venison before him. He raised his goblet, and Father Ulf lifted his with Nidfael and Thain's, echoing Lord Mornoth, "For the good of Northumbria!"

Later that night, after their guests departed for their chambers, the bishop's man entered at his usual hour, a shadow that solidified behind Thain's chair. Thain's neck prickled. The envoy's voice came softly. "It is best to know as much as one can about an enemy, my lord, inside the church or without. Not that any of them, tax-paying and law-abiding as they are at this hour, would know much of an enemy besides the brigands." He seemed to be waiting for something.

Thain said nothing. When the man did not continue, Thain let a hint of sharpness into his voice. "And this assists us, how?" His hands clenched the arm of his chair and his cup, and he shifted to glare at the black-clad messenger.

The envoy's eyes narrowed. "Since it has escaped your notice, the north has worsened since Lord Dain Cieri's daughter returned from slavery in the east. There is talk of oppression, and disregarded law in the southlands, and freedom." He shrugged. "Cierheld and the abbey guard their people as more precious than gold."

Thain frowned. "And whose fault is that but your master's?"

The envoy's thin frame ill-suited his black cloth, too rich a velvet for a mere churchman, even a deacon. But then he was Bishop Caddaric's man, in act and deed. The bishop would garb his creature as he did himself, even to a cloak of night. Thain allowed a slight curve of his mouth. The first of the seven deadly sins clearly gripped Caddaric. As for his envoy–the man looked down and folded bony arms across his small black-clad belly with a sniff–that one's indulgence was quite apparent. If ever he was employed in the shadows with a blade, he would be a hair slow unless he stabbed for the back.

The envoy's face held a tinge of red. "My lord, you of all young men understand the church must have its share of our fair island's abundance. Our blessed bishop receives the Lord's due for distribution. As is the way of the world, the strongholds have ill-guarded their own, thus their holds burn. That is no fault of ours." He dipped his head, scorn slipping around the edges of his words. "As for the burnings, we heard rumor that your hold knew something of it. I also hear this Father Ulf of Bolton believes the evil eye has come to Cierheld in the shape of its first daughter. Or he simply finds it politic to declare Lady Kyrin a heretic. One who associates with demons?"

Thain growled, "The burnings are your concern to ferret out. Any witchery is your master's. My concern is the northlords, who oppose us at every turn, on so reasonable a matter as the truth. Lord Cieri refuses to acknowledge the court's grip on Northumbria is slipping, despite the regent." He stood and paced to the window and back, green silk sleeves rustling. "Of course, Lord Cieri touts freedom and learning. It brings him the willing vassalage of lower men. He would have even the scullery maid learn to read! Tell me, what can a kitchen maid gain from the Vulgate?" He snorted. "But a churchman such as Father Ulf is far more careful of that than I! My uncle will see that ill idea wither before the spring."

The envoy smiled, tight and close.

Thain Mornoth shared his quick amusement with a shake of his head. His mirth died, and he continued, thoughtfully, "The regent recently seems more unwilling to guard his interests against grasping lords, even northlords with naught to their name but old blood, who reach for more." He raised a finger. "Notice, I do not mention the raiders who lurk beyond the great Wall in the north, waiting only for a sign of our weakness. Be sure to tell Bishop Caddaric that." He smiled his lips thin. "Of course, the brigands follow their own interests, and our good regent Golding simply loves peace, or his duties have already bitten him hard and deep, and it is not even last leaf-fall. Uncle Ludwin says the painted ones may come before summer. We may find each other allies." He tapped the dagger sheathed at his leather-clad waist with a finger.

The envoy inclined his head slowly. "Be it brigands or the painted people, it may be as you say; but the snows will come first." His expression chilled. "My master is losing patience. Lord Dain Cieri pricks his side. He is a thorn also to you of the house of Mornoth. If Dain was removed–God forbid, of course–and Lord Codi Golding was unfortunately not strong enough to survive news of treachery from such a trusted lord, who better to step into his shoes than your uncle, who knows the working of court and kingdom? Despite whispers I hear of one Durand Tolman who aspires to the seat of regent."

Thain raised his cup to hide his face. The brew had lost some of its bitterness. Gulping a swallow of honeyed mead, he lowered it. "Bishop Caddaric agrees something must be done if such unhappy events come to pass?"

Black shoulders twitched in a minute shrug. "Did he not have the holy impetus to send me? Your uncle's lands lie between those of north and south. My eminent master well knows the house of Mornoth stands between the lords, holding the peace. This Durand Tolman, well, few know his mind. Better a lord we know."

If his uncle rose higher than regent, who would take the place closest to the new king? Who but one of his house? Thain tapped his cup with his ruby signet. Unwarranted pride led to inevitable downfall. Strange, the envoy carried no prayer beads in hand, no outward sign of rank. A man should proclaim who he was to the world. His own ring rested on his forefinger, neither too loose nor too tight, though the jewel was rather small. He would remedy that as soon as he could.

But Alkborough, brooding on its hill above the Humber River, already occupied a key position, as did he when his uncle was allowed to speak in the ears of court. If they gained the court's regard with the bishop's favor, or even the ear of Father Ulf in Bolton Abbey, which Uncle Ludwin seemed to have secured, much would change. Despite the aspirations of Durand Tolman. Only over Lord Mornoth's unbreathing body would there be any more allowing in favor of the northern lords, of lands or anything else.

"I have also thought on how you may get word to and from this Father Ulf to your uncle without men's notice. That girl of Lady Ynglida's, now, Esther—the first daughter who threw herself almost under your horse's feet to gain Lord Mornoth's eye—she often tends to Father Ulf's simple needs at Bolton Abbey."

Thain's breath quickened. Bolton Abbey, close by Cierheld stronghold as it was, could not be handled without care. From abbot to monk, any churchman could turn in a man's grip, never mind that the hands that sought to wield him were worthy.

But if Bishop Caddaric saw their great vision and approved the small changes necessary, the church lands would extend themselves, would bring the hand of God upon every man, and rightful lordship to every town, stronghold, and hovel, not to mention the king's court.

"Ah! Now I remember why I pay you good coin." Thain drained the last of his mead. "You are right. Esther Govannon may continue to serve a worthy father she once knew as her confessor, without remark. A father who is an anchorite, a man in his hermit's cell, walled into a holy church, is secure from all temptations. She may carry more than offerings of food in her basket and return from such a pure errand unquestioned." He clenched his hand about his cup. "Do it. For something must be done. Any land is only as good as its king."

The bishop's man bowed his pale, tonsured head. "Under your care, Britannia will rise and thrive." He looked up, peat dark eyes glinting. "Then gold will not be uncommon. For the good of the kingdom, some must fall."

Thain stared darkly at the gathering shadows. "Even now Northumbria learns the danger of brigands."

6

# Torch Point

*And the light shines in the darkness, and the darkness did not comprehend it. ~ John 1:5*

"And I say you will!" Rolf felt at a distinct disadvantage, glowering at Kilden's imperturbable face a hands-breadth from his nose. "Seldon requires sword training by a hand other than mine, which is sore lacking any training of late. Just you remember that. Keep him from underfoot and busy this morn."

Kilden stared at Rolf. "He seemed to think your sword inspired when you first met him."

"You don't understand!" Striking at the icy fear and anger that spiked through him, Rolf erupted. "That was my ill-thought, murderous pride, wanting to prove myself. You know my skill is with the ash and oak, Kilden. It always has been. I'm not your squad leader. But Seldon is, well, he is not my enemy, yet I do not know him. But I'll see none pitted against a brigand without training." With the darkness of long-standing oak water, he said, "You agreed to Abbot Alton and the squad's wishes to serve as Bolton Abbey's guard for the present, not I. You train Seldon. Besides, the good father has me going after ink for his quill this morn."

Kilden growled, "Ulf was rather quick to say Brother Niel gets in the way of his own feet, that it must be you to run his errand."

Rolf's mouth tightened. "There is none other to find his berries and barks, none other who can boil his brew of iron-gall for his new translation."

Kilden's brow drew down. "Does this father cage you, or seek to break you, Rolf?" It was the quiet thunder before storm.

Rolf straightened under the heat of Kilden's ire. "This house is no cage. This place of God and my oath are of my choosing. Nothing and no one will break me."

Kilden did not budge. "It's not the good Lord pulling your rope so short."

Rolf hesitated. "He finds Seldon a fit scribe, for the moment."

"Then why is Father Ulf keeping you always tethered to his side? Seems odd when he hates you so."

Rolf's face burned. It was too true. "You think Father Ulf ill uses me, when Prior Dickon has better things to do than mix his ink? I'm the newest novice. Father Ulf has promised me a season's trial to prove myself."

Kilden eyed him. "I'm meaning no disrespect, but any man can see Ulf's ill will toward you who looks, and I don't believe he's a good man of the habit. Why do you not speak to your abbot, and work under this Prior Dickon?"

Rolf shook his head fiercely. "There is an order to things here. As there was in our...in Lester's squad. There are those who lead and those who serve. Kilden, Prior Dickon believes it unseemly that a brother who wishes to prove himself should move to another estate until he has kept his word in the first. He is right. If I am ever to gain Father Ulf's goodwill, I must be more faithful than any novice in the history of this abbey." He raised his shoulders in a helpless gesture. "He is prickly and set in his ways, but his hand at illumination has no equal. His translations are truly glorious."

Though the vermilion that graced Father Ulf's books in the scriptorium made Rolf swallow hard. The beautiful vines and scrollwork in lines of crimson forced him back, always back, to the day of his destructive anger and the flow of blood curling across Seldon's neck.

Rolf made a wry face. "Father Ulf also seeks to build a scribe school. He allowed Lord Mornoth to give coin toward it that may have gone better toward the hunger among us."

Kilden leaned forward, earnest. "My brother, let not this man deceive you. You were never meant for the church alone. God uses men in many places. May you not serve the church and your fellow men?"

Rolf shot him a look. "You think I ought to have joined a fighting order?" He shook his head and said, quieter, "I do not like Father Ulf, that is true. But we are brothers in more than the habit, whatever his ire says. He has sworn an oath to me and I to him, though we seldom speak of it. What he said this morn—a hungry stomach does drive a man to work harder." Rolf sighed. "I will mix his ink right well, as he asked, and eat later."

Kilden reached out and his fingers tightened on Rolf's shoulder. "And if the hunger is so great that there is no hand or mind left for the work?"

Lester said from behind, "Aye, tha' thought 'as been in my mind."

Kilden dropped his hand and turned. "You've the right of it, Lester." He rested his hands on his hips, watching as Lester offered Rolf a small loaf, an apple, and a bit of cheese.

Rolf took them reluctantly, and Lester said decidedly, "No man 'kin fight an inner or outer battle long, without somethin' in his middle."

"True." Kilden's voice was dour. "Let no desire for a home among these brothers blind you, Rolf. Some of 'em are well enough, I grant you. But better open-eyed and wary than blind and hunted," he said gruffly, and his green-brown eyes glinted. "You're never seeing bread from his table going to the young ones, and you never will. I know his kind."

Rolf's neck heated. He'd given the children as much of his own bread as he could and still work, then Father Ulf denied him the rest of his portion. His squad brothers yet cared for him. He eyed his hands, gripping the coarse brown bread and apple. His fingers were thinner, yet still strong. Men did change, he could attest to that. Even inwardly, they could change.

"What think you of Seldon?"

Lester clapped his shoulder with a great smile. "Ah! Seldon may right be your other half, learnin' to be a warrior, and a good one at that though his voice be an angel's."

Seldon, becoming what he could have been. Rolf's stomach curled. There was something more beneath Seldon's words, a carefulness to his actions, a watchfulness. What was he about? Rolf bit into the bread. He would do well to be wary on behalf of himself and his brothers. "Father Ulf will be visiting Alkborough stronghold often, it seems." It would give him time.

Kilden said slowly, "Alkborough troubles me. This Lord Ludwin Mornoth, he's got no love in his own hold. His men are uncommon clammish in mouth, and their number is growing. Not from among their own."

Rolf offered, "Father Ulf says the brigands are roaming, and Mornoth takes steps against their leader."

"Does he? But the brigand never strikes south of the Humber."

Rolf stopped chewing. "Aye. Never yet," he said thoughtfully.

He must look into it and send word winging among the abbey's brothers to keep a sharp eye and ear to the wind of gossip as they went about their work. His jaw tightened. The one who led the brigands must be caught.

"Might Lord Mornoth know if the brigands eye the abbey? Is it possible he purposes to protect his people by gathering men to his stronghold? I would ask Father Ulf, but he deems my questions foolish."

Lester laughed. "Abbot Alton 'as taken steps against all who would seek to 'arm the abbey. He could look far 'afore he found a better defender than Kilden an' the men."

"Aye." The pressure in Rolf's chest eased. The brigand would slaughter no innocents here.

A smile lurked around Kilden's mouth. "After you finish filling your stomach, I'll take Seldon for a bit, teach him the blade, if you'll meet me with your staff after you warm your knuckles against his ash."

Rolf's heart lightened further. "But no blades."

Kilden grinned. "Have I ever needed one?"

Rolf smiled. "Not against me. You always did beat me."

"And you led us as none other can." Kilden turned toward the stables. "Seldon!" he bellowed.

Odd, such a deep, reaching call from such a slender frame. Their Lord delighted in such oddities, found in odd places, in odd moments, where they fit strangely to perfection. Rolf grinned. He could count on Seldon getting a drubbing, and he was next. Never mind he must run about the woods for ink. He was among his own again.

§

Lord Ludwin Mornoth's messenger had come and gone from the scriptorium. Sweat pricked under Father Ulf's arms. The hour was come.

Why did he hang back? He had regent Codi Golding and the bishop's full support, even if Abbot Alton had not yet given the bishop an answer where he stood on the matter of the planned scriptorium. Father Ulf snorted. There was an old fool who would think on a thing till doomsday and pray until his breath came no more.

Such paths of foolishness were not for him. He smiled, a small, satisfied twitch. Events must be nudged, nay, pushed. Did not the ruler of heaven say a man must watch his feet and direct them on the path of life? He sought ahead to forge his destiny under the hand of heaven. The bishop had been right to take him from his moldering post of priest in Easby Church and from the archives to thrust him into Bolton Abbey. He'd discovered much more than the many things the bishop wished to know. He'd found his own way.

"Father." Brother Rolf strode through the door, rumpled red head high, breathing quick. "Lord Teth's stronghold is burned, and the brigand has struck at Lord Dain Cieri!"

Ulf snorted. "And you scent war, do you?"

Rolf flushed, and his jaw bunched. "The brigands killed all they could reach: men, women, and children. Besides innocents, they sorely wounded Lord Dain, who was helping with Lord Teth's harvest. The lord of Cierheld lies at death's door. Their first daughter readies the stronghold against raiders." Brother Rolf slammed his fist on the scriptorium desk, rattling quills in their holder. "If only we knew who the brigand is! He cannot take another stronghold!"

Father Ulf looked at Rolf's hand and then at his face, coldly, calmly. Rolf's old tensquad followed him these days as if he were a lord's armsman, waiting on his word, though Rolf was too dim of wit to see it. All but for young Seldon, who paid heed to wiser counsel. Ulf moved his inkwell out of danger and measured his words. "And how is that our affair?"

Rolf stared at him. "Our affair! Every man's pain is ours."

"Every man's pain, is it?" Ulf stroked his chin.

His unseemly novice would be out of his hair soon. Abbot Alton was about to give the foolish order for him to ride out to scout with his squad. Yet it could possibly be made to serve if Rolf touched the iron and broke his word. What would break that cursed stubbornness of his? It would take a mighty circumstance. But it was already in motion. His so-called brother had meddled enough.

Rolf's gaze flickered, and he shut his mouth.

Father Ulf sat back in his chair. "What, no verse to urge me to a different course, Brother Rolf?" His mouth twisted. He'd muzzled his wayward novice. Now to bind him. "A novice so near to taking his vows as you ought to be faithful. It must be clear you are worthy to assist in higher tasks to glorify our Lord, clear that you possess the control necessary to wield men and the quill. If you make it clear to all that Lord Dain's daughter does not follow in her meddling father's footsteps, you will do well. Meddlers who question orders are the bane of the church. Have you noted Seldon?"

"Yes."

"He does as he is asked, trusting those given a seat above him." Ulf leaned forward with a cold smile. "Do you understand?"

Rolf inclined his head silently then turned on his heel, his habit whisking after him, his hands clenched as tightly as his mouth.

"Ha." Father Ulf chuckled.

Humming, he rose as he searched for another book of parchment on the shelves behind him. He'd found the dagger to twist, it seemed. Seldon served him well. Watching Rolf's strong hands knot in helpless ire, with nothing to grip, was honey to his spirit. Though his novice had no skill for words, it seemed the Book drew him. Father Ulf rubbed his chin harder. Brother Rolf was entirely unfit for the church.

He had spoken to Alton. If the abbot did not see wisdom, Bishop Caddaric would soon dismiss him and Brother Rolf. Better yet, he himself would. Father Ulf allowed himself a grin. How he would treasure the look on Alton's face when he took the abbot's chair. Then would begin a reign of righteousness in the church, in dark Northumbria, and in the hearts of men. Then in all the world, as far as the church stretched. And who could say how far her reach might go?

A hand of days later, Father Ulf's ire clouded the cold air as the mare slipped yet again. "Heaven blast that witch, sorcerous whelp of a heretic!"

Brother Rolf's absence was the only good thing he could think of, as their party rode to meet the daughter of Cierheld. Father Ulf growled again, wordlessly, and Brother Niel's eyes widened.

Neil nudged his heels against his horse's sides to bring her crunching through the snow to his side. Ulf resisted the urge to nudge his own beast away. Niel always smelled of his work in the stable and followed his novice's meddling, though none would meddle much longer.

Niel wet his lips. Father Ulf glared, hoping to stay his words, but his brother's mouth opened, heedless of his displeasure. "Father, this gift the daughter of Cieri brings us, is...is it tainted? I would have naught to do with witchcraft."

Father Ulf rolled his eyes. Fools, he was surrounded by fools. "Brother Niel, how can any taint remain in a jewel of the earth, dedicated to our Lord and to his work? Especially such a worthy gift, soon to be blessed by holy water from the abbot's own hand?" Scorn laced his voice.

Niel nodded and looked back to their snowy road along the river. Father Ulf smiled thinly. Simple man, so easily contented.

Though his own heart also throbbed with his first contentment in some time. The brigand's latest raid on Tethold had severed the last tenuous tie between Father Ulf and Cierheld, in the sight of others. Cieri's first daughter had made her position clear to all men. She rode as a man, her unholy skill with death openly acknowledged. As a woman, she led her hold in heresy, and he was sure she dealt in darker arts. There was no debt of blood or family that could cover the sin of witchcraft. No one could blame him for what he had set in motion.

His sister Willa would see that, she must see it, living in the heavens, singing with those of clear sight. Even *she* would cast her daughter from heaven's gates. Father Ulf swallowed the bitterness in his mouth when he wanted to spit. Kyrin Cieri was not his niece, not in heart. The girl who used to pray with him at dawn was gone. As if she had never been, as if she had indeed died in slavery, as he had so long thought.

Now her suddenly discovered gift, with which she sought food for Cierheld, and the assistance of more men, would serve better than she knew. She sought the church and Abbot Alton as go-between, to take a generous portion of the abbey's gift for their service in the matter. Alton had various contacts in the south and north and could procure what was needed. Ironic, it was. As he followed heaven and the bishop, the daughter of Cieri's gift would serve better than she dreamed.

Lord Dain Cieri would learn what coin he had earned, harboring a witch who aided his seduction of men to heresy. As all would learn who followed them. Oh, how those who stood against the will of heaven and the good of all Britannia would pay, to their sorrow. With a sidelong glance at Niel through drifting snowflakes, Father Ulf settled in his saddle. By the snow-laden trees thickening around them, they were near the edge of Bolton.

He had ordered Brother Niel from the stables to accompany him, and Prior Dickon as Alton's representative, to assure the daughter of Cieri of the abbey's good intentions. Dickon knew better than to open his mouth without his order. They would meet the Cierheld witch and her party, receive the gift from her that was due to the church, albeit a larger share than she planned, and he would bear it to the proper hands. Father Ulf smiled.

Cierheld stronghold's windfall would go to a work far more worthy than the doomed struggle between the northlords and the southlands. Even Bolton Abbey must pay its tithe of affliction for the greater good.

7

# Dark Deed

*He says to you, "Eat and drink!" but his heart is not with you.*
*~ Proverbs 23:7*

The three men around Father Ulf were dark, white-dusted shapes, crossing the appointed meadow ahead that spread white and wide along the river. His horse followed, cold feathers of snow blowing against Father Ulf's face.

He'd claimed he feared another attack of the brigand, hence their meeting here with but a single armsman that Lord Mornoth said he could spare. He would have none of Brother Rolf's armsmen about to report. Ulf's mouth thinned. The witch had believed him and agreed.

Dim figures against the trees waited in the blowing white as Ulf drew nearer. Several of them moved forward. That smaller cloaked figure must be her, shoving through the snow after a dark-eyed armsman, a gangly boy, and another who broke trail before them.

Father Ulf snorted. At last, he faced her again. He had wondered how strong he would be, but he need not have worried. Kyrin no longer looked anything like his Willa, with little softness left about her. She walked in a cloak and trews. His niece deserved no courtesy for her unladylike, straight stare. He waited, silent, the twenty paces between them a narrowing sea of white.

The witch's lips tightened, and she stopped. Briefly, she bowed, and her voice lifted.

Father Ulf eyed her, barely noting her words as he raised an austere brow. His niece gave warning of the brigand and knowledge of Lord Mornoth, though nothing certain. He suppressed his grin. She must have no inkling she blackened the name of a high lord who had the support of the church. He must give no hint and compose fair words. His mouth flattened.

"It seems my thanks are due you. This scourge must be stopped. To sniff out evil at its source is a hard task for any man. Though," he shrugged, "we know the old king was ill fit to lead such a hunt." He shifted impatiently. "But I will speak no ill of the dead." The cold was beginning to bite. They would never find the brigand and his men.

Cieri's daughter nodded, short and sharp, as if she too wished to quit the place, and brought out a dagger. She took a small wooden box from her first armsman, removed part of the dagger's hilt, and tilted the weapon. The tinkling clatter from the box that followed reached Father Ulf's ears in the winter quiet. She bowed her head over Cierheld's gift to the church and payment for supplies. She hunched her shoulders, her fingers tight about the wood box, snowflakes blowing across her brown hands.

Father Ulf's breath froze in his chest despite himself. What if the witch thought she could better deliver Cierheld's gift to Bolton Abbey than he? In that box lay the rise and fall of many, and the hope of light for Northumbria, indeed, for all Britannia. It was as his messenger had told him and Alton.

Yet her armsman's hand hovered near his sword. The man's gaze was on *him*, not Mornoth's borrowed armsman, motionless at his side.

Father Ulf turned to Prior Dickon and tilted his head. "Assist her," he ordered. The small, round monk sighed and nodded, dismounting to step past the first daughter's wary armsman. Father Ulf composed his face and settled his hands in his sleeves. He must avoid being seen as a threat.

Cieri's daughter shoved the box into Prior Dickon's hands, whose mouth was open as he fought to keep from dropping it. The oaf. Father Ulf snorted. Had he never seen unset rubies, pearls, or sapphires before?

He sniffed and stiffened. The witch who had been Kyrin Cieri was following Prior Dickon's hurried path toward his horse. Father Ulf frowned when she stopped at his knee.

"Uncle, we would welcome you at Cierheld. My father is ill, as you have surely heard, and I..." The heretic looked down, knowing full well her comely wiles. "I find I do not wish to lose any of my blood, especially to ill will."

"Ill will?" Father Ulf leaned toward her, the fire he seldom allowed rising fast. He spat, "What know *you* of ill will? Speak to me again when you have lived without your lord of Cierheld, as I have endured the days without my Willa." She who had been of his blood would not catch him with a temptation so thinly veiled. She'd lure him close, then turn on him, as her father had. Perhaps it was as well that pleasing others had rarely, if ever, tempted him. But that she tried galled him.

Kyrin flinched, and Ulf affected to stare over her head at the hills. Willa had such a laugh, always a soft touch for him, and clear devotion for the church. If Lord Dain Cieri had not stolen her, the bishop would have taken them both under his wing, and Willa would have risen under the abbess as he did under the bishop. Together they would have brought order and plenty and righteousness to the land. Until she fell. But it was not Willa's fault. It was Dain Cieri's.

Father Ulf's hand tightened on the mare's rein. "God's pure work in flesh: tainted, twisted, driven to wallow in uncleanness, driven by her love of a man. To *heresy.*" He dropped his gaze to the one who had been his niece. The dark earring of jet in her ear cried of all that she was. The eye of evil of the far east. Heretic. Witch. But their fall had begun.

The daughter of Cierheld backed a step.

He grinned wider. "There will come a day when your heresy will be recognized." The armsman at his side stirred.

Brother Niel legged his horse beside them. "Father, we must go." He whispered for Ulf's ear, "It will be dark before we—"

"Then go!" The rising wind whipped away Kyrin Cieri's shaking voice. "Take Cierheld's gift and payment and go!"

Father Ulf pulled hard on his rein. No witch commanded him. Her first armsman stepped forward in threat, but he could do less than nothing. Bitter amusement pulled at the corners of Father Ulf's mouth, and he turned his mare and gave them his back. Lord Mornoth's man shifted his grip on his spear, his sheathed blade tapping his leg, and followed.

They rode away, Niel and Prior Dickon falling in behind, and the thickening snow first buried their tracks, then eased. A little later, the sky cleared to blue. Heaven had heard him.

Father Ulf led them on, into winding copse and vale, along a different route of return. None dared disturb his deep thought to ask about their way. At last, they reached the riverside again. From trunk and branch, late afternoon shadows crawled across the snow, and a crackling chill crept with them.

"Father, ought we not to be seeing Bolton Hill?" Prior Dickon said at length. He hugged himself and rubbed his arms, his breath steaming to mingle with his beast's.

Father Ulf pulled the mare to a stop and frowned, looking up the river and down the shallow valley. "We should," he growled.

And protectively laid his hand over the box in the leather bag on his saddle.

Mornoth's armsman looked at him expectantly. Father Ulf said nothing.

Brother Niel frowned. "I thought so too. But the snow changes everything so."

Eying the prior, Father Ulf said, "Prior Dickon has need of summat hot, I dare say."

Niel brightened. "We could all use a bit of soup. I've brought dried ramsons, and I've a bit of wheat. Then we can find our way back with better heart."

"You always bring the wild garlic," Dickon said.

"So I do." Niel grinned. "Brother Rolf rightly says it heals much ill in man and beast."

The armsman chuckled at that, and Dickon shook his head with a wry smile. "A bit of anything hot would go down well, brother, even if it be thick with ramsons."

Father Ulf grunted. "You can add my piece of rabbit from yesterday, and my sack of ramsons to yours, so long as you boil it well." He shrugged. "With this cold, the meat will not have spoiled."

Niel rubbed his hands briskly, delighted. "My thanks, father. We will sup well."

Prior Dickon nodded and pointed. "At the edge of the meadow there's a drier spot under that old fir."

The ancient tree's limbs were dead near the base, and they soon tore them off and started a crackling blaze. While Niel and the armsman tended to the horses, digging away snow from the grass in the meadow, Father Ulf put the ramsons and rabbit from his food pouch, and then Brother Niel's, into the steaming pot of wheat and water on the fire. Prior Dickon huddled near the flames, pulling an extra cloak from Ulf's baggage.

Father Ulf grimaced. "That cloak is meant for my investiture as anchorite."

"Truly?" Dickon felt the black linen between thumb and finger. "It's a good, thick weave. I am grateful."

Father Ulf nodded. *Wretch.* He cut the last of the white roots in his hands into the soup. He washed away the stickiness in the snow and rubbed his tingling fingers dry on his cloak.

When the soup was ready, Niel scooped it out into their horn ale-cups, setting each of the four horns hurriedly in the snow. With the last horn, he sucked in his breath and plunged his hands into the snow beside it to cool them.

"Hot enough, I see." Father Ulf reached for his horn and sniffed. He sighed. "*That* many ramsons turns my stomach. Here." He handed his cup to Prior Dickon. Dickon smiled at him, tremulous with shivers. Father Ulf waved off his thanks. "There's naught of charity in it, good brother, I but see no point in wasting it. I'll see to my beast."

Behind him, Dickon offered the horn to Niel and the armsman, who refused with smiles, lifting their own in salute. The three dug in and ate happily by the fire.

Father Ulf looked at the sky. Dark was less than a bell off, by the slant of the sun. The horses chewed hungrily, pawing at the snow Niel and the armsman had missed in the wide space they'd cleared. Ulf helped clear a bit from the grass, shoving with his shoes.

A cry brought him around. Niel was bent over Dickon, who retched horribly beside the tree. Ulf's stomach twisted.

"Is it the fever, father?" Niel cried.

The armsman stared, his hand resting on his blade at his side, though he could do nothing.

Crunching through the snow, Father Ulf reached them and felt Prior Dickon's flushed forehead. He glanced about them. "In this chill, we must get him back to the abbey."

"Aye." Niel clapped a hand to his mouth and dashed for the other side of the fir with a groan. He emerged, sweating.

"Come, we must get back." Father Ulf hurriedly gathered the horses, and, with the armsman's help, bundled Prior Dickon onto his horse. "I've been thinking on our path. I know the right turn now."

The armsman swung into his saddle, retched off to the side, and wiped his mouth.

"Yes, father, just let me get the pot," Niel panted. He secured the cooking things and groaned as he pulled himself across his beast's back. "It canna' have been the rabbit. You ate it yourself a few bells ago. Though you did say the smell of the soup turned your stomach."

The others mounted and rode strung out behind him.

Prior Dickon swayed and moaned as they trotted back up the vale. Beside the river, his voice rose. "The lily of death. The vale of the lily! It is...the valley...the lily."

He retched again, and again, and could not stop.

"Stay a moment, father!" Niel moved his horse to Dickon's and laid his hand over the prior's on the reins. "He's going cold, Father Ulf." His eyes were anxious.

"And he'll get colder yet if we don't move on." Such a blind mole deserved it.

Dickon cried out and stiffened. His legs locked straight, driving him forward across the horse's neck.

"Easy, Dickon. Easy, brother. We'll get you to Abbot Alton." Niel dismounted and looped his beast's reins over his arm as Dickon's teeth locked and his eyes rolled up. "This is more than over-ripe meat, father. It's a weakness..." Niel's legs wavered, and he fell into the snow, retching again. He crossed himself, fingers quivering.

"Tie him on if you must," Father Ulf said sharply. It would solve one possible obstacle.

Niel turned his head, huffing for breath. "How–how much rabbit did you put in?"

Riding up on the other side of Dickon and Niel, the armsman made a wild grab at the prior as Dickon toppled into the snow. The armsman was shaking violently. "No rabbit does such. Lily of the Valley..." He looked at Father Ulf, and his eyes narrowed.

Niel shoved to his feet and stared at them, swaying. "*Lily of the Valley?* Lord, save us! Father, where–where did you get the ramsons? I swear mine were only ramsons–I know them. How many of yours..." Niel bent again, his arms around his heaving stomach.

"Enough." Their confusion would have been pitiable, did they not stand against those who furthered the church and her welfare.

Staring at him, the armsman growled, "Who paid you?" And he gripped the hilt of his sword.

"Paid me?" Father Ulf's voice rose. The armsman was the one to guard against. The others were too weak. He weighed various actions. "You think I am your master's lackey, as you were?"

The armsman caught the import of his last word and jerked as if he'd been struck. "You've dealt with my Lord Mornoth as a brother yet you'd kill one who serves him?"

"I serve only, ever, the church. In this, our aims lie alike. He said he could spare you. I but took him at his word."

The armsman's face hardened. He tilted his head, grim, his gaze calculating. "Killing us gains you what? Ah. The jewels. The brigand strikes again in the winter night, leaving none to tell the tale. While one body is never found. For that to ring true, *father,* you'd have to stick a blade in us all." He drew his sword. "And for that, you'll taste mine!" He kicked his horse.

Father Ulf backed the mare and spun her, urging her away. Mornoth's armsman came on in a flurry of kicked up snow. Closing, their horses running shoulder to shoulder, he raised his blade. Father Ulf twisted and drove his dagger back below the armsman's ribs. The man crumpled, clinging to his mount. His horse turned and its teeth closed on Ulf's shoulder. With a cry, Father Ulf wrenched free and struck up under its jaw with his dagger. The horse rose on its back legs and whirled away with a gurgling whinny. The armsman fell, and his beast trotted a short distance and collapsed.

Breathing hard, Father Ulf dismounted and gathered up the tethers of the last two horses. Only his brothers stirred in the gathering dark. He would have need of his other cloak. He went to Dickon, who muttered, half-aware, and unfastened the cloak from about his throat.

"Don't touch him!" Niel struggled to rise, cursing him brokenly.

Father Ulf swung back into the saddle and looked down.

"N-niel!" Dickon's voice cracked, and his body curled again, a helpless blot against the white.

Brother Niel stumbled to his knees beside him. "I'm here, I'm here, Dickon," he gasped.

"Our Lord, my Lord....mercy." The prior's cry of pain trailed away.

Father Ulf said, "You serve our Lord far better in death than in life." It ought to comfort them, to serve so.

"Aye, I reckon we'll be seein' our Lord soon," Niel growled. "Do not think he does not see your treachery." He half rolled aside to retch, then settled Dickon against him, wiping his brother's mouth with a corner of his cloak.

Father Ulf snorted. "Treachery, Niel? I but pave the way for greatness. Greatness beyond your small thought." The smell of death rose around him. Father Ulf wrinkled his nose and wiped the blood from his hand and dagger. Next time, another would wield the blade. He would see to it. But he had a school to build, and a kingdom to save.

Hoof beats faded, and after a tortured time, quiet reigned beside the river. More snow fell, and the armsman stirred briefly, staggering across the shadowed snowy scape toward the brothers and his horse.

8

# Poisonous Fruit

*We were afflicted on every side: conflicts without, fears within.*
*~ 2 Corinthians 7:5*

"Keep a sharp watch." Brother Rolf slid from his saddle, staff in hand. His heart beat fast. There was doom here. He felt it and smelt it: blood and vomit and anger bright as copper fire.

"See to it," Lester said, and most of the squad formed a ring, looking outward at the trees, weapons to hand, long habit from the Wall taking root again.

They watched the woods and the water, their blades bared, Kilden with an arrow on his string. Seldon's feet thumped down on the other side of the snow-covered huddle of men who had not replied to their hail. Rolf moved quickly under the spitting torch Lester had lit with the coals he carried and held high.

Living shadows played across three iced cloaks, the hoods pulled down to shield the travelers' faces. Whipping at a corner of forlorn cloth, the night air also caught at Rolf's throat. If the brigands had dealt with these so hardly, their trail would be hot again. He would not return empty-handed to Father Ulf, though his heart sorrowed for these. This time, even Father Ulf must admit they had reason to find the brigand who terrorized the roads.

The white socks of the lone, partially snow-covered horse the group had huddled against had never been in *his* stable. Brother Rolf shook his head and pulled back a cloak one of the silent figures had extended to wrap around his companion. Breath failed him.

Brother Niel's hand fisted about the cloak edge, his fingers lifeless blue, Dickon within his arm. His brothers were frozen in a rictus that told its own tale.

Poison.

Rolf gripped his staff, and his soul went white hot, then deadly cold. Murder. What were they doing out at night? Had Father Ulf sent them on an errand, or had he also come? They'd been murdered.

His gaze flicked to Seldon, who lifted the other cloak. "This one's an armsman, struck by a blade."

Not Father Ulf? Rolf's hands shook as he stepped closer to the strange armsman. "Poison," he croaked, his voice so brittle he was distantly surprised it did not break.

"A dagger it was, I think." Leaning over, Seldon touched the man's blood-soaked side.

"My brothers were poisoned, but I don't need you to tell me what a blade wound looks like," Rolf snapped. "Your hand is more fit for the scribe table."

Seldon shot him a burning look, affront clear. "Says who?"

"Father Ulf, for one. Or mayhap you'd better fit the choir, with your lark's tongue?"

"That is no matter of yours." His eyes darkened. "This matter is ours."

"No matter of mine? Do you mean, this matter also will be none of mine?" Rolf grabbed Seldon's cloaked arm. "They are my brothers! And someone killed them." His throat closed. He'd been about to ask Father Ulf to let him scribe alongside Seldon, once he showed them both he could snare a brigand without resorting to an iron weapon. But it was for naught. Seldon took his chance of scribing from him, then he did not even care. "Whoever did this, I will bring them down." He shook Seldon's arm.

"A better question is, where is Father Ulf?" Seldon brushed snow from the armsman's shoulders with his free hand. "No brigand would leave behind such a weapon." He indicated a sword in the snow near the armsman's body.

Rolf released Seldon, who looked at him warily. Rolf had lost their last staff contest some time ago, due to his distraction over his scribing attempts. Seldon had not come to him again since.

Snow crunched as Kilden approached. He nodded agreement with Seldon's assessment, while Lester picked up the weapon that had fallen from the armsman's fingers to examine it. He looked over the bodies, lifting cloaks, eyeing their belts. "It seems as if nothing 'as been taken. What now?"

All eyes turned to Rolf. He closed his eyes. Abbot Alton was the one who had determined he should lead the squad on their first scouting foray, as he knew the area. He took a step away and drew a breath, staring into the trees across the meadow. Who had poisoned his brothers? If Father Ulf had been here, surely, he'd not gone for help, knowing it was useless. Better to stay and offer comfort. Regardless, he was not here now.

This could not be the brigand's work, not unless the band came on his brothers long after the poisoner, and they'd been startled away before they could rob the corpses. But there were no fresh tracks in the snow except their own. He'd noted that as they approached.

Unless the armsman had been one of the brigands, passing himself off as a traveler who wished to share their fire, and then administered the poison. But the armsman would never take it himself, and there was vomit on his tunic. Besides, the brigand had a band, all the hands he could wish. He had no need to wait for poison to do its ugly work. The armsman had drawn his sword. Who had he been fighting? Surely not Niel or Dickon. Rolf went back and peered closer.

His brothers were unmarked by any blade, their faces a tale of pain: jaws clenched, eyes wide, lips drawn back as their bodies arched in last agony.

Rolf stopped beside the armsman again. His eyes stung and his hand curled about his staff. "Do any of you know this man?"

Somberly, the men said they did not. Kilden looked, shook his head, and moved off in an ever-widening circle, searching for tracks.

Rolf leaned abruptly forward in the icy wind, and his breath came hard. They would never hurt any man, his brothers. Whoever did this would find justice, whatever Father Ulf said. Abbot Alton would concur.

Snow from Seldon's glove was melting on the armsman's pale face. Rolf's hand tightened in a sudden convulsion. The man was alive.

He would know who did it.

Shaking, Rolf dropped his staff and reached for the man's shoulders. Seldon glanced down and saw. His eyes widened, then his arm was in Rolf's way. "No, Rolf!"

Rolf gritted out, "He must tell us—"

"Not this night!" Seldon shoved him back, red patches on his pale cheeks. "He needs bandaging and warmth if he's ever to speak again!"

Rolf did not hear him for the blood rushing in his ears. "They will not die for nothing!" He snatched his staff from the snow and lifted it.

"Lester, stop him!"

Lester stepped forward. "Rolf, ee's right, brother."

"No! We have one chance."

Seldon rested his hand on his hilt and blew out a long-suffering breath. "You must not, brother. Father Ulf would say to take them to the abbey."

"First, we must find him!" Rolf glared at Seldon. "The armsman is the only one who knows where he is, where he went, who took him! Yet if you wish another lesson of wood against iron..." He thrust his staff toward Seldon's legs.

Lester slammed his torch down between them, scattering sparks, driving Rolf's staff into the cold white. "Enough!" His black hair and beard stirred in the rising wind. His form was dark around the sputtering brand that held Rolf's staff against the ground.

With a nod, Seldon stepped back. Rolf could do no less. He scowled, chest heaving. He could kill the whelp, all the more because he was right. Sudden despair blanketed Rolf, colder than the snow. His shoulders slumped.

Was he to lose everything? Seldon was better suited to his place, and he to the stable. Fear stiffened his back, forced a snarl from his mouth. Was that what Seldon had come for, to drive him even from his brothers of the abbey? That would be a complete revenge.

Lester glared at him. "Brother or no, yer our squad leader, at least this night. Don't make me regret it." He lifted the torch and turned his back.

Heart sinking, Rolf stared at him as he scanned the dark.

Kilden strode up and lifted his chin. "I found this." He held up one of Father Ulf's gloves.

Rolf's heart leaped. "Where?"

"At the edge of the road, where the tracks end, near covered in snow. A wagon and many horses passed after." He shrugged. "It could be the brigands; it could be others."

Seldon had tugged free his cloak and pulled it about the armsman. He looked up. "Rolf, your belt. It would slow the bleeding."

There was a hush.

So, his men held him to his place with words and expectation. To control the ice in his veins, or mayhap to show him the way, despite Seldon? Brother Rolf felt a sudden rush of tears and let out a breath. So be it. He would do what he could. He turned his head and surreptitiously rubbed his face with the back of his hand. Seldon looked away. *Whelp.* Rolf glared at his back, then stripped off his belt and moved forward.

He thrust his staff upright in the snow. "Kilden, mark us out a trail and see if you can tell how many were here, what kind of poison it was, and anything else we should know."

Kilden inclined his head and obeyed, mounting to scout the edge of the trees and the river.

"Lester—"

But Lester was already ordering some of the others to find wood and digging in his pack behind his saddle. The rest moved about various tasks, while some watched. Seldon held the torch.

The wind whipped the flame, and Rolf had no breath to argue. "Good, keep it steady." He rolled the armsman away from the dead horse. They must not be too late to learn what they needed. Rolf's gorge rose. He would hate to have to cut the armsman's throat later, if he had ties to the brigand. The lingering warmth from the horse's big body and his brothers was all that had kept the armsman alive for so long. *Lord, may he not be an enemy.*

Rolf glanced over his shoulder. The snow had buried all earlier tracks of the trail behind his brothers, but for vague dips and wells of the deepest horse prints. By their even spacing, he thought a rider distracted his brothers' horses from this place. He hoped it was Father Ulf. They could follow those tracks, but for the wounded armsman under his hands. Father Ulf, captive, killed, or running, was getting farther away with every flake of falling snow, an obscuring white wall beyond the illuminating torch flame.

The armsman did not die, but neither did he wake when Lester bandaged his wound next to the blazing fire. Seldon stared at Rolf when he ordered the fire lit, but none commented on it giving away their position, knowing it was for a life.

Rolf shrugged. The risk was small, with eleven in his squad, and well-armed. That is, well-armed if one discounted his oaken staff. Rolf smiled without humor.

A half-glass later, when Kilden reported on his long hunting circuit about the meadow, Rolf hissed through his teeth. They were confounded at every turn. As Father Ulf said, his choices went ill. They knew no more than they had, and he hadn't thought to send Kilden ahead to scout the trail before the snow buried it. He let out his breath carefully. "Kilden, you must take the armsman back to the abbey."

In the midst of adding the last blanket they could spare to wrap the armsman on his horse, Kilden paused.

Rolf said, "If we catch up, I'll know Mairne's prints."

Seldon steadied the limp man while Rolf held his first's gaze.

Kilden pressed his mouth tight. "I'll do it. Then I'll come back." His gaze was hard steel.

Seldon opened his mouth "I can—"

Lester shot him a dark look, and Seldon's teeth clicked together.

Rolf said, "I thank you for it, Kilden. My tracking is second to yours. But you are the only one with the woods skill to get back to Abbot Alton quickly enough with the armsman and my brothers." He gestured toward Niel and Dickon's still forms. "The rest of us must follow the trail, if we can." He hated to lose Kilden.

"One thing, brother." Lester tossed a stick in the fire and rose from his crouch. "Seldon says he 'eard one of Father Ulf's servants sayin' Ulf was to return with a treasure this eve. From Cierheld."

"Cierheld?" He'd heard Lord Dain Cieri was dangerously ill. After he'd been badly burned, his wounds refused to heal. Cierheld had called in the best healers they could afford, while the stronghold's people had as much of a pinched look as those in the abbey, the last he saw of them.

"Aye. He was to fetch it fer' the abbot. Part was to go to the church, and the rest was fer' men and arms the abbot would get from the south to 'elp protect the hold."

Rolf's gaze swung to Seldon, who held the armsman as if his life depended on his steady hands. "Seldon, what was the treasure that was to go to Abbot Alton?" Rolf's heart thundered. A large gift could change many things if services had not been carefully arranged beforehand.

"Jewels, he said." Seldon looked at the ground. "Gems she found in that strange, falcon-shaped dagger of hers. Kyrin Ci—"

Rolf ground out, "So, Dain's daughter found a treasure, yet they are not using it for a better healer?"

"It seems she did not wish to give all the jewels up. Her oath was called into question. In the end, it was decided she was to gift the jewels for Cierheld's needs and the abbot's fee, while the men of Cierheld gathered with their allies in the north. So, the man said."

Rolf's mouth tightened. Might the murderer be an enemy closer than the brigand and his band? Mayhap one of Cieri's men? Any who tried it would have to concoct an excuse to linger behind, and then wait for the poison to take effect. That seemed highly unlikely. Rolf muttered, "I do not think any would dare steal the jewels openly, unless..." Seldon looked at him, and Rolf said, "If one of Cierheld's men dared this deed and made his way back to Kyrin or even to Cierheld, he'd be questioned as to why he'd left his party. Unless it was that messenger, Lord Talik Wyman, as they call him now. No one would suspect him, always about between the holds at all hours."

Seldon hunched his shoulders. "He's off to the allies' camp, up north, leading Cierheld's men."

Father Ulf must have told him that. Rolf's mouth flattened. Seldon had been deep in Ulf's counsel and scribing of late. He turned from Seldon and spread his hands. "What think you, squad brothers? Father Ulf was here, on his way back from meeting Cieri's daughter with a treasure, and evil came upon him, Niel, and Dickon. The daughter of Cieri was the last to speak with them." Unless she herself did it. Cierheld had dire need these days, with a dying lord and father, and a hungry hold, nearly as hungry as the children in the abbey.

Seldon said, "Knowing she could accuse the brigands, did she plan to take back the jewels, and give the brothers a parting gift of food or drink?"

It was the simplest answer.

Lester chewed his beard. "It could be. Let us go an' ask."

"The trail leaves the meadow, there." Kilden pointed toward the eastern edge. "We might catch them on the road or find Father Ulf along the way."

If they found Father Ulf, it would likely be his body. Rolf shut his eyes. He could see the snow drifting to cover Ulf's frozen shape, mingling with his white eyebrows, raised in mocking doubt of him. Or Father Ulf might have eaten less of the poison and ridden further. Or did one of Cierheld compel Father

Ulf, who had left the armsman's sword behind when he gained a far worthier treasure? Did he gain with it his first daughter's favour?

"Let's follow the trail a little," Seldon offered. He grinned at Rolf in blatant challenge, taking the words from his mouth.

Rolf stiffened. *Why, Father? The greed and pride of men steals friendship, poisons loyalty, brings the necessity of killing for defense and for justice. I hate it. And the evil in my heart.* Where was the end of it–of the darkness? He must control it. But why did Seldon bait him? At least no one could mistake Seldon's rather golden voice for his own plain tongue. Yet he could make sure his words and his place were never taken again. Rolf shuddered, caught in a vision of Seldon falling into the snow by his hand. No. Never. Though he'd like to thrash him beyond crying for mercy. Was there not enough pain in the world? His brothers of the abbey were gone.

Now he must save who and what he could. How dare the daughter of Cieri break her word? She had implied honorable intentions. He well remembered their words as they spoke of her gift of the Vulgate.

*"Do you seek to bribe me, to tempt Father Ulf?"*

*"No, brother. I ask only that you let all read it, as often as they will, in Bolton church. And that you encourage our people to take comfort in it." Kyrin paused, then said almost to herself, "True comfort is much needed, with my land as it is."*

Rolf said, "We'll follow the road." Their only hope for truth was Kyrin Cieri. If he found Father Ulf with her or other sign of foul doing—his jaw knotted.

Seldon said nothing more, as Lester ordered the men to mount. The squad parted, Kilden riding with the armsman before him on his saddle, and the stiff bodies of Rolf's brothers lashed over Seldon's beast following behind, with a cloak over them.

Seldon followed Lester, and Rolf led the rest of the squad from the meadow, halting often to discern the trail, now clearer to see under a moon riding behind the parting clouds. The snowfall had ceased, and if the moon lasted, they might track Father Ulf all night.

The trail ended at the nearest road, as Kilden said, lost among a multitude of horse prints. Father Ulf's Mairne and the other two horses appeared to be following Ulf's earlier course, or, confused by poison, Ulf had become lost and simply kept to the nearest road. There was no way to tell which way he'd gone, or if there was another rider with him.

Seldon broke into Rolf's thoughts. "Whoever it was, they're long enough gone. This tracking at night is uncertain work. We might easily miss signs of anyone leaving the road." He waved his arm at the dim white stretch before them.

Rolf scowled. "It is true." If Lester had mentioned it, he could agree with better grace. They might also miss Father Ulf's body tossed behind a tree, covered by a skiff of snow. Though the ones they pursued, hopefully unaware they were followed, would likely camp. "We'll stop and move on with the light." Let Seldon find fault with that.

Seldon nodded, and Rolf glared at him. Lester soon had yet another fire going, and they huddled close for warmth, chewing on bits of stale bread they'd brought.

Seldon pulled his blanket around his neck. "How could someone steal from the church, let alone murder over it in such a way? It makes no sense! Poison and a blade? Is that not overkill?"

Lester grunted. "Anyone could, easily. Anger isna' sensible."

Rolf flushed and met no one's gaze, and an awkward silence descended around the fire.

Lester hunched his shoulders. "I meant to say, goin' by me own nose in me cups, I'd at times kill me own brother."

Across the fire, Seldon watched Rolf, sober. Rolf turned to the flames. He'd near enough killed Seldon at the Wall. He clutched his staff, wishing it were his quill, and he had a piece of parchment before him with the firelight flickering on it, with nothing more demanding than a letter to be written.

Kyrin's Vulgate now rested on Bolton's altar. She had given one gift freely, but if she withheld another by murder and deceit, she was not true, and he must get the jewels back. If Kyrin had Father Ulf's blood on her hands, she and her father would be a matter for the church. A matter also for him, under the promise he'd given.

*"Never think I do not watch you."*

*"I do not fault you for that." Kyrin's smile seemed to push back the shadows creeping across the ring. "All of us should watch for deception. The father of falsehood hunts us all."*

He'd said he'd watch and, in a sense, he was the abbey's armsman now, as a scout. By the abbot's own word, though, he bore no iron.

# 9

# Bitter Witness

*Why are you in despair, O my soul? And why are you disturbed within me? ~ Psalms 43:5*

Brother Rolf peered at his quarry through the empty eye-holes of a stinking mountain cat skin he'd flung over his head to disguise his features. Kyrin and her party rode along the road at the base of a white ridge clothed with scattered pine that rose opposite.

He'd not found Father Ulf. They had found a wood box, lined with silk, cast away beside the trail where Cierheld's men left the road to cut across a great loop of it. They were making speed, as they might well wish. Rolf gritted his teeth. If he was any judge, they were two nights from Cierheld stronghold, slowed by the snow that had fallen most of the night. It had given Kilden the Matins bells he needed to catch up with the men he'd gathered from Bolton.

Cierheld's men kept good order around their approaching first daughter. Even as Lester, the squad, and the Bolton men did behind him, farther back in the evergreens. Here the hills descended in low ridges, thick with trees, some bare of leaves. Rolf urged his horse forward. The moment for truth had come.

Kyrin Cieri's powerful, dark stallion snorted, as if sensing his thought, and reared with a scream. Did he know his mistress's guilt, black as his own hide? Brother Rolf tightened his grip on his spear. A stick in his other hand, he tapped the white sigil of peace he'd tied to the end of it against his leg.

Kyrin drew her blade, and her horse dropped to earth, pawing. Her first armsman's command rang out, and their men formed up, steel drawn, spears bristling. That stocky first armsman was Berd; he knew his voice. Rolf gritted his teeth. Why had Kyrin betrayed him? If she would but give up Father Ulf–*please, God, Ulf was not dead*–then he could show her mercy. He gained Berd as an enemy this day, if not the entire stronghold of Cierheld. If they brought war to Bolton Abbey, would that be evidence of sorcery in Dain's daughter? But he was putting off the confrontation.

He'd rather face anything than Berd's blade, or hers. But Father Ulf's fate declared otherwise. The prickly, hardened headpiece trailed down his back to end with a cat's tail. She could not know him yet, not in Kilden's spare set of soft-tanned tunic and leggings. On the road, she stared at him, waiting. The silence stretched. The pines whispered of treachery.

Kyrin shrugged, nudged her beast, and her men parted to let her through. His men were twice her number. Berd followed with his drawn sword across his saddle. A horse-length away, they stopped.

Those from Bolton, on horses little more than racks of hip and rib, spread out, a score at Rolf's back. Anger whispered among them. Most held ash spears. As usual, Kilden rode out of sight among the trees, his bow ready.

"Sir, what need you?" Kyrin asked quietly.

Rolf frowned, the furry edges of the cat skin concealing his ire. "I am Brother Rolf, no betrayer of a lord!" He spurred his horse forward and ripped the hide from him and dropped it.

"This day I am a hunter, and proud to be!" *You treacherous get of hell* choked in his throat.

Berd swung his horse in front of his first daughter. Rolf lowered his trembling voice. "You. False raiser of our children's hopes in Bolton! What say you before I take what was promised?" He did not look at Berd, who glared at him, deadly and ready. If he must use the spear he carried, he would use the butt. He'd taken up his staff in his other hand after dropping the sigil of peace.

"What do you say?" Kyrin's gaze was steady. He had her attention, right enough. "The jewels for the south people, Brother Rolf, they've been given."

"Have they? The law of the land falters. My warrior days are not so far behind me. Our Lord calls all men to do justice and ward the defenseless. This morn we found my brothers curled in speechless agony, slain by poison, and Father Ulf gone. How could you? Where are you keeping him? Or did you drop him when you finished with him for the snow to cover? By our Lord, I will whip your treacherous back for this!"

Her face admitted nothing but shock, and she added no word of surprise at his claim that he'd found his brothers this morn, though it was impossible for his party to have ridden so far in three bells, if she knew where they'd truly died. Rolf leaned forward. He must find the true trail. Every moment increased the gamble that Father Ulf would also die soon, if he was not already dead.

In one deft movement, Berd tore the spear from Rolf's hand, then whipped the edge of his blade to Rolf's throat. He growled at the angry stir of Rolf's men, "Be still. I would not murder a man of the church."

Rolf swallowed against the chill edge and glared into Berd's snapping eyes, unmoving. *Kilden, hold your hand,* he prayed silently.

Just as surely as Berd held his blade, Kilden had an unseen arrow aimed at the armsman's heart.

If Berd was so anxious to silence him, might Niel and Dickon's deaths be his doing? Or was he only defensive of his first daughter? Rolf drew breath and readied himself. The first daughter of Cierheld must answer for other lives than his. He could not falter now. Another moment would tell.

Kyrin flung out her arm. "Stop! Brother Rolf, I gave the jewels to my uncle early last even'." She swallowed hard but did not look away from Rolf's stern gaze. "Our meeting lacked fair words on his part, it is true. But there was no treachery. Might the brigand under Lord Mornoth have struck again?"

"Hah!" Rolf straightened. There was the crux of the matter. "You would know more of that than I. Has not this robber ceased his attacks since the lord of Cierheld took to his bed? Or would you deny that knowledge also?"

"Have a care for your tongue, man," Berd gritted. "Our lord took his death wound protecting you. He has only ever served his king."

That did not sound like treachery, but his brothers were dead. And someone dared steal food from the mouths of hungry families, even dared to steal Father Ulf. Brother Rolf narrowed his eyes and smiled at Berd in challenge. Berd looked back without a twitch, his dark gaze steady and cold as frost.

Kyrin held up her hand. Berd lowered his blade, tight-lipped. Rolf could not keep back his short smile and a soundless sigh of relief.

Lord Dain's daughter swung down from her horse, giving him her back. Hiding guilt or did she trust herself to him? Surely, she trusted her back instead to Berd. Her hands whitened on her saddle, but she faced Rolf again with decision. "Brother Rolf, my uncle may have been taken. Or he may have left the trail where the new snow hid his tracks, or those of his attackers."

New snow there had been in plenty, but Father Ulf was not a woodsman, who sent Rolf to get his herbs for ink, though Seldon served him more often, of late. Kyrin followed the same trails of thought he had, or she had the lie prepared.

"Give me proof of what you say."

Kyrin lifted her chin. "I have none. None but my men's word, and the question of what we do on the road without Cierheld's walls, if we did not fulfil our word."

Where was the truth, and Father Ulf? He could not fail in this. Rolf grimaced, watching them all, and Berd tensed as Rolf said, "Then some of us will die here. Better now than of hunger." He had almost rather fall here himself.

Kyrin's gaze sharpened as she took the measure of his determination. "Wait! I will give better than proof! Take me and..." Berd caught her eye fiercely, but Kyrin paused, considering the youngest in her company. "And Jost, as prisoners for Cieri's word. Take us with you and hunt down Father Ulf."

Berd turned. "No, my lady, you cannot. I will stay."

Rolf glared at Berd as he whipped his gaze back to him. Berd rightly guessed he would like nothing more than a chance to question his first daughter on far more than theology.

"Berd, I will endanger no one else for my uncle. Besides, I doubt not Brother Rolf will find him quickly, mayhap exchanging his ill-gotten gain for coin, for the brigands have never yet dealt in poison." Kyrin's voice was bitter, as dark as Rolf's heart.

Though her hostage offer and concern for her men weighed in her favour, her last words cast it away. His own thought echoed her doubt. As Jost legged his horse toward them, Rolf protested, "Do you have so little faith in a father of our abbey?"

The daughter of Cieri looked at him sadly. "Do you have so much? My uncle is different from the man I knew. Bitterness devours him."

Rolf shut his mouth in a flat line. He had noted the stiffness between them during their brief meetings he had witnessed. He could not gainsay her. The question remained: who stood to gain by murdering his brothers? Father Ulf would gain nothing but loss of the church's trust if he took such a course; he would never hazard losing his share of the coin he'd reap after Abbot Alton exchanged the jewels. It seemed the first daughter of Cierheld would reap trouble.

Her black earring winked at him in the sunlight. Rolf frowned. He could do nothing but remain alert for any sign of a guilty party, for a sign of Father Ulf or the brigands, and press forward. He was Alton's watchman, tasked with being his arm for the moment. As a representative of the abbey, he was also a dispenser of God's judgement and a guardian of Kyrin's soul, and every man's. Had he been deceived by her?

"I could never speak before your father again if I let you go," Berd protested. "I am your first armsman—"

"And it is not your decision." Kyrin's cheeks reddened. Berd straightened.

Every moment, Father Ulf's trail grew colder. If in the end it was a Cierhelden, and he must arrest him, far better it was Cierheld's first armsman who rode with them as proxy, than Kyrin Cieri.

Rolf said stiffly, "I will take this Jost, and him," he indicated Berd with a tilt of his chin, "and count it enough, Lady Cieri. It is not right that a stronghold first daughter ride with us. Your armsmen will not be harmed, for I hold *you* accountable. I pray that my judgement was right about you, that you do no witchery here, and I will find you at Cierheld, your word redeemed." He would find the guilty one, whoever it was.

Rolf spun his horse on its haunches, ignoring Berd. He felt the first armsman's stare burn holes in his back. That bridge to learning and a companion of the staff was thoroughly burned.

"One thing, Brother Rolf." As he turned sharply, Kyrin continued, "I will wait for you here two days. Also, be wary of any men of Lord Mornoth and Nidfael Keffer's. Mornoth supplies the brigand."

The brigand and his band? If Lord Mornoth sought advantage over the northlands, and the brigand was in his pay...Father Ulf had been regularly attending to Lord Ludwin Mornoth's stronghold. But Mornoth would gain little but enmity if he took a man of the church for any reason. Cierheld likely knew more of Lord Mornoth's designs than they revealed.

"They may have my uncle. It is probable they have much of your lowland goods."

Behind Rolf, Seldon muttered hotly, "I knew it!"

"We'll get 'em!" Lester cried. "Whoever they be." He looked darkly at Kyrin.

"Peace!" Rolf raised his hand. Kilden yet kept himself hidden; that was telling. "We will ride to look into it. Lester, as you love me, ride with the lady. I will not leave her with her guard under strength."

Lester dismounted and walked his horse toward Kyrin. Her cheeks turned pink. She rightly guessed Rolf sent Lester among them as his eyes, but she did not refuse. "Fare you well," Rolf said to her, then nodded curtly to Berd. The first armsman looked away and swallowed his retort. Rolf shook his head slightly, uncomfortable. Honor alone kept such a man silent.

"My lady." Berd saluted his first daughter, sheathed his weapon, and fell in at Rolf's side, his horse pawing the ground. Rolf ignored the first armsman's tight-lipped silence when Kilden joined them and took the lead, searching the snow as they rode back along the trail yet again.

Kilden found the first sign of their quarry at the edge of a large meadow off the road. He lifted his arm, turned to Rolf, and jerked his head toward the trees. Father Ulf's unshod horse, among others, had left the trail where Berd had stopped Cierheld's squad earlier, to dig snow away from the grass to provide the horses' feed. Kilden could not tell in the thawing snow if more than the monks' beasts had passed that way. Rolf flicked a hand signal, gave a low order, and the men of Bolton slipped through the trees and bracken in a wide net on either side of Father Ulf's tracks.

§

Kilden dismounted to trail Rolf and Cierheld's men. He approved Rolf's taking the lead in the pursuit. Berd was too wise to cause trouble, but Jost was young, and if the boy believed all he'd heard...Kilden shook his head. He'd heard much himself, of treachery between men and holds. They were near enough Pately Bridge and Keffold, Lord Nidfael Keffer's lands, who was often at Lord Mornoth's table. If the leader of the brigands hid in Nidfael Keffer's woods he might come and go, unmarked by most.

Fire smoke tickled Kilden's nose. Rolf stopped as he noted it, and Kilden smiled to himself, but glanced sharply from side to side. Their necks prickled alike at any hint of danger.

He watched Rolf follow the marks in the snow and look often into the trees. One of Bolton's watchmen and Berd walked hard on his heels. Smoke could travel far from a fire that made it. Did Rolf ache for his monk's habit? Though rough, the habit likely did not chill him with cooling sweat as the tanned skins he'd loaned him did. Kilden snorted. Rolf's books and the abbey were softening him. The signs were there. But toward a better man or a worse? Toward taking his place, or into the likeness of lackey Dugar? The need for riches and power drove too many to become as Mornoth and Dugar's ilk, bowing the knee to bishops and circumstance rather their rightful lords.

One of the Bolton watch edged toward Rolf, and Kilden eased closer, with a furious hand signal for silence. The man did not see him. Fool! They were on the hunt. It was no time to speak.

"Brother," Bolton's watchman whispered to Rolf, "Cierheld has always been true."

Rolf made a wordless sound at the misstep, evidently agreeing but grudging Berd his wide grin. Kilden glared at them. Between the three of them, they would give the entire squad away.

Ahead, the road to Pately Bridge passed through trees. Over a small rise, the watchman stepped upon a patch of snow. His feet crunched across the crust. Kilden stopped before he neared the dangerous spot, and Rolf and Berd stepped to either side. Rolf pursed his mouth. Kilden scowled, and the watchman took another crackling step with a wince.

"If they see me, they'll kill me!" The voice was indignant.

Father Ulf! Berd and the watchman froze. Kilden tensed, nocking an arrow, while Rolf's head snapped toward the sound. The wind shifted. The noise of many men and beasts was a hum of voices and a shift of bodies, punctuated by the clack of daggers on dishes.

A lower, nearer voice growled, "I tell you again, no one will know you in that tunic! Find out when and where any southlanders will ride to Kem Landyl's hold in Beeth to join Cierheld. There should not be many, since you have their promised coin. Remember, it is half your payment."

"And not near enough. God's house requires—"

"Prate not to me of your house!"

Kilden half-lifted his bow and crept forward. Smoke and mist drifted, heavy and close to the ground with the cold. Good, it would conceal their breath.

When Kilden stopped, Rolf eased beside him and peeped between the leaves of a low-growing oak, Berd almost standing on his heels. Kilden shifted, scanning the edge of the copse.

A horse and rider faced a scarecrow in the road. A ragged thatcher stood just below the rise, bits of straw winking about him. He tipped back his wide hat and caught at it as it began to fall. Kilden's mouth tightened. Ulf jammed the hat on again, his back partially toward them, reed straight. There was a grin in his voice.

"Lord Cieri and these cursed northlanders will have an unexpected greeting at your hands, my lord." He blew on his hands. "That nest of rebellion has been fat for far too long—"

Lord Mornoth's restive white stallion pawed the ground. The lord scratched beneath his conical helmet that shone in the afternoon. His strong face was deeply graven, heightened by his yellow beard. He would look better with an arrow through him. Kilden squinted. Beyond Mornoth, squads of spearmen, swordsmen, and one of archers rested, scattered about the snowy ground. Their cook fires marched out of sight along the road.

Rolf slid back behind the trunk of the tree and sat. Kilden lowered his bow and met Jost and the first armsman's eyes. They'd heard all they needed, as had Rolf. They looked away when Rolf rubbed at his eyes.

So far, they were undiscovered. Kilden watched Ulf, Lord Mornoth, and the edge of the camp opposite, thinking. His anger quickened. Father Ulf betrayed them all, against all reason.

Rolf could not speak for Father Ulf now, even if he wished. His brother had wanted nothing but Father Ulf's approval and peace between them. But Ulf had turned from that path, and Rolf—hah! Kilden's frame shook with a soundless, dry laugh. Father Ulf did not know his novice. He could never make Rolf depart from his oath, for he was loyal to a fault. Kilden knew it ate at Rolf that he had been so deceived in Ulf. Now Kilden met Berd's eye and his mouth thinned. The daughter of Cierheld would be in doubt of them no longer. He wondered if the house of Cierheld knew more than they told of Lord Mornoth's doings.

But Lord Mornoth had three wildcats and an implacable boar by the tail in Rolf and his squad. Lester would be spitting-mad when he returned, as was he. Kilden nodded. Ulf had thrown in his lot with the brigand, who plotted against the king's strongholds in the north, mayhap against the king's regent himself. What did Father Ulf know of Lord Mornoth and the brigands, and the rape of their strongholds? Now was the day to capture a traitor, and the man lurking behind him. In that moment, Kilden knew Lord Mornoth must die.

## 10

# New Traitor

*The name of the Lord is a strong tower. ~ Proverbs 18:10*

It was far south of Lord Mornoth and his men, after the Nones bell had rung in kinder places, when Father Ulf rode into the snowy vale where Rolf and his squad waited. Seldon and Berd leaped from cover at the forest's sunny edge. Berd went for the horse's rein, while Seldon took Ulf from the saddle with a grunt of impact, down into a whirl of snow on the far side. Rolf's men moved up. Those of Bolton watched, leaving the tensquad to the business they knew best.

Staggering up, hair wild, his hood swept back, Father Ulf spit snow and screamed, "No! I've Lord Mornoth's—" He caught sight of Rolf.

Seldon lifted Ulf to his feet, restraining him.

Rolf clenched his hands. "So, you thought us the brigand's men, did you? But we are not who you thought." He motioned at those around him. "Are we? And you have Lord Mornoth's *what?* Sanction to betray honest men to their deaths? *They were our brothers!"*

Ulf crossed his arms and lifted an arrogant brow.

Trembling, Rolf raised his spear and whirled the butt around to strike the disguising hat from Ulf's head. Father Ulf did not flinch, and his lip curled. Rolf could hardly speak. That he had been so close and not known him, this man whose charge it was to lead and protect. "Murderer and traitor," he said thickly. "Abbot Alton will deal with you."

Ulf shrugged. "And with you, I deem." He looked meaningfully at Rolf's spear.

Rolf stood his ground. "My word is true. It will remain so." He must make it so. The spear in his hand could be used two ways, and he wielded only the wood. The cur deserved to be run through, but it would not be by him. Abbot Alton had ordered him on this disastrous scout with Kilden and the rest and ordered that he not appear unarmed. Rolf scowled darkly. When he returned, he would speak with Alton of that, and much else besides. His mouth twisted.

Father Ulf had given Abbot Alton lies of him, and doubtless more lies to Bishop Caddaric about the abbot. Had he spoken of Seldon's wish for training with the blade, of Rolf's own desire for weapons despite his oath, and of budding heretics in the church and out?

Seldon took a firmer grip on Father Ulf, and Rolf's smile was grim. From the men's expressions, any of them would remove Father Ulf's miserable head at his word. Cierheld's young Jost ached for it, his hand on his dagger. But first they must learn what was afoot, and with Father Ulf, an indirect attack was the best way. Rolf looked at him a long moment.

At last, he said, "Abbot Alton will rebuke Lord Mornoth for consorting with such as the brigand in unholy alliance."

Father Ulf's back straightened, and he lifted his head. "Have you ever wielded men like swords? How can you not see this alliance works for our betterment? Some things must be sacrificed for the good of all men. Alton refuses to acknowledge what those above him see clearly."

"Those above him, such as the bishop?"

Ulf took a sudden step forward. "Rolf, I may have been too hard on your skill with scribing. A warrior's hand is not shaped for such work. But if you can see the higher path, the mercies for all, the good gained, I know the bishop will find a place for you to fitly repay your worth."

"What mercies for all?" Rolf asked.

"The hand of God will bring order to the land. That is a mercy, is it not? It will mean food, safety, learning, and prosperity! You asked for the same for your children of the abbey."

Rolf frowned. "And who determines what God desires?"

Father Ulf snorted. "He who leads God's house, of course."

"Did he sanction the death of my brothers?"

Ulf's gaze slid aside, then came back to him. "We must do what is necessary—"

*"Necessary?"* Rolf said heavily, "I know little, but this I do know. You have allied with men intent on evil. What is necessary is the very thing you have sacrificed. Loyalty and honor and truth."

Father Ulf spat, "What know you of our high destiny, the goal of the church in the service of our Lord? Bishop Caddaric intends to achieve—"

That was one name confirmed.

Rolf said slowly, "Is our Lord's hand too slow to accomplish your designs?"

"You are a mere novice. You know nothing!"

Rolf looked around him at the others and back at Ulf. "We know you deal death by lying hands. Our betterment, pah! Brother Niel and Prior Dickon are gone. But our Lord will see justice done, now or at the end of time." The spear in his hand did not comfort him, his fist white about the wood. Looking down at it, he said in a low voice, "Wrongful blood builds nothing good."

A sly laugh brought his gaze up. "Ah, you're as poor a warrior as you are a novice!" Father Ulf grinned at him. "Far less are you a man, *Brother* Rolf. Every man upholds justice."

He dared falsely juxtapose justice and the man Rolf was, seeking to drive him from his oath? Or did the good father simply wish to die quickly?

"You are not true." He stepped forward, cold as the North Sea. Some answers they would get out of Ulf later. Some they needed now. "Where are the jewels?"

"Jewels?" Like a turtle, Father Ulf drew his head back as far as he could from Rolf's out-thrust chin and icy glare.

Seldon took up Rolf's question with a vigorous shake of Ulf's habit. "The gift of Cierheld for the abbot, *priest.*" At Ulf's silence, he said, "Oh, you have nothing? Come, let us search your horse." Seldon spun Father Ulf and forced him toward his beast, Berd yet holding its rein.

"And we'll search you." Kilden slung his bow over his shoulder. He stripped Father Ulf's cloak and then his outer robe over his head.

Rolf's friends closed fierce around his enemy. He watched, relieved, as Berd dropped Father Ulf's saddlebags from the horse and opened them under the squad's gaze. Bolton and Cierheld men crowded closer.

"There." Seldon pointed to a small bag tied about Father Ulf's linen under-tunic. He lowered his blade from Ulf's throat to cut the cord, while Kilden deftly removed Father Ulf's dagger from the other side of his belt. Rolf drove his spear butt into the snow, plucked the bag free, loosened the leather tie, and poured the contents into his hand.

"Six," he said. "A ruby, two white pearls and one black, and two blue stones." He shook his head. "Such beautiful things, to be worth so much death." He lifted his gaze. "Before justice finds you, Father Ulf, you will tell us who plots against our Codi Golding, and Abbot Alton, and the house of Cieri. Answer me this. Who schemes against our fair Northumbria? Who would bring down Britannia?" If Lord Mornoth conspired against the regent as well as Cierheld—was that the dark pattern he'd sensed?

Father Ulf was pale, sweat gleaming on his forehead. He hunched his shoulders, feverish eyes on his treasure.

"Umm." Seldon moved to Rolf's side. Berd and the others looked over his shoulders. "Are those blue ones sapphires?"

"Mayhap." Rolf showed the blaze of colorful stones around then shook them back into the bag. "Abbot Alton will know their quality. And Lady Cieri and her lord father will be pleased we have caught the traitor."

At his last word, Father Ulf stiffened. "Now, Seldon!" he shouted. He tore free of Seldon's grip, shot across the circle, and scrambled onto his horse's back. He kicked it for the trees, its hooves throwing up clots of snow.

Rolf swung toward Kilden. "Shoot him—" An arm slid around his neck and a blade pricked behind his ear. Seldon yanked him back from the others.

*Seldon.* Rage swelled in Rolf, and sorrow as he staggered backward. *Not another traitor.* Seldon slowed a moment to whisk the bag of jewels out of his hand and tuck them in his belt. Then the dagger returned to Rolf's neck and dug slightly deeper. Ready, if any of the others made a move. Rolf held very still.

Berd stayed where he was. His eyes flicked between Rolf and the escaping rider. Whatever the armsman's suspicions, Rolf trusted the Cierheldens would deal with whatever came to pass.

Kilden faced Seldon in an attacking crouch, drawn dagger in his hand. At his swift signal, Jost and several others trotted after Father Ulf, while the squad closed in on Seldon. Watching them, Seldon slid his blade delicately around Rolf's neck to rest on his other shoulder.

Rolf's throat tightened; he could not swallow. As soon as Father Ulf escaped, Seldon meant to cut him open from collarbone to ear, to make him feel the edge where his blade once bit Seldon. Immense sadness clawed at Rolf. *No man's heart is safe.* Neither was his Britannia.

The abbey, the north, and the children. These traitors must not take them down. As Father Ulf said, there were things every man must fight if he were a man. With iron or without.

Rolf stared hard into Kilden's eyes. *Be ready.* "Get him!" Rolf shouted. And surged to the side, desperately reaching for Seldon's blade.

Seldon's eyes widened as he turned with Rolf. He whipped his arm back out of reach then in. Rolf folded over the blow to his belly, and Seldon's kick to the back of his knee drove him down. He couldn't get his breath. He shuddered.

But there was no slicing pain, no wet-spreading warmth under the hands he clutched to his middle, as his lungs strove for air. Seldon had struck his stomach with the dull spine of the weapon. Dimly he realized there was only the prick of a blade again at the back of his skull. The whelp wanted to draw his death into an execution. Why hadn't Kilden taken him?

"Back!" Seldon cried.

From the corner of his eye as air finally wheezed in, Rolf watched Kilden tilt his palm in a signal. The squad halted their closing circle instantly. Jost stopped his pursuit of Ulf, and Bolton's men staggered to an uncertain pause. Across the vale, Ulf slowed his horse, watching. His face held the superior smile Rolf hated most.

Berd eased toward Kilden. Rolf caught a ragged breath. They were too far away. Neither were close enough to save him. Yet he would not die on his knees before a traitor, mewling before his men.

He straightened carefully to his full height. To his surprise Seldon let him rise, only keeping the dagger hard against the back of his neck, icy cold.

Father Ulf crowed across the silence, "Your men see how the wind lies, even if you do not, blind *brother.* You will not behold such a loyal change of oath again, nor any man's oath to you renewed."

"No!" Seldon shouted, "We will—"

But Rolf was already moving. He lunged forward, reached up with a long arm as he whirled, found Seldon's wrist, and stripped the sharp blade away with his bare hand. He raised the dagger to Seldon's throat. Red dripped from his stinging fingers. He rasped, "You will *not!"* Those who depended on the abbey would find their trust kept.

Blood and iron filled Rolf's vision, then horror took him. *"Ahh, my Lord!"* He flung the dagger down. His angry gaze held Seldon's, which was full of grey consternation even as Seldon whipped free. "Not for you, traitor," Rolf gritted.

Jagged grief and anger coiled in a single tear that wet his face. He braced himself. "Do your worst, I willna' break my word." His Lord would uphold him.

Crouching but a breath away, his nemesis held a second dagger wide. Waiting.

Seldon dropped his arm and gave him an open, beautiful grin. "I am not what you think." He tossed his dagger into the snow beside Rolf's right foot, where it disappeared. "I am no traitor. Ask Lester when next we see him. It was his plan that I feign to work with Father Ulf, to smoke out the rat in the abbey. No, Brother Rolf, your debt is long paid." His voice lowered, solemn. "There never was a debt. But Lester wanted you to know

I hold no grudge." He shrugged, and with a crooked ghost of a grin, held out the leather bag. "Your heart is true." He dropped the jewels in Rolf's hand and gave him his back, turning toward Father Ulf.

Rolf stared dumbly, as every line of Seldon hardened.

Kilden closed his mouth with a snap. He thrust his dagger into its sheath, swung wordlessly toward Father Ulf, and freed his bow.

Seldon called, "You think all men can be bought, Father Ulf? As Lester said, now we know. I follow a worthy man. He has my oath."

Ulf sat on his horse, his arms carefully wide, motionless under Kilden's leveled arrow and granite face. His voice cracked. "How can that be your choice? He is beneath you even now in sword skill!"

"He has my oath, for he will not break his, even on pain of death. Blind as he is, your brother holds his honor." There was a glint in Seldon's eye.

Rolf choked. No matter the impudent whelp conspired with Lester, he could not thump him with his spear butt. Not yet. Had he and Lester spoken of Rolf's refusal to lead, and Seldon's growing ability? But whatever Seldon was, whether he meant to take his place or something darker, he was no traitor, though Father Ulf remained to be dealt with.

Berd stepped forward, soft and calculating as a mountain cat. "A false father who betrays a first daughter to underserved bloodguilt, let alone a father who murders his own brothers, will not be held blameless. Let us see if there is further proof of your treachery." He stalked to Ulf's saddlebags in the snow. He lifted out a waterskin, writing implements, and a few sheets of parchment, which he tossed aside, then another small bag and opened it. It rustled, and Berd sniffed at it. "Hah! Wild ramsons." He handed the bag to Jost.

"Well, let's have the father's garlic with our bread and onions warmed over a hot fire," Seldon said, with a grin. "Ramsons are near enough garlic, no matter that they're wild." He called to Rolf, "Brother, was it not a wrinkled Eagle commander who said a man can live strong at home or at war if only he has garlic or an onion in his belly?"

"No man I know, though the Roman Eagles did use garlic for strength and to ward illness." Rolf's smile flickered. Seldon twice refused to plunge a blade in him. Not that day at the wall, nor this. *Your heart is true.* Rolf picked Seldon's dagger out of the cold white snow, found the other he'd thrown aside, and wiped the red clean. "In a man's belly, onion, ramson, or garlic becomes naught but rank air, be he a man of the most golden tongue on earth." He held the weapons out to Seldon, and said for his ears alone, "Take back your blades, and your oath. I thank you, but I may not accept them."

Seldon said nothing, merely looked down, and eyed him sidelong. There was more at work than the oath he had given. What else did he know of the treachery coiling about them?

"Your words are true, brother!" Berd laughed and held out his hand to catch the bag Jost returned, raising it with a shake. "But then, ramsons and onions give strength to body and will. If a man, say a new squad member, but sweeten his golden breath with mint and apples, most could bear to listen to his drivel at a mid-day meal. Then they'd throw him in the snowbank to let his voice sweeten the night. By strength of said body and will, his oath must be tried." He shrugged in elaborate unconcern.

The men of Cierheld chuckled at the joke. Seldon turned red as his hair and tucked his blades away. The squad roared; the men full relieved to have Seldon proved one of them. They crowded in, slapping his back and pounding his shoulder. Rolf gave him a nod.

Lester, the idiot, had told no one, not even Kilden, of his plan to unmask the abbey's rat and prove Rolf's loyalty. Nor of the deceit Seldon had played to the hilt, pretending to be one of those rats. *As Lester said, now we know.* Rolf glanced down at the bag of jewels in his belt, then at Seldon. Had he and Lester possibly suspected him? It mattered not. The whelp's honor was regained in the eyes of the squad.

Rolf's cut hand ached, blood running. As he hunted about him for a bit of cloth to wrap it, Kilden said mildly, his bow negligently trained on Ulf, "I'll eat ramsons cooked or raw, hot or cold. And cold they'll be iffen' you don't get a move on, first armsman. This bird we've caught will look well tied against that log. Mayhap while we eat, you can persuade him to sing for us?"

"It would be my pleasure," Berd said. Young Jost grinned and hurried to Berd's side to assist in whatever way he deemed best. If only Seldon followed orders so well. Had he meant what he said? And he had not said what oath, precisely, he gave.

Rolf cut a bit from the top of his hose to bind his wound while the men scattered. Three went for water, more for wood, and some for supplies while Seldon lit a fire. Rolf gathered up Ulf's steed and led Mairne among their beasts, brought to the edge of the trees and surrounded by an alert guard of six men.

The mare whuffled uneasily. "Easy, easy sister." He stroked Mairne's neck, his touch leaving streaks of blood on her dun neck. Under Kilden's sharp watch, Jost tied Ulf on his side on his cloak, spread in the bright snow.

Father Ulf raised a sardonic brow at Kilden, who stared at him, near unblinking, bowstring relaxed but ready to shoot in an instant. "You will die, all of you who serve the spawn of evil," he said, then turned to Berd. His face darkened. "The heretic and his brood will be eradicated, and this upstart king, whoever he be."

Jost only gave him a black look and bound his ankles to his hands behind him. Berd said, "That will be remedied. You will find we know somewhat of Lord Ludwin Mornoth's coils, and you will speak of any others in the plot against our stronghold, our regent, and our king to come."

"I will speak of nothing. And do you think to mete justice?" Father Ulf choked on weak laughter. "What know you of justice, oath-breakers who obstruct the will of heaven?"

Rolf stirred. Berd knew more than he'd said, and Father Ulf's confidence set unease growing in his belly. His words of a king to come might prove the most poisonous thing in the cup Father Ulf offered.

Rolf said, "At the end of my staff, if naught else, you will be taken to meet the law, the law of God and man. You have spilled unlawful blood."

"Think you so? Your oath is already broken by your thirst for blood. From ash to iron—"

"I will listen when you speak words of worth." Rolf abruptly moved to stand near the fire, while Berd checked the cords about Ulf's wrists and nodded to Jost when he found them sound.

Father Ulf tugged against his bonds fruitlessly and cried, "Lord Mornoth will triumph, for we are the finger of heaven!"

Rolf frowned, turning. "The finger of heaven? God gives no one the order to murder or steal bread from children. And you, I think, mean darker things."

"The Word must go forth and spread—"

"And our Lord has not the power to uphold his own Word, and work in men's hearts as He will?"

"Oathbreaker! You are naught else—"

"If so, I will answer for it. For me, it will be as God wills. But that is neither here nor there, to you." Rolf eyed Ulf levelly. "Where is Mornoth going to strike? Who is the brigand? It might go easier with you if you answer." The brigand might be more willing to talk of the one who hunted the lifeblood of Britannia. And of the coming king.

Ulf pressed his lips together.

Young Jost stood guard while Berd joined Rolf at the fire and slid a pot of snow on the flames to heat. Rolf hoped Berd did not press for questioning Father Ulf here and now. He'd rather break his oath by killing him outright than torturing him. That he could not stomach. Better they found another who wished to talk.

Berd growled, "He will answer, one way or another. We may find the brigand and Lord Mornoth together." He poked the fire meaningfully, and sparks flew. When Rolf looked at him sharply, he said, "Brother, did you mean what you said? You'll bear no weapon but a staff?"

Rolf accepted the change of subject. "Aye. I've enough to learn, wielding the ash and the oak." He hesitated, then reached after his courage. "If you give me leave, after we've taken this traitor to meet your first daughter and dealt with Lord Mornoth, I'd learn more of the staff from you and Kyrin. Your first daughter's staff has, well, a life of its own in her hands." It surprised him, the depth of his anticipation, when all the future was uncertain.

Berd's mouth pursed in a slight frown. "If it proves well." He looked up, his brown gaze piercing, back to the hunt. "Do you lead these men? Do they follow you?"

"I do not." Had Berd no eyes to see his refusal of leadership, and Kilden's orders to the men?

Berd pressed, "Do they follow another? What of Abbot Alton? Who holds his allegiance? These are uncertain times. I ask on behalf of Cierheld."

"I must speak with Abbot Alton before I say more." He dared not give Berd surety before he knew himself.

"Ah." Berd stood and gripped his shoulder. "Then once your allegiance and your place at the abbey are settled, we will speak of the staff, and truth."

Rolf stiffened. His allegiance lay always with truth. His place, that he did not quite know, but he must give Berd some cause for trust, to receive it. All the more, considering the first arms-man's dying lord, his maligned first daughter, and his threat-ened stronghold. Rolf considered. "I can tell you our abbot has tasked me with overseeing the defense of Bolton Abbey." That was all the insufficient proof he could offer at the moment, with affairs unknown between the regent and Abbot Alton and Bishop Caddaric.

Berd crossed his arms and fingered his chin. "What are you going to do about the bishop?"

A straight shot to the heart. Before Rolf could open his mouth, Kilden broke in. "Laggards, you'll miss your strength if you swallow naught but cold air with your yelping, and our bird will never sing!" On the other side of the fire, he waved the bag of ramsons at them, an onion in his other hand.

Berd touched his belt where the ramsons had been. His brows drew together. He smiled at Kilden, a predator's smile. "Oh, we will lose strength, will we?" In a curious skittering of feet, he leaped over the fire-circle, feinted to one side, and snatched the bag from Kilden. Only blowing snow told the tale of his passage.

Rolf blinked. He'd never seen a man move so. It was what he looked forward to, such secrets, and more, from Cieri's daughter.

A few strides past Kilden, Berd pulled out a handful of the ivory white-scaped bulbs with a grin.

"You sneaking fox!" Kilden leaped for him.

"You're the fox!" Laughing, Berd deflected Kilden, who sprawled at his feet. The others chuckled, even those watching the horses.

Father Ulf turned his face away. Jost shot him a glare. He roared with the others as, on his feet again, Kilden made a wild grab.

Twirling, evading, Berd rubbed papery scapes free to drift on the wind and held up a single bulb to admire. Kilden's eyes blazed; he seemed far angrier than the jest warranted. Had he heard Berd's words to Rolf and taken offense? Rolf held his peace. When he did not know, silence was wiser.

Berd popped the ramson in his mouth. "Pah!" He spat.

Kilden lunged. And gained the bag and lifted a handful toward his mouth, glaring at Berd, disregarding the scapes.

"No!" Berd struck Kilden's hand, scattering bulbs of garlic across the snow, then slipped the bag from Kilden's grip, every limb containing a sudden deadly grace Rolf recognized.

"Why, you greedy—" Kilden growled, but Berd was gone.

The armsman fell to his knees at Ulf's side. His face was pale and cold. His dagger menaced Ulf's stomach, while his other hand dangled the ramsons before Ulf's nose.

"Stop!" Rolf rushed to his shoulder. Not in time, he knew, if Berd meant to finish what he started. "By our Lord, what mean you—"

"Ask him. Ask him what he means by carrying Lily of the Valley bulbs hidden inside a bag of ramsons!"

Kilden yanked the bag from Berd and spread some of the bulbs in his hand. Broke one and sniffed it, broke another. "It's so." His weathered eyes narrowed.

Berd's backhand blow across Father Ulf's throat left him coughing. "When I am endangered, so is my first daughter." Utter scorn laced his voice, and his dark eyes burned. "I expected the dangers of the road, but not this, not from a man of God!" He turned to Rolf. "He gave them the poison!"

A black weight bore down on Rolf's shoulders. *No man's heart is safe.* He felt suddenly utterly weary. "I should have known. The fault is mine. We should eat, take council, and leave in the morn."

Berd watched him, but other heads nodded. Kilden dumped the rest of the ramsons and Lily of the Valley and ground them to paste under his boot, that they might not grow in the spring and fool a traveler hunting wild ramsons. Soon after, the men ate roasted meat, bread, cheese and cold onions, quiet and subdued.

At council around the fire afterward, all had little to add but a bitter wish that they'd left a scout to shadow Lord Mornoth. Berd dispatched two of Cierheld to follow Mornoth's forces, and they left immediately. Everyone else spent a rather restless night. Rolf's bandaged hand pained him less than his thoughts.

When the sun rose, Rolf motioned for Seldon to help Jost tie Father Ulf over Mairne's back while he spoke with Cierheld's first armsman. "The poisoner is found, and his reward will find him. The abbot will see it done. You may be sure of it."

"Yes. I am certain of it." Berd's face was blank stone. "I will see it done. You will first give him to us."

Rolf looked him in the eye and thought, *What more do you know of Father Ulf's treachery?* But the trust between them was fragile. Instead, he said, "We will exchange the jewels for the 'promised coin' for more men for your stronghold. The payment will reach the south. But we would be indebted if your men would keep us abreast of Lord Mornoth's movements."

Berd paused. "What does your Abbot Alton know of these matters?"

That doubt of Alton brought incandescent rage. Rolf reined it in hard. He drew himself up and stepped close, nose to nose. "My abbot knows naught but that Cierheld brought us a gift for payment and exchange; until I bring him word of murder, and robbery, and traitors. Of us all, first armsman, Abbot Alton's tongue most closely aligns with what is good. In heart he follows hard after truth, for he loves our Lord. Let all of Cieri know it. As does your Lord Dain. I trust there is justice in him also." Rolf paused, his lips pressed tight. "I followed so hard after the poisoner that I was blind to the given word of your first daughter. I sorrow for that. I will tell her so." Berd said nothing, and Rolf nodded. "Ah. She is someone you cannot speak for without leave. But we have ever been allies, the abbey and Cierheld. May we remain so. You and Kyrin may take Father Ulf, if you will return him for the abbot's justice."

Berd inclined his head, his look stony. "It is well."

Rolf watched him walk away, and motion Jost to take Ulf's horse in hand. After this, he'd give over any scouting around Bolton to Lester and be responsible for no more forays. They could not ask him to fight without bearing a weapon of greater strength than wood, and that he could not do. His heart was not safe.

Seldon and Jost flanked him as they rode for the road and Kyrin Cieri, and he must have looked fearsome in his thoughts. Jost swallowed when he caught his glower, but Seldon glanced across him at the young guardsman with a wink. Young Jost did not look reassured.

Neither was Rolf. Lester and Seldon had spoken together concerning him. He wondered if Kilden had said aught, and what it may have been, and what Abbot Alton would say about his slain brothers and his giving Father Ulf over to Cierheld.

## 11

# Broken Oath

*Take hold of instruction; do not let go. Guard her, for she is your life.*
*~ Proverbs 4:13*

Brother Rolf rode into Bolton Abbey at the head of the squad. The cowl of his cloak shielded his face from the stinging sleet but could not shield him from his thoughts. Who would have thought the first daughter of Cierheld and her armsman would stir such a hornets' nest in the north with Lord Mornoth, let alone in his soul? She'd proved her words true, and worse, Berd proved the church false. Proved *him* false, for his suspicious blindness. He ought to have sought the truth before he accused Kyrin Cieri. He ought to have asked her how things stood, showed trust. He had not meant to be false, but he had been. Had he left Berd with enough assurance of Abbot Alton's support, despite his cold anger that Berd's doubt of the abbot sparked?

He had given Father Ulf to Cierheld, to those who would make him talk. And whatever he or Berd thought of each other, the first armsman would bring Father Ulf back to the church for sentencing. Rolf reached up to touch the small bag at his neck. Kyrin Cieri had given him the jewels he carried over his heart. In moments, he would see them safe in Alton's hands.

The children would live. And the north would carry on the struggle. From what Kyrin said and Berd hinted at, the fate of the north might depend on how much Father Ulf had involved the church in the plot that deepened around them. How deep did Ulf's treachery go, and where did it run? Were there other undeclared traitors in the pattern, even among the lords? The bishop of Richmond was near certainly involved. Berd also seemed to think Thorgil bore watching, though he had not said why.

Rolf frowned. The first armsman wrested an oath from him before they parted, to watch the woodcutter. He would do so, and speak with Mornoth's armsman that Ulf had wounded, if the man lived. Rolf glanced over his shoulder. His men rode at guard behind him, his squad again, for the moment. He could not grant the oath they wished him to give, but they had never tried to deny theirs to him. And concerning Seldon, one oath older than them all had been renewed, the silent oath of men who defended each other's backs.

Night had laid its frozen hand over the land, sucking the heat from man and beast as they went through the second gate. The men of Bolton had left them at the edge of town with a rousing cheer and gone home. Home. Rolf stared down at his staff as he halted before the abbey stables. He'd broken his oath at its heart and to the letter. For a moment, he had meant to wield the dagger.

The whispering feet of children pattered in the shadows. The oldest boy rushed out and held Rolf's mount. Rolf swung down and nodded in answer to the question on his thin face. The staff in his hand was cold as iron. He touched his breast where the warm sack from Cierheld stronghold rested. "We rescued the first daughter's gift from a traitor. Ask Mial to heat a hot drink for us, if it be naught but tea."

The boy's eyes lit when Rolf rested a hand on his shoulder. With a smile he rushed away, all trust. That one carried himself with uncommon eagerness to serve. Faithfully serve. Rolf's sigh shook him to his toes. He must speak with Abbot Alton. His brothers' deaths must not be in vain, whatever befell him after the telling.

He nodded to Lester. "Take them in."

None the worse for his easy ride with Lady Cieri, Lester grunted and waved the others inside. Wet and cold and hungry from their long pursuit and the longer ride back to the abbey, his men obeyed. No, not his men, Lester's men.

Seldon lifted his head and looked back at Rolf, as tired as the rest of the squad. "There's your escort of shadows, fit for an armsman." He gave a small smile as he pointed at the children crowded around the stable door.

*An armsman I am not, nor a worthy brother.* Rolf turned silently back toward the church. The older children walked behind, hugging the dark places. The raids on their strongholds had taught them caution.

Rolf entered alone.

Past the candle-lit dimness of stone aisles and wooden seats, Abbot Alton rose from his knees before the altar, lifting his thin frame with difficulty. He sat on the nearest bench with a sigh, and Brother Rolf sank down beside him. He laid aside his staff. At last, it had warmed to his grip. A lump formed in his throat, and his words tangled behind it.

Alton looked from the wood to his face, the wrinkles deepening around his sharp old eyes.

Brother Rolf's breath came short. "I have not chosen the iron, but I broke my oath. In the moment, I did not realize I had. Though the only blood the iron drew was mine." It was the utter, bitter truth. He could not meet Alton's gaze but stared at the abbot's wrinkled brown hands under the yellow light, clasped in the lap of his simple habit. "I cannot seem to keep what I swear to," he continued miserably. "I do not know what Father Ulf told you before, or what Kilden said when he brought the armsman, Niel, and Dickon back, but the fault is mine. I should have known what Father Ulf was. I was closest to him. I told Berd of Cierheld that."

Alton gestured at two linen-draped figures that lay near the altar, each with a lit candle at the feet and head. "My son, your brothers lie there. They are with God. Tell me what you know. Tell me from the beginning."

Rolf's hand closed on the bag inside his tunic, beneath his habit. It was time to trust. He bowed his head.

§

Lord Ludwin Mornoth did not seek to quell his fierce smile. Britannia was in his grasp. He who had warmed the throne was out of play for eternity, and even better, the newly instated Codi Golding would soon be a reed to his hand when he brought his men south of the Humber. Father Ulf had fulfilled his purpose. He was being taken to his just reward, if a trifle unwillingly.

Mornoth frowned. He could have used the jewels that interfering scraggart of a monk carried away, back to his spineless abbot. But all churches would soon be in his hand. His mouth broadened in a grin. Cierheld thought to gather allies in the north, but even now the trap closed about Lord Dain's stronghold, soon to exact payment for that error. Payment long overdue was in motion among the northern strongholds. He would be king. Thain had his uses. If he continued to serve well, he might make him steward.

He turned his horse toward the lower north road and Cattraeth, his companies wheeling onto the Eagle's broken stone way after him. Bishop Caddaric would answer his call.

Lord Gadral of Aysgarth, Lord Fresen, and Lord Landyl would learn to pick their allies more wisely in future. It was the hour for the Northumbrian upstarts to find their place under his rule.

§

"What of the jewels my Lord Mornoth was ready to murder for?" Mornoth's erstwhile armsman watched Brother Rolf, pale hands clutching his blankets. He'd been tied to his bed by fever in the infirmary the last nine days. The wound between his ribs had been much aggravated by the heaving caused by the smaller dose of poison he'd ingested, and he had bled much. But he was on the mend, and strong enough to talk.

Rolf smiled. "The gift was recovered, and our abbot has exchanged the jewels for our services, men, and goods, as was arranged." His gaze sharpened. "Why?"

The armsman glanced down, frowning. "Lord Mornoth, I mean the traitor, dealt with a double tongue with many. If he ever hears I spoke of—"

"He will hear naught from me." Rolf's mouth was a grim line.

The armsman beckoned Rolf closer and whispered in his ear.

Rolf shot to his feet. "Why did you not speak of this before! He and the brigand are in this foul plot against Cierheld?"

The armsman eyed him warily. "He is, as my name is Henges Aelwin. I give every oath on my blade 'tis so. Everyone in our hold knows his lackey Lord Keffer marches for Cierheld. You must tell your abbot. But of this brigand you speak of, I know nothing."

"He hunts our people, preying on our kingdom, and I fear he means worse."

"Others about your abbey have inquired much of these brigands, but I am not sure who it is safe to speak to after your Father Ulf stabbed me. That young man of yours, Seldon, and your cook have asked after these brigands you mention, but my Lord Mornoth is the one to watch. He is dangerous."

Stilled by shock, Rolf took in the armsman's worn face full of regret and ran. "Abbot Alton!" he called. The abbot was not in his quarters, nor in the refectory, the garden, or the church. But the Book on the altar was gone.

Dashing inside the scriptorium, Rolf found Alton poring over the Vulgate on Father Ulf's desk. He halted, gasping, "They mean to take down Lord Dain!"

"Who does?" Alton stiffened and looked at him keenly under his grizzled brows, his aged hands gripping the Book.

"Lord Nidfael Keffer, even as Lord Mornoth marches for Cattraeth."

"Where the northern lords gather with Cierheld's forces, while this Lord Nidfael Keffer stalks Cierheld stronghold when it lies vulnerable? Are you certain?"

Rolf's hands closed. "The armsman tells me the bishop of Richmond has spoken with Lord Mornoth often. They know too well Lord Cieri is the beating heart of justice for our people in the north. Lord Nidfael is Mornoth's close ally."

Alton bowed his head, running his hand over his crozier. The unblinking eagle of John faced the watchful lion of Luke atop the official staff of ash that leaned against Ulf's desk. "We have not the men to stop them?"

Rolf drew a deep breath. "Not by a frontal defense, but with Lester and the squad, and the men of Bolton, there is a chance."

"No. The men of Bolton must ward their village against the brigands. Yet the tensquad is not enough." The Abbot raised his hand to still Rolf's protest. "You may take your men and go to warn Cierheld. Raise the stronghold against our enemies. It is time to fight."

Rolf's skin prickled. "You cannot mean that. Scouting with a spear was one thing. This is folly. You know what I swore."

Alton's smile was gentle. He tapped a page of the Vulgate. "I believe you may have given your oath in error, and your vow in misunderstanding." His old eyes sharpened. "Tell me, have you found your heart come to heel since your penance with the lash this last seven-day?"

Rolf flushed and swallowed, fighting the urge to roll his shoulders against the lingering burn of the half-healed weals. "No, father."

"Well then, I find that one more goad in my heart," Alton said, with the decisiveness of a scythe through wheat. "You will not take up the penance again. I forbid it." He watched Rolf, sober. "Lord Dain may be right. Our striving to keep the law of God is for naught. What was that verse Father Ulf quoted at you one morn in the refectory?"

"That the just shall live by faith?"

"Yes. He twisted the application. By 'faith,' he meant those who believed his idea of heaven's commands. But taken the way God means it, it is true. Ulf did not finish the rest of the Holy writ. 'The just shall live by faith, and that not of themselves, it is the gift of God.' And that gift is a real gift, without thought of payment." Alton stroked the parchment. "Have you not punished yourself with the lash for taking up the blade with the intent to use it, even though your hand was prevented? Father Ulf disregarded this word, that 'the letter kills, but the Spirit gives life'. But you have felt this lesson more than I, these last few days. You have not found life in the letter of the law. It condemned you." His faint smile was pained.

Rolf's heart pounded. "The flesh must be subdued, must it not? And God's commands kept?"

"Yes. But we cannot do it: we men are constant sinners. In heart, if naught else. We cannot change ourselves."

When he struck the hat from Ulf's head, in his heart's eye, his spear end flashed, and the traitor's blood flooded the snow. Rolf's brow furrowed. "I am a warrior no more; now I am a blade in your hand."

"That is true. But open your ears. Even the oath you took to obey does not give the strength to fulfil or the liberty to discern what God desires of us. And we cannot keep the good we desire to do, is it not so?" Alton looked at him steadily.

Rolf looked down.

"If these things are true, then all our work together is despair of pleasing God or rebellion against him, until, as Paul said, God drives us to fall on his mercy. The law is but the taskmaster to bring us there. To our knees. There, with Christ, we can do all things." A smile crept over his face. "To be counted pure and live out of love is a blessed privilege. Then we can truly love him who died for us. That is blessed freedom. And you are not free. You are driven by fear. As am I."

Rolf's mouth tightened. "Nothing drives me but my flesh, the flesh I must eradicate, and to defeat the same stinking corruption in others. Nothing drives me except that my land is full of trouble and terror and treachery! One traitor is being dealt with. Others remain." Lester would lead the squad. *He* would do as he'd committed himself to do. He would please God. Alton would see. "I must fight my demons as I may."

"Can I do less, my son? Any less than take his gift and fight evil as he bids? Can you do less than that?" Alton's eyes were gentle. "Tell me, do you still fear yourself so much that you will not trust our Lord with your fear? He alone can warm the coldest heart."

Rolf blinked. He was no good if he could not hold his anger in check, as a man should. Was his abbot going witless with overmuch study? "That is a man's charge, to govern himself. His own word in the Book says it."

"Ah." Alton lifted his hand. "That is true. But how is it to be done? His Book seems to say His blood worked our salvation in us, and we are to work out the fruit of that salvation. For he works within us both to will and to do of his good pleasure." He smiled wryly and pointed to the Book. "See, here. What does it say?" The crimson letters shone dark and deep.

Rolf forced aside thoughts of Seldon and blood welling between his fingers. He leaned close to the fresh-smelling parchment and read slowly, "I do not nullify the grace of God; for if righteousness comes through the law, then Christ died in vain."

Alton said slowly, "Give yourself to him in trust. This time swear no oath. Ask him for strength to take up both the truth and the iron in our hour of need, for he has given them to you. Both the sword of the Spirit and this blade of earth." He stood and lifted Rolf's sword from behind the desk. "At this moment, he has set you on a different path than your oath. But take not my word for truth. Study the Book and see if it is not so. Behold the long reach of the law, and the farther reach of forgiveness. Faith is the key. Trust in *him."*

How could God leave him nothing to do? Pushed beyond bearing, Rolf backed a step and cried, "Do you give yourself to heresy?"

"No. I give myself to truth. Read it for yourself." Alton moved forward to lay his hand on Rolf's shoulder.

Rolf shook his head. His eyes stung. "Do you say my heart is not true to you and to my brothers? That I would not die for our Lord, for my oath?" His voice shook. He could *not* give in. It was all he had left.

"No. No, my son." Alton laid down the blade on the desk behind him and gripped Rolf's shoulders, his old hands strong. "I think no such thing." His face creased in a smile. "It is because your heart yearns to be true, that I pray you may understand.

"I mean 'the letter' may reach to our sacraments, even to the 'grace' of salvation we thought we began to earn at our baptismal font. But his gift of faith, it appears to conquer everything. Our work cannot. I must search it out further. And so must you. His very Word," he touched the Vulgate gently, "compels me. I think it likely nothing should be added to his grace, nor truly can be. We have deluded ourselves. We only ever earn ourselves death." He paused. "Is he not sufficient? That is the question." He stared at Rolf, burning with quiet fierceness. "Is his love not sufficient? The price he paid? How does any man dare think to add to God's work on the tree? I dare not."

Then he sighed. "Now the stakes are greater than you and I alone. Are we to let the innocent die, for lack of a warding hand? Do not let your oath drive you to evil. Will you strain out a gnat and swallow a camel?"

"No."

He took up the sword and laid it in Rolf's hands. "Our Lord said, 'It is finished.' We love because he loved us. You must go and do the same. Love with heart and head and hand."

Rolf stared at the abbot, aghast, then at the weapon across his palms. He did not question God's love or law, but his abbot's fitness this moment, and his own weakness. Both weakness of the heart, and his hand that had barely begun to heal.

The abbot turned, muttering, "It matters less whether you bear a blade, and much more why you bear it, or do not."

Rolf wondered at his abbot's resolve. Nothing would surprise him after this. But was what he said true?

Alton's voice was a rustling whisper. "Our righteousness is as filthy rags. That point we have got right in the church, though we negate it on the other hand so often. But his sufficiency we deny. Both salt water and fresh from the same spring, when it ought to be faith working by love." His voice trailed away, and he shook his head suddenly and urged Rolf toward the door. "Come, my son, we will speak of this again, but you must go with all Godspeed. More lives than ours are at risk."

As they hurried down the path, Alton said quickly, "I also have talked with Henges Aelwin. Though not completely open, he did imply there are spies around the regent that replaced Codi Golding, and he swears Father Ulf meant to turn the church upside down in search of heresy. How does Ludwin Mornoth fit with this aim? How far would Father Ulf take such a purge when he would murder those guilty of nothing?" Alton shook his head again, his eyes deep and sad. "I will render temporal judgement when Lord Cieri returns him."

Rolf panted, "Berd guards his first daughter well. Kyrin holds secrets we do not yet know. But I judge he is our ally in this tangle, and Cierheld, as well." He wondered if the abbot would accept his assessment, or should, since he'd proved faulty in the matter of Father Ulf. Had his heart's struggle with the dean blinded him to the wider possibilities of Father Ulf's ambitions?

The abbot halted at the inner abbey gate. "It seems the bishop may be compromised. You must be my hands and eyes now, Brother Rolf. The evil in Britannia must be stopped. It may require our blood. Mine for the truth of his Word, and yours in battle. Or, if our Lord graces us with victory, then we may think of this school for scribes, among other things. It was a good aim of Father Ulf's, though he meant to twist it to ungodly purpose." Tears gleamed on his cheek. "Go in his grace." Alton raised his hand in blessing. Rolf knelt, his sword point down before him.

"Be my hands in Cierheld and wherever else our Lord takes you, but first be his. Remember, his love fulfills the law."

It mattered not at all that the abbot had forgotten his crozier in the scriptorium. He was a man who followed justice and truth, and the love of God shone through him. Rolf swallowed hard. Could he do less? He would obey as best he could, as far as he could see what was true. He looked up into his face. "Yes, my father, I will." *Lord, let me keep my word to him, and to Cierheld—and to you.* It was time to redeem his word to a certain first daughter. It was time to fight, though exactly how, he was not yet certain.

Alton lifted him to his feet. Rolf said, "I will ride to aid Cierheld as I may, but who will stay to ward you?"

"I do not think the brigands will trouble the abbey, as they doubtless have bigger fish to net at the moment. I have secured our payment of Cierheld's coin where it is needed, and Ludwin Mornoth is occupied to the north. After we lay your brothers to rest, I believe the new regent is in need of my presence. Durand Tolman appears to be of a different mold than Codi Golding. The lords may find him less biddable than they wish. Especially if he pays heed to our Lord's Word. I will go to him. And I will stop by Cierheld and take Father Ulf. He will face the regent's judgement. I must think; I may also have some fault in the matter."

Rolf grinned at Alton's gentle, strong smile. With men such as this to fight for it, Northumbria could not fall. "Take the black gelding. He is swift and canny."

"I will do so." The abbot sobered. "My son, wear your blade with intent, for has our Master not said, 'Defend the defenseless?' You may commit murder if you do not save the one who needs saving. Remember the spirit of his law, to love your neighbor as yourself. Do not give in to any fear."

Rolf nodded. "So be it." Could such a freedom be true, to bear a blade at his Lord's very word? Could the spirit of the law go deeper than the letter? Had that thought not crossed his mind when he first heard Cieri's daughter, at her confession long ago? He must search it out when he could. Yet somewhere within a voice whispered, *Never enough. You must be more, traitor.*

## 12

# Infernal Weapon

*Rescue the weak and needy; deliver them out of the hand of the wicked.*
*~ Psalms 82:4*

Those words wove about Rolf's mind as he and Lester and the squad thundered along the road to Cierheld. Mairne carried him well, without a stumble, and he urged her on despite the pain of the lashes across his back. Many lives lay in the balance. He must be enough.

Near the stronghold, they slowed from their alternate gallop and trot to a walk. Kilden, who had gone ahead, urged his horse out of the trees and the heavy mist. He pointed. "They attack the gate in force, and ring the hold two-deep. The scouts will not bother us."

Rolf nodded and led the squad off the road, where they could cut across the fields and behind Cierheld's mill. The mist curled about them. He exchanged a glance with Lester. What he was about to do was foolhardy by any combat standards. "Sound the call."

Lester lifted the horn by his side and winded it: clear, earth-shaking, and rich. As the squad drew into tight formation with Rolf at the point, Seldon moved behind him. The standard Seldon bore clung wetly to its pole. Rolf did not look back at him again. There was no moment to unfurl the standard if their charge did not shake it loose.

"For Lord Cieri!"

At the head of the squad, Rolf raced Mairne toward the four ranks of Keffer's men about Cierheld's gate. Kilden broke away from them to use his bow to good effect. At the forest's edge, he turned to wave forward unseen squads behind them. They did not exist. Or did they, in ranks of bright spirits no man could see? Rolf sent up a quick prayer, lowered his spear and braced as the line of swordsmen before him screamed defiance. Hooves thundered about him. His anger must never undo him again. *Lord, help me.*

Mairne swerved to avoid an attacker's blow and Rolf's shaft slid home, knocking the man backward a good six lengths. Rolf pulled his spear free as Mairne leaped forward with a shrill whinny, straight for the next line. She'd been born with battle in her blood, and her spirit rose with his. The grin on his face felt fierce. The spear fit his hand as if it had never left it.

"Jorn! Lord Jorn!" The cries rose from Cierheld. Though in error, they could not but help foster welcome confusion among Keffer's ranks.

His men were through. But if his squad was to live, they must gain the gate, or be crushed against it by superior numbers. Rolf swept his arm around his head. Lester sounded his horn again, gathering the squad tighter. Lord Keffer's forces withdrew briefly. Enemy squad leaders shouted, and loud horns blatted from the rear near the tree line.

Cierheld's gate opened even as Brother Rolf neared it. He led them inside the first gate at a gallop, and came to a sliding stop, his blood pounding. In moments Kyrin Cieri stood on the inner wall, near the second gate, Berd beside her. Scowling, his right arm bound to his side, Berd said something to his first daughter.

She frowned and Rolf heard her reply. "If the occasion warrants." She lifted her chin as Berd's look grew more stolid and grinned down at Brother Rolf.

Berd's mouth thinned, and Rolf caught a few of his next words. "...you'll use any weapon. Even one ill fit for your hand. He has turned his back on war..."

Brother Rolf tensed, and Kyrin said lightly, "But not on his brothers."

Rolf repressed his grin. *I also wish your first daughter well. On behalf of Abbot Alton, my own word, and as I hope to learn from her.*

Berd shook his head, but with a shrug, he waved Rolf further in. A Cierhelden opened the inner gate, and an archer stepped onto the walkway. He lifted his weapon.

What doubt of him and his men was this, after such proofs as they had given? With a scowl, Brother Rolf spun Mairne back toward the gate, and Lester and Kilden swung with him, in leather and mail.

Berd raised his eyebrows in question and motioned the archer back, calling, "You are well come to Cierheld, Brother Rolf."

Had it been a mistake? Rolf shot Berd an austere look. Mistake or no, the armsman was altogether too amused.

"My pardon, Brother Rolf." Kyrin bowed. "Your assistance is timely."

Rolf's stiffness melted. She at least was properly sober, the soul of courteous welcome. "No offense taken. Yet." He glared at Berd, who made his face expressionless.

Later, while Rolf rested on the wall, watching the woods where Kilden had disappeared on foot once again, Kyrin found him. She soberly met his eyes. "You saved us many lives. Though now you are in the same trap, I thank you."

Rolf looked down. "I thought you a traitor. And worse, in my more shameful moments. And then, we didn't try to stop Lord

Keffer, lady, to the church's shame. You don't shelter a viper; you crush it." He sighed. Though Abbot Alton had been right they had not the men, still they should have set their minds to deal with Lord Keffer long ago, when he first began to hang about with Lord Mornoth. But they had no proof, and he had come to see the pattern too late. "I would have harried him when he retreated into the woods, but my men are too few." He stared at his hands, rubbing his fingers and thumbs together. "I turned to the quill because of my hot blood, and now it is different." Suddenly, all was different.

"Yes. But Rolf, you've given us a chance. If Jorn comes..."

Rolf grinned. "Ahh, you thought we were Lord Jorn's. To my sorrow, we are but ten, retired from violent service until now. I would redeem our numbers if I could." At least he could keep his word to her. He tapped the stone, dimly remembering something Seldon had once said, something about necessity and the Eagles' tactics. "Do you have much porridge meal?"

"We have plenty, Cernalt says enough for five seven-days. Our meat will give out first, if they siege us."

"I heard you're out of oil but for the pots above the gate. If meal is boiled, it sticks well and burns long." If they were sieged, and it was not lifted soon, a little more meal would avail them nothing. Lord Ludwin Mornoth would snap up a stronghold through whatever means came to his hand, and his hand held many men.

Rolf drew a hard breath. All Kyrin had told him confirmed, in more deadly terms, what he and Abbot Alton had learned from Henges Aelwin, and the polite nothings of Bishop Caddaric. Lord Mornoth would likely come here after Cattraeth. As he would come for every hold in the north. Lord Mornoth must die. But must it be by his hand? Yet he might perish with Cierheld then it would be of no concern. The thought almost relieved him.

Bells later, the alarm horn alerted the watchers on the wall. Four tensquads of pikes approached with a form of polearm high enough to reach the wall. Brother Rolf ran for the gate. As he went, he grimly downed one of Lord Keffer's men scaling the wall with an awkward sword thrust. The man tumbled away, screaming.

A great judder of the earth drew every Cierhelden to their feet from their brief respite over a last meal, as the roar yanked Rolf's gaze to a rush of dirt, a fountain in the sky. The sound hurt his ears and beat against his entire being, stinking of sulfur and fire. A dark bloom hung above the outer gate.

Gaping, limbs tingling, he dropped the pot in his hands. He did not hear it hit the stones. The blast had smashed the stone in terrible power. The smoke was vile. A black powder misted around the edges, as bitter as horehound. Dazed, Rolf dropped his sword. Men and women dashed from the stables below, streamed from the kitchen and hall toward the gate. Rolf staggered forward to grab the next batch of boiled meal he'd prepared near the portal.

Lord Keffer's men poured inside Cierheld. They streamed around the outer gate, which hung from a hinge. A few gained the wall. Upon the wall walk, Rolf turned to meet the first man, throwing his emptied pot at the black hole of the man's soundlessly shouting mouth.

The rest of his squad was scattered. In the melee below, Seldon and Jost fought back-to-back. Seldon glanced up at Rolf, and Rolf found his sword and struck another man down. The turmoil across the yard converged on the inner gate in strange silence. The few enemies who had made it inside struggled to draw it wide, while Cierheldens jumped from the wall and desperately ran forward to close the wood span.

Berd was not in sight...no, he fought below, his bound arm forgotten. At Berd's side, the first daughter of Cierheld wielded a sword. Rolf watched in awe.

She was a living force to be reckoned with. Her heart and will directed each parry, thrust, and back-slash, leaving a swath of wounds that did not always kill, but never left an enemy on his feet. If he could wield a blade like that, he would be a fighter, indeed.

"'Ware!"

Rolf ducked aside from the bellow in his ear. Lester lashed by him to take out the pike aimed at his throat and followed up his strike to sweep away the last man on the gate wall. Rolf nodded his thanks; he'd acted as heedless as a new recruit.

Below, Seldon gave him a look filled with fear. He still hid something. Kilden would never see such a pup in his place. A friend like Lester was a friend forever. But his squad...Seldon was not ready to lead them. Along Cierheld's wall rose a roar of triumph. They'd repulsed the enemy yet again. Rolf forgot Seldon and returned to the fray.

Among the circle of Lord Keffer's men who drove for the gate, striving against Kyrin Cieri, a man raised his arm. His yell was muffled to Rolf's half deafened ear. "Death to Cierheld!" White streamed from his helm to match the white horsehead on his breast. Keffer's men surged forward.

Berd stumbled before the inner gate. As Kyrin's first arms-man fell, he threw himself forward, disappearing under the feet of the men trying to get at his first daughter.

"No!" Rolf's cry rose with Kyrin's.

Then a horn blew. The stones under his feet came apart with earth-rending force. He spun from the wall and down into blackness.

Rolf woke. His head ached. His ears throbbed. Oak branches waved above the pallet he lay on. The air was cold. Beside him, Lester hunched on his heels, his voice a reverberating thunder that pierced bone and grated on flesh. Rolf winced as he raised his head.

"It's good to see yer yet with the livin', brother." Lester grinned and wiped at his eyes.

Rolf smiled as he could. On the far side of the hall steps and across the yard, the gates were a blackened shamble. A portion of the wall had tumbled and scattered about the yard. Charred edges of wood and stone bore silent witness to destruction. A scent as of the stinking pit reached his nose.

Rolf turned to Lester, swallowing, and coughed on his dry throat. "Berd, Seldon, the others?"

Lester stared through the demolished gateway. "This ants' nest is well and truly stirred, brother. The rest of the squad is well, naught but flesh wounds. But it's best ye know, the lord's daughter..." He paused, and Rolf clenched his hands, waiting. "By a blessed stroke, Lady Cieri brought down Lord Keffer with her bow. But she was hit mortal hard in the head with a pike. She lies in the hall, neither dead nor wakin'."

So, she'd rallied the hold beyond the end of hope. There was no immediate danger now, by the lone sentry he saw on the wall. Berd would never believe that, watchful as he was. "And the first armsman?"

A red-haired young woman nearby, tending a man who'd taken a blade in his thigh, paused. Her green gaze was also intent, waiting on Lester's reply.

"Berd?" Lester shook his head. "He's in the infirmary. 'E may live. Though if he'll wish it, if 'is first daughter dies, I don't know."

The red-haired woman bit her lip and turned away. Rolf thought she brushed back tears. Were they for Berd, for her first daughter, or for both of them?

He did not have time for his own tears. He was Abbot Alton's hands. He must stand in for Berd, must keep that demonic weapon from coming to bear again if it were in his power. *Defend the defenseless.* He pushed himself up on his arms.

"Easy, brother! Ye took a hard fall." Lester put a large hand on his shoulder.

Panting, Rolf glared at him. "Find Kilden and Seldon. Get the squad together. We've a war to fight, and I'm not hurt mortal." The healing lashes on his back nor aught else would stay him.

They rode out within a bell. Kilden's mount loped ahead and to the left, Lester after him, moving to their other lead flank. Rolf looked about as the sound of hooves approached from behind. Seldon and Jost slowed on his right. Rolf gave them a small smile, and they rode without speaking, while the rest of the squad and more Cierheld men trailed behind, all who would defend the heart of Northumbria.

Rolf patted Mairne's neck. She'd had a patient ear for his wonderings back in Alton's stables. He rubbed his fingers together meditatively. Strange, his hand itched for his quill and a pot of royal blue ink for the Vulgate translation in the very hour he bore a blade instead of a quill.

He rubbed his aching forehead. Blue would complement the red ink Father Ulf had used so liberally in the Vulgate. When it was finished, Abbot Alton must see to it that both the common translation of the Book that Kyrin brought saw every church's altar and the Latin, despite wherever Father Ulf meant to hide away their Lord's Word in hidden splendor. The Word was sent to grace men's hearts. *Do you still fear yourself so much that you will not trust our Lord with your fear and your anger?* He could wish Alton rode beside him now. Then he could ask him more of what he meant. *Driven to mercy.*

Sore inside and out, Rolf forced a grin at Seldon, riding beside him in the afternoon sun. "That weapon of Mornoth's knocks a man about the ears. But I believe its elements are of this earth."

Seldon grunted. "One of Cierheld's men saw a runner with a cast iron pot in his hands. He shoved it against the base of the wall just before it came down. Some vile device of Mornoth's."

"Probably from his trade in foreign parts. If it was an invention of Britannia, someone would have heard of it. Or he stole it." He looked at Jost. "You know well that Lord Mornoth must not reach Cierheld, in vengeance for Lord Keffer. The house of Cieri must not fall. For the sake of the abbey and all the land." *If Lord Dain Cieri passes from this world, his daughter must take up his mantle. She must not sleep until the last trump, God forbid. She must know I have kept my word.*

"Mornoth will use it against our allies in the north," Seldon warned.

Jost said, "I fear he will. It may be an invention of the east. They have been perfecting the art of warfare for millennia. Kyrin would know, were she not struck down." He colored and looked away. He was very young.

"Aye. We must see it stopped, and if we can, take one of them undamaged, to see how it works." Seldon turned to Rolf. "Did you know Lord Mornoth has mercenary help from the west—his bowmen and the like?"

So, he had been deep in Father Ulf's counsels. Rolf said lightly, "Oh, aye. Which means Kilden will not always be close to guard our backs. He'll be off hunting archers."

Seldon bristled. "I have no need of his guarding. But do not we guard each other's back?"

Jost straightened in his saddle. "When will we meet them?"

Rolf said, "What's in the squad, stays in the squad. Lester sees to it." Seldon did not seem to be after simple ambition, for he offered his oath, yet still he weighed Rolf. Rolf continued, "As for Mornoth and his forces, Jost, we'll be at Cattraeth in three days if we pass through Coverdale. Lord Mornoth may not expect us from that western vale. With us and your tensquad, we will sow discord and doubt—"

"We'll carry the fight to bite their flanks as a hungry wolf," Seldon broke in.

Jost laughed. "And beat them mightily about the head with your staff, Brother Rolf!"

Seldon said shortly, "We must kill them before they kill us, and we will do it as we have always done, with spear and blade and bow." He did not look at Rolf.

Seldon once approved a staff as an excellent weapon. Why did he jab at him with words? Was it because he lifted his blade on the wall? Rolf felt a growing chill within and bowed his head. He was trapped between who he had been, this place between, and who he would be. *"Will you strain out a gnat and swallow a camel?"* Rolf cleared his throat and turned pointedly to Jost. "As Abbot Alton said, I will uphold Cierheld. That means following Lord Dain and your armsmaster's plans, Jost."

The young armsman brightened. "The news of our victory over Lord Keffer ought to bolster our men's arms against Lord Mornoth. We'll fight through our enemies to their sides." He smiled, satisfied. "It is good to have brothers at one's back."

Rolf said nothing. If they came in time, and their allies were not already overrun. If news of Kyrin's fall did not overwrite Cierheld's victory. If he wielded his staff well. He did not wish to think of using the blade again.

Seldon looked from one to the other and growled, "What of the brigand and the abbey?"

Rolf frowned. "Abbot Alton has not forgotten the brigands." Neither had he. "It is thought of," he said shortly. *Never enough, traitor. You must be my hands now. Drives us to fall on his mercy.*

Seldon picked at a scab on his forearm, where a sword had scratched him before the gate of Cierheld. The blood ran, and he drew the Chi-Rho on his skin.

Rolf's stomach clenched. Seldon did not draw idly. He came from the painted people indeed, to think of such a red ink, on such a strange and ghastly parchment.

Sigil of their Lord's name in the Greek tongue, the Chi-Rho, the X and P painted directly one upon the other. Some believed it had power. Seldon had once asked him of things that could hold power.

So, he had learned the Chi-Rho. He had also learned to align his body and weapon in balance, for he'd gained skill with the sword and staff. The staff Rolf had promised to teach him, though Seldon came not after their last lesson. It seemed ages agone. Rolf had not asked him back, bitterly thinking him busy with Father Ulf.

Rolf swallowed. Father Ulf was foiled well enough. Seldon was proved true, though a goading thorn. But how he stood with him, Rolf knew he must ask Lester close questions. Or would it be better to speak with Kilden? He still felt there was more to Seldon than met the eye.

"Tell me, Brother." Seldon studied the graceful script on his arm. "We saw you take down the man above the gate. You seemed to do well enough. Do you still hold that you wield a blade so ill? We would welcome you back to lead us."

"Whether I wield it ill or with skill is not the point!" Seldon's challenge sliced Rolf deep. He'd told them all how Alton released him from his oath, and near commanded that he bear weapons, though he was still conflicted. Could Seldon not see it pained him? Words rushed up Rolf's throat, and he said abruptly, "Any man can stab with a sword or spear. But when and how and whether I keep my oath or break his Word, that is what is in question. I am a man, and I do seek justice, and if you place any trust in Father Ulf's words, then or now, you've yet to learn of the darknesses of men."

Seldon dropped his arm and looked at him, his hand brushing the hilt of his sword. "That device is dark enough, with Mornoth behind its use. If we stop him, it is well." He shrugged.

Deeper pain hit Rolf. Seldon did not understand what he sought and had lost. Right standing with God and man. That might have been his arm brushing a sword, and his skill honed in Seldon's place, as if he had never left the squad. Someone must replace him. If it was any other but Seldon, wearing Rolf's shame on his skin, he would be content.

13

# Brigand Betwixt

*Sharper than any two-edged sword...piercing as far as the division of soul and spirit... ~ Hebrews 4:12*

With a fling of his hand, Seldon cast aside beads of blood, and his laugh rose. "That did itch so, brother, like the evil one himself clawing at my skin. But we go to stop these 'darknesses of men.' There, my blood will serve a better purpose. It will help bring in the coming king." He raised his arm for Jost to admire the Chi-Rho and grinned at them. "This will drive off evil better than my blade, which does not lack the swiftness Kilden beat into me. Lester says I may soon surpass him."

Rolf snorted. "You know nothing if you think a sigil will drive off evil of any sort. It's our Lord who does the driving, and he is not a power at our beck and call. He does not answer to lines drawn in blood or to words of a spell, or to rote prayer, for that matter. But an honest cry from a man's heart, that now, he hears."

"You are a man of God and prayer. But I forget. Surely, your quill wields more power than any sigil or spell, sword or staff?"

Seldon once upheld those words before Father Ulf on his behalf. Now Seldon taunted him with them. Kilden had not sparred with him for the past two seven-days. Had his squad leaders said nothing of Seldon's skill, for pity of him?

"Oh, I know well enough you've not had much use for your quill of late. My uncle in the tribe once said, "Seldon, someday you'll learn you must only please the gods." He tapped his bloodied arm. "This should please my uncle. With Constantine's sign from heaven, the Byzantines conquered. Surely you may mark us all with the Chi-Rho, and keep your men from harm?"

"No." Rolf gritted his teeth. He hated sigils like the Chi-Rho, twisted from their true meaning. Twisting anything from the purpose for which God made it in an attempt to control any source of power was deception. It was ignorance, or worse, malice. Which did Seldon mean? Or did he simply mean to draw his ire for some purpose of his own?

Seldon stared at him in high astonishment. "Why not, brother? You must be good at something, for the abbot to keep you! You must have at least the little skill required for the Chi-Rho!"

It was ire, then. He was pulling no blow. "God was never our errand boy." Blue and green and gold ink would flow after Alton set him to finish Father Ulf's scribe school. He would find a substitute for Seldon's skin for his quill. Rolf almost grinned. Mayhap calfskin? Then Seldon would cease his mocking challenge when he saw the beauty of his scribing.

Seldon sighed. "The Chi-Rho is a small thing. But you will raise your blade beside me, Rolf. Then your fear will be gone for good and all." He nodded. "I'll keep you from harm. Even if you do not yet dare to turn your back on me, brother, since you would not allow my oath." He watched him carefully.

Rolf laughed. "You think I fear you?" Seldon knew nothing of the haunting, niggling tension, of his bitter thoughts of failure. Of his abbot's words that would not leave his mind. *We cannot change ourselves.*

Seldon frowned. "Why else do you avoid me? When you're with the squad, you always look to Kilden and Lester. You fear something, or someone. It wasn't Father Ulf, perchance?"

"Mayhap you ought to fear what I fear," Rolf said darkly.

Seldon stared at him. "Do you truly fear the blade? If so, we're sky and earth apart, brother."

Rolf growled, "You ought to fear losing your place. Kilden does not suffer golden-tongued fools. Nor Lester." He needed no more brothers, wanted none. He had the squad, for the moment.

"I have no place to lose, only to gain." Seldon tossed his head. "Or is it the blood that makes you turn pale?" He peered at Rolf.

The blood. Rolf flushed. When a man feared himself, it was something he could not escape. It seemed Seldon had learned how to twist the subtle knife. Ulf taught him well. How deep had he been in his counsel?

"Hah! Seldon, never were you a lost scion of one of my uncles, a half-brother or cousin! Of that, I am sure. You are no brother of mine. But you wish to know what I fear. I fear I might kill you with a misplaced blow! You were under my blade once and did I teach you nothing with my staff?"

"Not as much as I want to learn! It might surprise you how little I would fall under your sword now, if you wield it so ill as you did on the wall! And that stick of yours is a twig!" Seldon flung it at him.

"Now I hear what you truly think." Rolf regarded him stonily. "You're a fool. And you are right, exactly so. My stick is a twig. Hence, I will not cross blade or wood with you."

Seldon's nostrils flared, and his face whitened. "I'm not such a fool as you!"

"For refusing your oath? Or is it something to do with this king you mentioned?" What had Father Ulf told him, if anything?

Seldon struck his thigh with his fist. "You will not see—"

"See what?" cried Rolf. "What cursed blindness came over you that day that you follow me about like a milk-hungry calf? The sword I am not ready to teach. And as I said, you are not ready for it, if you must goad your teacher to prove yourself."

Jost rode wide-eyed on the far side of them.

How had Seldon gone from offering his oath to this? Seldon handled a sword like he never could, and a spear, even the bow. But not the staff. Rolf sighed. Brother, hah! But there was no comparison. It was as Kilden told him, Seldon was destined to lead, and as Ulf said, he was far above him in sword skill.

Seldon lowered his voice, a flaming wick pinched to a smolder. "I saw a man with my life in his hands give it back, in the heat of battle. I saw my brother—my twin—the man I want to be. Despite your cursed fears, you must teach me something. I do not believe it possible my forgiveness will be for naught."

The men riding behind were out of earshot along the road that twisted through the trees. Jost looked away, whether to spare him or Seldon, Rolf was not sure. He leaned forward. "Kilden and Lester school you well enough, since you call my staff a twig. I will not teach you the blade in heaven, on earth, or near hell!" He meant every word. "Heaven has no need of blades. On earth, I will not spill blood unless I must, and thank God, I am spared the fire of retribution for breaking my oath. Or so Abbot Alton seems to think. You cannot make me do otherwise."

"I've heard brothers oft do the like."

"Do what?"

Seldon cocked his head. "Anger each other, come near to blows, then teach each other." His suddenly solemn face held much of the imp. "You're my brother in spirit, if naught else. You're calfish yourself, you oaf." He grinned. "I've made you want to strike me down this moment with that stick of yours. It is useless to deny it! I may cross blades with you for the squad. I will be as you. I will be even better. Even to the Chi-Rho." With that warning, he thundered ahead to catch up with Lester.

"I'll risk it with wood only!" Rolf clutched his staff, glaring after him, with a shake of his head at Seldon's laugh that drifted back.

The whelp could never surpass him with the staff, though he had in all else. All else but his men's hearts. Rolf eyed the pommel of the sword at his side. A fool Seldon remained. And he supposed he was one too, since he wished to knock Seldon off his horse. What would his Lord above have him do? Definitely not let loose his frustration on his companions.

He twisted Mairne's reins hard then laid them carefully flat, grumbling over his breath at Seldon's departing back, "Prove it if you must, if you can."

Jost swallowed, the slight Cierhelden's throat bobbing. He seemed unable to tear his eyes from Rolf's hands. He sighed silently in relief when he saw Rolf would not pursue Seldon, and Rolf forced a grin for him and flipped his staff up. There, he'd brought the challenge down to future blows, a challenge Jost and the others would understand.

He'd have to make sure their match came to staves. His Lord himself said it was right to flee temptation. Rolf's mouth soured as he nudged Mairne back as she swung her head aside from the path to eye a bit of grass. Pain twinged in his hand. He wished Berd would recover the use of his arm soon, at least enough to show him his first daughter's secrets of the staff. Most of all, he wished her to live and show him herself. Then let Seldon try him. But Lord Ludwin Mornoth and his fearsome weapon must be stopped first. Britannia must not fall.

They came over the wooded brow of the hills around Aysgarth stronghold. Its walls rose on the northern side of the dale, at the end of the long bowl of rolling grass amid an ocean of ancient trees. The oaks here were hale, their boughs widespread. A dark column of smoke thickened the air before the gate on the south side. Aysgarth was besieged.

Cierheld's colors flew before the south gate, facing them, where their men engaged two tensquads of spears.

To the right, a line of bowmen advanced slowly through the woods. Further below, the shouts of men and clash of arms rang among the boles of oak, ash, and alder. A long block of defenders in black rallied before the east wall of the stronghold, their ranks three deep, waiting. It was curious they did not fight alongside Cierheld's squads massed before the southern gate. Moving across the open killing ground between his squad and the stronghold, three squads of Mornoth's pikemen ignored the Cierhelden's and strode around them toward the first line of defenders in black along the east side, close to the woods.

Why had the Aysgarth forces come out from behind the safety of gate and wall? Unless it was a costly, last-ditch defense against pikes and archers in the open in an attempt to defend against something more deadly. Rolf exchanged a glance with Kilden.

A thin finger of woods extended between those guarding the gate and the Aysgarth squads to the east. Among the trees, a bit of white flashed. A horse's flicking tail. Rolf caught his breath. A small, mounted force moved stealthily toward the left flank of the defenders in black. He knew that bright horse and dark helm, and the ambitious heart beneath.

"Foolish," muttered Kilden. "Lord Mornoth is between his bowmen and his enemy."

Witless indeed was Mornoth's move, except he bore a roundish bundle before him on his horse, wrapped in a dark blue cloth. Rolf stiffened. By the strength of the blade he was given, it would not be. Not another gate and wall sundered, the children to flee the bodies and the blood and the fear. Cierheld remained untaken. So would Aysgarth, if a few more men could stop the fearsome flame.

"No time," Rolf whispered. He slid his spear from its thongs beside Mairne's saddle and put his staff in its place. "To me!" He cried. Kilden, Seldon, and the squad formed up behind him. Jost fell in behind Lester on Rolf's right, with those of Cierheld.

"There." Lester pointed.

Below them a hand of men in black flitted on foot between the alders and thick trunks in desperate pursuit of Mornoth. They would be too late, even if they had an archer or two.

Kilden grunted, Lester nodded, his dark eyes tracing the route below, then both stared at Rolf. He knew their minds, as if their last battle together were yesterday. If they moved round the archers' flank below, they could ride down through the finger of forest and slip between their enemies' forces. They might overtake Mornoth before his bowmen realized who they were.

Rolf looked at his men. Their eyes were steady on his. Seldon's grey gaze was almost smiling. With a shiver, Brother Rolf inclined his head. Seldon returned it, and the squad rode down the slope at an easy jog. Jost leaned forward, eyes flicking watchfully over the stronghold and the woods and their enemies before it, his men eager behind.

As they rode, Lord Mornoth's archers loosed a volley toward the gate, and another. Cierheldens fell. The rest closed ranks. Hemmed in by arrows, they edged back toward the hold. By the crashing of weapons over the sound of hooves, and the roar of men's voices, most of the defenders inside were on the far side of Aysgarth. Rolf shared a dire glance with Kilden. Had Lord Mornoth planned a three-pronged attack? Was there another black cauldron of destruction on the far side? But they must deal with Mornoth's pot of hell first.

Along the steep rocky hillside and thinner cover, through heather and down into the thickening trees, ever down they rode at a steady walk, listening to the echo of, "Cierheld! Lord Aysgarth! For the lady!" And their opponents' answering screams, "A Mornoth, a Mornoth! For the church!"

The church indeed. "Seldon," Rolf said quietly. As his horse wove around an ash, Seldon shook out the standard, and the abbot's silver cross on blue unfolded over them. If some from the bishop were here, it might conceal their purpose for a time. Rolf realized how very many needed them in the hold, and all he could give with heart and hand. He had been given weapons for this time. His oath had been wrongful.

They were past the archers and kicked the horses into a trot, then a gallop. Moments later, Lord Mornoth's rearmost man turned his head. He blinked and opened his mouth, but Rolf's spear took him from his mount. Kilden winged an arrow after Lord Mornoth. It struck an oak at Mornoth's back with a wicked 'thwap'.

Mornoth cast a glance over his shoulder. "Hold!" He cried and spun his horse.

Mornoth's men turned, checked at the sight of the flapping blue standard and Brother Rolf's Benedictine robe rucked up over his trews and tunic he wore beneath. They stared at his weaponless hands, then at the men around him.

Rolf stood in his stirrups and raised his arm. "For our Lord!"

As the squads closed, spreading their net, two of Mornoth's squad fell to Kilden's arrow and Lester's heavy blade.

"A Mornoth! A Mornoth!" Lester bellowed, adding to the confusion.

Rolf urged Mairne around the edge of the melee for Lord Mornoth. A lancer galloped between them. Rolf thought only of the one who had ordered Cierheld destroyed, and who meant to kill again. He batted at the lance and looped his arm around it, tucking it under his arm. The lancer fell from his saddle with a yelp as his weapon pulled him free. Rolf reversed the long shaft. It was near enough a spear. With a curse, Mornoth drew his sword. He clutched the bulky bundle of his terrible weapon in his other arm.

Rolf feinted at his shoulder and Mornoth deflected it, then Rolf neatly changed direction and pierced the blue cloth with the lance tip. He lifted the round bundle away. The lance bowed, almost ripping from Rolf's hands.

Lord Mornoth grabbed wildly at his prize, missed, and spurred straight for Rolf, sword high. Rolf nudged Mairne aside and let his burden slide off the lance gently, just in time to catch the full jolt of Mornoth's horse as it crashed into him.

A snarl marred Mornoth's lean face. Mairne reared and struck with her hooves. Rolf found himself sliding away from the mare as Lord Mornoth's sword came down. He landed on his back on the ground. The blade thumped across Mairne's empty saddle, and she kicked out again with a fierce squeal, ears flat. She snaked her neck around to bite Mornoth's mount and took a chunk of flesh and mane. The horse bucked. Ludwin Mornoth flew off. He landed heavily on his feet and staggered toward his prize that rested in a bush.

Brother Rolf struggled up. His lance lay a short distance from the inhuman device—too far for him to lunge for either of them. Kilden and the squad strove to keep Lord Mornoth's men back. Jost and the Cierhelden's were gone to help their brethren. Yanking his torn habit over his head, Rolf tossed it aside.

"Weren't you to be further north, my lord?" Panting, he edged forward, empty hands spread.

Fallen branches snapped as someone stepped from the trees at Rolf's back. "Weren't you to be a brother at Bolton Abbey?"

The voice was smooth and scornful. "Unless that simple-minded abbot at last agreed to the bishop's order? Does the church attack us by mistake?"

Rolf spun. "Dugar!" He shifted back, not to be caught between the bishop's armsman and Mornoth. With quick gestures, Kilden was gathering the rest of the squad against the pikemen and bowmen approaching through the trees, drawn by the noise. He was out of arrows. There were too many against them.

Rolf's heart caught and stuttered on. If only Jost had not left. Where was Lester? He needed him now. The bishop's perfidy was certain.

"So, have you gained more skill with that blade than the lance?" Armsman Dugar nodded at the sheathed sword at Rolf's side, his eyes as cold as Rolf remembered. They bore a wicked spark, as his mouth bore a toying smile. "Did you think us brigands, perhaps?"

Rolf gripped his hilt without taking his eyes from the two who faced him. *Did you think us brigands?* Dugar might as well be; he made a pastime of preying on others. He was in fit company with Lord Ludwin Mornoth.

Mornoth changed his grip on his sword and crossed his arms with a chuckle. "You know this man, Dugar? Get him out of my way. Our business lies ahead."

"We know about your devilish black powder!" cried Rolf. "It will never reach this gate, nor Cierheld's." What did the fearsome weapon take to ignite its power?

"Is that so?" Lord Mornoth sighed happily. "Then we will have another stronghold to visit on our way to Bolton, to free our good Father Ulf. Cierheld must fall."

He did not know Abbot Alton had taken Father Ulf with him to face regent Tolman, who was not an absolute fool. Rolf hoped the newest regent would not be a fool. But the children and those left in the abbey...Ludwin Mornoth meant to attack. Of course he did; he was a brigand in heart.

Rolf drew his sword, wounded hand aching. Dugar sniffed eloquently. Lester was not in sight.

The armsman took a slow step forward. Rolf glanced at the lance, then dashed for it. Dugar smiled. But Rolf stopped short, drew back his arm, and threw the sword like a spear, with a desperate prayer. He followed it in, his dagger hand low.

The sword hit. Dugar stumbled back, clutching at his neck. Red blood spurted. Rolf saw with relief there was no need for a second blow. He scrambled for his sword that had fallen behind Dugar and came to his feet.

Beside the willow clump, Lord Mornoth held the blue bundle like a babe of innocence inside his black-clad arm. When Rolf rose, he laid it softly behind him. Mayhap a blow would loose its blast. The tip of Ludwin's weapon lifted lazily in a serpentine weave. "You say you're not good with a blade?"

"No," Rolf admitted, trying not to tense. What he would give for a spear, or his staff. Every lord trained with blades almost from birth.

Mornoth sprang. Rolf did not know how he kept his head and limbs in the fierce clatter and shriek of steel. His enemy was far stronger than he. Sweat ran into his eyes. They parted.

Ludwin grinned as Rolf panted. Blood darkened Rolf's sleeve and flooded his left boot. He still felt little pain besides his hand. His blood thundered through him, shaking him. He took a step and his leg buckled. He shoved himself up. He must be enough. Then a body crashed into him from the side, knocked him back, and turned to engage Mornoth with a furious yell.

Kilden—but it was not him. Rolf spun around on his good leg. Seldon shouted something and drove Lord Mornoth back, and back. The pot lay deserted behind them. The pot.

Carefully placing each step, Rolf approached Mornoth's prize. Then it was in his hand. Something whispered under the blue cloth, inside the heavy iron. The lid was sealed with wax, like a cork. Rolf cradled it. Everything felt curiously distant.

Pain ripped through his back. He looked down with a groan. A blade tip extended past his chin, then dragged a shuddering breath from him as it withdrew from his left shoulder. It grated on bone. Thank God it was not his scribing arm, he thought dimly. The blue bundle dropped from his hand with a thud.

Behind him, Mornoth said, "One more step and I'll kill him." Rolf could feel the point in his lower back. Mornoth held his shoulder from behind, bracing to drive the weapon home.

*Fool!* He was no longer an armsman, that was certain, so unaware of his surroundings. *At least the powder does not kill when dropped.*

The pain in his pierced shoulder bloomed, swallowing that of his slashed arm and leg. The small bite of Mornoth's blade at his back was that of an ant. Suddenly dizzy, Rolf leaned forward as the familiar cold prowled through him, the rage of despair. He could claim that burn of an incandescent wish for destruction. His own, Mornoth's, or both. He could draw it close and kill the traitor. The anger brooked no obstacles. He looked up.

Seldon crouched before them, sword out, his eyes stormy hot as he met Rolf's. His gaze darkened and he looked past Rolf. "Give it up, Lord Ludwin. Do not kill a man of the church. Or suffer the wrath of God." His voice was hard, mouth pressed tight.

Mornoth laughed. "Wrath of God? Tell me, what is a man, if he does not choose his own destiny? I have chosen mine. I will be king. Britannia will rise from her ashes of incompetence and doddering impotence. This one," he shoved Rolf's shoulder, "will also choose." He chuckled. "Your brother is no great fighter. Dugar said he was squad leader. I am surprised."

Rolf strove for breath and said nothing.

Lord Mornoth shook him hard. "Come, I have not every bell of the day to wait upon, as you monks do, with endless room for prayer. Carry the pot for me. Now."

Seldon watched, ready. Rolf smiled at him, swaying. He and Seldon were nothing alike. Yet the whelp proved true. Rolf stumbled, his body faltering.

His earthly blade was gone. Only the sword of the Spirit, of truth and the Word, remained. *Traitor. Never enough.* It was true. He never had been. He knew it now. His shoulder was on fire, his life leaking away, the cold growing. *Trust him.*

A vision of the Vulgate swam before his eyes. He clutched at it. What verse was it, ah, that knotty Celtic letter he admired and struggled to write. "I can do all things through Christ." That was what Alton meant. Christ. He bridged the gap, in mercy, forever. It could not be, but it was. To be trusted, or not. *My Lord is enough.*

"I am not enough," Rolf breathed. "But he is." *Lord.* The last of his guilt melted. *I yield.* He smiled faintly and looked Seldon in the eye. *In him I am enough.* He was free before his maker. That grace meant two things.

Rolf leaned down for the pot. He gripped it carefully. Spots flashed before his eyes. A warmth sputtered in his belly. The ice was gone. In its place was the comfort of peace. It was a growing flame as he straightened.

"Well done, my good man, well done!" crowed Lord Mornoth, mocking.

Rolf lifted the pot, hugging it to his chest. He turned. And threw himself across Mornoth's legs. Ludwin cursed, stumbling back.

With a yell, Seldon lunged. His sword darted in.

Rolf held the pot close as he hit the ground, and tucked his knees up and rolled away, guarding it between his forearms, along with a stick he caught as he spun. He rolled rapidly until an alder stopped him. Gasping, he shoved himself to his knees with a groan and one arm and managed to thrust the pot deep within the shrub.

The sound of blades at his back lessened. Rolf swallowed against his parchment-dry throat. "Take him, Seldon!" he cried. His voice cracked to a whisper. "Defend the defenseless."

Seldon cried out. Sight whirling, Rolf pulled himself up by the stick that had lent itself to his grip and staggered. The top was sharp against his wounded hand.

Seven lengths away, Mornoth stood over Seldon. He lifted his sword for a great downward stroke. At the edge of the trees across from them, Kilden leveled his bow, face tense. The arrow might not stop Mornoth's blade.

Even as Rolf realized what he held, with two great steps and a leap, he sprang. The wood struck true.

Mornoth twitched with a grunt. His weapon drove into the ground, just missing Seldon's legs. As Rolf thudded into him, they both fell atop Seldon. Men rushed forward.

Rolf trusted Kilden was there, and Lester. His weight would hurt Seldon. He rolled once more. It took all his strength. Blackness drew in.

14

# Brother Found

*The one who loves his brother abides in the light. ~ 1 John 2:10*

"I got a piece of 'em!" That was Lester's roar. There was a pound of footsteps, a tugging, and a disgusted grunt. "Help me get 'em off 'em!"

Several crushing weights left Rolf. Closer by, Kilden said mildly, "For not being a fighter, he gets it done."

"Aye." Seldon's voice was tight. A warm hand closed on Rolf's. He gripped it weakly. "He's waking! Open your eyes, brother, you're too stubborn not too. Come on," Seldon chided.

Rolf realized he was squeezing his eyes shut against the pain that wrapped around him and squinted. There was light and trees and faces above him. Seldon.

He met the whelp's anxious gaze, felt his hard grip on his hand, and found himself with a sudden desire to laugh. "Brother?" he queried softly and smiled. An irritated scowl crossed Seldon's face, but he did not let go.

Then Rolf smiled up into Lester's worried eyes and turned his head slowly. Lord Ludwin Mornoth lay sprawled to one side, no threat to anyone, the pot set carefully near his head. Guarding pot and all, Jost threw Rolf a salute. Rolf blinked at him. Others of the squad walked into his view and gave him heartfelt grins. He smiled back as much as he was able.

Lester gripped his good shoulder, and then Kilden shoved him aside, hefting the bag of herbs they carried for wounds. Most of the men scattered, some to guard them, others to lay the bodies on the ground straight, some to other tasks. At the moment, Rolf did not care.

Seldon did not move. Rolf drew a long breath and held it against a cough, which would probably make him cry. Not in front of Seldon. He grimaced. "You...did it." Never again would he call him 'whelp.' "You have your place."

"I don't want it, not at this price." Seldon loosed his hand, not looking at him.

"Price? What price?" Rolf cocked a curious eye at him, while Kilden helped him sit straighter and cut away his robe and tunic, then swiftly crushed ferny leaves of yarrow. He packed the herb around Rolf's shoulder and tightened a bandage that made him grit his teeth.

Seldon opened his mouth as if to say something, then closed it. At last, he said, "That you are not enough. You near gave your life for me."

Rolf protested. "I did not—" and caught his breath on a burst of pain.

Seldon said hurriedly, "When I was with the tribe beyond the wall, I always wanted to come back. My second mother loved me, but her husband never let me forget I carried the blood of *finn gaill,* the light-skinned foreigners. The man was not important to my errand, and I...never mind. When he set that captured brother of yours to teach me a little scribing, I learned the Chi-Rho." He looked down, pulling at his boot. "With the squad, I found a place, of a sort. Then, at Bolton Abbey, I found you."

Seldon stared at him. "You are a brother of soul, and I—I want to be your brother." The hunger was naked in his face.

He surely wanted something, but he did not know what Rolf knew. True brotherhood meant trust. Rolf struggled to hold himself upright. "You're daft," he said fiercely. "What are you not yet telling me? Spit it out."

Seldon said low, "I know. Our first meeting changed me. The sword will give me what I want now, but you *are* enough, in our Lord, to lead any man." He glared at Rolf just as fiercely. "You are a man of unbending honor, when you are in the right."

"And why does that matter?" Trust was so simple, yet so hard.

Seldon drew a deep breath. "You must judge me."

Lester crossed his arms on his great chest and looked down at him, while Kilden did not pause in his exploration of the sword wound in Rolf's leg. Rolf waited. He knew there was something else. Telling the truth was harder yet.

"I was sent beyond the wall when I was young, to gather any word of import for the king."

Rolf drew back slightly in surprise.

"Then the king died, and I did not wish to carry news to the wrong ears. My teachers dinned it into me that fighting men and brothers of the church know most about the currents sweeping the world, and love to speak of what they see. I heard conflicting reports of the regent, so I stayed with your squad brothers. At first, we went to the bishop, but I did not trust him. Then we sought you out. You were no exception." He grinned suddenly.

"And what did you learn of me?" Rolf cocked his head with a hiss.

Kilden paused as he slathered a yarrow salve across his leg As Achilles had from ancient time, his squad-first used it for healing men.

"I learned there is more to sword skill than I thought. I hope my balance has improved. I also came to know it takes even more skill to discern traitors and trustworthy men than to know a good blade or a staff." Seldon pursed his mouth, staring at the ground. "Of you, I learned you are worthy of much."

Rolf grunted. He distrusted this sudden communicativeness. "What of the coming king? Do you serve him?"

"I do not know." Seldon looked up. "If he is worthy. But you are worthy of leading us in search of him. Should we not have a rightful king, rather than a regent?" His grey eyes were piercing.

He gave away much with those words, *Worthy of leading us, in search of him.* And, *I do not know.* The gazes of both squad leaders fixed on Rolf. "No, ye *don't* know, ye fool!" Rolf burst out. "All of ye!" Lester frowned as he went on, "I willna' lead in war unless I must—"

Kilden held him from getting to his feet, both hands on his chest. "I know. We mean to follow wherever *you* go. We will be your sword arm. Hasn't that abbot of yours shown good sense in electing you to be his eyes, ears, and hands in these treacherous times? He'll be amenable to us staying on in his service, and finding the king, too. You will see." He smiled and tucked the end of a bandage in place about Rolf's arm. Rolf gasped. His shoulder was setting into flame hotter and deeper than his arm and leg.

Lester barked a laugh, dark eyes twinkling. "Never thought I'd see the hour ye didna' talk proper! Ye're back with us, lad!" He clapped a hand on Rolf's good leg, then was abruptly serious. "We're travelin' together again. An' now that's all I care about."

All of his squad brothers watched Rolf, and he found a stinging in his eyes. Wincing, he raised his hand. "Alright, alright, I'll cede that. But not this." He turned to Seldon. "What I mean is, you *have* my place. You must understand. Lester and Kilden would suffer no one as they have you. For all the mercy they give me." He growled the last words, as Kilden released his blood-soaked arm with a tug that shot fire through him.

"But...but, you *cannot."*

Rolf lost patience. "Cannot what, whelp?"

"You cannot give up your place! You are my brother!" His face whitened under his red hair, and he jerked to his feet. Desperately, he said, "You can't, because you are my brother in truth. Our father-by-blood left you a small holding, but he did not marry my mother. That is why they took me beyond the wall. I will not take your place!" He spun and put his back to them, every muscle tight, breathing hard, fists clenched.

Rolf gaped, staring at his back. He swallowed, and said softly, "Is that so?"

"Yes!" Seldon swung back, tears on his face. His voice was small, and defiant with shame. "I did not wish you to know there was more to me than my work for the king." He swallowed hard. "I would not have you hate me."

It was the truth. Rolf relaxed. "My brother," he whispered in wonder. That explained so much. That was why Seldon gave him his oath with such a sidelong look and baited him. He had never meant to take his place, but to be like him. Rolf smiled. "But that is all the better. Now we will learn together!" His joy was a well springing up.

Seldon stared. At last he gave a crooked grin. "Is that all you think of? Learning?"

Rolf couldn't help it. He laughed, gasped, and laughed again. He reached out and pulled Seldon down into a one-armed hug. "You are worth more than all the lands and learning I could ever gain of this life. I have a brother!"

Seldon gave a half-choked laugh of relief and returned his embrace. Then pulled back. "I still mean to beat you at staves, someday."

"Never." It was a declaration that spoke better than any oath. Here was a brother who would always have his back. But his squad brothers...Rolf glanced about hastily. They looked none too shocked; pleased grins graced their faces.

"I'm sorry," Seldon said, drawing his arm across his face. "I didn't know until Abbot Alton told me. He suspected. He made a search in all the church records from the Humber to just short of the wall."

"You and Lester knew, when you pretended to conspire with Father Ulf?" That hurt, that none of them had told him. Rolf looked down.

"No! I found out just before we left for Cierheld. And then you know how things were." He shrugged, awkward. "I was not sure of you."

Neither had he been sure of him. "Ah. That is well enough, then." He would not mention barbs cast between brothers.

Lester said solemnly, "Your abbot thought it best it come from Seldon." He sighed. "None of us were sure of much, or knew what ye wished, brother."

That was true. He had not known what he wished, himself. It was a day of discovery. Rolf drew a shaky breath and looked up at them. "The sword is not for me. I always knew it, I think. Far better you take it up, Seldon. My blade will find its home in your hands, for far better purpose." He sank back on his elbows, blinking.

Kilden leaned close, green-brown eyes sharp. "Are ye faint-ish?" Seldon looked alarmed.

"No. I find the quill now calls me more than iron, unless there is need." Out of breath, he tried to smile. "Though I will keep my hand in practice with the spear. I still want a bout of staves with Berd, or his first daughter—"

"And why would you want that?" Another voice broke in. It was a commanding voice, a lord's voice.

A tall young man strode toward them, with a hand of men attending. Most of them were clad in leather and chain armour, holding doffed helms. The young lord wore black. Cierheld's sun and moon was embroidered bold on his breast, and sweat plastered his straw-colored hair awry, a plain helm under his bandaged arm. A wiry, dark-haired, dark-eyed man stood beside him, taller than Berd. He, too, looked at Brother Rolf, awaiting his answer.

Rolf let his head hang back. "I do not know you, my lords."

"But we know you."

Seldon's mouth quirked. Rolf scowled at them all and sat up again. Seldon stood and bowed deeply. "Brother Rolf," he said, "allow me to present Lord Talik Wyman, and Nith, first arms-man of the house of Cieri."

Rolf flushed, and, clinging to Kilden's arm, gained his feet. He bowed shakily. "Forgive me. I fear I do not give you courtesy. I would wish to learn the wiles of staves from your hold, and particularly your first daughter, whom I have met." He devoutly hoped to see her again.

"And our Lord Cieri?" Nith's gaze was a spear, pinning him, seeking deceit.

"He also lives, a little recovered, it seems."

"So." Talik rested his hands on his belt. "Our lord and our first daughter have need of us." The men behind him muttered agreement, gripping their weapons.

Nith inclined his head and said shortly, "All is not as it seems, Brother Rolf." He gestured with his chin. "When my scout reached Aysgarth ahead of Lord Mornoth, the outbuildings were already in flames. Someone raided here, taking advantage of Lord Cor Gadral's absence. He has taken his seat now, but someone else schemed to take his hold. That bodes ill."

Rolf gazed into the distance. "He said to me, 'Did you think us brigands?'" Had there been brigands? Rolf wondered.

"Who said?" Nith's gaze sharpened, if that were possible, as Rolf eyed him.

"Armsman Dugar Isen was with Lord Mornoth. We fought. He came from the bishop, I cut him down." Rolf looked to Seldon.

Seldon said shortly, "He's dead. I had the men throw his body in the pit with the others."

"Describe him." Nith waited. Talik watched Rolf closely.

Rolf hesitated, gathering words, and Seldon said, "A thick man with a strong nose, a black beard and—"

"What of his feet? Their size?"

"Ah. Rather small, like a woman's." Seldon shrugged.

Rolf rubbed at his arm, which stung and ached under the bandage. He'd not noted Dugar's feet. But such things were no longer his to worry over. He only bore the iron at need, at his Lord's command. He gave a faint smile, then sobered.

It was like Dugar, to laugh over his confusion. But Dugar Isen would trouble the children of the abbey no more. He must have been the leader of the brigands. It fit, since he could go where the bishop pleased. Or had his forays been without Caddaric's specific knowledge, but with his tacit approval?

Nith folded his arms. "Dugar is not the one who struck down our Lord Dain."

Not the brigand who burned Tethold stronghold, and struck at Cierheld's lord? Rolf stared at Nith and gestured toward the wall. "Did not the brigand strike at Aysgarth? And Lord Cor Gadral?" If the brigand had not been dealt with...Rolf turned his head so fast his vision spun. Lord Wyman must protect the abbey.

Kilden steadied him. "Easy, Brother."

Talik's gaze, very like Seldon's, bored into Rolf. "No, Dugar did not strike down Dain. The brigand's men rove like wolves. I have tracked their leader. His feet are three hands' width long."

*Three hands' width.* The pain of Rolf's wounds made him shake. "Will you...guard our abbey?" Had anyone spoken to Lord Wyman of his long hunt for the brigand and the poisoner through the snow, and his uncharitable meeting with Kyrin Cieri?

"We will."

"You have my thanks, and Abbot Alton's." Rolf sighed and leaned against Kilden's arm. Mornoth was dead, and by the men and the allied banners he saw through the trees, they had the victory. There remained only the mopping up of stray men by the tensquads. Doubtless, Lord Talik Wyman wished also to be on his way. But they must know their danger. Then he needed to lie down. He drew a deep breath, pulling in his scattering thoughts. "There were several explosions at Cierheld when Keffer's squads attacked. Has anyone searched those Mornoth sent around the other side of the stronghold, to be sure he did not seek to use that weapon in more places than one?"

"Yes." Talik gave a short nod. "When the first pot burst against the front gate, we sent runners to watch each side. It is how we found you." He considered him, fingering his chin.

With the fire in each breath, Rolf could not bow. He inclined his head. "I have come to serve at my abbot's word. With staff, blade, and quill. Abbot Alton of Bolton gives you all grace." He traced the sign of the cross in the air and found Seldon at his other elbow with the abbey's standard. Pride in him, and thankfulness for such true men, brought a shaky grin to Rolf's face.

Nith gave him a military salute and glanced at the banner with a respectful gesture. Lord Wyman bowed. "We accept your service, with all thanks, and pray we find a man or so among the captives with knowledge of these brigands and their leader. We would confirm the safety of our lands, including Bolton Abbey. You should also know that the new regent, Lord Durand Tolman, is of stronger steel than Codi Golding."

"We have heard so. Abbot Alton anticipates it with great pleasure. He will welcome you."

Not long after, Rolf pushed aside the remains of a bowl of stew. He chased down the last crumbs of a loaf and a cheese wedge with a cup of wine heavy with herbs, which he lifted from a small wood table. No comfort had been too much for the savior of Aysgarth after the battle, not even a tent. He had rested a while through the afternoon, while Seldon had raised Abbot Alton's standard above it. Then Seldon brought in the stool Rolf sat on, while others of the squad gathered a fresh robe from his pack behind Mairne's saddle for him, a bed of skins, a blanket, and the table. At last Lester set a trencher before him.

He had protested, thinking of the other wounded while they served him, but Kilden assured him they were well looked after. He said, eyes bright, "We have a leader, and we have not struck amiss." Then ducked out of the tent with a rare, wide smile.

Rolf wondered if there was a Book in the hold he might read from. Fewer lives had been lost than might have been. Yet every life lost was a grief. Later, he would need to speak over them in their burial place. The Word of his Lord above never returned void of comfort, assurance, and strength.

Seldon directed the men to start fires and prepare supper, while Lester took up guard outside the tent door. Everyone else left quietly, leaving Rolf to his food. The wine and simple bread and cheese tasted better than he could remember. His staff had been placed beside the bed, against the back wall. The bed-place looked soft and inviting with a silver-black wolf's fur. His shoulder would hurt less there. Thankfully, Mornoth's blade had missed his vital parts. But he did not want to move and ignite the pain, subsided at last to a throb.

Footsteps came close. There was a low voice outside. "I must speak with Brother Rolf."

"Yes, my lord." Lester sounded as if he knew the man. Rolf stared at the door.

Lord Wyman ducked through the tent flap, past which Rolf glimpsed the walls of Aysgarth, reddened by the light of evening.

He began to push himself to his feet, but Talik shook his head. "Do not trouble yourself. You've earned your rest, though I come to ask for a service." He frowned.

A service of the church, or a personal one? "How may I serve you, my lord?"

"We must notify the bishop of Richmond with all swiftness, before this rot spreads further. He must be informed of Mornoth's fall. It may stay his hand if he sees the plot broken open. Do you know the mind of Abbot Alton well enough to quill a letter regarding the bishop in this matter?" It was a formal request.

It was Rolf's turn to frown. A complaint formally lodged in the church was a testament of a kind, but it had little strength behind it, beyond being a written witness. A letter of reprimand held more authority if it were signed by one of rank in the church. Was that what Lord Wyman wished him to scribe?

Talik inclined his head respectfully. "There will be copies made, of course. At least three, one of them to go to Abbot Alton for approval, one for the regent, and one for myself."

Relieved, Rolf nodded. "Yes, my lord, I can do that." As the hand of Abbot Alton, he must carefully consider the possible outcomes of every word he penned.

"Have you the head for scribe work this evening?"

Brother Rolf lifted the spoon from his empty stew bowl. "As you can see, my scribing hand is yet able, my lord." His other wounds were ignorable compared to the bear chewing at his shoulder, but scribing would take his mind from it for a time. Would the skill he had gained in a season of unrest and treachery be enough, before the herbs in the wine took effect?

"Ah, indeed." Talik smiled and stuck his head outside. "Get me four sheets of parchment, quills, and ink. Not dry, mind you."

Lester passed on the order, and the noise of celebration outside receded as the men moved to a fire where they would not disturb them. Talik himself whisked Rolf's supper remains from the table, and a waiting servant deposited the writing materials and departed.

Rolf lifted the quill Talik set before him. The white goose feather was pristine, the tip finely cut. He drew a breath. "So, you wish one letter addressed to Bishop Caddaric of Richmond, and three copies. This one I will make with a postscript for Abbot Alton. I am ready."

Talik cleared his throat. "Begin in this way, 'In the year of our Lord...'"

Rolf bent over his work, and the ink smell rose around him with its hint of iron.

"Why do you smile?" Talik was watching him.

Rolf gave a twitch. As the pain grated through him, he dared to speak his mind. "I was thinking of the ink. This iron does not stab the flesh, but pierces the soul, the mind, the heart. In this moment, a quill is sharper than a blade. By God's grace, the steel of heaven upholds the iron of earth. Against a bishop and treachery."

"Hah!" A grin flashed across Talik's mouth. "It is so, indeed. Tell me, what did Dugar use against you?"

Rolf cocked his head. "My lord, it was Mornoth who sought to overthrow the regent."

Talik leaned forward. "Did Dugar say anything else to you?"

"Naught but mock me—" Rolf stopped short.

"What do you remember?" Talik's voice was sharp.

"He said the bishop had given orders to Abbot Alton." Rolf sat back a little, carefully. "That means, between Bishop Caddaric and Lord Ludwin, they took into account that Alton and Bolton Abbey opposed them. What orders did the bishop give Dugar, I wonder? And to Mornoth?" He closed his eyes. "It is well you go to guard the abbey."

Was there another rat, another traitor? It could not be his other brothers. He could not think it of Mial. Worse yet, it could not be Seldon.

## 15

# Final Foe

*Love the brotherhood, fear God, honor the king. ~ 1 Peter 2:17*

In one stride, Talik gripped either side of Rolf's table, his face very close, hard with intent. "You look no fool, Brother. Tell me what he said. The daughter of Cierheld will find her hold safe when she wakes, that I swear—"

"No, my lord!" Rolf stood abruptly and had to grab the table with his good hand to avoid falling. He huffed out a breath and looked into Talik's eyes with effort. "Do not say so! Oaths bind us by the letter of law, without room for keeping the heart of our words. Let your 'yes' bind you to simple truth, to the limitless power of our God who upholds it, and you. You will serve Kyrin best so."

Talik stared at him, releasing the table. "You gained this knowledge how?"

"I bound myself with an oath years ago. But it was he who released me this day to truly keep it. My Lord above has released me to love him, and through him, you. It was his power that brought our enemy down. He laid Mornoth low. Or I would be in my abbey yet, or lie in this ground. Along with all who seek peace and right."

"I see. Our enemies will also know that I love the peaceful, when I bring down their schemes. I will protect those I love."

Rolf closed his mouth. Those grey eyes held no contempt, no malice, only determination. Rolf nodded again, jerkily. It was a word in truth. "Dugar said, my lord—"

"Call me Talik."

"As you will, my Lord Talik." Rolf's fingers slipped around his quill, and he wiped them on his trews. "As I said at our first meeting, Dugar thought I mistook him for one of the brigands I had been hunting."

Talik's mouth hardened. "Did he mention nothing of Thorgil?"

"The woodcutter? No." Brother Rolf eyed him. "Your first daughter's armsman, Berd, also spoke of him. He asked me to watch him. He supplies the abbey with wood, and sometimes messages." If Talik knew ill of Thorgil Axen, he would know of it as a defender of Bolton Abbey.

"Has your watch borne fruit?"

"We have placed no eyes near his house, for he would know it. During his duties, we've seen and heard nothing suspicious."

Talik said, "You must watch him closer yet. I suspect he has ties to this brigand."

"If he has anything to do with the brigands, I will discover it. Though it was not they who killed my brothers, but a traitor among us. Or do you believe Thorgil is also an ally of Lord Mornoth, and you have done nothing?" But he had best watch his tongue. He bowed his head. "Forgive me, my lord."

Talik smiled a small smile. "Did I not say you were not a fool?" He crossed his arms. He seemed rather to approve of Rolf's curiosity, and his caution. Rolf sighed in relief.

Talik tapped a finger against his arm. "Write to the esteemed bishop what words you think your abbot would aptly use. Tell the bishop that all commands to support the traitor and those under him must stop, for Lord Mornoth is fallen, as God is our witness. List the names of myself and our allies in the north. Tell him that the northlords will see him give his account before Lord Durand Tolman, who is to be invested at the next council. Now, with my thanks, I will leave you to your work." Talik nodded and went out.

Rolf stared after him, bemused. Cierheld's ally placed much trust in him without question, but then, he was more than a novice these days. He was the abbot's voice, his eyes and hands. Rolf bent over the parchment. How would the abbot begin?

*My lord bishop, I mourn a deacon's perfidy, to betray both his coming king of earth and his king of heaven for a lord of this world. Father Ulf has lost his soul, though he now recognizes I do not carry the crozier in vain. The kingdom of the soul is fragile, especially so when sold away from its rightful Lord for ill gain. Often does our greatest strength become our greatest weakness. His was desire for progress as he saw it.*

*I hope you have not fallen into the same trap. The tide has changed since Lord Ludwin Mornoth's fall, as attested by the allied lords of the north, who sign this missive. I hold forth hope you will renounce Mornoth's unholy alliance against Northumbria and its people. In which case, I am certain the new regent, Durand Tolman, will not be unreasonable, for he knows what service you have been to the church and our Lord in former years. If we deal with the danger now, it need not become a matter for the Archbishop. I retain all hope you will see the truth, and pray you will assist me in this matter speedily.*

*With every authority vested in me, your brother in our Lord, Abbot Alton. Peace be with you.*

*Set down by the quill of Brother Rolf, my voice and hand, acting for Bolten Abbey in all its affairs, since the recent loss of my prior, Dickon, and Father Ulf. The lords of the north have directed me to add that they will hear your statement before the next council, and Regent Durand Tolman.*

Rolf paused as he neared the bottom of the page.

*I do attest that these words are true, in the fear of God, as he is my witness: Lord Talik Wyman.*

He had given him a signed blank writ. Rolf shook his head. This was trust, indeed. The other allies would sign it soon. First, he would have Lester take it to Lord Wyman for ratification.

A rustle outside brought Rolf's head up. A thump. He levered himself to his feet, reaching for his staff. "Lester?" No answer.

There was a muffled curse, rapid steps from further away, and a grunt. And the *shring* of iron meeting iron. Rolf stepped to the back of the tent, grabbed his staff, and lifted the heavy edge with the tip. He slipped out in an awkward crouch, dragging his right leg. He rose, staff in hand, teeth gritted.

The nearest fire was down to a hill of coals against the approach of night, lighting two shadowy figures. Weapons glinted between them. Neither was Lester's giant form. They spun, locked together. One kicked the fire into a shower of sparks, and his hair shone as red as the garish light. Seldon. The other was clad in black trews and tunic, gleaming dull in the firelight. Above the concealing cloth wrapping his face, his eyes were beady. One arm lashed out swiftly with a dagger. The man reminded Rolf of a crow at evening, beak stabbing at his prey.

Seldon leaped back, holding his own. The men spun past Rolf again, not seeing him in the tent's shadow, intent on each other. Rolf hobbled after them. Lester's bulk lay motionless near the front of the tent, at the edge of another fire pit.

The assassin turned his back to Rolf, stalking Seldon, pushing him toward the coals. A step back and forward, a testing of Seldon's guard here, a dart of a blade there. Seldon's weapon skittered from his hand as he stepped clear of Lester's bulk. The assassin turned with him, blade seeking. Rolf took a step and swung, short and hard, at the back of the man's head. With the *thunk* behind his ear, the assassin folded facedown over his small black belly, an empty linen sack, dark limbs asprawl.

Seldon picked up his sword and straightened, panting. Rolf leaned on the staff in his hand, knees weak.

"So, you save me again, brother." There was a grin in Seldon's voice.

"I never said I didn't know the staff. I rather think it knows me." He smiled in the dark.

There was a rush of movement. "Ye're no good with a sword!" The vicious yell rose directly behind Rolf. He knew he was dead even as he twisted. At the edge of sight, an axe descended. It would shear through his staff like bread.

The axe haft crunched, wood against wood, driving down his arm he held helplessly over his head even as Seldon crashed into his back, and another arm flashed up to support his. Then Seldon shoved him aside and thrust his blade past Rolf's ribs. The attacker gasped and slid off the edge to the ground. Rolf raised his trembling staff in reflex, not sure their enemy was down. Seldon moved forward, but their second attacker, also in black, remained still.

Behind them, Lester stirred and put a hand to his head. "Hunh, he 'ad a swipe like a bear," he muttered. He rolled over to his knees. Then he saw Rolf, and Seldon before him with a bared blade. His great hands closed. "Hai! Squad brothers!" he roared, and stumbled up.

"All is well, Lester. He kept me from the axe." Rolf's mouth pulled up on one side, as he indicated the assassin at their feet.

From the shadows, Kilden said, "That was the way of it." He stepped into the light and dropped another log on the fire, his bow in his other hand. Rolf gave him a solemn nod.

Kilden ignored him. "So, one squad leader saves the other, and turnabout. I'd say that's as close as brothers ever get."

Kilden walked closer. "You stopped an assassin, Seldon. Now we will know the face of evil behind all this."

"But Rolf took Mornoth," protested Seldon. "And the assassin. I only helped with this one."

Lester grunted. "The strongest leads. That may be the way of your 'eathen tribe away beyond the wall. But 'ave ye not learned in our squad that strength of 'eart is more needed than strength of arm? Is it not so?" He asked it of them all, for the men gathered, drawn by the noise.

Amid the exclamations and growls of men yet arriving from the other fires at a trot, Rolf faced a growing circle. "Aye, it is so." He laid his arm across Seldon's shoulders. "My brother is well fit to lead you. Train him as you did me, and he cannot do worse. Indeed, he will do better. God has called me to leave the blade for the quill. I will lead you from there with the iron ink. Each to lead in his own sphere."

"If you're a man of the church, you may find iron ink more deadly than a poison blade, or a blade in the dark," someone quipped. Wood thrown on the coals kindled to flame.

Rolf's skin prickled. Indeed. Who commanded the assassins, and had they wanted ought besides his death? The bishop's letter yet lay on his table in his tent.

"Seldon, help me." He limped to the side of the tent toward the first man in black, and Seldon leaned down to pull away the cloth wrapping his face. The others followed. None knew the man.

"What of the second attacker?" asked Seldon.

As they turned, one of the men shouted, "He's gone!"

Rolf rounded the corner, and Kilden looked up from his study of the ground. "He's bleeding."

Rolf met his eyes, saying nothing. He must know who they were.

"Aye, we'll find 'em. You two 'ave done us proud this night." Lester looked from Kilden to Seldon and Rolf, then around at the men. His dark eyes gleamed with firelight. He thrust his great fist toward the star-scattered sky. "Hai! Squad brothers! To the fight!" An echoing shout rang around them.

Even Nith, watchful and solemn at the edge of the tents and the darkness, arms crossed, raised his fist in honor of the ancient call.

"Seldon, you will lead." Rolf turned to Seldon, who clasped his forearm firmly, with a rather dazed look. Warmth spread through Rolf, deeper and gentler than the familiar cold anger. Strength of heart, Lester had called it. It beat the chill hollow. He smiled at his brother.

Seldon nudged his side. "When that shoulder heals, we'll see the mettle of your wood against *my* blade." He was grinning.

"Sure you will, after I learn a trick or two of Lady Cieri and Berd!" Rolf rather thought Kyrin might recover.

Nith strode closer to clap their shoulders. "May it be so! But first let us find this assassin. He must not endanger our lords!"

Under the great cheer breaking out around them, Seldon turned to Kilden, and Rolf went to check the missive. Soon Lester bore it to Talik, when he went to beg a mount from him. At last Rolf found his bed, his tent under double guard, and smiled up into the darkness. Their Lord was merciful. Seldon was learning, and so was he.

The following turn of the moon, Brother Rolf saw many changes. Lord Talik Wyman and Nith having moved their forces to Cierheld days before, the rest of the northlords departed for their strongholds. As soon as Rolf was able to sit Mairne for more than a half-glass, he and the squad also departed Aysgarth, carrying Lord Cor Gadral's heartfelt thanks and commendation to Abbot Alton.

They rode into Bolton Abbey triumphant, to join in much celebration. A message had reached every town and village before them; the first daughter of Cieri was mending, with her lord father. Abbot Alton said it surely was a miracle. Rolf was glad, though his shoulder and other hurts were healing at the usual mortal speed. But he did not grudge Cierheld a whit. He also was mending within, which was a miracle in itself.

Rolf was about his new work in the church when he heard a stir at the front step and the sound of feet. He looked up from the Vulgate, quill in hand.

Berd strode toward him. But it was not Kyrin Cieri who walked in his wake. This woman was burned dark by the sun, her red-gold hair full of fiery hints, fair in a blue kirtle. Her greenwood gaze met Rolf's straightly.

*Ah.* Rolf set his quill down on the altar. It was Kyrin's sister, closer than blood. She who wielded a quill as a scribe and married a prince of the desert lands. There was talk of her prince, once an unbeliever who became a Christian. She had traveled across the sea, it seemed.

Rolf bowed, mystified. "You are well come, Lady Alaina."

She smiled at him. "You have used our Vulgate for the people, as you said. Kyrin could not come this day, but she has spoken of you."

Rolf reddened under her approving regard. "It was what any man ought to do." He blushed again and turned in desperation to Berd. "Is Cieri's daughter yet so ill she cannot ride?" he demanded.

Berd smiled. "She's as able as I, but I left her in better hands than mine. Lady Alaina and Tae Chisun, a warrior from the East, rode to Cierheld some seven-days ago. As her foster father, Tae keeps my first daughter well." He smiled. "We are beset by talk of combat and wagers at table every night. The only person missing is you." Rolf blinked. Berd continued, "There are nightly wagers between Tae and Cernalt. That's our old first armsman of many years agone, from before Nith's time." He wagged his head with a comical, heavy sigh. "Only a bout of hand-to-hand will settle it. Soon, Tae will also test Kyrin for top rank in her fighting art." He nodded at Alaina, his dark eyes agleam. "The Lady Alaina, also. Then you will see staff and stick work, brother, that will set you afire." His grin held a spark of challenge. "It's a wondrous system of thought, how the body works, turned to attack and defense at need. It's a wonder to see, with naught of witchcraft in it."

Rolf scowled. Father Ulf's charge of heresy and witchcraft against the house of Cieri had been abolished, unofficially as yet. But he could never miss such a display of the staff, no matter what others thought. "I will come. Someone from the abbey with knowledge of warfare ought to witness this fighting art called Subak. I will speak with the abbot. I'm sure he will agree."

"It is well." Alaina bowed her head then looked up, hesitant. "I also came to bring you word. My lord husband and I, we see many manuscripts taken from many lands over the course of history in Araby. Or we will soon, since we have come again into the good graces of the wazir, adviser to the caliph. Their libraries are large. We seek to preserve and record some of these writings for the good of men. My sister and Tae thought you may wish to see them for translation. It has been mentioned that Abbot Alton has put you in charge of plans for a scribe school?" Her gaze became direct. "May I send some of the manuscripts to your school? You would not mind if the name of the scribe on some of the parchments was mine?"

Rolf drew himself up. He knew that feeling of being counted and found wanting. "No, my lady, I would not count your scribing amiss. None may disprove any hand my Lord has made and approved, especially a daughter's." He touched the Book under his fingers. "This is all the proof you require of your faithful work and skill."

"You have proved faithful also, in more than words."

Rolf's face heated.

Berd broke in, "I hear you killed an armsman, one Dugar, and Lord Mornoth, in our defense."

"Yes. By God's grace."

Berd nodded. "Lord Talik sent me to tell you it was either Mornoth's men or the bishop's who tried to kill you. Come to Cierheld, when you may. I would cross staves with you. It will be good to learn together."

"My thanks." Rolf hesitated. But the time for distrust was past. "In the north, Lord Talik also told me Thorgil was not to be trusted. But before we returned, our woodcutter had already disappeared with all his belongings. Brother Mial guesses he left us when the abbot departed for court. For his crimes, Father Ulf has requested he be walled early away from the world for his tenure as a holy anchorite." Rolf frowned. "The bishop sent for him after he received the letter your Lord Talik dictated to me." There was a sour taste in Rolf's mouth. "Esther of Halwende has attended Father Ulf. Since he claimed to repent, she was given leave."

"I see. But you do not trust him." It did not seem to surprise Berd. "It is unfortunate the bishop intervened. As an anchorite, Father Ulf will be sought by men of high repute. I do not think a man such as he turns so quickly to good. There is also this I must tell you. The wazir himself has come from Araby to remove our first daughter's earring of slavery with his own hand. So that evil eye is dead." Berd shook his head. "There is yet unrest about, brother. We've caught one troubler of our kingdom, dealt with Lord Mornoth and his evil weapon, and driven the brigand underground. Yet one assassin was not caught. Watch well. For any man or woman who walks where they ought not, who speaks what they ought not. The brigand may return."

"I will watch."

Alaina gazed at him, her green eyes intent. "Kyrin will come when she can. Watch also for the falcon, and the tiger who haunts my sister's steps." She laughed a little. "Pay little heed to my maundering, brother. I have always feared her falcon blade."

"And this tiger more?" Rolf cocked his head, intrigued.

She sobered. "Aye. Though I've seen it but once, on a hillside when I was full of cold fear."

Recognizing her grip on the staff in her hand, the lithe strength of her limbs, he did not think she would fear easily.

She went on, "Wisdom, perseverance, and love are powerful weapons of the heart. The tiger," she shrugged, "it is but a symbol of the evil one we have all been given means to conquer. By God's grace alone. He will destroy the works of the evil one."

Rolf looked at her and smiled. "You are wise." So, Kyrin Cieri had overcome the eye of evil, as men saw that jewel. Did they see Him who she walked with? Rolf shivered, not with cold or fear, but awe. He had caught one glimpse of a depth of mercy that yet filled him to tears. He had also watched a soul fall and seen the destruction of a kingdom within. But the outer lands and many men had been saved.

Seldon stepped inside the door of the church in his blue and silver tabard over dark trews. Checking on him and his guests. Rolf flicked him the hand sign for no trouble. His brother was now head of the abbot's guard, which Lord Durand Tolman had authorised for the present hour of unrest. The guard was made up of his old squad, for his brothers would stand at his back and the abbot's against any enemy. It was enough.

Berd cleared his throat. "This Esther, first daughter of Halwende stronghold, she is not a friend to Cierheld. Esther's lady mother also has some ties with the church."

"Ah. Lord Talik told me some things, yet it seems he concealed more." Rolf looked at Berd sharply. "I think there are more of you who ferret out men like Mornoth, to protect us and the coming king, whoever he may be. Is it not so?"

"It is so."

"And you do not wish to give me names. I think there are hidden depths to you."

Berd shrugged. "With no names, none can be found and killed. But any man would find he'd grabbed a bear by the tail who touched Cernalt—" Berd halted and red crept up his neck. Suddenly he looked as young as his years, despite his broad shoulders.

Rolf grinned. "Who did you say? But it is no matter, we will find the brigand and his men. And any other who seeks the life of Northumbria," he said darkly. Then he sighed. For the moment, things were right with the world. As right as they could be until he gained the next, where there was no evil anywhere.

But there was much for him to do between. Watching for the good of all men was his task. He would watch as he could for the sake of his people. In every moment, in his Lord, he was more than enough. And then the moment was vast. His blade had passed to Seldon.

His quill waited.

§

*The hour of Britannia's history between the Wolfship invasions and the great peace is often formless. Lost in the Northumbrian mists, much is unrecorded that it would be better men remembered. Who now recounts what was lost in a stronghold gone up in flame in the hot battle over a king's seat, or tells of the greater prize gained by a man's spirit?*

*My quill writes for this kingdom, and this man, among many. But the good brother of Bolton was right. Our destinies are not our own. An accounting will always come, for we are not alone.*

*It has also been discovered that Berd, first armsman of Cierheld, had a part in the following Chronicle of the Falcon that none imagined. But that is another tale.*

*—Alaina Ilen, consort and scribe to Prince Faisal Ben Salin.*

# Falcon Dagger~Prologue

*Here recorded is a clash of souls in a tale of treachery, courage, friendship, and love. A conflict of hearts caught on the field of earth, between hell and heaven. The first whisper of events began in a missive from Kyrin Cieri.*

§

*To my good Brother Rolf: on behalf of the house of Cieri, I extend all greetings in our Lord. May this missive find you well, with your Abbot Alton's plans for the scribes' school at Alkborough well in hand and nearing completion. My lord husband, Talik, will give you all welcome when it is time for the building to receive teachers. I will be glad when he has prepared Alkborough for our arrival with its lands and people, and bids us join him.*

*Alas, I am confined with child for the coming months. Do not mistake me; I mean not that I regret our child or bearing an heir for my husband and Cierheld. I deeply love them both. It is only that I sense tension in the present peace. I especially felt it during the hand of days in winter that I spent at court, in things said and not said among conversations, some concerning the regent. There lurks a hidden danger that brings to my mind the tiger that stalks in the warm dark.*

*If the falcon dagger should return, whom would it oppose in our kingdom? For that loyal, true bird fights every lie, and there are many about the regent. To his credit, he refuses every hint of kingship from those at court, and protests he is only a steward for the king to come. I wonder, does he have in mind his son? The boy is not yet old enough to show what kind of man he will become.*

*As for untruths, I could wish Esther and Lord Thain Mornoth did not smile at me so. The thoughts behind their approval swirl dark and strong as eels, while their teeth flash swift as snapping wolves. There are many who speak less fair of Cierheld and mean us far better.*

*I could wish the falcon dagger were at hand again, and myself fit to wield the blade. Soon enough I shall be too cumbersome to move, I think. These thoughts may be but the foreboding of a body working upon the difficult and most blessed task of childbearing. Do not pay me overmuch heed, my friend.*

*Yet our Master of the Stars is always with us, and He has gifted Cierheld with many good friends. Among them, yourself and Abbot Alton and the regent. There are many hearts, hands, and eyes warding us.*

*As always, we pray for your prosperity and peace. Of your good will, lift us up likewise.*

*May our Lord bless you, and all who wish the good of our people and our fair Britannia.*

*With my own hand, Kyrin Cieri, first daughter of Cierheld and soon, Lady of Alkborough.*

*Please pass this missive to my sister of bread and salt, who will send it on to her second father and mine, to let them know of our affairs, and that they are in our hearts evermore.*

§

*As Brother Rolf asked of me, I sent this missive on to Tae Chisun by swift courier. We all share each other's letters, bound by the most tender of ties. That of shared blood in battle, of love, and of friendship.*

*But the foreshadowed conflict began too soon, before the heir was born and could draw a first breath.*

*—Alaina Ilen, consort and scribe to Prince Faisal Ben Salin. (Fragments of this letter were later returned to me for inclusion in the Chronicle and are here pieced together save for the reply of Tae Chisun, which I left out for reasons of my own.)*

# 1

# Falcon Dagger

*The heart knows its own bitterness. ~ Proverbs 14:10*

The last star faded into green and blue, washed with gold. Beyond the stronghold wall and the gate, a wren warbled, herald of a new sun. Berd turned from the fields and forest to face the morning, and the hold he warded with his life.

From the moat and mound outside to the wall of uncommon stone beneath his feet, nothing was out of place in the stronghold. Nothing.

The crenel was cold against the back of his leg as Berd squinted into the warmth. His skin was numb where neither leather nor linen cushioned his helm and light mail shirt. The five men of his half squad were silhouettes around the wall. A damp breeze stirred. The hold was quiet.

Berd tucked his chilled hands under his arms and eyed the long barracks along the east wall, beyond the smithy. The smell of Cook's roasted pork would rouse the men. Berd's stomach rumbled. Soon there would be crisp pork slices, new bread, cheese, and mayhap a sweet apple from last winter. He watched the barracks door, yet in shadow, for the first movement.

A voice whispered from the stone at his feet. "The sword is gone."

Berd started and gripped his hilt. Heart pounding, he stepped to the edge and stared at the shadow that had crept so close without his knowledge. He knew that voice.

Dark hair framed Kyrin's upturned face, pale in the grey. It lent her an elfin air. The first daughter of Cierheld stood close enough to take his booted foot with her blade.

"I was going to walk in the garden, but the sword is not above the hearth. We have a thief." She crossed her arms. Her cloaked form showed the new life of the heir she bore.

"My lady." Berd clenched his fist.

Who would dare take the blade from Cierheld's very hall? Straight and costly steel, the weapon was cousin to Kyrin's old falcon dagger that once saved Cierheld. The sword was of like curious forging, a rippled pattern of watered steel, of perfect weight and balance. During the war between the southlords and the northlords loyal to the regent, the keen edge disappeared.

Then it had been found again, at great peril to his first daughter. Now it was gone again. More was out of place than the Damascus blade.

"I'll wake Nith." Berd's neck prickled. Everything that happened in the hold on his watch was his responsibility. If only he had known before Kyrin that the blade was missing and raised the alarm. More than half of the hundred fifty men usually quartered in Cierheld had been assigned to their sister holds, Fenwrd and Alkborough. But Cierheld's first armsmaster and a few men remained.

"I wished to tell you first." Her amber gaze was steady.

He yet held her trust. Berd lifted his arm in silent signal to his men, not to alarm the intruder. Most of the hold was visible from the north gate, and he scanned it swiftly. The thief might wish for more than a blade.

The mews were silent. A lone stable boy made his way to the stables. The chicken coop and sundry edged them, then the smithy and long barracks along the east wall. At the south end of the yard, before the straw archery butts, a few chickens scratched in the dust near the sword posts where he trained daily with the squads.

Closer, the well and the washhouse abutted the kitchen's rear wall. Across the dirt lane from them was the great hall. Naught moved among the neat rows of carrots, cabbages, and green herbs he could see past the corner.

He instructed two men to guard the gate and descended from the wall. "They'll keep watch from above. We must get you within, then we'll search the hold." If he was to find the thief there was no time to lose.

Kyrin's light brown eyes darkened. "I'm still able to protect myself, at least as well as any warrior—"

"We do not know the thief's purpose. You now have two heirs to care for: yourself and the one you bear. Later, you may speak of this with your lord father, if you wish. Or your husband. But I am your first armsman." She and the household must be protected before he roused the rest of the men.

She scowled but turned in a swirl of cloak and kirtle and strode toward the hall steps. Berd followed her inside, searched swiftly upstairs and down, and saw to it that her Aunt Medaen and the women and servants of the house barred the great door behind him.

At the wall, the watch had seen nothing. None had passed the gate. The thief was yet within Cierheld.

If they were quick, they would catch him. Or was it her?

Esther had stolen the blade the first time and seen it gifted to Kyrin's disgruntled Uncle Ulf. As he rushed across the yard toward the barracks, Berd frowned. He wished he knew more of that monk's attack on Kyrin and Celine.

The newly instated regent let Esther of Halwende off far too easily, though her involvement was discovered late. She was a rapacious vulture, that one. But Esther retired to her mother's estate at Halwende. Nothing guaranteed she would bide there. She had recently returned to the regent's court.

Berd left the wall and rapped at the door of the armsmaster's quarters at the south end of the barracks. In a moment, Nith Nulduin, Cierheld's first armsmaster, faced him, blade in hand. He was stern, tall, and dark. The shorter, grizzled Cernalt stood at his shoulder, his old, scarred face inquiring, a chess piece in one hand.

Berd informed them of the thief.

Nith gave sharp orders even as he belted on his blade. "The patrol will return soon. We'll have enough men to mount a proper search. I'll roust the others from the barracks. Five men will go with me. I'll station them to cover every entry and exit in Cierheld yet remain in sight of the wall. Five will go with Cernalt, and Berd, you and your half squad will hunt through the outbuildings. When the patrol returns, we'll do a sweep outside—"

Cernalt cut him off, inclining his head. "Berd should stay in your sight."

Nith looked at him with a frown. "Hawkmaster," he said slowly, waiting.

Cernalt stared back, impassive. "As he was on watch, the sword was entrusted to him. It is gone. Since he is ranked first among my missive squad as well, I say he should stay close to the hold with you, while I take four tensquads of our five to search the roads and surrounding woods for the thief. He must not be seen walking free without a watcher."

"I concede keeping him close." Nith glanced at Berd. "But to leave us to guard the wall and search within with one tensquad? We cannot call for more from Alkborough or Fenwrd."

"No." Cernalt had a mulish tilt to his mouth. "There is no time to call in any of the other squads. We must find the thief."

"Speak plainly."

Cernalt straightened, not looking at Berd. "He should be relieved of duty. Keep his men with you at all times." Old, revered hawkmaster and retired armsmaster that he was, Cernalt yet held steel. "It is for you to search and to guard, and put the men's minds at ease. He is under suspicion. He must not be shown unusual favor."

"But taking the sword may be a diversion," Berd protested. "A ploy to take you away from the hold. To leave us under strength, and our first daughter vulnerable."

Nith and Cierheld's master of hawks both swung to look at him. Berd stiffened. "If I took it, would I ask you to leave more men?"

Cernalt said mildly, "And if this also is a diversion?"

Berd reddened. Cernalt was nominally in charge in the absence of their lord and lady of Cierheld. "So many years, Cernalt, I have gathered threads of information between the holds for Cierheld's use, and news from others that arise around the regent for you. You have known me since birth. Now you doubt me?"

"I doubt all until proven guiltless." He'd meant it when he bade Nith keep him close.

Berd glared at him, then turned to Nith. He cleared his throat and said formally, "You have trained me all my life, first armsmaster. You will leave more men to keep my lady, surely?"

Cernalt's light blue gaze was icy. "Do not test us. We are not unwise, boy."

Berd's breath came hard. "Do you truly think I took it?"

"All saw your yearning for it after Kyrin found it in the stream, before Esther stole it." Cernalt watched him with the sharp, piercing gaze of one of his own birds.

Frustration choked the words from Berd's throat. "Yes, it is a splendid blade! But may none overcome a destructive desire? Don't you understand? It has been taken again. I must find it! And she must be protected!" A tensquad would not be enough to protect the hold and his first daughter.

"There may very well be more to this than meets the eye," Nith frowned.

Berd looked at him in hope. "I am certain of it. There is some deeper scheme at work. You are first armsman to our Lord Dain, as well as first armsmaster to our hold. Surely you see that someone works against the house of Cieri in this." Nith must believe him.

The armsmaster eyed him. "We will find them."

Cernalt said, "What does northern blood bring?"

Berd's brows drew down. "What?"

"Northern blood," Nith repeated Cernalt's question, staring at him, curiously intent. "What does it bring?"

"She brings more than a snow-haired child," Berd said drily. That was a clever shot, better than many he had aimed at the archery butts that rose at his back this past winter.

Nith's mouth flattened, and he looked at him as at a particularly dull student. Cernalt crossed his arms. "Tell us, since your wit is so tender, what does Kyrin's northern blood bring *to the line of Cieri?"*

Berd drew in a breath, glaring at Cernalt. "Northern blood brings," he said slowly, "question."

"Lackwit," Cernalt said, "it brings far more!"

Berd swallowed. "I know it. It brings question of how well old northern blood mixes with southern, and what ties of power a reinstated lord of Alkborough may forge with a daughter of Cierheld. The rest you know, master spy."

Cernalt's eyes narrowed. "Never call me that aloud."

Berd straightened, flushing. "Yes, sir." He ought to have known better, especially with Lord Dain and his lady overseeing repairs at Fenwrd with Meric on the coast, and Kyrin's husband making ready their new home at Alkborough, renewing ties with his people and lands long denied him. Worse, young Lord Thain Mornoth, nephew of the traitorous leader of the last war, was asking questions in the regent's court of burial mounds robbed on his land, and there was talk of a seller of stolen treasure. Berd frowned. He would be one to watch.

But he could not accuse Cierheld, now that they also had suffered a stolen blade from olden days, though how it had ended up in the stream where Kyrin found it, he did not know. Cernalt had mentioned naught if he ever thought the weapon was taken from a burial trove. Cernalt suspected him of taking the Damascus blade, as the old fox must until they found the thief. Did he believe he had stolen the blade before and given it to Esther? But it was Cernalt's way to seek out all and wait for the opportune moment to catch an offender.

Yet why did his teachers waste time, speaking of northern blood, of Kyrin's ancestors from beyond the wall? Nith bore much of that old blood himself.

It was clear they expected him to know something he did not, or Cernalt tested him. Berd sighed silently. His days of late seemed one long trial, a string of many tests, which he failed far too often. Nith Nulduin was his commander, and armsmaster of Cierheld stronghold. Was he now to be his guard?

The old retired armsman walked past Berd, never looking at him, on his way to rouse the men.

There was a step behind them, and Berd spun, hand on his hilt. Kyrin nodded to him and called to Cernalt, "Old friend, stay a moment." Cernalt turned and bowed, his eyes sharp. Kyrin lifted her chin. "Berd would never steal from the house of Cieri, no matter his desire for a sword fashioned by a master craftsman."

Berd opened his mouth then shut it. His throat was tight. That cut deep. His first daughter should not have to speak for him.

Again, he felt something out of place. He saw it in Cernalt's noncommittal face; he felt it in his bones, in so many little things slightly awry. Yet there was nothing he could point to as proof. Nothing.

Kyrin and the old armsman spoke in low tones. Berd listened with half an ear as Nith summoned his men and gave them their orders. Cernalt was never suspicious without reason. And Berd wanted that blade, as well as the man who took it. On Kyrin's behalf, as well as his own. It might mean her life. If someone could take the sword, they had access to the hall, and everyone in it.

Unconvinced by remonstration, old Cernalt took the returning patrol that the men on watch halted at the gate. Soon after, he left near everyone in the hold equally disgruntled.

Nith had sent one tensquad to sleep in reserve in the barracks, while a second squad from the night patrol pulled an extra shift on the wall. All because of Berd. Their angry looks and muttered remarks just out of earshot bore heat. The search within Cierheld had proved fruitless.

Berd sighed. Afterward, Kyrin watched him with worried eyes across their staves as they sparred. She had returned to the hall moments before to rest and study. *De Re Militari,* the Eagles' ancient manual of warfare, Alaina's translation of the Vulgate, and Tae's book of Subak, which bore no name, were among her favorites.

But Berd had yet to finish his morning drills. It was three bells after Prime and he had another hand of drills to go. After the thrust and parry techniques of the ancient Eagles' way, came the training in the long sword. The training blades were twice as heavy as his steel.

Gritting his teeth, he put his whole body behind the blows of his long wooden practice blade against the post before him. His oak weapon flashed into a deadly sequence: a crushing cross-body blow through the collarbone, a reverse cut below the ribs, then a twist and downward slice to the tendons behind the pine 'knee' of his enemy. That was one man down.

Fast and whipcord strong, Nith had already completed his routines and beaten his post into submission. Now he bent his long frame over the well stones at the back of the washhouse and splashed his black head. He came up and shook back his hair, flinging water. Nith always finished before him.

That did not irk Berd. He panted at his work, thirst growing. The first armsmaster of a stronghold ought to be quicker, stronger, and more wily than any armsman. Berd's grin cut short.

The thief irritated him to no end. The thief who stole his first daughter's blade from the heart of Cierheld. Who cast his oath as Lady Cieri's personal armsman under the shadow of doubt. The person or persons who endangered the house of Cieri.

Berd's jaw knotted as he swung into another sequence. He should be out hunting the blade and the one who took it with the rest of the men, not caged, worse than useless. The thunk of his hundred and seventieth strike shuddered through the post.

It did not comfort him. He had wielded all his skill against his wooden enemy from Prime bell to Terce. It availed nothing.

One would have thought the third hour of the morn would bring news if it did not bring rest. It did not. But if anyone saw anything of note without the walls, the retired armsmaster would learn of it. Over long years, Cernalt had woven a ring of hearts within and without Cierheld loyal to Lord Dain Cieri. All news came eventually to his ears.

Berd drew a long breath through his nose, and quietly out. *He* was yet loyal, though the head of Cierheld's missive squad was uncertain of him. Sweat ran down his face. As Nith so often said, he must fight with patience. He turned to a series of thrusts against the enemy that stood between him and the cool well.

At last, his wooden edge thudded into the pine neck one last time, and he whipped it back to readiness behind his shoulder. His speed belied his hot face and dark hair, as prickly with sweat about the ends as a hedgehog's. "Ho, Nith, my arm tires. Are you fixing to swim?"

Nith turned, dripping, with a bare lift of lips. He studied his charge, as if he discovered somewhat of interest, cocking his head. "You are relieved of your place as squad leader," he said softly.

Berd gave him back a blank stare. He should have expected it. Nith bruised his heart on top of the marks Kyrin dealt him earlier with her staff. His thoughts were sorer than the purple on his pale skin. Words deserted him.

Mildly, the armsmaster indicated Berd's weathered post. "Use your wit to bring him down. Never let your enemy recover. You must outlast him. If his heart still beats after the blow that dropped his hose about his ankles a moment past," he added dri-ly. Then his voice left all jest. "First armsman, you must become a blade. Every blade must be tempered, honed, tested. Like the weapon you seek."

Only one who knew Berd well would notice the tension about his mouth and realize his anger glowed white hot. "What would you have me do?"

"What you have always done. Protect Cierheld with all you are. If you are strong enough, seek the sword and those who took it."

Berd's eyes narrowed. His first armsmaster removed him from the squad and asked if he was strong enough? Carefully, he said, "You mean something other than disobeying Cernalt." He would contribute no wedge between those who led and warded Cierheld's men in trust. That faith, that love, must not be broken. All had given their oaths to a higher Lord than Dain Cieri.

"You will know when the time is right to leave." Nith smiled at him crookedly. "It is good if you do not harry Cernalt. There are many questions that need answered. And Kyrin must be protected. At our hour of need, return to us. For the heir will be of two different bloods, like a blade of two metals."

Berd said thoughtfully, "If our Lord makes a man able to strike two such different elements into a strong blade..."

"An heir can be forged so, also." Nith's gaze was steady.

"Such an heir would be a weapon indeed, with an edge keen enough to protect this hold." Berd grinned at last. "I see you will forge my mettle under Cernalt, so I may help temper Lady Kyrin's heir in turn."

"Yes. Yet remember that when one sets out to teach another, he learns most well himself." Nith paused, then shook his head with a wry smile. "It is well you govern your heart this morn."

"Ha! It strives to govern me. It is not only northern blood which would not dare any tempering but yours and that of heaven, to be true steel." Berd sobered. "I will take your tempering, also." He bowed his head.

"Is that so, armsman? Then trust no one till they are proved." Without warning, Nith flipped his dripping linen towel from the well-edge into Berd's face.

His hands came up against the sting with an indignant, "Ow!"

Nith laughed, turned his back, ducked into the well again and came up blowing. He wiped his face on his arm. "I fear the heir also will be forged in fire, as his lady mother has been. The southlords about the regent do not rest. They seek any cause to bring Cierheld down, so they may strengthen their own positions. Even a few of the northlords. And then there is the matter of the king to come. They are afraid." Nith's eyes were piercing. "Many seek security, advantage, and their own will."

Berd swallowed and turned away to hide the sudden wet in his eyes. He understood the fear of ruin, never mind the coming king and the larger battlefield of intrigue. He remembered the day long ago when Kyrin disappeared.

They had not found her body in the charnel heap that had been Lord Fenwer's hall. The rain hissed and spat against the hot ash and stones of the partially burned stronghold where they found her mother's remains instead. They thought their first daughter lost.

But Kyrin returned from both sand and sea, still holding her stronghold key. She had not lain beneath earth or wave, her bones open to the sun. As she would not lie now, for any scheme of man. He swore it. Regent or no regent, king or no king. But how quickly things could change. He remembered the pain.

A hand grasped the back of Berd's neck, and he spun with a silent snarl, warding against Cierheld's loss. And found himself thrusting Nith back over the well stones toward the water.

Nith did not resist. Berd let out a breath. Wise of him. Then, shocked to his core, he released him. He dared lift a hand against his armsmaster. He looked down. What had come over him? "I ask your pardon first armsmaster—"

"No," Nith said. "It shows your readiness. But you withdraw your hand too easily." He stepped to the side and in a trice Berd was in the same position, his back straining against the rock. Nith shook him hard. "Do not be certain of any man until he is proven!"

Berd swallowed and said faintly, "Yes, sir."

"After you have the upper hand, then you may decide if mercy is the right course. Not before." Nith pulled him up roughly. "You have my pardon, first armsman. Now drink."

When Berd finished with the cool, pure water, Nith smiled tightly and shoved him back toward the training ground. "The post grows complacent. Put the fear of Cierheld into its heart. Tomorrow, I will test you with blade and shield." He did not wait to see his order obeyed but walked away up the lane between the kitchen and the hall side door.

Berd knew he would be tested indeed.

2

*He trains my hands for battle. ~ Psalms 18:34*

Hardly had the door thumped to when Celine stepped out of the washhouse, a basket of laundry on one hip. Green eyed, a blue tunic and dark apron gracing her shapely form, she tossed back hair as fiery as her spirit. "By the noise you two make, one would think you'd found the thief." She waited, her alert glance inquiring.

Berd's brow creased, and he dropped his sword hand to his side. She was always watching him, and always training. She knew the ways of a staff from her foster father, Hal, and currently studied Subak with Kyrin when she was not in a spat with her, as Celine was at times with everyone. She was prickly, but she grew in skill. Celine had heart.

Once gagged at a traitor's hands, tied hand and foot, immured with her companions to linger with them in a slow death of thirst, walled in dark stone from the world, she had chewed through the ropes of the others first. He admired that.

Her companions had not had time to untie her before he and the rest of Cierheld arrived to face their enemies without, and spring the trap set for them. Father Ulf was killed, and his underlings fled. She had passed through the uncertain dark and survived. Now she could not train hard enough, long enough, or gain knowledge enough to expunge her fear of helplessness. But when she smiled, she could warm a room. She would understand.

"Just training," he said.

"Just training?" Celine eyed him, scornful. "You think I am so dull of wit?"

"No. It is just..." He scrambled for words, and with relief fastened on what came to mind. "My Lady Kyrin—she is not careful enough. My Lord Talik would have hard words for me if I did less than ensure her safety and the heir's. I am her first armsman." It was true enough, and he suddenly felt the weight of the world on his shoulders.

Celine nodded wisely. "Ah, so that is your reason, is it? Six months handfasted to Lord Wyman and three months with child, and Kyrin practices the bow more than anything else these days. Not careful enough? The heir is too precious to risk in our usual rigorous Subak practice. So, we do the tamer exercises and focus on footwork." She pushed back a stray copper strand and snorted. "And what is that to you? You speak with Cernalt, and Nith, and you train, while we cannot." Her eyes sparked. "All you think of is your precious place. A first armsman must do this; he must do that! And why must *you* be the one to find the sword? Are you the only one able to defend this hold?"

Berd stepped back a pace. "Of course not. I did not mean to anger you."

Celine set her free hand on her hip. "Are soft words your only answer? I thought more of an armsman. At least one such as you."

Berd gritted his teeth. What did that mean? "Every armsman among us must train with the sword, short sword, spear, and all other weapons. This evening, Nith will lead the hunt, and there my bow will serve well. As will yours, if you will come. The table cries for meat from the chase. We are all part of Cierheld." He shrugged. "We all do what we may."

But Celine was not done. "So, our enemy gains our hold; do you not defend the walls?" She motioned at the ramparts, the men's barracks, and the packed dirt yard between the long building with its many doors and the great hall, overshadowed by the huge oak before Kyrin's window. Her lips quirked. "Can you even defeat that post you have been after all morn?"

There at last was a small smile, at his expense. Berd felt his face heat. "Why speak of what you cannot do at all?" She never worked at the posts. It was simple fact. He thrust his wooden blade through his belt and reached for the wet towel Nith had left on the edge of the well with a mischievous twist of his lips. Wringing the towel, he pulled it taught with a snap and moved forward. He would try a last time to show her what he meant.

"Oh, so now you use a weapon I know, since I'm proficient in no other?" Red-faced in turn, her chin high, Celine dropped the basket and yanked out a fresh washed tunic, back-stepping as she twirled it into a hard rope. She stretched it cross-body, one hand high, one low, ready to attack or defend.

Berd straightened. "Celine, I don't mean so! You know what you're about with a staff, just not a blade. Mine is too heavy for you." He popped the towel experimentally, with a smile of challenge. "This is more fitting and cuts me down to your size."

Celine turned grim. "Come then, if you know what you're about with that bit of linen."

Her tongue was too quick for him. As Cernalt and Nith were too quick for him. He felt always behind this day. Even his first daughter was ahead, and he a moment late. There was no word of the thief, now long gone, he was sure. Berd's frustration boiled over. "Can you not laugh for once, Celine? I mean no ill!" He sprang in.

Celine brought up the tunic, blocking his first strike. "Testing, armsman? Well, I am good for far more than following at your heels. What is it you say, as a 'laughing maiden.'" She danced away then as they traded blows, neither of them landing more than a stinging slap to hand or shoulder.

"Laughing? You've yet to smile!"

But she had been studying her footwork. Moving nimbly, Celine tried for his shins then his face, out to win, while Berd used distraction but stuck to his chosen target, a spot over her heart. At last, the snapping towel and tunic tangled, and Berd yanked. He would have pulled her over if he had not let go in disgust.

"These are no good. Why not take this to the archery butts, where I will gain a little skill?" If only she would take the peace offering. She had a natural aptitude for the bow. But his offer seemed to offend her.

She drew herself up, defiant, red-cheeked, and blowing. "Not on your life! Give me a blade my weight, then try me."

"But I don't—" He didn't wish to thrash her; she was completely below him in sword work. She was seas apart from Kyrin's level, though she tried with every fiber.

"I'm not good enough, you think?"

In her current state, one of them was likely to be injured. And it was not likely to be him. "I'm not the one to spar you in blades." It was the diplomatic answer.

Celine clenched her fists. "Then what of the dagger?" she said sweetly. "Or unarmed combat? Kyrin taught me how to choke a man from his senses."

But he knew the counter to the choke hold, and he was stronger. "How about the javelin?" he offered. He would make sure it was at a target they could both reach, where aiming true became a matter of finesse more than strength. If she could just gain a little wisdom and use her head with what strengths she truly had, she would be an opponent worthy of any man's steel. He had the feeling she could be deadly with the bow.

Celine stopped breathing. When she spoke again, her voice was low and utterly determined. "You avoid me, but I can be as strong as you. I *will* be. I'll find the sword first." Her glare was furious. "You'll see."

He stared at her. How much had she heard between him and Nith? "Celine, use your head. The name of Cieri has many enemies."

"Huh! And I thought Talik said Kyrin should keep the name Cieri because it is known to the regent." She was sober for once. "That bond must be strengthened. Yet Cieri is not my name." She added more lightly, "Lord Mornoth and his men molder under Northumbria's leaves, but does not Thain ache for a place of power at court again, for men to speak the name of Mornoth with honor instead of scorn? Esther Govannan is often at his side. Do you mean those enemies?"

Berd licked his lips. Nith warned him of trusting, and Celine had once followed Esther. "Who speaks of such enemies?"

"Cernalt."

Ah. Berd frowned. He had read the last batch of reports, and there had been no mention of Esther or Halwende. How long had Cernalt been removing information from the bag of messengers' missives before he saw them? Had he concealed this from the rest of his people or Berd alone? Evidently, he had not hidden it from Celine. Cernalt had stopped trusting him before the sword was even taken. Berd forced out his breath, along with the pain. Had the suspicious old fox scented a traitor then? But he must find another source of news before he left the hold.

Still, Cernalt had never yet proved a liar. Berd said softly, "What he said is true. It is also true our lord and lady and

Kyrin's heir, whoever that may be, must not be disappointed. Cierheld is in our trust. None may find us complacent or weak. We must be ready."

The heir would find him waiting, first armsman to Kyrin Cieri. But first he must find the sword, and the one who could walk so fearlessly in the heart of an enemy hold. His hand tightened on his wooden haft. Berd was fast enough with his hands, but not quick enough on his feet in thought to ever speak at court. He dared not trust those there, with disastrous result. He would not trust easily; he would learn when to have mercy and when to strike with justice. But could he track the thief, though the trail led to court and beyond?

Celine was smug. "You mean Kyrin's heir will need an armsman who knows what he is about?" It seemed she thought the same.

Berd shook his head. "It is true I am not Nith or Cernalt, but I must do what I can." He sighed. He would go to where Kyrin found the sword in the stream beside Samson's burial place and follow the weapon's trail to where it had been left in the chamber of stone. He must trace the thought of their old enemies and try to discern the path of their current aims. "We must all do what we can."

"What can I do?" Celine challenged.

"You are a worthy companion to Kyrin. In some ways, you are closer to her than I. Guard her back."

Celine's face flooded with red. "How dare you mock me!" She shoved him, hard, and aimed a strong kick at his thigh, where it would do no permanent damage but hurt mightily.

Berd slid past her on instinct, inside the attack, so close he caught the scent of violets in her hair. He saw she was crying. "I do not mock you!" he said in dismay from behind her shoulder.

"I hate you!" She spun and swung a fist, clumsy with emotion, and he grabbed her wrist.

"Don't you understand?" Berd shouted. He lowered his voice. "No one will expect a woman, besides Kyrin, to know anything of war craft. You have a mind sharper than my spear, and the wit to use it. Far more wit than I possess. That is one thing Cernalt has taught me. *Everyone* has places they are strong and weak in areas of weapons, attack, and defense." He caught her other arm and gripped her hard, pulling her closer. "You must understand, your strengths are simply different than mine. You are stronger in those ways. Find them. And protect Cierheld." He was breathing hard. He wanted to shake her. "You would not last long outside the hold, alone."

Celine looked up at him, eyes swimming, and shivered in his hands. Then she bared her teeth and said fiercely, "I am strong! I will protect Kyrin and find your cursed sword! Neither you, Esther, nor Lord Thain Mornoth will keep me from it!"

Berd let go. "Find your gifts, or finding the sword will destroy you." He clamped his mouth shut and turned back to his post. His hands were always faster than his head. He was a fool. She would truly hate him now.

"How can you say such things?"

Her voice brimmed with passion and outraged curiosity, yet his reasons were not for her. Berd paused in his fierce glare at his feet. It bothered him he did not know. And then he did.

He turned, looking up. "I can say such things, and follow Cierheld, because it is right. The line of Cierheld pursues justice, and mercy, and kindness. Kindness to all in Northumbria. That is worth all my blood and breath, every scrap of honor I possess. You could also say I love my lady, the house of Cieri, you—all our people." His almost helpless gesture included the hold and its environs.

"Love us!" Celine scoffed and clenched her fists. "You love the blade far more! How was it lost, I wonder?"

Rage shook him. She thought him careless in his duty, or said it just to needle him. She pushed too far. "Armsmen," he ground out at last, "defend those they ward to their last breath. Some say beyond. That is foolishness. I must do what I can in life. It is not for me the sword must be found. I do not covet it for my honor or what it may bring." He would love to wield the blade. Any man would delight in a finely honed weapon that fit the hand and the heart.

"Then may the best of us win." She raised her chin.

He had to challenge her on that. "If we both go, who will guard Kyrin and Cierheld?"

"Is that not your place, first armsman?" she said archly.

He gave her one fulminating look and turned away. His place was between those of Cierheld and every threat. Now that threat was wrapped up in the missing blade and the one who took it, and if Cernalt thought their old enemies were involved, and Nith told him to pursue it, he had best pay heed. With an effort, Berd breathed deep. Surely Celine knew better of him than what she accused him of. No true armsman would seek anything or anyone above those he warded. Unless it was a matter of their Lord above, or wrong and right. But it would not come to that.

All Cierheld had been forged in fire. They had come forth true. Now came the tempering. How he hoped the plotted threads of their enemies' designs did not lead to court. It might be there that his courage would fail. As had Celine's courage, in a different way. She sought the courage to embrace who she was created to be, to find joy in the heart she was given. Yet courage could be gained, and a heart regained again. More, he was not alone.

Now the post called, and the first attack. Berd drew his blade. It did not matter that it was wood. It would soon be steel.

3

# Friend and Foe

*A friend loves at all times. ~ Proverbs 17:17*

Celine stamped through the small side door into the hall. That man was infuriating! As if the cat got the cream, and licked it calmly off his whiskers, so superior, sure it was his by right. Kyrin's first armsman was so certain he was stronger, faster, better with a blade. Better than an orphan who came late to training. Celine glanced at her rosy arm clasping the basket to her side; her skin still stung from one of Berd's chance hits. But she had gotten in a couple of her own.

She stared at her basket in sudden dismay. He'd so distracted her she'd forgotten to hang up the wash. Her mouth tightened. That meddling *boy!*

His last look before turning his back had been full of angry disappointment. As if he expected something more of her. Celine quivered with indignation.

As if she would ever leave Kyrin's back undefended. Myrna must take her place. Celine slid the basket into the corner with a defiant thump, ignoring the raised brows of the nearest serving woman. If she meant to find the sword, she must begin now. She would hang the clothes later, after she spoke with Myrna. Lifting her skirts, she made her way swiftly up the stairs.

Myrna had taken Lord and Lady Cieri's chambers gratefully while they were away, since their door opened first on a short hall, with Kyrin's chamber at the far end. Opposite her, Celine had Meric's chamber, while he was away overseeing and designing repairs to Alkborough and Fenwrd. Celine tapped once at the first doorway off the stair landing and went in when a clear voice invited her.

Myrna sat before a high, thin window with a bit of mending or embroidery. Celine did not care to inspect her needlework so closely as to tell which, beyond noticing it was dark linen and the thread bore the fuzziness of blue wool. Celine made a face. She hated threadwork.

Myrna looked up, her round face as pale and gentle as always. She rested her work in her lap, her grey-blue eyes alert. "What is it, Celine?"

Celine pressed her lips together and sat on a nearby stool, back straight, bunching her tunic and apron in her hands and flattening them again. She burst out, "Do you pity me, Myrna? Am I not strong? I don't care what he says, I will not be a pitied orphan!"

Myrna blew out a breath. "Have Esther or her minions gotten to you again?"

"Yes...no, not for some time." Celine refused to touch her hot cheeks. "She is back at court, with no time for me. Not that I want it."

Myrna looked at her sympathetically.

"Truly, I don't. She never did think much of me. When she took the sword and helped those who sent us to die, she proved that..." Celine's eyes widened. "Myrna, what if *she* stole the sword again?"

Myrna frowned down at her needle. "How could she? Never could she get inside the hold without notice, unless she dressed as a servant. Even if she did that, her manner would give her away. She can no more drop her haughty ways than a mouse can its whiskers." This steady assessment came with a shrug of pretty shoulders under a fall of dark brown hair, a nimbus of highlights flowing across it from the window.

The thought of Esther as a fierce mouse made Celine cover her mouth with a hand, choking back a laugh.

"What? She would give herself away," said Myrna. "I don't believe she would risk it. She sends others to do the dangerous things for her." Her face pinched and darkened.

"I know." Celine looked down. Myrna had once been a moon quietly willing to mirror Esther's bright rays, basking in the warmth of approval she deigned to bestow on a lesser person in her orbit. But no longer. "We have learned better, and Kyrin is a true friend."

"Yes." Myrna gazed out the window sadly. Was she thinking of all the moments they had laughed at Kyrin, when they were young? Celine hoped not. Myrna had never been cruel, not on purpose. She had not understood the import of her words, sometimes. Esther had known, and known full well. She took delight in it. Celine balled her fists. She herself had merely been weak.

"Do you think Kyrin would be up for practicing footwork again this even'?" Myrna looked at her hopefully. "I think I will have the strength for it then."

Myrna struggled still with the illness that sucked the energy from her like a leech. But it could never take her heart.

"Kyrin is always ready for another drill, especially now, before she grows too large to move easily. But could I ask you something?" Myrna might even appreciate being of use, grateful that Celine considered her able to guard Kyrin. At least, Celine hoped so.

Myrna stared at her. "Of course. What is it?"

Celine swallowed. She would be worthy to walk between two first daughters. Even Esther would have to admit she was strong, no matter that she no longer spoke to her, except with a look of indifference that could reach across a room like a slap. Now that it came to it, it was hard. But she must show her, and Berd, and Kyrin, show everyone that she was worthy. Celine looked Myrna in the eye. "Will you keep Kyrin's back while I am gone?"

"What?" Myrna gripped her sewing hard. "Celine, what foolishness do you mean to get yourself into now?"

Celine's shoulders drooped. "Berd thinks little enough of me, and so much of his swords." The bitterness in her words surprised her. "He says I'm not as strong as he. So, I am going to find the sword." She looked up. "I'll find it first."

Myrna's brow furrowed. "But why? You need prove nothing to him."

"I am strong. I will not be defenseless again. Ever." Celine yanked a thread from the edge of her apron. From Esther to those at court, their enemies would also learn she was to be reckoned with. "I am not to be left in the shadows. I am not sorry I chose Kyrin's company instead of Esther's." As Berd said, Kyrin was kind, kinder than she deserved. A true friend, and so strong herself, though forced to walk gently for a time.

"But you are strong," Myrna protested. "With a staff you are the match of most men—"

"Not like Kyrin."

"Well, no." Myrna sat back. "Of course not. No one is equal to Kyrin. But she's had more training."

Celine smiled. "You are generous, Myrna, and I love you for it. You keep me from becoming as wolfish as Esther, I think."

Myrna shrugged, and her face colored. "Well, I will do what I can for Kyrin, though there are others far more suited to defend this house. But what did Berd say that made you think he does not esteem you?"

"He told me to use my head, and that Cieri has enemies, among other things." *Find your gifts, or finding the sword will destroy you.*

Myrna swallowed. "He is right. Not about you; you most always use your head. But about our enemies."

"Concerning them, Myrna, if any came for Kyrin, you would have an advantage. Your seeming frailty hides a will of steel. Rather like Kyrin's falcon blade."

"Go on, flatterer!" Myrna said with a smile and a shooing motion.

"I do not jest, Myrna, or not entirely." Celine drew a breath. "I trust you. I do not trust Esther. Never again. And now that she is so much above me, she's taken up with Thain Mornoth. We saw them at court, do you remember? He has a hard mouth, though his words can be sweet enough when he wishes. Mayhap they are alike in that. She suits him, I think."

Myrna grimaced, then sighed. "I know. You may have a point. But I would not see you hurt again. And Berd? What else did he say?"

"He said we must all do what we can."

"Oh, Celine—"

"He did not mean it ill, I think." But he had meant she was not a worthy blade companion. That she could not forgive. Though now she felt a little ashamed. *You mean Kyrin's heir will need an armsman who knows what he is about?* He had winced at her words.

"What do you mean, he did not mean it ill? When he knows what Esther did to you! What those men did to us? He ought to know how you would take it! Do what you can, my foot!" Myrna stood, her mouth a thin line. "You *will* find the sword first. We will count it a test of sorts. And he will learn our mettle." She lifted her head, determined. "I know just the armsman who can help."

Celine was curious. "Who?" Since Cernalt had banned Berd from the inner ring of his missive squad for the time, she knew few would speak openly to her now of any matters they heard concerning Cierheld. They all knew she trained with Kyrin's first armsman often.

"You remember Henges Aelwin?"

Celine brightened. "Yes, the armsman Brother Rolf asked Cernalt to find a place for, after Lord Mornoth meant him to die."

"Yes. He's a good man, though he seems a bit at ends lately, with his wife and daughter and the new babe gone from Alkborough to Halwende."

"Halwende?" Celine raised a brow. "Why would he send them there?"

"He didn't. Apparently, a friend arranged it before Henges knew of it and spirited them off. But he says they are well enough in Esther's employ. His wife is glad of a place, as there was no room for them here, and he is so often gone on Cernalt's errands between the holds. I could see he yearns to visit them."

Celine grinned. "Kyrin used to complain of the same long days, when Talik was off and about carrying his messages."

"Now he's a lord again, in his rightful hold. Lord Talik Wyman of Alkborough." Myrna smiled. "He bears his name well."

"He does that. But I wouldn't envy a cow who lived with Esther, far less anyone staying there as a servant."

"No." Myrna looked down. "She does not expect a cow to understand, only to bow to her will. Every servant she expects to bow to her will. And understand and acknowledge her right to rule over them. Even those she names friend."

Celine looked at Myrna with new respect. She had learned much of the ways of those in power, or those who thought they wielded power, and of those who yearned for more of it, these last seasons, for all she avoided the regent's court these days. She said thoughtfully, "I used to think it was because her mother was the old king's mistress, that Esther thought so much of her right to order things as she wished. Now, I am not so certain. She loves to order others about."

There was a spark of fire in Myrna's eye. "She loves power over others and hates those who deny it to her."

"Like Kyrin."

"Yes, like Kyrin. And like us. Be careful of her, Celine, and all who walk with her. I do not think we have seen the end of her terrible calculation yet. When she sets her mind on a thing, all she can touch are wielded toward that end, whether they will or not. She often sways them without their knowledge. She is a mistress of deceit." There was a sad glint in her grey eyes and deep anger in the tremulous breath she drew.

A step whispered outside the door with a patter of claws on wood. Kyrin swept in, Gwenich at her side. The noble hound kept careful pace, her head high, liquid brown eyes alert. One of Kyrin's hands rested on the Saluki's shoulders, the other on her own belly, swelling these near nine months since the fall she wed Lord Talik. It was another summer since Alaina and Tae departed, and delicate vines and embroidered flowers adorned her roomy blue tunic about the neck and sleeves. "Why do you say mistress of deceit, Myrna?"

The dress, Gwenich's uplifted head, and Kyrin's intense stare brought a long-ago name day suddenly to Celine's mind.

That day when Kyrin became first daughter and defied Esther over Berd's hound. She'd heard the story afterward. Ever since, Esther had sought Kyrin's ill. Celine sighed.

She herself had thrown all her discontent and uneasy bitterness at Kyrin after her return from slavery. Until her own brush with death, when Kyrin's forgiveness renewed their friendship. Then the one she once counted a friend decisively wished her ill as well. Had Esther ever truly counted her a friend in her heart?

Kyrin looked between them. "Who is calculating deceit?"

Celine reddened. "Esther. Kyrin, why does she seek power at the cost of us all? We used to do everything together."

Kyrin drew the remaining chair closer and sat, a faraway look in her eyes, a curl of hair already wrapped about a finger. Celine hid her smile.

At last Kyrin said, "Evidently, to her, power is worth more than people." She lifted a hand in a simple gesture at the rich furs scattered about the room, the embroidered tapestries on the wall. "Things are worth more." She rubbed the carved wood arm of her chair, staring down at it. "It is easier when there is someone to blame for your misfortune. You must admit, Cierhheld and I have been somewhat at the center of everything that has ever foiled her plans. There is a kind of pleasure in thinking of another as beneath you." She looked up at them then and grinned. "I suppose she is doubly angry you gave me welcome since I got back."

Myrna leaned forward, brightening. "You came out of nowhere and spirited me away from Lord Keffer after he captured me for Lord Mornoth and tried to wield me in marriage against my brother, Lord Bergrin Jorn." She paused, out of breath. "He tried to turn the title of Jornhold into a curse... in the mouth of all the other lords of the north. That began her downward spiral. When she went against you."

"Hah!" Celine shook her head. "I think it began the day you could first talk, Kyrin, and you refused to speak to her, or laugh at her pulling the hound's tail, down through every moment you have stepped between us. From our days at our embroidery, to after you were taken away, you never thought like her. Then you came back and upended her world again, drawing every gaze after you. Whether in enmity or goodwill, none could ignore you. You and Brother Rolf destroyed Lord Mornoth and saved Cierheld and the north. Then you kept Myrna and Nell and I from a most horrible end." Her mouth grew dry as old stone, remembering.

Kyrin's hands tightened on the chair, and her mouth flattened. "There were many others. If it had not been for so many who were lost, where would we be now? I remember Twr and the others who died for me, for all of us. Still, we must go on." She swallowed. "I must play my part in the world well, as the Master of the stars leads, or all will end in ash.

"He taught me that. And I try never to forget. Only he gave me the strength to go on when I was a slave. He gives us strength still." Her mouth trembled. She walked in memory. "Our Maker showed me how to endure, what a loyal heart is, and the swift power of commitment. All bound in the falcon, against the tiger that would bring us to despair in darkness and flame." She looked up, sober. "Now the falcon is with Tae Chisun, in honor in the far East. I miss Samson, but I am glad for Truthseeker. They both remind me."

Celine shifted on her stool. "I like your falcons as well as any." She shrugged, and thought, *I don't need the help of bird or man. I must prove myself, hold my own, shape my path.* She went on, "I need no falcon, Kyrin. I will not be a weight about your neck, as Esther says I was about hers. I will take nothing from you."

"I know this is a point where we differ, my friend, but I do not think ill of you for it." Kyrin smiled. "You will come to see the truth, I think." Then her small jaw set, and she lifted her chin. "Berd told me he means to find the sword and our thief. He has my full backing. We must regain that blade and know the currents of thought about us among the lords. Only then can we keep this stronghold, Fenwrd, and Alkborough, safe." Her hand moved to her rounded belly.

Myrna said, "We must know our enemy." She fingered her needle with a frown.

"Yes."

Celine said nothing. The sword and the currents shifting about it would wait for none. She must leave soon.

Myrna nodded, as if her mind were made up. "Esther may have retired for a time at Halwende, but she is not idle. Thain ever seeks the regent's ear. I heard talk about that blade you found in the stream, that it may have come from a burial place. Some think you ought not to have touched it, though you never sought to sell it. She will use that. Words are her weapons."

Celine frowned. "Do you think someone took it from Cierheld for the regent?"

"No." Kyrin let out a breath. "They would have asked for it before seeking to steal it. And I would have given it with a good will. I had hoped for peace after our last battle. But this smiling amity about the regent, where few speak their true minds, seems even more..."

"Deadly?" Myrna offered. "I've felt it too. A lingering, creeping coldness under the light laughter." She hugged her arms about her, the embroidery in her lap forgotten.

Celine watched them. Such fears should not be the lot of her dearest friends. It had to end. She would end it, and walk with them, their equal at last.

"Celine." Kyrin's gaze was sharp. Celine swallowed. Had Berd given her away? "What do you think?"

"I—I think we should each do what we can." They were his words. By rights her face should be aflame, her cheeks heated so. If things kept on as they'd begun, she might be a cinder yet by nightfall.

"That is true." Kyrin's wry smile was a trifle forced. "You get about the hold more than I, these days, Celine." She rose with a groan. "I need to finish adding Tae's book to my memory. That I can do. Then I can get back to teaching Subak, once the babe comes. I think my lying in may be soon. Thankfully, I have most of my strength yet, and I have not been ill." She turned toward the door.

"Kyrin," Celine stood, reaching after her. "I hope you know, I'm sorry about before. I never meant to be like Esther."

A small frown grew between Kyrin's brows for a moment, then it cleared before her smile. "You're a mite prickly at times, Celine, but you show me every day how you've changed. You were never quite like her. You work hard at Subak and everything you put your hand to." She grinned. "Sometimes I worry you work too hard. And that is not why I love you back, you know." Her impish grin melted into the utmost seriousness. "You are of most high worth, Celine." She touched her arm, and Celine held her breath against sudden tears.

She swung toward Myrna to hide her face. Kyrin knew that she loved her as her own blood. "I'm glad you think so," she said a little hoarsely. She cleared her throat. "I'll just speak with Myrna a bit, then I've the wash to finish that Berd kept me from hanging."

"As you wish," Kyrin said softly.

She left, Gwenich following her with a small whine, and Myrna stared at her work in her lap then cocked her head at Celine. "Should you consider going with Berd? To find the sword, I mean? It appears the intrigue about the regent has grown thicker of late."

"Myrna! How can you say so? Berd is the last man to want me underfoot, by his own word!"

"Well," Myrna said, and considered her needle, digging at the wool, picking at the threads with the point. "He is strong, good to have at your back, and he'd be there at your side for you to prove yourself too. You could test him when you wish, as you wish." She looked up, all innocence.

Celine threw out her hands. "That is scant comfort! I was going to say, 'I love you' too, but it seems a little past the moment."

"You love me, or Berd?" Myrna's mouth quirked up.

Celine's mouth dropped open, her eyes widened, and she bristled. "I have never been less than your friend, and his, I suppose. It is certain I love you. Him, I have never loved." She put her hands on her hips and finished wryly, "Or a treasure such as a Damascus blade."

"Test him well." Myrna gave her a dark look. "He should not doubt you."

"I will."

"I am to introduce Brother Rolf to the herbalist, Margye, tomorrow. Since I told him how she's been teaching me of healing herbs this spring, he wishes to see if she will consent to teach at the school. I am sure she will accept. Henges will be there. He loves to hear of the Alkborough school and doings thereabouts, since he used to be an armsman of the hold. Will you join us? Then you may meet him. I am sure Henges will be pleased to help any way he can."

Celine nodded. "That would be well. Thank you, Myrna." So, her task began. She would speak with Henges and learn all she could. He once served Lord Ludwin Mornoth, before he'd been consigned to die at Father Ulf's hands. They had that in common. Henges also had neighbors, friends, and brothers in arms in Alkborough as well as in Cierheld. Who knew, his reach might even extend to the circle of the church. After all, he had ties enough to Brother Rolf. She wondered what he knew of Esther. But far more important, she must beat Berd along the sword's path.

§

Myrna watched Celine slip out the door and could not help the twinge of pure envy that ran through her. How long had it been since she felt the vigor Celine showed in every step? After her second capture beside Celine and the others, she had weakened. The strain had been too much when she was just beginning to recover. She did not know if her illness could be reversed now.

She was bound to small things that took up all her days; needlework or practicing a few moments with Kyrin. Whenever she went out to gather medicinal plants with Margye, it drained her for several days, though she was eager to learn under the healer at the school, after Kyrin's lying in. Sorrow filled her. When she felt most sick, she had no will even to study De Re Militari, which Brother Rolf had copied from Meric's book for her, let alone ability to apply it.

She had no sigil, like Kyrin's falcon, no one who loved her like Kyrin's husband, Talik, no one like Nell's lord Bergrin, or Celine's growing relationship with Berd. Even full of sparks, and blind to it as Celine was.

She pressed her hand to the window and murmured, "Duty has many branches, and love is one of them. Neither alone makes a whole man, but both together. I hope he is worthy of you, Celine. For that, he must learn to risk loss and lead. And I, I must learn to be content. If only I had the falcon dagger, something to remind me of courage."

4

# Counter and Coil

*I have become estranged from my brothers. ~ Psalms 69:8*

Henges Aelwin strode toward Berd in the dusk, quaking inside. He knew what the first armsman wanted. It was but Nones since Celine spoke with him of the Damascus blade, asking him for any news of it, past or present. Now it neared sunset and Vespers.

How many people must speak with him about the stolen weapon before he reached his bed in the barracks? Would Cernalt also find him there, or would he have time to think of a way out of the deadly trap closing in on him? He wiped a thick arm across his sweating face.

Berd grimaced as he neared. "Ho, Henges. A word, if I may." He indicated the side of the smithy. Henges' shoulders sagged with relief. At least no one would overhear them there, with the smith hard at his work on clanging metal within.

"Yes, sir." He stepped out of sight around the side of the building, but Berd gripped his shoulder and steered him back out in full view of all in the yard. Brow furrowing, Henges waited. Whatever the first armsman was about, seeking to speak with him in full view of the rest of the hunt that straggled wearily across the yard, Berd could do no more than what had already been done to him. Could not hold a greater threat for him than the one that stalked him now. But he was a good man; taking a man's wife and children to bind him to his will would never cross Berd's mind.

Berd glanced at him, kicked at a rock, looked up at the wall then finally back. "You are a good man, and loyal." The scent of sweat came from Berd, and his strung bow remained over his shoulder. He had not even taken the time to remove it before searching him out.

Henges crossed his arms. "Lord Dain Cieri took me in when my need was greatest," he said gruffly.

Berd nodded. "You know Cernalt has deemed me unfit at this time to ride among his missive squad. I agree; we can both see why. I have leave to hunt the thief. Therefore, though Cernalt may not be seen speaking to me, I need to know all the news between the holds, the regent, and Halwende. Along with any talk concerning the stolen sword or tidbits among the other lords you think I may need to hear. Indeed, it would be best if you give me all you can." His face was haggard. "For the life of Cieri."

"Yes, sir. I will." Henges could promise that. He would do all in his power for those who had taken him in and treated him more than fairly. He did not promise who else he would tell, or not tell. He could also ask why the first armsman of Cierheld did not search out his own news, but more lives than those of Cierheld rode on what he did not say. Two lives, most dear.

Berd stared at him, seeming to catch the drift of his thought. "If Cernalt or Nith asks, you may tell them all I have said to you." A smile pulled up one side of his mouth. "Our hunt was rewarded." He motioned at the hunters milling before the stables, the bodies of a stag and a hind bound over the mounts that a young armsman led around the garden toward the kitchen and the Cook's dressing knife.

Henges swallowed hard. "Yes, sir." Hares and a few birds adorned a few other saddles. It had been a fruitful hunt. As fruitful as his own this morn. Curse the black-hearted wretches who forced him to deceive such a man as Berd in the slightest. But he would outwit them yet. If he could but bide his time, they would fashion the web they trapped themselves in.

"Do you understand?" Berd peered at him closely. "I need news, and I will hide nothing."

"I do, sir." He could not tell him what he wished to hear. "Cernalt says nothing was found outside, no sign of theft in the village or unusual traffic on the road. Whoever took it got clean away." He prayed it would be enough, oh how he prayed. If he held his threads of knowledge loosely, wound them skillfully, if he pleased both Berd and whoever held his heart in cruel, unfeeling fingers, he could at last bind those wicked hands. This man could help him do it. Berd would help him with all his heart, if he knew all. But he dared not tell him. Still, could he point him toward their enemy indirectly? "Sir, would it not be better to watch those who oppose Cierheld?"

"Such as who?" Berd looked at him sharply, and Henges called himself seven kinds of fool. "Does Cernalt have any proof of who plots against us?" Henges grimaced and shook his head, and Berd said, "Until we have proof, we can do nothing. I will find the thief."

Henges licked his lips. "Sir, aside from the lady and others who asked about the blade, I'm sure you'll find it, if anyone can."

"A lady asked about it?" Berd took a sudden step forward.

Henges shrugged in surprise. "Why, it's natural they'd want to know if aught had been heard of the Damascus blade. Lady Myrna is studying medicine with that old herbalist Brother Rolf of Bolton Abbey accepted, and there are the roads to think of, with the brigands about."

Berd cut him off. "Herbalist? When did he get here? Who knows him?"

"Margye is her name. Lady Myrna and our first daughter both vouch for her. She seems harmless enough and is joining that school of Lord Talik's in Alkborough after the heir is born. There's not a harmful bone in her body." He drew himself up a trifle. "That I'd swear." He would have no old woman harried on his account.

Berd relaxed with a grunt. "You are probably right. Forgive my suspicion."

"Not at all. Lady Kyrin's fire-haired companion was as kind as Lady Myrna, asking after my good wife as she did—"

Berd's head jerked up and his face tightened again. "Celine? What else did she ask you?"

"Only if Lord Ludwin ever mentioned the blade, as she was trying to track its past history for recording." He shrugged again. "He never did, leastwise, not in my hearing." That was true enough. "He did mention the brigand, and Brother Rolf got a mite impatient when I said that."

Berd scowled. "Is he mixed up in this?"

"Who, Brother Rolf?" Henges was aghast.

"The brigand."

Henges sighed. "That's for wiser heads to tell than I. Brother Rolf means to send his brother Seldon and his old tensquad to escort Lady Myrna back to Alkborough when the time comes." He'd said enough. Best get along before he said too much. "If there's naught else, sir, I'm for a bit of ale and my bed." He wished for rest, warm and dry, before the gray-black clouds massing above brought rain, borne on a sweet wind that was a harbinger of more than storm. It brought dangerous change it its wings to more than he, even if only he knew it.

"Did you have any word of the blade for Celine?"

Henges shook his head. "No." He was like a dog with a bone, that one. "There was naught I could tell her." Not when those precious to him hung in the balance.

"Very well." Berd nodded. "My thanks. I will be about, mayhap at odd times and in odd places, and I may wish to speak with you privately. Be ready." He squared his shoulders, and his hands tightened as if he faced imminent battle instead of one sweating armsman.

"Yes, sir." Henges inclined his head. This man he could respect. He thought deep, and far ahead. He held more of a lord's mettle than many he could name.

Berd gave him a good night and strode away, his broad shoulders slightly bowed, though he answered a call from one of the nearby men cheerily enough.

Henges had to swallow more than once to ease the dryness of his throat. Things were in motion that could not be undone. He entered the barracks. None were about, and he went to the fire, staring into the coals. It had been allowed to die down in anticipation of toasted bread and cheese after those on the hunt returned.

The feast would begin tomorrow, though he had no belly for it. He picked up the nearby fire iron and stirred the coals, listening. None approached the barracks door, or stirred in the sleeping rooms, though there was a noise of horses, weapons, and laughter in the yard.

Swift and silent, he stretched the iron up toward a small shelf tucked high inside the great chimney for the sake of those who cleaned the soot yearly in the spring. The end touched something hard with a dull 'ting'. It was safe.

Henges thunked the fire iron against the nearby stone till a bit of ash filtered down and whistled tunelessly, a bored armsman waiting for his meal as he poked about the fire.

Cernalt brushed through the door, his arms full of several round loaves and a wheel of cheese. "Well, Henges, here's for a bite and an early sleep. Stir that fire up a bit, will you? The rest will be in soon enough. I sent the boys for some apples, so we'll have a couple moments of peace before the feeding frenzy." He grinned, his face crinkling.

The loaves were shortly cut in rough slices on the hearth by Cernalt's dagger; the cheese carved into wedges. Henges waited for questions or talk of the sword, his fingers locked about the iron, but Cernalt said only, "The boys are bringing some green willow sticks from my Thelmae. Then we'll have a proper feast."

Henges nodded, while his stomach did a slow roll, and Cernalt glanced at him.

"Is aught amiss?"

"No." Henges tried to keep his voice even. The old armsman's sons faced no greater peril than a missed meal if they stayed too long. They did not labor to please another for their very life. His breath caught, to keep back the rage and the helpless tears. He breathed through his nose, long and slow, and turned his back to settle the fire iron with care against the wall. His hand was white on the handle.

"Well." Cernalt cleared his throat. "I hope Berd flies true."

"What?"

Cernalt looked at him wryly. "I've been training falcons longer than you've walked this earth, and he is ready to fly on his own a bit."

"Aye. You can't hold a bird too tight." Henges thought grimly, *Or an armsman.* "He seems to hold no enmity for you, despite your pushing him from his eerie for wrongful suspicion."

"You're right," Cernalt agreed. "One must cast them high, and in time of battle, give them a glimpse of prey and the enemy."

Henges turned slightly, ready to lunge for the fire iron.

With unconcern, all his attention on the bread he edged toward the heat, Cernalt went on, "There are many twists and turns to a falcon's flight, until it finds the right course, the true opponent, and commits to the stoop and the swift, flashing kill."

Henges added a piece of cheese to each bit of browning bread. The old fox meant more than he said. Or he himself was merely jumpy as a hare, knowing his guilt. But if Cernalt suspected him, surely the old armsman would set someone to watch him? If that someone was Berd, could he turn the first armsman to his enemies' disadvantage? He must be careful; there were none he dared trust. He must not touch the hidden bundle again until it was called for. So his instructions had said. He would save his family and Cierheld, also.

Squatting down by the hearth, Cernalt smiled at him as the smell of toasting cheese rose around them. "There are good choices open to us all," he said, his gruff voice not unkind. "If we but have the courage to fly against the storm. First, we must be willing to go from our nests." He sighed. "I remember something our first daughter said once. If it is God's wind beneath our wings, we will not fly astray. And there is a storm coming; I can smell it. Keep your ears open. My messengers have never had greater need of their ears." He looked up at him, sober. "There is one thing I cannot abide, and that is injustice. There is one person who has damaged this hold beyond repair."

Henges tensed.

Cernalt laughed. "Oh no, I do not bring up your old lord's doings. I do not cast his treachery in your face. It was none of yours. Now you serve Cierheld, and a worthy master."

Henges could not help averting his gaze to the bread and swallowing hard. He hoped he served him. He meant to, in the end.

Cernalt slapped his shoulder. "Together, we will catch the thief, and those who mean Cierheld ill. They will answer for their wrongs, and nevermore prey on us or any other."

Henges turned, his heart in his eyes. There was hope. "Yes," he said hoarsely, "they will."

"Go on, eat." Cernalt motioned to the bread. "I saw your look; you're hungry. My sons are late. This will teach them the hours wait for no man, and one must be wise and swift in the moment." He picked up his own bread and cheese, juggled it from hand to hand, and took a huge bite. "Mmm, that's good." He continued around his chewing, "Thelmae's cooking beats all. As you doubtless swear your Mary's does." He swallowed. "But there is something about bread cooked over an open fire with a companion in arms that is like no other food."

Henges' heart swelled. The house of Cieri held him to its breast. He almost spoke then. But he had spoken once before, and his lord betrayed him when he knew too much. Worse, this time if he uttered words in the wrong ears he would seem a threat to Dain, the lord of Cieri. Better he use caution, better to wait and watch as the fox himself said, for the right moment. He would speak when the fly was well in the web.

Two mornings later, Cernalt arrived early in the barracks and soon ordered him off with a letter from the first daughter of Cierheld for Brother Rolf, from Kyrin to her second father in the East. She was concerned for him. They had not seen a reply to the missive she sent in early spring. As Henges readied his horse, a prickle of flesh rode up his back. With the sword taken, the game of wits had begun.

The road was long, and he stopped by the river just outside Bolton to freshen his face and hands and let his horse drink. The willows rustled behind him. Henges spun, short sword out. His mouth flattened. He knew the man, though he had not seen him since more than a winter past.

"You're a mite quick with yer' edge." Thorgil was a heavily muscled man with flaxen hair straggling across his broad shoulders. He regarded Henges with an unpleasant grin, arms crossed. A dagger hung in a sheath at his left side, an ax hung strapped across his back, and he also bore a sword. That was new. His hands were as thick as the rest of him and heavily callused, as if he was more used to the weapon that peeped above his shoulder than the long blade. The ax haft looked worn, but the newly sewn sword sheath creaked slightly when he moved forward, looming over Henges. "It must be you're fearful of the brigands said to haunt these lands. By Thor, that's rich, coming from you."

He had never had anything to do with the brigand, though Lord Mornoth had. Henges lifted the tip of his short blade a little, ready to step to the side and thrust. "What do you want, Thorgil?" The smell of wine hung on him, instead of the usual ale such a man would imbibe. He was a trifle drunk, though it was not far past midday. The abbey would soon ring for Nones. What could he possibly want? Surely Thorgil knew he served Cierheld ever since his traitorous lord cast him out of Alkborough to die.

"Ha. You have the gall to ask. Did you do as you were bid? Mary will take it amiss if you did na'."

Henges stiffened. "How did they dare touch her?" He took a step forward. "What have they done?"

"Naught, yet. If you did as yer' was told."

"So now you run messages for filth."

The tall man spat noisily and said nothing.

Henges' jaw worked. The missive had said only that his wife and children would die if he did not follow instructions, and that someone outside the hold would contact him again. Thorgil had once been a woodcutter, sometimes a messenger, a jack of all trades, and rather a vagabond about the roads. But he had helped Father Ulf in a kidnapping before. If he had come alone, and he knew who stole his Mary away... Henges sprang to the side, his point threatening Thorgil's kidneys. "Who did it? What do they want? Tell me!"

Thorgil turned with him, a smile flickering about his mouth.

"Did you do as we told you?" Another voice broke in from behind.

Henges froze and lowered his weapon, turning slowly. He'd seen Thain Mornoth last winter, hanging about near the regent. Young, with a rather pale face neither strong nor weak, and a short crop of chestnut hair. His eyes were the same brown shade. But the dispassion in them made Henges shiver. He sheathed his weapon. He was not bound to give especial courtesy to one unproved, without place.

"It's Lord Thain Mornoth, to you." Thain lifted his chin arrogantly and dropped a hand to the silver chased blade at his side. A brilliant sapphire ring gleamed on his hand. "You once served the house of Mornoth. Despite your new allegiance, you will serve me still. Your treachery was not against me, was it?"

Those eyes could never be called warm. They dared him to say nay. Henges worked his throat. At last, he got the words out. "I have it. It is well hidden." He bowed slightly. "I am at your service, my lord." He must not antagonize them, or those he loved would pay for every imagined slight.

Thorgil looked pointedly at Thain. "Did I not tell you? He names you 'lord'. Your fame has reached Cierheld's ears." His grin was rather malevolent.

Thain ignored him and looked down his nose at Henges. "You will bring it to Keffold stronghold soon."

"But I was to secure it only, and I have more news," Henges protested.

"Ah, news." Thain was studying him. "So, what is this news, armsman?"

Henges swallowed. "Berd, first armsman to Kyrin Cieri, is hunting the blade. He questions all who ever had contact with it."

"What did he find out?"

"I told him nothing of it."

Thorgil stepped aside as Thain circled the armsman like a great cat, head cocked, waiting for him to bolt under the pressure of the threat of his regard.

Henges held his gaze and did not move.

Thain halted, and his voice was soft. "Such news will not pay for the neck of your snotty brat, or the head of your beautiful wife. We already knew those of Cierheld would look for what you stole. As part of Cieri's messenger service, you can bring me more. Serve them, and the house of Mornoth better. Convince your armsmaster that they hold your oath yet give all you learn to me." He leaned close and whispered, "Or I will take the head of your brat myself." His breath stank of fish, though his teeth were white.

Henges' nostrils flared. The nephew meant to finish what his uncle began.

Thorgil cleared his throat. "And, armsman, if you dabble with thoughts of asking anyone for help, know that the bishop has declared you under his eye, and the regent would pay much to know yer' name as one who once served Lord Ludwin Mornoth."

Henges cared little for his own life, but Mary, little Ellen, and the babe ought not to be caught in such coils. His breath came fast. He dared one low word. "You also served him." To his surprise, Thorgil threw back his head and laughed.

He grinned at Henges, shaking his head. "I have served many places, in many ways. I serve the house of Mornoth still. And now, my ears reach into Cierheld." His amusement faded, and he glanced at Thain. "A brigand must needs hear many things of the roads these days, to steer a safe course."

Thain inclined his head in acknowledgment with a triumphant smile.

Henges' mouth dropped open. This disgraced young lord was the leader of the brigands? But it all fit. The brigands' strikes that avoided Cierheld's patrolling armsmen every moment, never preying on Bolton Abbey or Alkborough or Halwende. Even Thain's reference to the Lady Esther, who was often at court. It all fit. For all that the regent and Cierheld worked together, still the brigands had eluded them, robbing travelers here and there, never taking a large enough prize to bring all in the land against them at once.

Thain glared at Henges. "My men are far fiercer than an armsman who draws weapons on a whim and grows soft carrying messages," he sneered. "Especially one who bows before the threat of a blade. With others coming to our cause from the south, our ranks will thicken, with little need of such as you."

Henges flushed but put aside the insult. He must know more. "You say I am a threat to both the regent and the bishop," he countered. "How can that be, a lowly armsman such as myself? How would my word ever stand against such lords of men, even on your behalf?" It was always best to know an enemy, so said the book that Tae Chisun, that strange armsman of the East, left to his first daughter. So said the manual of warfare, De Re Militari, of the ancient Eagles. So said others, and he agreed. "I wish only for my family's safety." Who would dare join the brigands that Cierheld had devoted itself to eradicating?

Thain indicated Thorgil with a gesture of his chin. "If you give us what we need, there is no need to drop a word in either the bishop's ear or the regent's. No need to show them who may pay for past destruction, while they avoid chance of future damage." He tapped his ring finger against his belt. "Keffold stronghold is worthless, though I hold it as I may at the regent's word." He shrugged, affecting carelessness, but his lip curled. "I am told it is to keep me out of trouble and under Regent Durand Tolman and Cieri's eye. It matters not that the regent denies me the right to replace the white horse head of Keffold with my own standard." His voice dropped. "But Alkborough is mine. All will say my name with respect when the traitors are revealed. I said it once, and I will say it again. The house of Mornoth will rise."

Henges kept his hand from his hilt with an effort. It was not the moment.

Thorgil grunted then said to Henges, "Bring yer' charge to the forest about Keffold, near the bridge."

Thain snorted. "I saw that blade once. It is no Northman's bronze weapon."

"No," Henges said. "But fighting men rove far, and they of all men covet a good blade. Who knows whence it came?" He shrugged.

"Tell me something I don't know, fool!"

Henges said slowly, "What the blade is matters less than how it is wielded. By a worthy hand, or not."

"Ah," Thorgil broke in, "but you will swear by all you hold holy that it came from a place of the dead. Of yer' suspicion that those curs of Cieri stole it from a burial mound, who would as soon sell the sole possession of the dead for gain, no matter the spirit they leave in torment. Bishop Caddaric will back you, if yer' speak for us."

"But there is no evidence! Cierheld is loyal, and well do all know it at court."

Thorgil growled, "There will be proof enough, by Odin, yer' can be sure of that. You will obey."

Thain's voice purred. "If you do not, Lady Esther of Halwende will bear your son a special gift and leave your wife alive to see it. Or we could choose your daughter. Who else will your Mary blame but you, who left them to such a fate?"

Henges dropped his gaze, afraid of what they might see in his face. He could not fail, on pain of death. He could speak to no one.

He must gather news as he never had before, on Berd's authority, and yet withhold from him what he learned. The knife was at Mary and the babe's throats even now. He did not suppose they would let Ellen live long. He could make no mistake. "Very well." He bowed and strode toward his horse, then stopped. "I would know Mary and my son and little Ellen are in good health." He humbly added, "When may I expect word?"

Thain barked a laugh. "They are well enough. For the moment. The first daughter of Halwende needs a fair hand to help her, in place of her faithless companions who follow Cieri." He drew himself up. "Know that I am not faithless." It was a direct challenge. "The house of Halwende may soon join its fortunes to mine. See that you do not stand in our way."

Hearing the unspoken words, *then all will be well,* Henges lowered his head. "Thank you, my lord." Only it would not be well, and he knew it. But he was not certain where his own allegiance lay; he only knew it was not with evil.

Thorgil watched him, a cruel smile playing about his mouth. He followed Henges toward his mount and stopped him, ran his hands over the saddlebags. "What message do you bear this day, and where?"

Fingers numb, Henges allowed him to pull out the sealed parchment from Cierheld to Rolf in Alkborough then Tae's land. He hoped it held no important news.

Thorgil read silently and handed it to Thain.

Henges' throat dried, and his hope sank. Since when did a woodcutter learn to read? He must have deeper purpose than to read messages to better serve his master.

The young lord frowned after he finished the parchment and tapped it against his chin. "This changes things. We must move quickly. Thorgil," he began, "that man from the East must not—"

Thorgil cut him off. "I will see to it." His eyes were narrow and dangerous, and he was watching Henges rather than his lord.

Thain snorted and said arrogantly, "So send it on then, and see that you get the right man for our task."

Thorgil nodded. The armsman stepped back before he realized the cold hate in Thorgil's face was not for him. The man did not love his lord. Thorgil slapped the parchment in his hand. "Reseal and deliver it to Alkborough. Bring your gift to York instead of Keffold, well concealed, mind."

Henges inclined his head and swung into the saddle. He had a feeling his hidden prize was called out far too soon. Whether it meant ill for his enemies or himself, he did not know.

5

# Court's Call

*A soothing tongue is a tree of life. ~ Proverbs 15:4*

Outside Cierheld a Seven-day after the sword disappeared, Myrna slowly followed Margye's bent and brown form through the tall grass close to the streamside.

"Ah, here it is." Margye beckoned, her wrinkled face alight. "We'll dig a few roots and take a few leaves. Knitbone is good fer' so many ills."

Myrna came closer and touched the long, prickly leaves, nudged a bunch of nodding purple flowers. A bee buzzed away. "Is it any relation to wolfsbane?"

"Bless you, no! Have ye never seen wolfsbane? You must add a sketch to yer' book."

Myrna ducked her head.

Margye shook a finger at her. "The flower of aconite puts one in mind of a purple hood. Could ye picture Brother Rolf in one wi' his red hair?" She laughed, a pure cackle of delight. "Hence its other name, monkshood. Tha' plant has its uses, yet I hate it. Aconite so easily poisons instead of heals." She sighed, staring down at her left hand, absently rubbing an old injury that had left her last two fingers curled, skin fused to her palm. "In small portion, after a thorough boiling or steaming, mind you, wolfsbane can calm the mind, lower an agitated bloodbeat, or help pain. Yet it can also kill, and tha' quick. Poisonin' with the raw plant leads to stomach grippe, then the poor soul may get pain in the chest, tingling of the limbs, dizzy in the head. Sweetish but acrid, numb yer' mouth, it will. The breathin' worsens with a weak bloodbeat until the breath ceases." Her dark eyes sharpened. "Promise old Margye, ye'll not go after tha' plant yerself. It must be handled carefully, so as not to kill."

"I promise. I've no need of such."

Margye nodded. "Tha' book of yours, does it have a name?"

Myrna colored, but her head came up. "I call it Salves to Soothe and Save. I hope to find something in my learning to help my weakness, besides the medicine my brother gets from the apothecary."

"A good name. If ye don't mind old Margye askin', what recipes do yer' have in it?"

"Mostly of this knitbone." Myrna tugged a leaf free, careful of the prickles. "Comfrey in hot oil infusions. With rosemary added, it helps pain of the skin, with lavender it aids sleep, or one can add peppermint for deep pain. I know so little of herbs as of yet. Kyrin has told me of a fruit called orange with wonderfully invigorating properties. It grows in the Araby lands. Mayhap we may see some. Meric is soon to receive a shipload of trade goods from there."

Margye nodded, a gleam in her eye. "A new herb or fruit is always good to add to yer' knowledge. As fer' knitbone, as its name says, heal bone, it will. And much else. Ah, bodies and bones and babes, the herbs be given to us to heal."

Myrna bowed her head. "There is also an oil blend the brigands hereabouts are said to use. Hence its name, thieves' oil. I hope I can discover its making someday. And I will learn from you all I can."

"Ye will, tha' I can promise. We may also ferret out this secret recipe for thieves' oil." Margye smiled, her silvered dark hair bound back as her seamed hands dug into the damp earth beneath the knitbone. "But back to tha' monkshood. Know tha' charcoal from a smelter's hut, clay, or a bezoar stone from an animal's stomach, powdered and administered in pure water, if the poisonin' be caught in time, may seize the wolfsbane and carry it out of the body. If the poison dose be not too high. As fer' knitbone, the root cannot be given to yer' Lady Kyrin, since she is with child. It may bring on the pains too early. The leaf is safe enough."

Myrna touched the soft petals of the knitbone bells again. She had always been blessed with a good memory. She would write down Margye's words and keep them close. Kyrin's babe would come soon.

§

Celine slipped lightly down the length of the broken pavement, toward the old site of Fenwrd's stronghold hall now open to the sky, eager to leave the over ambitious steward. On their right rose the repaired and expanded hall of Fenwrd within its wall; a vast structure she knew loomed above the lonely sea that she could hear crashing out of sight below the cliffs. The steward hastened after her, sputtering.

"But the lord and lady and even young Meric have gone to the seaside to inspect those who began their trades with us. A weaver and his family, descended from his grandfather's grandfather, have lived on Fenwrd lands since they fled Teth's hold when the raiders burned it. They value the patronage of our stronghold. As do others, and rightly so. It is not proper you should wander about in our cellar without my lord's leave."

"But it is certain I have Lord Dain's leave. I am Kyrin's companion." Celine stopped short to inspect the man, from his thick shock of graying hair and florid face to his stocky legs and large feet as he strode after her. He looked more like a farmer than a steward of anywhere.

"But you should not go beneath alone, and I may fetch whatever you wish from there," he protested. "Some of the walls below are unstable."

She highly doubted that any walls near the food stores were left so under Meric's insatiable curiosity and penchant for building up whatever came into his care. Celine rested one hand on a hip and gave the steward her most dangerous look. "I am on my lady's errand."

The steward swelled with a long breath. "That is not the point. There is another who said the same."

"I know my own way down." She brushed him off with a wave. "I will not trouble you further."

"But—"

"Unless assassins yet lurk in your passages, after wine?" She raised her brows and lifted her staff, taking a step forward.

His mouth snapped shut, and he straightened. "Very well. Do as you desire."

"You have my thanks." Celine relented. "I will break no wine bottle and touch nothing. I simply wish to see the new cellars. They and your storerooms are safe from me."

He nodded curtly and stopped at the ruined tower stair, now much shorter than Celine remembered. There were only a few sun-brightened stones left above her head to mark its once sturdy presence. Doubtless it had been torn down for its stones which were then used to repair the cellar rooms below, one of them the place where she was imprisoned with Myrna, Nell, and Alaina. But the old fire-scarred door to the passage and the room where Father Ulf once walled her in was gone. In its place was an oak portal, thick and heavy, at the stairs' foot, barred on the outside.

Beyond that threshold, the stones had seen Kyrin's capture and her mother's fall at the hand of Araby slavers. More recently, they had almost witnessed Celine's death. But enough of that. She shook herself with a low growl of irritation.

The steward was walking back toward the hall, his tunic bright in the noon sun. There was no one else in sight. No tiger lurked here, not in the black shadows left by the high sun, nor any falcon. No hawk's call rang down the wind. Celine drew a breath, lifted the bar and stepped through, the echo of Kyrin's ode to the falcon in her ears. *Falcon of loyalty, by blood and high decree, your heart led mine to Majesty.*

The door closed with a thump behind her. She straightened her back, sniffing. The chill scent of wine, aging cheese, and the first summer berries tickled her nose. Her stomach woke. It was near enough the abbey's hour for Sext, though the bell's rich tones would never reach this hold.

She strode down the passage, lit by a few torches, before she reached the room she wished never to see again. Another wood door loomed before her. She leaned against the outer wall for a moment to catch her breath. Her heart beat hard, and her hunger was gone.

Within, she would confront the fear that haunted her still; that someone would overpower her again and take her back to the cold and the dark, and, this time, leave her alone. Thorgil's cords bound her. The stinging pain wound around her wrists, her ankles. Again, she could not move, she could not fight. Only her voice was left.

"Kyrin," she whispered. For her, she would dare dragons. Celine reached for the iron latch. The metal was warm. It pulled sharply inward, as if the room meant to swallow her.

She let go and sprang back. Thudding into the opposite side of the passage, she lifted her staff.

The flickering light of the nearest torch did not illumine the dark silence within.

"You?" The voice that sliced the blackness was light and yet scathing.

Her breath caught as every nerve froze.

"Celine, what are you doing here?" Berd stepped into the light. His dark eyes snapped, and his voice lowered, dangerous. "Did you follow me?"

How dare he? Always he confronted her, always in the right. Celine lifted her stave and slammed it down, the sharp thrum through the wood in her fingers a comfort. "How could I, mud-brain? Since you disappeared from Cierheld four days agone, and I got here in three?" She glared at him, her breath quick. "What do you do here?"

"What do you think?"

They stared at each other.

Berd shrugged. "So," he said.

Even as Celine broke in, "We're on the same errand, I see."

Stalemate.

He looked away, turning slightly, and she caught sight of the blade he held reversed, concealed along his arm. His hands were swift. He had been ready to strike. Her anger boiled. "Who did you think I was, Esther?"

"Who knows, not I." It held vast weariness. "You could indeed have been from Halwende. Or one of Bishop Caddaric's men. He sent one of his crows not so long ago, a man in black, as an assassin after Rolf. As I feared, it appears the sword is just one small thread of a much bigger tapestry."

A shiver of pure chill ran over Celine. If someone was going after even those of the church, none were safe. "Why Brother Rolf?" she demanded.

"He is loyal to no man but the rightful king, or all who hold authority from him. That makes him dangerous."

Celine's brow furrowed. "But we have no king, and the regent is a good man. Surely Brother Rolf is not seeking rebellion against him. Abbot Alton would never stand for it."

"No. I mean, Rolf serves God first and men second, though he and Kilden's squad keep watch for such a one as may become king."

"Ah." Celine leaned on her staff. "Cierheld is much the same." She resisted the urge to shrug, as he had. She'd heard whispers the regent's son was fit for the king's seat, but he was yet young.

"Joined together as family allies—with the local church and Cierheld inland, Alkborough near the Humber, and Fenwrd on the coast—who knows what is possible for the house of Cieri? Trade with Araby and other lands, a strong presence to deal with the south, a clear voice behind the regent." Berd spread his hands, returned his dagger to its sheath, and leaned against the door he pulled closed behind him, studying her.

His words were clear enough. "That is what you meant by enemies." Excitement sharpened her voice. "You mean those of the south seek to tear apart the accord between us in the north and the regent. It all comes back to him, and ties to power and the coming king, doesn't it?"

"Not entirely. There are some unknown threads that run under this door." He kicked the oak behind him gently. "The question is who holds the other end, and how we threaten them."

"I can think of one person. And you, most of all, know one way we threaten them." But she must learn his true purpose, what he sought under the cover of searching for Kyrin's blade.

Had he had something to do with its disappearance? "Nith spoke of northern blood, and you of a snow-haired child." She looked at him and pushed hard. "Is that what Father Ulf saw? The danger of an heir in Kyrin? An heir to the throne?"

Berd straightened, arm brushing his dagger. "What do you mean?" His gaze was suddenly dark, intent as he looked down at her.

Celine licked her lips. "Only that Esther—" she began.

Berd was on her before she could do more than twitch her staff an inch. He rammed her against the stone. His weight shoved the breath from her. Worst of all was his face. "Esther will what?" he growled.

But Celine could not get breath to speak. The threat of him bore down on her, irresistible as crushing rock. Her staff thunked into the side of his head, but it was a weak blow, hindered by his arm. She lost the staff, clattering to the floor. She had not meant to push him this far. Helplessness rose, and an animal growl of her own in answer. Memory descended. Darkness and pain and hopelessness that gnawed at her, even as she chewed the ropes that bound Myrna.

He leaned closer, and his warm breath on her neck tore all thought from her. She did not hear what he said. Desperation filled her. She went for his nose with her teeth. He pulled back; she thrust a knee up. Then she had a hand loose, and spit in his face, making a wild strike for his neck. He disengaged and backed up several lengths. Only then did she realize a low keening sound came from her, of rage and fear.

He looked at her in horror.

Celine's breath rushed in and out, too fast. She closed her mouth and drew herself up. He thought her in Esther's circle. He would never trust her again. She could not be weak, not in front of him. And he had told her to guard Kyrin's back.

She did not know why, but that broke her. What came out was the moan of a wounded deer instead of the wolf's howl she wished to claw free of her throat. Then came the tears. She turned from him, facing the wall. Shuddering, she strove for control, fingers digging into the stone.

"I am not Esther," she choked. "I left Myrna to guard Kyrin. I must take back the blade. You will not stop me, nor Esther, nor any man!" None could drag her back to helplessness again. She would die first. That scared her. Head down, she dragged in air, fighting panic. She must be strong. She must think, find a way to convince him she would never follow Esther.

"Celine." Berd's voice was low, calm. He had not drawn nearer, was not too close. His threat diminished. She pushed down the sobs and turned slowly. He waited. When she dared look up, she gulped. There were tears in his eyes. "I am sorry."

A wind of storm shook her like a tree, leaves of feeling and confusion falling fast.

But Berd was not done. "What were you saying about Esther?" The words were gentle.

Maybe he did not quite distrust her. Celine wiped her face, left the leaves where they fell for later sorting. Rather than testing him, the truth poured out of her. "I was saying," she stuttered, "Esther wa-wants power. Kyrin is in her way. Even more, since the regent paid Kyrin such attention at court last winter as the future Lady Cieri of Cierheld. Alkborough is hers now, and she has a strong lord at her side. With her brother ruling Fenwrd on the coast with access for ships, as you say, and the prospect of trade with the wazir, well, Esther sees the threat of Cieri growing. All men see it." She stopped and gulped again.

Berd's nostrils flared. "True. Why stop there? Trade with other lands brings riches. Meric is looking to sign on more squads to train, to fill the regent's request for skilled men. But the other lords, notably in the south, may also wonder what things we may learn, what may come of joining Kyrin's knowledge of Subak and De Re Militari, what secrets Tae's book may hold that we have not plumbed yet."

"Oh." Celine paused. "Do they think we strengthen our holds to overthrow them? But how could they?" she burst out. "We have already fought one war, and we seek only to defend ourselves and avoid another!"

Berd said dryly, "People often suspect others of what they do. They hunt for power and renown and riches for their own sakes. Therefore, so do we." There was an ironic glint in his eye.

"That is why Esther wants Thain, and why she gathers all men in her hands that she can. She wants power."

"Yes. And how the thief and the sword play into this mess, we need to know."

He uncannily echoed her thought. A messy stew it was, if he sought the weapon for coin, or the thief for acclaim in the eyes of Cieri. There were enough others striving for their own ends. Still, someone must find that inconvenient blade.

Celine sobered. "In the light of our conversation, Cierheld appears ambitious indeed." The implications sank in, and fear filled her. What right had Esther to start this, to hurt them, and with them all of Britannia? None. She said in a low voice, "But we must have proof, something more than speculation, rumor, or our experience." She stiffened. "We must go to court."

Berd let out a breath. "I had hoped not, but the threads run there." He stared at his hands. "I had thought," he said softly, looking up, "that Esther may have held the other end of your thread. Or her mother. Like flower, like bud, those two."

Celine swallowed. "No. Never."

"I am glad I was wrong. But I should have remembered this place would be a battleground for you." He set his jaw. "Be that as it may, the regent is soon meeting with the southlords in York; something about a grain dispute. Thain and Esther are sure to be there. We must find out their webs and tear what we may."

The dark fire in his eyes shocked her. Celine knew then it had been fierce sadness at her betrayal that sparked his anger moments ago. Now he held potential deadliness in mind, against the enemies of Cieri. She felt a sneaking gladness she would walk with him.

Berd's voice hardened. "The sword's trail is cold. We must leave the thief to smoke out those behind him."

"But what of the rat? He and the blade are bound together."

His head jerked up. "What rat?"

"The rat in Cierheld's walls, who carries news where he ought not. The one who stole our lady's weapon must know his name." She needed that weapon as proof. Of what, she shied away from examining too closely. She did not flinch when he stepped forward, though memories assaulted her again. She pushed them back.

That day was not this. Berd was not Thorgil. he did not mean her harm. He probably never would. Though she straightened on instinct.

The armsman picked up her staff and rested it against the stone beside her.

Celine made her voice even. "The rat is as much a danger to Cierheld as those behind him."

"Whatever schemes are designed against us, you can help me. Together, we are stronger, wherever the trail leads." Berd reached out to touch her hand tentatively, giving her time to evade him if she wished.

She need no longer fear him, not in that way. But she felt more vulnerable than ever. Celine drew back. Stronger together? Her heart twisted, and she looked aside at the weapon she had lost to him. "How can I possibly help you?" She had shown herself weak in body and spirit this day, a creature of tears. Besides, did she wish to follow him, or find the sword herself?

A small voice inside her said he made her weak, he had broken her. But that was not true. Somehow, she could not be angry with him for it. Rousing the darkness in her heart had not been his purpose.

Now there was too much danger to those they both loved. Why had she not been born a boy? The fire of her anger banked, leaving determination. The reason she must find out, as her life unfolded. But one thing was undeniably clear. "I am not yet as strong as you."

"You are. In your own way." He suddenly laughed. "You will grow stronger, Celine, never fear. You wield your heart well enough. You are learning to use this." He touched the side of her head, stroking her hair as he dropped his hand. He whispered, "In some ways, you are far more powerful than I. You have a strength of spirit some cannot reach."

She gave him a small smile. A little warmth bloomed inside. "Though not your strength of arm?" She raised a brow.

"No, never that." He was laughing, though serious, also.

"Hmmph." She would show him. Somehow, the thought did not have the sting of desperation it used to carry. It did not matter so much now that she found the sword first. It mattered that they found it and uncovered their enemy. For Kyrin. For them all.

Then she would have work enough, for every bit of strength she possessed.

6

# Gambit's End

*Keep deception and lies far from me. ~ Proverbs 30:8*

Berd watched Celine riding ahead of him on their second day on the road to York. When they left Fenwrd last even' after requesting supplies from the steward, they had run into a rainstorm. The rain had not been particularly cold, so they had continued, heads bent under their hoods, bedraggled red hair peeping from hers. The rain pattered in a soothing music on ash and oak and bracken, rattled upon his hood and trickled down his chin and the streaming manes of their horses.

The morn had dawned chill and misty, so before they rode out of a quiet camp, he'd seen to it Celine donned her hunting leathers and applied another layer of a waterproofing mix of beeswax and a secret ingredient of Nith's to her brown boots. She had waxed her bowstring with the same, as had he, to protect them from the wet.

Celine's mare was a spirited gray beast that mirrored her rider's mood. She tossed her dark mane, and Celine patted her neck, speaking in a low voice. He could not make out her words. Berd smiled. Celine had taken every weapon she owned on this journey.

Her dagger was on her leather belt, her staff in carrying thongs along her horse's right side. Her bow, a recurve after Kyrin's design, of about the same weight, rode proudly on her other side in its upright case, and her quiver was slung across her shoulders. He would have to convince her to dye those white arrow feathers. They stood out over her shoulder under the trees like the goose they were taken from and made a target of her back.

He nudged his brown gelding with his heels and trotted up beside her. She turned her head, green eyes catching a stray beam of early sun. Her face was truly beautiful, so bright and alive.

Berd cleared his throat, awkward now it came to it. He touched the tip of his longbow. Best not to mention the feathers at first; he had criticized her enough. "I can shoot a little, but Kilden is a master. He is better even than Lord Dain."

She regarded him with surprise.

"I have been trying to think of something that may suit your hand. Some weapon, I mean." Heat crept up his neck. "If you train under Kilden, you will soon surpass me, and mayhap even Kyrin. No one can deny you have always been good with the bow." He stumbled on, words swift. "When I went with Brother Rolf and his old tensquad to bring down the traitor who answered to Mornoth, I discovered Kilden was Brother Rolf's right-hand man. He's a terror with a bow, by all accounts. He brought down game by more difficult shots than I can tell. I would not have him as my enemy, not for all the regent's gold."

Celine twisted her horse's mane in her hands with a frown. "Durand holds court in York, and you say he wishes to show favor to the southern lords. Or at least to let all know he has no fear of residing so near the Humber and the south. He sends the message he holds a position of power and means to keep it. Let us say, for the king to come." She looked at him sidelong.

Berd shifted uncomfortably. "Yes, that is probably so. But it's been eating at me—I mean, I ought not to have questioned your loyalties. You left Esther for Kyrin before there was any gain in doing so. You have been loyal to us all over a thousand moments since last summer." He grimaced. "Yes, you were unfriendly to Kyrin, at first, before you were taken. But you changed. You were always loyal after. With such a history, you should have had my trust. So let us leave aside talk of training and intrigue for later. I give you my trust now. We should have that in the open between us." He waited with bated breath.

Celine's mouth pursed. "You are entirely infuriating; did you know that?"

Bewildered, Berd said, "What cause do I give for offense?" He had a feeling the arrow feathers would have to wait, along with trust.

"We reach York in a few bells, and you speak of yesterday? You are quite wrong if you think I am concerned with my lack of skill now. This is not a good moment to deal with my failure." Her voice was tight, and she looked away. "Though I am grateful for your trust, I would rather hear what you plan to tell the regent about our unexpected visit. You say you were advised to arrive before the council of southlords convenes in another Sevenday. What reason should we give? With respect, but contrary to yourself, I believe it is time to consider intrigue."

Berd grinned. So be it. "Then we will leave my questions for the moment while I answer yours. You are thinking ahead, as Nith would say." Later, they would come back to training and trust.

She smiled at him, and Berd settled into the saddle in the deep contentment of conversing with Celine without heat. It had been too long.

§

Celine's mind was busy with Berd's revelations, and they broke their fast briefly by a stream while the horses drank. They finished their bread and meat in the saddle and rode into York around Nones. The gate was open, and the guards passed them through with barely a glance at their arms and the sigil of Cierheld over their breasts, a shield halved by a red arrow, dividing the sun on blue from a moon on black. The hour had come to bait the trap, and only the bells could tell what they would catch. Her heartbeat quickened. At the door of the Thirsty Man, an inn close to the town hall, they dismounted.

Berd soon paid for their lodging, and, after depositing their things in their rooms, they left the surly innkeep and his lad to stable the horses while they walked across the street to the hall. It was a long, tidy structure of stone topped by a wooden upper story. As they neared the entrance, a bit of bright thatch from the roof wisped down, catching on the respectable green tunic and kirtle Celine had donned. She glanced up but saw no one. The top layer of thatching looked new and evidently had not had time to settle. Someone had not secured their fastening of twisted hazel.

It made her smile as she brushed the golden stem of wheat off her skirt, remembering her adopted brothers rethatching their cottage under her foster father's vigorous instruction, his red-haired, bearish figure moving about the edges of the roof, while her brothers laid down a new layer of wheat thatch on the steep pitch and combed it down to shed the rain and snow. She had applied the hazel switches to the thatch that time. With a deft twist, bending each twig and driving the ends deep on each side to secure the straw bundles. She could see Berd at such work, smiling and laughing with her foster father.

Berd was not smiling now. He strode beside her, sober and watchful. He had left all his weapons in his room but for his dagger, and she had done the same. They were on a peaceful errand.

Up the steps and just within the hall door, a guard gruffly asked their business.

"I have news for Regent Durand Tolman, concerning his men in training at Cierheld." Berd gave his name, and Celine hers.

With a sharp look, the man motioned them inside and bade them find a seat. They sat quietly side by side on a bench behind a table on one side of the long room. There was no one at the opposite table, or at the great board at the head of the room. The rushes underfoot were new and spread with fragrant rosemary and various mints. Celine's hand strayed to her dagger under her kirtle. She blessed Kyrin for showing her where such weapons could best be hidden. The hilt was comforting. At the moment, she would have welcomed the falcon dagger itself and, far more, Kyrin. She swallowed, trying to wet her dry throat. She hoped their gambit paid off, but couldn't the guard have at least offered them a drink?

"See? They are here. It is as I said." Thain's voice held an undercurrent of triumph. At the regent's side in the doorway, Thain Mornoth stood with one hand on his belt, a goblet in the other. He saw her watching him and lifted it in salute. He smiled, an unpleasant smile.

The regent strode to the table, his hair the color of ripe wheat.

Celine had all she could do to ignore the arrogant young lord at his heels, rise, and offer her curtsey to the regent.

Beside her, Berd bowed. "My lord regent."

Six armsmen filed into the room and halted, two attending the regent on either side, two flanking Berd and herself.

"He is the one," Thain continued. "You must arrest him, my lord. Justice demands it."

Berd did not deign to notice him. Celine tensed. Berd pressed an elbow against her arm, and looked at the regent, as if inquiring his pleasure. "My Lord Tolman?" he said formally. "I have news from Cierheld for your ears."

Durand held up his hand to Thain. "Let us hear them before we judge." He lifted one foot to the bench. "But all in good time. Sit, sit, you must be weary from your journey." He smiled, regarding them with a quick hazel gaze. The regent wore a sword and dark clothing of the best weave. His only ornament was a ruby on a gold chain about his neck and a twin ring on his finger. He was young to have a son of nine summers.

Celine sat, fought the urge to fidget, and held her head high. "We are not so weary, my lord, we but came from Fenwrd, and camped on the road. We came only to deliver news."

"Well, you must at least be thirsty. The day is warm." His brow furrowed. "What is our guard about, not to offer you a drink in common courtesy?"

Celine lifted a graceful shoulder. "Doubtless we surprised him at this afternoon hour, though I would be grateful for a sip of ale."

Berd nodded in curt agreement.

Durand hastily stood and called for a servant, and shortly there were cups of cool, frothing ale on the table before them. Celine nudged Berd when Durand turned away to speak with Thain and his men. She smiled at him pointedly. Berd colored and took a deep drink. When he came up for air, the regent was watching him coolly.

"So, what is the news from Cierheld?"

With a dogged air, Berd said, "It is for your ears alone, my lord." He was a mere armsman adhering to protocol.

"I see." The regent glanced at Thain.

The young lord inclined his head stiffly and left.

Without preamble, Berd stood and faced the regent. All traces of the stolid lackey were gone. He was alight in every fiber. The regent's armsmen stirred.

Berd ignored them. "My lord, someone stole Kyrin Cieri's Damascus blade near a Seven-day ago. We do not know who, but Nith Nulduin, first armsmaster of Cierheld, bids me say he believes there is mischief afoot."

Celine would not like to be Durand, under that hot gaze, as if he should know something of that mischief.

"There always is." Durand sighed, waved a hand, and his armsmen retreated just outside the door. He ignored Thain's protest that came faintly to their ears and said, "How do my men fare?"

Berd looked at him in gentle challenge. "Did you not hear me, my lord?"

"I did, but I wish to inquire after my men. He who aspires to victory should spare no pains to form his soldiers. How goes the training?"

"Ah. You also know Flavius' work in De Re Militari. Their training goes very well," Berd said. "They grow more skilled by the day. Soon we will have the greatest body of armed men ready to defend Northumbria, trained very like the Eagles of old. Meric is ecstatic." Berd grinned. "He sees the chance to direct men in experiment with all kinds of weapons, ancient and new." His smile died as he locked gazes with Durand.

Esther swept through the doorway. "There you have it. He said it himself." Her words held light humor. With a swish of her kirtle, her light purple mantle covering a lavender tunic, Esther approached and dipped a deep curtsey before the regent. Her voice darkened. "Cierheld does not respect the dead." With a worried frown, she continued, "My Lord Tolman, can you ignore such a statement? All these heard it." She indicated two of the regent's armsmen behind her. "Why, my Lord Thain even has proof. I trust he told you of it?"

Celine clenched her fists in her tunic but said without heat, "What is it you accuse Cierheld of?"

"Oh, what a goose I am. I did forget that part. Lord Thain must remind me. He speaks so much better than I." Thain appeared at her elbow as if bespelled. Esther tittered. "My pardon, my lord regent. Please let my Lord Thain explain."

A smile played about the corners of Thain's mouth. He cut a handsome figure in dark blue. "We mean we have proof that Cierheld has stooped to robbing the dead." He turned to Durand, apologetic. "Though I trust my house has given no further cause for offense of late, my lord, if I may allude to past misdeeds, now Cierheld, in like manner, desecrates my ancestor's land and makes Alkborough a further nest of betrayal." His breath was quick. His hot glance raked Celine and Berd.

Berd clenched his fists. "We do no such thing!"

"Then what do you there?" Thain shot back. "What is the purpose of all your maneuvers, your messengers that travel so thick between the three holds? I swear, I do have proof of your grave robbing."

Berd said nothing, jaw set. Celine's nails hurt her palms. Berd would never speak a word of Cierheld's missive squad or Lord Dain Cieri's business without leave. She ached to have Esther to herself for a quarter hour. Halwende's first daughter would have put Thain up to this. And what was she about, wearing royal purple, even of the lightest shade?

The regent crossed his arms and fingered his chin. "This is a matter for the council," he said at last. "I will not receive accusations of Lord Dain Cieri that he is not here to answer. We must uphold the law."

Celine's smile did not reach her face. Their gambit looked to be successful, in part.

Thain stepped forward. "Of course, my lord. But there is more. This man is directly involved. Lord Dain may not be aware of his treachery. Let me send for the proof I hold at Keffold, and then you may wish to question this armsman further."

Celine glared at Thain. If only Kyrin was beside her, or Myrna, even old Medaen. Though she could not speak, having another ploy to play, they would, and eloquently. Myrna would be quite convincing about how Thain's actions would reflect badly on the court's perspective of him and the regent.

Celine's gaze flew to Berd's face. If only he would defend himself. He could not be guilty. His eyes held hers with deep sadness. It could not be. Why did he not speak a word? But she gave her promise to keep up the mask of a simple first daughter's companion so she could be free to listen and act if necessary. She could not ask him what loss or danger he steeled himself against, what made him flex his hand as if he ached for a blade.

Esther said acidly, "At least contain him until the council." Her face softened, and she laid a hand on Durand's arm. "In calling the council, my lord regent, your wisdom is revealed. Many heads may make a wise decision, after the facts are heard before the lords of the south, as well as the north. Though we know where their sympathies lie."

The regent grimaced. "The house of Cieri has proven a worthy ally. I will not be soon convinced of ill doing by any of Lord Dain's house, though I will confine his armsman until the council. But not a moment longer than necessary." He turned to Berd, his stern face inquiring. "Why do you say nothing? Do they indeed bear proof of your guilt?" He did not look like the thought gave him pleasure.

Berd drew a deep breath. "My lord, I may speak with none but my Lord Dain or Armsmaster Nith of details concerning my actions." His voice was even. "As to Lord Thain's accusations, they are not true, for I have done nothing against Cierheld or you, my lord. Whether I can prove it is another matter." He looked straight at Celine, and his mouth pressed into a tight line.

*An armsman who knows what he is about.* Celine could bear no more. There were things an empty-headed companion might say to retrieve a failed gambit. She lifted her chin. "If he has deceived us, you may be sure my hand will be first against him, my lord." She hoped Berd did not take her words to heart.

"But you," she spun on Esther, "you have always disdained my first daughter. What gain do you seek from the house of Cieri? Kyrin and all of her line work only for the good of Britannia. They see beyond their own people." She arched a brow. "I ought to know; I hear far too much of it." There, that would put a bee in the regent's ear, and Berd's.

Thain set his goblet on the table with a thump. "The good of Britannia? How can it be for the good of our people to teach stable boys who care nothing for words to read, to the neglect of those who can make use of such learning, such as those who will be councilors, lords, and even the king to come? These small minds know nothing of the Vulgate or statecraft or leadership."

He snorted. "Who believes a cowherd or a serving maid, even the goodwife of the inn outside, can have anything of import to say, any insight to direct the clearer vision of those over them?" He threw up his head in defiance. "How can it be wise to make mercenaries into a force stronger than our own? Is it any wonder gold and men flow like water through Lord Dain's hands?

"Worse, to steal from the dead to support his foolish aim to endear himself to common men is despicable. Companion to Kyrin Cieri you may be, but it seems you are as blind as she. No waste is good, especially coin to teach the poor. It does not benefit the church, our people, or our land. Can you not see? All must submit to rule and take up their proper purpose and place."

Esther listened to the man who held her arm, mouth parted in awe as she stared up at him.

Thain laid a hand over hers and smiled down at her. "It is our right and duty as lords to uphold our ruler, and to act for the good of all, when they do not know it themselves. Greater minds must rule those beneath them. Is it not so, my lord?" he said this last to the regent.

Celine did see. The man held a vision of greatness that had no hope of anything but men's destruction, in a twisted Paradise on earth born of his own imagining. To gain it, Cierheld must fall along with all who held Britannia the fair and true, as a worthy ideal in their hearts. This man wished to be king.

Berd spoke at last. Every line of face and body again afire; he was yet wary. "My lords, it is not my place to speak of Cieri's goals. I can speak what I know. I am one of those *common men,* and I serve the house of Cieri to my last breath."

Celine lifted her head, proud she stood with such a man. He would not desert Cieri, and Cierheld served the regent. His words were a challenge and a promise to all who would oppose them, and a declaration of loyalty to the regent, if he but had the wit to see it.

Berd went on. "Is not every man given the common light of God at birth: in mind, heart, and hand? I have known many men, and I tell you, there are few with a greater heart or mind than Nith Nulduin, though his skin is black, and Dain Cieri, though his skin is white.

"They are brothers akin, and the most humble of men, though one was born in the dust, and the other within stronghold stone. I also will follow the light God gives. If I can be like them in a tenth of their ways, I will count myself blessed. It is a privilege to serve them, especially when they have given oaths to Lord Dain, and he to a man like you, my Lord Durand Tolman. We all serve someone." He paused, and said in a low voice to the regent alone, "Do we not serve the coming king? Both he of earth and He of heaven?"

The regent considered him gravely. "You give me food for thought. In the meantime, I regret you must rest under guard until the southlords have joined us. I promise you, no stone of proof will be left unturned."

Berd paled, but he bowed his head. "It is well. My thanks, my lord."

"Oh, and Celine may attend you, as she wishes." The regent smiled at her, and Celine gave him a heartfelt curtsey, murmuring her thanks. Esther shot her a look like a dagger, and Thain pursed his lips but said nothing.

Four armsmen escorted Berd out between them in the regent's wake. Celine stepped up beside him. Berd gave her a grateful look, but she said nothing, staring straight ahead.

Only after the armsmen left them in the cell of the guardhouse, Berd relieved of his dagger and behind bars, did Celine let out a long sigh and lean against the wall. "Why did you not ask the regent to send a messenger to Lord Dain?"

Berd's head shot up. "He would not have reached Cierheld."

Celine sprang to grip the iron between them. "What have you found out? What do you know?"

"Only that our gambit had the not entirely unexpected result of drawing our enemies' ire. But I did look for Durand's support." One side of his mouth tilted, wry. "He must have a reason."

"Yes. But why did he not acknowledge Nith's word of trouble?"

"I fear he knows of some danger, or senses it, and calls Cierheld to his side."

"Using you as bait." Celine said with disgust. "Then why not send a messenger?"

"He did. He left you free." Berd smiled, and it showed his teeth. "The regent knows Kyrin would never leave a companion of hers untrained. Thain also knows it, mayhap even Esther. They will watch you, try to trap you."

Celine gulped. Neither Dain nor Kyrin would leave one of their own to a trumped-up court.

Berd let out a long breath he did not mean for her to hear. "But we must wait a little. See what further move Thain means to make."

"Do not discount Esther."

"Never fear; that is where you come in. See if you can walk the middle road with her, or let some of your tart tongue loose to good effect, and fulfill their expectations of a bumbling companion." He grinned briefly. "You made a precise strike, to plant question in the regent by asking what Esther wishes to gain." He moved closer. "Be careful. All know you must have some training. But they do not know how much." He tapped her forehead with a light finger. "In this, you are an arrow in Cierheld's quiver."

"Yes." Celine looked down. "I will show how inept I am in every way."

"Not too much," Berd warned. "Remember, you've always been good with a staff, and Esther will sense it if you act unlike yourself."

"I know." Celine reached for his hands that gripped the bars, sliding her fingers around his. "Be careful yourself." She turned her back, reached under her tunic, and withdrew her dagger. "Take this. Not all men are honorable."

He said nothing but took the weapon and lowered his head. His breath warmed her hands. His murmur was almost inaudible. "For this moment, the tiger sows. Ambition glows, when men rise, a kingdom to dispose."

Her whisper joined his, "Falcon, though evil rises to oppose, your call I disclose." It was from Kyrin's ode.

She remembered the last line of the stanza and thought, *You are true as the coming snows.*

7

# Harry and Hunt

*Their sword shall enter their own heart. ~ Psalms 37:15*

Thain stared up at the corner of his room and the shadows drawing down. Someone might come for him in the dark before the council assembled. He knew Cernalt's reputation.

Thorgil had made it very clear that the old armsmaster, though retired and master of Cierheld's birds at present, was the most dangerous man in Cierheld, for he was the mind behind the messenger system between the holds. Thain had also heard whispers that Cernalt's missive squad carried more than messages. First armsmaster Nith was a close second to the hawkmaster, for he oversaw the armsmen in the field. Worst of all, Dain Cieri was a master of chess, for he knew how to loose his men to their own devices to get the best strategy and tactics from them.

But he was not without wits of his own. His man would see that Berd spoke when he ought and then was silenced when the moment came to gain his rightful seat. Thain rubbed the ring on his finger. Esther was a worthy woman, though overly ambitious at times. She might need a strong hand. Cierheld's missive squad must also be dealt with. He must speak with Henges about that.

There was a light knock at the door, and he smiled slightly in the dimness and rose from his bed. "My lady, is aught amiss?"

Esther stepped inside. "Is all in place?"

"Yes. The regent likes the idea of a grand hunt before the councilmen arrive. He will bring a select number of the northlords, and we are invited, of course. The daughter of Cieri's companion is also to come. You will not drive her away. Do I have your oath on that, my lady?"

"Of what use is Celine to you?" Esther watched him, her blue eyes narrow.

Thain shrugged. "We must keep her occupied and under our eye, and in the regent's mind, also. You may put your guile to work and find an opportunity to expose her undependable character to our lord."

"That will be a pleasure."

They smiled at each other, and after a quick embrace, Esther turned for the door.

Thain stopped her. "Though we are betrothed, my love, we have not yet gained our end. Walk carefully around the man who has sworn to help us. I do not trust him."

"But of course, my lord. When have I ever trusted amiss?" Esther paused. "Do you trust him to do his work? We paid him well enough."

"He will do as he is told. Still, Berd is rather a thorn until he takes care of him."

Esther gave a low laugh that prickled his skin; it was so deep and venomous. "You forget, I have known this armsman far longer than you. We have a history." She raised her chin. "The proud boy will receive his just deserts. But why waste a body, warm or not?" She gave him a pert curtsey and swept from the room.

Thain lay back down. Sometimes she chilled even his blood. But he was strong enough to manage her. Esther distrusted mayhap even his oath to her. He wondered if he could trust hers.

He flung the light linen cover to the side. It was too hot in these mean quarters, while the regent basked in the lodging that contained two windows at the other end of the inn, under the evening breeze that he knew stirred outside with the coming of night. Thain could smell the approaching shadows in the cooling oaks and hear the call of an early owl.

Oaths were made to be broken when one outgrew them, or if they became too small for what they contained. Power made its own way. It was inevitable. He fingered his chin. New oaths would soon be forged by all.

§

The sixth morn after their arrival in York, Celine stepped softly through her training routine, making no more sound than the whisper of cloth socks across the floor. She'd moved her pallet to the center of the wood span, after taking Berd's weapons from his quarters. She had slept ill these nights, starting at every noise, and risen early, wishing Berd were on the other side of the wall.

Now she stared at his bow and sword lying beside her own white feathered quiver and staff on the pallet, and wished she had a blade of her own, even her dagger. Still, she was glad Berd had it. She pulled her mind back to her training.

She shuffled at the pallet at attack speed, leaned down to grasp the hilt of the blade, and lifted it with a grunt of effort. As she spun to guard position, the steel edge wavered before her. Berd was right. It was too heavy.

A light sweat on her skin, heart pounding, but still breathing evenly the way Kyrin taught her, Celine spun back and replaced the blade. If only they had the sword of Damascus steel. It would cut through much of their enemies' plans.

Was Berd at all used to his cell, or had he slept as ill as she again? It was time to find out, though it was barely Prime. She finished the quieter footwork drills as best she could in the small space and padded to the door to pull on her boots she'd left in front of it as an early warning of attempted entry.

Downstairs, she attempted for the sixth time to regain Berd's coin he'd given for his room. The innkeep refused, and Celine glared at him. "You owe him a room then, in all rights, when he is released. The first night I told you he would not be staying, and I had removed his things."

The man looked as dour as his dirty apron. "If he's freed, then we'll see."

Celine drew herself up. "You will see, so you shall. Kyrin Cieri will not take it kindly you have treated her companion and her first armsman in so dishonorable a manner." With this dark warning she left him, fuming that she had to resort to using Kyrin's name.

The innkeep shrugged, and that troubled her. Cierheld seemed to have an unsavory, or at least powerless, reputation in this place. Deep in thought, Celine left and made her way toward the guardhouse in the first light. She swung around a corner and smacked into a small boy. They both parted with an oof. She rubbed her elbow, staring at his blond hair as he grimaced, scrubbing at his head. She'd never seen that hair, yet something seemed familiar...

The boy shook off his pain and bowed. "I am most sorry, mistress. Forgive my heedless rush." He glanced at her with a hazel, wary gaze, as if fearing her wrath.

"Not at all. I was the one in haste." She smiled at him. Those eyes, and the dark tunic and trousers. Even a small ruby ring on his hand. This was Durand Tolman's son. "Forgive me, I was on the way to see a friend who is in trouble, and I was thinking too hard of what to say." She smiled again, rather sadly. How long had it been since she was as young as he, and only feared a social misstep at Esther's heels? He grinned in relief, and she curtseyed. "I am Celine, young sir. What is your name?"

"Corin Tolman, my lady." He bowed again.

"I am no lady, only companion to Kyrin Cieri." It was a relief to speak plain words without having to layer meaning in them, good or ill.

He took them as plainly as she meant them. His eyes widened in awe. "You serve Kyrin Cieri? Is she as good without arms as they say?"

"I know not what they say, but she has bested several men, my foster father among them."

"With what weapon?"

"Staves and hand to hand."

"I would like to see this Subak." There was pure longing in his voice.

"Mayhap you will, someday. Cierheld makes no secret of our training."

"You train with her too?" he breathed.

"Yes, though I only learn footwork and sometimes the bow, at the moment. I deeply wish to learn blades. But that will have to come later, and after her babe."

He nodded wisely. "You're not strong enough. Isn't that what they always say?"

Celine laughed and bowed to him. "Then we shall have to learn the war bow first, with a draw beyond our years, shall we not, and prove them all wrong?"

He laughed with her, and they made their way toward the guardhouse. "I may even have a chance this day," Corin said.

"Father says we need meat for the council tomorrow. We will hunt the forest with Lord Thain and—" He broke off, for Esther waited for them before the guardhouse, her face thunderous.

Had she seen their entire interlude? Celine lifted her chin. Corin looked at her, quick and sharp, and said in a low voice, "If you will come, meet me at the stable." Louder he said, "I must get my horse," and dashed away after a flashing bow to Esther.

Celine walked up to the first daughter of Halwende, who regarded her, features serene again, blue eyes deep as the dawn sky. And yet, she kept faith with none.

"So, had a word with the youngling, have you? Did he enlighten you to anything besides the beauties of his horse?"

Celine shrugged, dispensing with the curtsey she had been considering. "Naught but the usual. Boys are so avid about shooting and the like."

Esther choked on her snort. "You were so from the beginning."

"Was I? I seem to remember embroidery until I near died of repeating the same stitch. Except for listening to you scheme how to entrap the most handsome young lords. Not much has changed, I deem." Celine said this with a cheery air and slipped around Esther and into the guardhouse. Esther's mouth hung open, and she did not follow.

Celine assured herself Berd was well, notified him of Corin's invitation, and left for the stables. There she found another woman overseeing the saddling of two horses, a white mare and a grey gelding. "Pull that girth a little tighter," she instructed the stable boy. "It will be our necks and the mare's if the saddle slips." Her black hair framed a comfortable face, and she dipped a curtsey when she saw Celine. "My lady." She eyed Celine's tunic and trousers with curiosity but without shock.

Celine explained she was no lady for the second time that morn and asked her name. "Mary, at your service." The woman dipped again and smiled.

Celine paused as she readied her mare with the bridle above its ears. "Are you Henges Aelwin's Mary?" The woman affirmed it, and something clicked in the back of Celine's mind. Her mouth tightened.

The first daughter of Halwende was in this hunt. She hoped Esther did not have Mary under her thumb, as she had so often manipulated her. The first daughter of Halwende was prone to prey on anyone who did not serve her, and torment those who did. It would be an interesting ride.

Too soon, the regent and the rest of the hunters appeared. Thain and a few other lords and their ladies surrounded Esther, and then the stable was a flurry of orders, harried stable boys, and small mishaps with various mounts. At last, they were off, about the seventh hour, just before the Terce bell.

The regent led them out, Corin at his side, and the rest followed. Celine rolled her eyes, long since mounted and waiting. Mary shared a grin with her.

Esther called sharply, "Mary, did you bring the water flask? I must check it and make sure you added enough mint. I hope you did not forget the bread and fruit to break our fast with the regent."

Corin heard and rolled his eyes as he looked back at them. Celine shook with laughter. She kept it inside, for she did not wish Berd to suffer on her account. He would have laughed.

But Berd was not at her side. And neither was any other. Men and women talked and jested in scattered groups along the cavalcade's lengthy ride to the edge of the trees. For a while, she enjoyed the morning air and the sun on the waving grass. Finally, the aloneness surrounded her.

Pushing it back, her hands tightened on the reins. She did not need company. Tae Chisun used to say, "Never be unaware," and "Better safe and alive than sorry and dead." She checked that her bow and staff were in their places ready to hand, tugging at her furred ankle cuff and one sleeve to cover her movements. After Tae said his piece, Berd would have told her she could either be the goose or the fox. Then he would glance at her bright hair.

Celine sighed. She knew the leathers she wore would become too hot by Sext bell, but if they were blessed by much game this morn, the hunt might return early. Besides, she had nothing else suitable.

By Sext, the sun high overhead, Celine was heartily tired of Esther's constant jabs and the long, fruitless hunt. In the course of the day, they had brought down nothing but a few birds. She wished she were alone again. Her mare walked between scattered trees near the end of the great circuit they had carved through the forest. They would have another two hours' ride across open ground before reaching York. Years of woodcutting for building and winter fires had pushed back the forest's edge. Corin urged his mount away, dashing off with enthusiasm for the hundredth time into a thicket a long arrowshot ahead.

Everyone was weary, though the regent seemed cheerful enough. Most of the hunt walked their mounts, with a lazy eye to anything that moved, not expecting game so late in the afternoon. The armsmen about the regent, and those bringing up the rear, talked easily with those closest to them. A laugh rose.

The sun was baking Celine. She was sure she smelled anything but pleasant.

Esther smiled. "Is it not a beautiful day to escape our stale quarters? The shade is so delightful." She looked around and drew a deep breath, eyes dancing, though Celine saw beads of sweat on her brow. Celine closed her mouth, not wishing to snap at her. With a smirk of triumph, Esther eased her beast's rein and dropped back beside Mary and another lady. Celine's scowl must have been eloquent enough.

She did not know what made her glance up. They had drawn even with Corin, now off to their right. He circled a hazel thicket, bow ready. He gave an excited call.

A pheasant burst in thunder from right before his horse's feet. It reared, and Corin released his arrow, which went wild. He dropped the bow and grabbed for the horse's mane.

There was a flicker, a shadow of movement in the thicket behind him. Then it was gone. It was not a bird.

Too quiet. Too high above the ground to be a deer. Could it be a man?

Celine's senses abruptly widened. Closer to the front, birds exploded from cover. She heard the regent, his men, and the twang of bows. Staring at the shrub at Corin's back, she slid an arrow from her quiver. Nocked it, resting her bow across her thighs.

There. Another movement, a deeper shadow against the green.

"What is it?" Esther halted beside her.

Then Celine saw the outline of a man's forearm and a bow. Aimed at Corin.

She lifted and released from half draw, kicked free of the saddle and stumbled, spun down to one knee. She had a second arrow. Shot. There was a shriek, cut off by her third arrow.

Then she had a fourth and rapidly searched the trees around them at full draw. The men at the rear scrambled closer in confusion. All Celine saw was her hand on the bow and the head of her arrow as it flashed past them. "On guard! Guard them!" she cried.

Corin had heard the man scream and now hurtled back. His eyes widened as Celine swung toward him.

Something struck her between the shoulders. Her arrow loosed. Desperate, Celine twisted her wrist. The shot missed Corin by an arm's span. Celine surged to her feet, running for him, striving to protect the one person she knew was innocent.

The regent's first armsman knocked her sprawling. Then three others had her pinned.

"How dare you attack our prince!" Esther slid down from her horse, panting, dagger drawn. The others drew closer, the alarm spreading. A horn called. Hooves thumped on the leaf litter.

The first armsman gave Celine one hard, steely glance. "Two of you, hold her," he snapped. "The rest, to your posts!"

Celine lifted her head. "Guard him!" she cried. "Find the regent!" She gulped in air. "Watch the trees; there are men!" A horrible thought crossed her mind. The brigands had the numbers to try a master stroke.

In short order, the rear of the hunting party was a knot, women in the center, horses and men braced about them, bristling with weapons. The hunters in the lead had formed their own protective circle and moved to join them. They had fifty lengths to cross. At least there were no bodies on the ground.

The armsmen held Celine on her feet between them, but her gaze was only for the trees, moving from cover to cover. She did her best to keep Esther also in view. Halwende's first daughter had not sheathed her blade.

There was silence. The forest was still, and then the first armsman stalked toward Celine. He gave low orders to his second, and the other men remained on guard. When he reached her, Celine swallowed hard before the first armsman's furious stare. At least there was no sign it was the brigands. She hoped she had not made a mistake. If she shot one of his men who had been guarding their flanks, who aimed only to bring down the pheasant... Her stomach turned.

Esther shoved closer, wary of Celine, keeping her dagger between them. "She attacked Corin! I saw it with my own eyes. She deserves to be walled into the darkest hole in the kingdom!"

Celine glanced at her. "Of course, you would say that, my lady." Every word dripped derision. Her voice shook. Sweat trickled down her back.

"Who was hit?" The first armsman was looking over those nearby with a critical eye.

"I saw no one hit," Esther shouldered in. "It was only by heaven's grace Corin was not."

The armsman stared at Celine, waiting. He was going to hear her out.

Corin slipped through the press and stood beside his father's men. At his dignified nod, the men holding her let her go and stepped back. Celine curtseyed.

The only warning she had was Corin's alarmed, "Watch out!"

Somehow, one of the armsmen standing near Esther fell against Celine, dagger in hand. On reflex, Celine stripped it from him. As she had been trained, she skittered back, detaching from danger, and found herself outside the circle. Lead arm guarding, dagger hand at her side and ready, she looked for further threat. Men raised weapons.

Esther shouted, "Shoot her! I told you she tried to kill him! Shoot her!"

Even as a bow twanged and an arrow hissed past her ear, Celine dropped flat. When she drew a shuddering breath of pungent leaf mold and there were no arrows in her, she opened her hand and released the dagger. She waited.

It took all her will to remain face down. When would sharp iron pierce her back? Was there another assassin left in the trees? But she couldn't think of that. There was nothing to do but show complete submission.

Corin was yelling. "She did not shoot at me! Lady Esther kicked her in the back!"

"Of course I did! She was aiming at you, my prince!"

"Armsmen, weapons down! Cease, you two!" bellowed the first armsman.

Footsteps sounded nearby. Celine tensed.

"Get up." The regent's voice was quiet.

Celine rose, slow and careful. Those hazel eyes were bright with anger. He held a drawn sword. The armsmen on either side also held drawn steel. They looked ready to kill her on the spot. She regarded the regent levelly and waited again. She had acted against the threats she saw on instinct. But this was no moment for fiery word or action. She so hoped none of this reflected on Berd.

"Who did you shoot?"

"The man in the hazel thicket."

"Which one?"

She turned her head, found the clump, and indicated it with her chin. "That one."

The regent motioned, and one of his armsmen left at a trot. He reached the thicket and gave a shout. The first armsman dispatched his second, and in moments they had pulled a man from the shrubbery. The men removed his sword and rooted around for his other weapons. He was clearly dead. But he was not the regent's man, unless they had taken to wearing black.

Celine let out a breath of relief. White goose feathers stood out, revealing her arrows pierced him through the arm, side, and neck. They carried him to the regent and dropped him at Celine's feet.

She stared at him. After the first arrow, she aimed at where she had thought he stood, concealed amid the leaves. Her last arrow had taken him through the neck, a blessed shot, seeing it had to get through the hazel stems without being deflected. She cocked her head. Or maybe it had deflected into him. She shrugged, a bare shift of shoulders. The thought was protection against the inevitable.

The man wore a mask. None seemed to know him by his slight, short build, including her. "May I uncover his face?"

The regent nodded.

Celine knelt, untied the black cloth at the back of his neck, and rolled his head face upward, feeling a strange need for gentleness. She froze, the silk crumpled in her hand. The assassin had dark skin, slanting eyes, and short black hair, straight as knives. Like another man she knew. Yet he did not have the white streak in his hair that Tae bore above one ear.

Who was he? He could not have anything to do with Cierheld, though from the East. His clothing was deep black, even his skin blackened with something like charcoal. Hands shaking, she untied the black sash and pulled it free. The strange wraparound style of tunic fell open, and two bits of torn parchment, wrinkled from much reading, slid down his bloodied side.

Celine smoothed the first and read, lips moving silently.

*To my good Brother Rolf: on behalf of the house of Cieri, I extend all greetings in our Lord.*

*May this missive find you well, with your Abbot Alton's plans for the scribes' school at Alkborough well in hand and nearing completion. My lord husband, Talik, will give you all welcome when it is time for the building to receive teachers. I will be glad when he has prepared Alkborough for our arrival with its lands and people, and bids us join him.*

*Alas, I am confined with child for the coming months. Do not mistake me; I mean not that I regret our child or bearing an heir for my husband and*

*Cierheld. I deeply love them both. It is only that I sense tension in the present peace. I especially felt it during the hand of days in winter that I spent at court, in things said and not said among conversations, some concerning the regent. There lurks a hidden danger that brings to my mind the tiger that stalks in the warm dark...*

Part of the letter was missing, probably Tae's reply. She looked up at the regent, lips numb.

"Well?"

"Someone has been stealing more than blades. Why does he have my lady's letter?" She handed him the scrap.

He read it silently, sent her a hard look. "Could this have been done without your knowledge?" His gesture included the dead assassin and Corin. "So you would be able to deny it all?"

Celine got up so swiftly Durand's armsmen tensed. "No! I know my people. The house of Cieri would never do such a thing."

"Are you certain?" Thain left Esther's side and walked closer, a lazy smile on his face. "How is it that some stranger from a far land has taken things into his own hands? To eliminate a threat?"

One of the regent's armsmen said something in his ear. The regent started, took the assassin's blade, which had been wrapped in black, and turned to them all. He removed the cloth.

Esther cried, "The Damascus sword!" Every lady, lord, and armsman craned to look.

Celine gaped.

"So," the regent said slowly. "We find the blade that was stolen from you on this man. This assassin who is from the same Land of the Morning Calm as Tae Chisun. Oh, yes." He smiled thinly at her surprise. "I make it my business to know what I can about those who hold power. Has Cierheld been selling weapons, the blades of our dead, to other lands? Are we so dangerous to your nefarious trade that my son must be killed?"

"My lord, you misunderstand the letter—"

He said softly, *"... concerning the regent. There lurks a hidden danger..."*

"That is what I mean. You misunderstand," she began, but Corin interrupted.

"Father, she killed him to save me!" He protested.

"Yes. It is apparent Celine is innocent in this. But what of the house of Cieri and Dain's first armsman?" Durand put a gentle arm around Corin's shoulders. To his men he said, "Bind her, but treat her well. We must question Berd of Cierheld."

She had lost the sword before she touched it. There was nothing she could do except use her head. "You will find him innocent also." Almost against her will, Celine's gaze went to Corin. He gave her a worried, hopeful smile, pale hair shining in the sun.

Her lips twitched in a small answer. He was alive. That at least she had done, and with a weapon she knew. She would have to get Kilden to show her the finer points of shooting from horseback like the steppes riders.

Esther snorted. "Is not the blade and this stranger proof enough? Though I, for one, would also hear what the missive said of hidden danger."

Celine lifted her head. "Cierheld is not involved in this. I would wager Tae is not either." Some faces around her were suspicious, some closed, others worried. She threw up her hands. "Why was the letter torn? There is another explanation!" There had to be.

Thain shrugged. "There usually is. If you care to wager your life on it."

8

# Armsman's Trial

*Do you see a man skilled at his work? He will stand before kings.*
*~ Proverbs 22:29*

On the ride back, Durand's first armsman chose to ride beside Celine. She did not know if it was his presence that made Mary brave Esther's wrath, but she was grateful. Since her hands were tied in front of her, the serving woman gave her regular sips of mint water from Esther's flask.

Esther rode up at one point and said in a low voice, "They know what you did. I will see you get everything you deserve. It will be the dark for you, without companions."

Celine's hands were cold, and her heart sank. But she ignored Esther, as if she had not heard. The armsman watched, thoughtful, but said nothing. To protect Mary, Celine said a brief thanks and bent her mind to Berd.

It was clear the rat in Cierheld was just the beginning. Who could have orchestrated such an assassination, and set it up so others would blame Cieri? Did Thain and Esther have the resources? They had no ties to Meric's harbor he had widened near Alkborough for the wazir's ships, or to the wazir's men, let alone any of Tae Chisun's. Besides, Mary had told her Thain and Esther had been at court since Kyrin last saw them there, save for a hunting trip or two of Thain's, lasting no more than a few days. Did the regent seek occasion against Cierheld? Was the rat the regent's man? Or even the bishop's?

If it was Cernalt or Nith who had turned traitor—but no, if they had planned to take out Corin, there would have been more men—and they would not fail. But she was grasping at straws, uncertain even of the needle.

In the stables, the first armsman untied her from the saddle and helped her down, hands still bound. He set her in a corner and bade Mary stay by her. "Don't move."

Celine nodded, then, remembering Nith's remarks about insolent armsmen in training, said, "Yes, sir," with an attempt at crispness. Though she was not his armsman, she represented Cierheld's forces at this moment. Lord Dain would want her to respect him. She thought the man had also kept her from an arrow in the back. He raised a brow and grinned, shaking his head. In that moment he reminded her of old Cernalt. She hoped they were not enemies.

A half hour later, most of the horses were unpacked, brushed down, and their riders departed for supper and a horn of mead, goblet of wine, or cup of ale. The first armsman had left them to his second to escort to the guardhouse or the inn; Celine was not sure which. Esther had not protested the pre-empting of Mary to stay with Celine. Likely she thought Mary would learn something of use to her.

Celine was almost past caring. She wished to bathe and change, her leathers sticking to her skin, but she feared the regent would not wait for night to bring Berd to trial. If she was right, she would need all her wits about her. She backed further into the corner and sat with a groan on a barrel.

A hand gripped her shoulder from behind, and Celine jumped, barely biting back a scream. "Henges?" she gasped. "What are you doing here?"

"Hush, there is no time." Sweat on his forehead, he jerked his head at the door. Outside, the second armsman was instructing the guard about the watch. Mary's gaze locked on Henges. He smiled tenderly and indicated the door again.

Without a word, she moved to it, tears beginning to stream down her cheeks. She wiped them and stepped out. Her low, inquiring voice rose, something about bathing for Celine.

Celine gripped Henges' hand in both hers, awkwardly because of the ropes. "Henges, you have to take a message to Cernalt and—"

"No, my lady. Take these to Berd, tell him to wait for me. I will make all clear." He shoved what felt like a ball of parchment and a dagger into her grasp. Then he slipped to the back door. It was not yet Nones, and the shadows grew across the yard.

She tucked the sheathed blade against a palm and the parchment inside her leathers with her other two fingers as best she could. Then she turned her attention to the weapon. And almost dropped it. The dark eyes of the falcon glared up at her, fierce and uncompromising, wings and talons reaching.

Kyrin's falcon dagger she had given to Tae. Henges had acquired it somehow, and evidently meant it as a message for Berd. Did it mean Tae was here? He could not have sent the assassin. Whatever else it meant, danger was afoot, and she had best go cautiously. But she was strong, as strong as Berd, wasn't she? Celine's hand closed on the falcon.

No, no, she wasn't. The armsmen who bore her to the ground, leaving ample bruises she felt all over, was proof of that. She never would be as strong in that way. Not in arm and body.

In a different way, she could be tougher than any enemy. Berd had seen it all along. She could be strong in spirit, in endurance and resilience. Her old fear of Esther and newer dread of dark places, even her defiance of men's strength, were bastards born of fear of helplessness. The sword of men was too heavy for her, in more ways than one. *Find your gifts, or finding the sword will destroy you.* At last, she understood.

The first gift was from the Master of All. She needed his help, far more than what any bright edge or strength of thew could give. With his power and wisdom molding her, she would never break, not irreparably. Another gift was her budding ability with the bow. What could she become if she bent all her energies on it, the staff, and Subak? How skilled could she become?

A smile spread across her face. It was blessed relief. Never mind Esther called the staff a peasant's weapon. The strain of trying to do what she could not lifted. Celine felt light and free. Free from driving fears, free to explore who she was, with room to grow. But that would have to wait. Berd needed her, and Cierheld. She was strong.

Esther had best beware.

Mary returned, tight-lipped when she saw Henges had left, but she said nothing. It seemed the regent wished to do things properly, for the second armsman soon took Celine to the inn and waited outside her room while she bathed in a hastily brought up tub.

The warmth was delightful, and some of her aches faded. She soaped the sweat away, thoughtful. Berd didn't pity her. He never had doubted her. He'd been attempting to treat her as an equal when he told her to pursue her gifts. It was what he expected of everyone. No one really pitied her for being an orphan but herself. She considered it a drawback, when it was her gain. Kyrin never had seen her as a poor orphan. She took her into her family before she was old enough to know what the name meant. Only Esther ever put on a show of pity, simply to irk her. Myrna was really the most to be pitied, and yet she took the least pity on herself.

Celine's eyes stung. She would have a word with Kyrin about it. The falcon blade would do Myrna good, as it had her.

Celine climbed out of the bath too soon, then it was Mary's turn. While Mary washed her hair, Celine dried her own. Mary was a woman of wonder. She did what needed to be done, never questioning Celine, though she had to be itching to know what Henges said. Obviously, she loved her husband, and worked with him, even while uncertain about what was happening and afraid. She was a jewel. Celine opened the door a crack to ask the armsman to have the inn help bring another length of linen for Mary's drying.

Mary brought out a small jar of salve. "It's mostly knitbone, but it will help you heal faster, my lady."

"Oh, you mean boneset?"

"That is another of its many names."

Celine smiled and sniffed the jar. It smelled of olive oil, mint, something earthier, and somehow of bees. Myrna would know more of such things.

Mary whispered, "It was not enough to save my Ellen. The stomach grippe took her. One day she was such a bright spirit, running about, and by even' she was gone. I sent for the healer near Jornhold, but Margye was away. I did not know how to tell Henges, and earlier there was danger. How do I tell him?" She looked up at Celine, tears shining in the lamplight.

Celine's throat tightened, and she took Mary's hands in hers. "Oh Mary, I am so sorry." She pulled her into her arms and their tears mingled. "You are wise, and you will find the words when the hour nears."

Mary dried her eyes, sniffing. "Thank you, Celine. But we must look to this night and protect our families as best we may."

Celine gave her a small smile. "Yes." Mary had not called her lady, and it warmed her heart.

They dressed with care. Celine donned her best green tunic, skirt, and kirtle, embroidered with blue, and slid the falcon dagger beneath. She was going to a different kind of battle.

§

Berd stood when the regent's first armsman stamped to his cell and regarded him with a grim eye. "Up, the regent calls you to trial." Four armsmen stood at his back.

Berd looked at him in utter surprise. "But the council is tomorrow."

"The regent bids you give your defense."

"What has happened?"

The armsman stared at him. "Best you tell Regent Tolman, after the attack on his son this morn."

"On the hunt?" Berd asked sharply. His mind raced as he stood. What had they done with Celine, if they suspected him and the house of Cieri of an assassination attempt? "Is Celine well?"

"Better to ask if my young lord is well." It was a growl.

Berd jerked. "Is he harmed? What of the regent?"

"It is fortunate your young lass has some skill with a bow. Come. You will learn the rest soon enough." The armsman would say no more, but bound Berd's hands behind him and escorted him to the hall.

Durand waited, seated at the head table, severe in black and silver. Another table had been moved to face it, and the first armsman deposited Berd behind it, hands still bound, without a bench. The third table had been cleared from the room, and twenty armsmen stood along the walls. There was no one present but Celine, Thain, and a few other lords and ladies with their armsmen. They sat on a bench placed against the wall fifteen paces behind him.

The regent noted his glance. "This council is closed. Only those involved in what happened this day are here. Esther's testimony has already been taken, as she begged leave to depart. We will hear the evidence and judge if you will reach the council on the morrow."

"My lord." Berd let out a breath and inclined his head. Neither Nith, Cernalt, nor his lord or Kyrin were present to consult. Here, now, he was the face and voice of Cierheld. This was a trial he dared not fail.

The regent beckoned to his second armsman and said something in his ear. The man left and returned with Corin, a trifle pale but composed, resplendent in scarlet and gold. Berd looked him over quickly. He did not seem to have even a scratch. He sat in a chair beside his father. Berd's shoulders relaxed a fraction.

Durand eyed him narrowly. "We will first ask you if you ever had or have any knowledge of ill intent against me or my house."

Berd's brow furrowed slightly. "Only suspicions, my lord. The usual complaints by the occasional drunk, and whispers of unrest. These we have heard."

"What was your answer to the problem?"

"That I cannot say, my lord. We are seeking the root of it." Berd would have spread his hands. Being tied, his shoulders lifted slightly.

"Has Bolton Abbey anything to say? And why is it you have not yet brought this brigand to justice? Can it be that you foster this unrest? Or at least are not opposed to it? The brigand first rose to be a thorn in Lord Ludwin Mornoth's time."

"Rolf and his brother Seldon's squad, under Kilden, yet seek him. We speak often. The escape of the brigand and his band was our greatest failure, my lord," Berd admitted.

"Do you think the brigand attempted to murder my son, Corin?" The regent's shrewd gaze pinned Berd.

Though he was innocent, Berd found himself sweating. "I do not know. Yet. I have not been told what happened, what the attacker looked like, or any detail I could use to identify them."

"Celine, come forward and stand beside the accused."

Celine did so, head up, back straight.

"Tell us what you saw." Durand sat back, elbow on the arm of his chair, stroking his chin.

Celine drew a breath. She smelled of sweet mint, and Berd breathed in, and took courage. Then Celine told all assembled how she saw the threat to Corin and shot the assassin. All in the room hung on her words, for she spoke with spirit and conviction, without accusation. After the moment when the assassin fell, the regent held up his hand. "That is enough. Corin, will you tell us what you saw?"

The boy steadily related how, after a scream, he turned back for the hunt and saw Celine spinning toward him with a drawn weapon. Esther struck Celine in the back, forcing her to release her arrow prematurely. When Corin reached the part where the dead man was hauled out of the bushes, the regent again held up his hand. "Thank you, Corin. First armsman, please tell us what this man looked like."

Behind Berd, the armsman said, "My lord, he had three arrows in him, placed where my best archer could not, at that range and in a thicket of hazel. He was not of this land."

Berd felt a stir of pride and looked down at Celine with a small grin tugging at the side of his mouth. She must have felt his gaze, though she did not look at him. She colored and raised her chin higher.

The armsman went on, "He was from the far East, by his look, his tunic, and most of all, his weapons."

"That will do." The regent turned to Berd. "Do you know such a man?"

Anger sprang up in Berd. Durand sought to trap him. Celine had tensed. He kept his voice soft. "No, my lord, not for a long while. I have known one man from the East, who returned there near a year ago. His name was Tae Chisun."

"You have not seen him since?"

"No."

Durand snapped his fingers, and two armsmen brought in a linen-wrapped figure, which they laid on the table before Berd and Celine. They pulled the material from the assassin's face.

With relief, Berd noted each feature, wishing he could see the man's dress and weapons for himself. He looked up. "I have never seen him before, my lord." The tips of the man's boots beyond the shroud were curious. The black leather divided the first two toes from the rest.

Corin eyed the body with fascination.

The regent waited. Berd added nothing. At last Durand sighed. "Then how do you account for this?" He lifted a blade wrapped in black and set it gently before him on the tabletop.

Berd looked at it and back up at him. "My lord?"

Celine stirred, resting a hand across her stomach as if she felt sick.

Durand revealed the weapon, never taking his gaze from him. Berd's mouth dropped open. He looked from the assassin to Celine and back to the regent. He swallowed, searching for words.

Thain spoke first. "How well he acts the part, my lord regent." He strode to the table at Berd's right, masterful. "May we ask how this man of the East came by the weapon this armsman says was stolen from Cierheld? Who among Cieri has been deceiving us?"

Durand said heavily, "It is said Lord Dain knows all that goes on in his holds. But perhaps there is an ambitious armsman among you who would take his lord's place, or find some gain without his lord's knowledge?"

The words struck Berd like fists, and he curled his hands at his back. "First Armsmaster Nith Nulduin and Cernalt are good men. In no way are they treacherous. Neither is the family of Cieri. I trust each of them with my life. I have known them since I was born, as they have known me." There was too little air in the room. "We have suspected there is a rat within Cierheld's walls. He must have taken the Damascus steel. We will find him, and when I do—"

"You'll what?" Thain smiled at him, a cat with a mouse, toying. "Will you accuse an innocent man among your own ranks to cover your perfidy? Will you give another's life for yours? The regent has promised a life."

Berd stared at him. "Lord Dain will never agree to give any man to death unless he is worthy of it."

Thain turned to the regent and indicated Berd with a wave. "See? He has said that his Lord Dain's authority is greater than yours, my lord regent."

Berd's mouth dried, and he cursed his clumsy tongue. "I meant only that my lord will convict no man on another's word alone."

"That is just." The voice was young, and the room rustled as all regarded Corin. The boy stood at his place, pale head up, eyes flashing. "I am the one they tried to kill." He pointed at the assassin. "His crime was apparent. He paid for it. No man should be executed on the word of another. There must be proof."

Thain smiled. "Do we listen to a child? Is there time for unseasoned council when an unknown enemy is in play?"

Berd scowled. The arrogant man did not quite dare name the regent's son a puppet. But for all that, Corin's words were kingly.

Corin was not done. "Is it true?" he asked.

Thain raised a brow with the patience of one humoring a slow mind. "Is what true?"

"Is what I said true?"

Someone coughed, and Thain reddened. He held out his hands in appeal. "There may be an unknown force on the road to York this very moment!"

Before any could say more, there was a knock at the door. The first armsman looked to the regent. At his nod, a guard opened it, then announced, "Henges Aelwin, my Lord Tolman, of Cierheld's missive squad. He claims he bears important news."

"Then let us hear it."

Henges gave his sword to the guard and strode inside, across the room, and stopped beside Thain. He bowed to the regent.

"My lord, I bear heavy news."

"What is it, man? Out with it!"

"Very well, my lord. I came with a message but overheard somewhat of doings involving Cierheld." His mouth pinched in distaste as he eyed the weapon before the regent. "I know not how that bright edge disappeared from Cierheld, but I do know this man," he indicated Berd, "has dealings with those who buy weapons from unsavory places. I believe they come from Alkborough burial mounds, my lord."

## 9

# Letter and Land

*A throne is established on righteousness. ~ Proverbs 16:2*

The hall erupted, men and women murmuring, Corin intent, the regent watching all.

Thain cried, "From the land of my fathers? Here is proof! Treacherous cur!" He spat at Berd.

Celine reddened, fists clenched. "It isn't true, none of it!" She glared at Henges. "How can you take such lies in your mouth?"

Berd was the only one unmoved and silent. The danger about Cierheld and the regent had deepened. If he must, he would take the fall for Cierheld and draw out their enemy. But Henges was about something. Yet he could not, for the sake of all, trust too easily. He would prepare for treachery or loyalty.

Ignoring Celine, Henges continued, "My Lord Durand Tolman, we will subject ourselves to your judgment in this matter. Bishop Caddaric will provide the final proof of the truth of Lord Thain Mornoth's assertion."

"Yes, my lord," Thain said. "It is fortunate church business brought him from Richmond this past day. He has sufficient proofs."

Durand Tolman surged to his feet. "Does he?" His face darkened, and though he leaned on the wood four lengths away, he loomed over Henges. Then he bent his regard on Thain. His voice came very softly. "How do you know that? What has the bishop to do with this matter?"

Thain swallowed, and his mouth opened, but nothing came out. He licked his lips. "My lady," he began, with a glance over his shoulder.

The regent did not let him finish. "I am speaking to you, not Lady Esther." He picked up the Damascus blade and prowled around his table to Berd's. The room was silent as a tomb. He stopped in front of Thain. "The bishop has been a far worse traitor than your uncle. Do you know why?"

Thain said nothing.

"Corin," the regent said, "Why did Bishop Rylan Caddaric deserve death the day he allied himself with the house of Ludwin Mornoth?"

"He broke his oath," Corin said slowly. His voice was steady, without defiance or fear. "He lied to our Lord above, as well as his lord on earth." He hesitated, then said, "He failed everyone in Britannia. Every boy such as I, who depended on him."

"For what?"

"Protection against the evil he knew." With that, Corin called all in the room to account.

The regent slammed the sword point down into the table. Accusers and accused jumped. "This also is true." He stared each in the face, ending again with Thain. "I gave you grace, Lord Thain Mornoth, not to doom you with your uncle. You have refused it."

"What evidence do you raise against me?"

"Your certainty of the Bishop's mind on this matter. For you already appraised him of what was to happen here, did you not? He ever plays the long game. He knows I will not suffer a second misstep."

Thain had courage, for he tried to brazen it out. "Bishop Rylan Caddaric bears the heart of the church. He has spoken of another thread of rebellion fomenting among Cieri's holds. I hear much of Brother Rolf and the school Dain put in his heretical hands. There they call themselves Christian, and do not hold good Catholic teaching. My lord, between that divisive heresy and the crimes brought against them, how can the house of Cieri not be treacherous? Where there is smoke, there is fire."

"Why are you unwilling to wait for the council's judgment and proof? Is the fire set by an enemy within?"

Thain's face hardened. "My sigil is raised. It is my right." He looked around the room between his accusers, proud and pale. "The world must be reset. The torch of a new day will lighten the minds of men."

Berd thought he also meant to gift those small minds he was so fond of despising with burning.

Releasing the quivering blade, the regent stood to his full height. He paced to one side and back, attention on Thain. "In the last hand of days, you said all men must submit to rule and their proper role. What is yours?" He did not say under his rule.

Thain's mouth worked. "Dain Cieri and his line will bring in misrule. He will use the blood of his line, a child of the north and the south, to bind Britannia. He gathers too much strength. He is of the old ways and despises the new. I would not see you betrayed, my lord." He bowed. "I would put Lord Dain in his place."

"Do you submit to my rule?"

"Yes."

"Then it would please you to learn I have no intention of stopping Lord Dain? Unless he indeed contemplates treachery. He runs his holds well and brings prosperity and trade."

"By letting every man work to reach whatever level he can in this world! It is disorder and every evil thing!"

The regent tapped his chin. "Mayhap we have not heard you out on this matter. What order would you bring, my lord?"

"Those in the north would stay there. The south must be free to govern its own affairs. In the course of seasons, the northlords may be brought to see the vision of the south and accept it." Thain paused. "Each must learn to work for the good of his lord, that the whole may be served."

"And who is the whole?"

Disbelief deepened Thain's voice. "Why, we are." He gestured at himself, the regent, and the lords and ladies in the room. "Those who have the sight to embrace the way forward! Dain is a jester in court clothes. He will destroy us. Since he rose, the kingdom has gone to the dogs!"

The regent waited.

"Even now they snap at our heels, as does this armsman, a blind hound, in blind obedience to a greedy master!" He gestured with his hand, and the sapphire gleamed blue. "His thought that men are equal in the eyes of God is a lie from the pit. His lord grasps above himself and would pull us all down with him. It cannot happen. My brother southlords would agree. Alkborough will not suffer hands of northern blood to rule!"

"Though it be the will of the council?"

"They must be better taught."

"How taught, my lord?"

"By whatever means necessary." Thain glared at Durand, omitting his title. "Cieri is cursed."

"And where does your Lady Esther of Halwende come into this?"

Thain bristled, someone on the bench laughed, and he said through clenched teeth, "My lady is no concern of yours, though she is of the same mind. Halwende is willing to help teach those who wish to learn, my lord. I believe even Bishop Caddaric would redeem himself in this. Your son could learn much under him." A light gleamed in his eyes.

Corin swallowed hard, and Durand's eyes narrowed. "First armsman, bind him. We have heard enough."

As the regent's armsman gripped Thain's arm, Henges said, "There is reason to believe he is also the brigand."

Several things happened at once.

Berd cried, "What?"

Thain whipped out Henges' dagger, jerking away from the regent's armsman and taking Henges with him, pinned against his side by an arm around his neck. Thain's edge lay at Henges' throat.

A woman screamed, "Henges!"

The regent barked, "Take them!"

"He is Cieri's man!" Berd shouted. "Let them go, please, my lord." Duty demanded he risk the loss of all. If the regent could only trust him thus far. He looked him straight in the face, all defenses down. "I am no traitor, my lord. Let me take his place."

The regent nodded, giving Berd a sharp look.

Thain's lip curled. "Come then, hound." He shifted, wary. "Try nothing, or he dies."

Berd walked to him. Thain released Henges with a shove. He stumbled into the regent, which worried Durand's armsman.

The regent steadied Henges, who gave him a nod and turned to fasten an unblinking stare on Thain Mornoth. Without a word, Berd gave the young lord his back. He half expected ripping pain through his kidneys.

Thain's arm slid around Berd's neck almost lovingly. He was slightly shorter and dragged against Berd's windpipe until his eyes teared. "You weaken yourself, thinking of other men. You prove yourself a true dog of Cieri."

Henges and the regent's men waited, poised to move, but Berd shook his head.

Thain's warm whisper beat against his ear. He was chuckling. Berd's skin crawled. "You will do more than buy my freedom. But I will be equally glad to kill you." Under that warning, Durand's men allowed Thain to maneuver Berd through the closest armsmen with hands on weapons, past the wary lords, and frightened women behind them.

Before the door, Thain tightened his grip. His edge bit Berd's neck until he gasped, "Back, back!"

The door guards moved.

Thain paused. His gaze swept the room. "Mary, come here," he ordered. A black-haired woman stood and edged closer.

Celine cried, "Mary! Don't!" and Henges lifted one hand in entreaty then dropped it.

Mary stopped a length away. "What do you wish?" Her eyes were on the floor and the herbs strewn there.

"Attend my lady and assure she is well on her road. You know the way, and the cost of deserting your place."

"Yes, my lord." Mary curtseyed and slipped through the door without a backward look.

That instant, Berd moved. He slammed Thain back against the wall with all his strength and dropped, tucking his chin to his chest. With a grunt, Thain flung out his left arm for balance and pulled his right inward with the blade as Berd spun to face him. The armsman did not feel the slice across his forehead that just missed his eyes, only the force of the blow. Then Berd was on his back on the floor. He rammed a heel for the soft spot between Thain's legs. He hit the wall instead. One of Durand's armsman had closed with Thain, drawing him away. The man sagged. Thain slid a dagger from the man's side and turned for the door.

"Lord Mornoth!" Berd yelled, trying to slow him.

But Thain Mornoth was out and away into the evening with a shout of triumph.

Berd curled, and jerked his body through his bound arms so his hands were in front of him. He scrambled for his feet, the other door guard hauling him up as he swiped blood from his eyes.

"Pardon, my lord." Celine bowed to the regent and hopped lightly onto the table. One foot on either side of the assassin, she seized the Damascus blade, and yanked it from the board. Her cry rang across the hall. "First armsman of Cieri!"

He flung the blood from his face as the guard scrambled away, and she threw the weapon to him with a heave of both hands. He caught it hilt first.

In a moment, his bonds parted. Berd spun the blade and smiled. Perfect in balance and weight, as it had always been. Here was no cunningly made copy. This edge was keen for battle.

Henges strode to him and saluted. His face was white.

He blurted, "Sir, please, take what I tell you to Armsmaster Nith and Lord Dain. A large force of men in service to Thain Mornoth has come over the mountains."

"How many?" Berd frowned.

"Archers a hundred strong, sir, and fifty with polearms. The other hundred are swordsmen. But they also have five squads of cavalry. There is no time to tell the other lords. They will hit Cierheld first, with his brigands, and then this hall."

With one hand, Berd shoved him toward the regent. "You must warn Cierheld! Give Lord Tolman all you know. I must find Thain."

Henges fell to his knees and caught his arm. "I left it too late! Now he has my Mary in his coils, and Ellen and the babe are with Lady Esther. They will kill them!"

"That is why I must find him, for all our sakes! The brigand must be stopped!"

Henges cried, "He sent the assassin! He will take down the regent and Britannia. He will blame it on you and Lord Dain Cieri!"

"How do you know this?" Berd yanked Henges to his feet and propelled him toward the regent. "Tell us," he ground out, "all you know."

"I gave a missive to Celine; did she not give it to you?"

"In it was what?"

"My proof of Thain's treachery!"

"Why did you not speak of this earlier?"

Celine pushed between them, red hair rumpled. "I tried to get it to Berd, but there was no opportunity!"

Corin eyed Henges curiously.

The regent fingered his chin. "You are the rat."

Berd spun on Henges. "You! You stole the sword and put my Lady Kyrin in danger? You betrayed us! Why? When you are so indebted to Lord Dain!"

"I did, for my Mary. You must save them, and little Ellen!" Henges' breath caught on a incoherent sob. "Or he will cut my son's throat."

Berd cried, "There are other daughters and other sons at risk!"

"I see that now." He stood before Berd, bracing as if for a blow. "These pitiless schemers have woven their web. We may catch them in it, if we are quick."

"What have you told them," Berd whispered. "How long were you in the brigand's pay? Have you been hand in glove with them all along?" Anguish twisted inside. He advanced, driving Henges slowly back to the wall.

"Only since the sword, I swear."

Berd gripped the Damascus steel. "You endanger my first daughter." *Trust no one till they are proved.* He glanced at Durand, who nodded. Berd gritted his jaw and closed his eyes. He opened them on Henges, who saw his sentence in his face.

"It is just to kill me." There was unutterable sorrow in him, but the armsman did not flinch. "Have mercy on my family. They had naught to do with any of it."

"That, I believe."

"Then what of Mary?" Henges looked from Berd to the regent and Corin. "And my son?"

Berd leaned closer and said, harshly, "What have you learned of loyalty?"

Henges looked away in misery. "It is possible Lord Ludwin Mornoth saw my flaw when he sought my death. A divided heart is none at all. I did not see it, then. I see it now."

Berd sighed. "How is it possible to serve through life without a challenge of loyalty? It means you think more than other men. Tell me, and think carefully, who do you serve above all others? Now that you have turned back to us with all you are?" He watched him close.

Henges swallowed. To his credit, he did not look at Berd's weapon, but straight in his face. His voice steadied. "Sir, I would serve the right, and never be swayed from it again. That means I serve Cierheld. I would see the threat of Mornoth and all who join him ended forever."

"And if Cierheld or those who lead it turn to evil? As may happen at any point?"

A quiver began in Henges' hands. "Wings to fly," he said to himself. And louder, "Then, then I serve him who judges all, in the end. Him who will see that right rises over wrong." He did not take his gaze from Berd's face.

By the gasps in the room, more than a few expected his death. Rigid, Henges waited.

Huskily, Berd said, "You learned late, but you learned." He laid his hand on his arm, and looked up. "Here is a new forged man, sharper than this steel. Now, tell us what you know of Thain's doings."

Henges passed an arm over his face. "Yes. Let me think! I must set all in order before you. You cannot misunderstand." He drew a tremulous breath.

"Late this spring, Cernalt sent me with a missive from Kyrin Cieri for Brother Rolf in the abbey, to be passed to her sister in Araby, and thence to Tae in his country. It was over a tenday ago I first learned who held Mary.

"Then Thain ordered me to bring the sword to him soon. Cernalt had given me another missive to take to the wazir's ship docked near Fenwrd for our first daughter of Cieri. I stopped by Fenwrd stronghold and spoke with Meric of trade opportunities, inspected the vessel at anchor just off the coast, and slipped the missive to the shipmaster at the same time. A bear of a Northman, he was. Then I disembarked."

He gestured at the dead man from the East. "On my way here, this one attacked my night camp. He took the weapon you hold." He nodded to Berd. "When I woke, he was gone, but I had a leather bag ripped from his shoulder. In it was a dagger, and a torn scrap of a missive. Go on, my lady, read it."

Celine went bright red and turned her back a moment to retrieve something from her tunic. She unrolled the balled piece of parchment. Her clear voice pierced the room as all strained to hear.

*... If the falcon dagger should return, whom would it oppose in our kingdom? For that loyal, true bird fights every lie, and there are many about the regent. To his credit, he refuses every hint of kingship from those at court, and protests he is only a steward for the king to come. I wonder, does he have in mind his son?*

*The boy is not yet old enough to show what kind of man he will become.*

*As for untruths, I could wish Esther and Lord Thain Mornoth did not smile at me so. The thoughts behind their approval swirl dark and strong as eels, while their teeth flash swift as snapping wolves. There are many who speak less fair of Cierheld and mean us far better.*

*I could wish the falcon dagger were at hand again, and myself fit to wield the blade. Soon enough I shall be too cumbersome to move, I think. These thoughts may be but the foreboding of a body working upon the difficult and most blessed task of childbearing. Do not pay me overmuch heed, my friend.*

*Yet our Master of the Stars is always with us, and He has gifted Cierheld with many good friends. Among them, yourself and Abbot Alton and the regent. There are many hearts, hands, and eyes warding us.*

*As always, we pray for your prosperity and peace. Of your good will, lift us up likewise.*

*May our Lord bless you, and all who wish the good of our people and our fair Britannia.*

*With my own hand, Kyrin Cieri, first daughter of Cierheld and soon, Lady of Alkborough.*

*Please pass this missive to my sister of bread and salt, who will send it on to her second father and mine, to let them know of our affairs, and that they are in our hearts evermore.*

Celine smiled aside at Corin. The boy grinned, and his father gave him a proud nod. Berd bowed his head slightly, with a small smile. The boy had shown strength of character, and a will to do right. Several of the lords and their ladies also smiled.

Celine turned back to the letter and sobered. "My lord, Tae appended his answer." She handed it to him, and he squinted at the script. Berd itched for its contents, but she must have a reason not to read it aloud.

"Hmph." The regent made a noncommittal noise and cleared his throat. "It is past Compline, and I am satisfied this assassin was none of Tae Chisun's or Cierheld's doing. That does not absolve you, Berd of Cierheld, of the charge of stealing weapons from the dead."

"No." Berd stared at the sinking sun outside the door. "My lord, may I draw my own blade before you for a moment?"

Durand inclined his head. "You have my leave."

Berd took out his sword and slid home the Damascus steel in its place. With his own across his hands, he stepped forward and laid it on the assassin's body. "I leave my blade in your keeping. This night I must ride for you, for my first daughter Kyrin Cieri, and for Britannia. I will return and submit myself to your judgment if a higher does not find me."

The regent nodded briskly. "So let it be." He beckoned to his first armsman. "Darren will accompany you with five armsmen. Thain knows he must first deal with the house of Cierheld to gain any foothold in our lands. The rest who are with us will be sufficient to hold York if we must. God give you speed, an overcoming arm, and may he smooth your return with Armsmaster Nith and my squads."

Berd bowed. "It shall be done, my Lord Durand Tolman." He cleared his throat, though all could hear the pride in his voice. "My lord, I also beg leave for armsman Henges of Cierheld to depart after Lady Esther on the road toward Keffold and Halwende with Celine. They will free his family. With her help, I am sure they may steal them away."

"It is granted. My men will follow as soon as possible and arrest Lady Esther Govannan, with orders to take her to the nearest convent. There she will bide till the council can sit in judgment. I will also send word to every village and hold of Thain Mornoth's treachery."

Henges grinned, and a huge weight appeared to leave his shoulders. He drew himself up and saluted in the Cierhelden way, fist to his heart, and forehead, with an outward flick of fingers.

"I am happy to assist," Celine said. "I will bring my bow." Her smile was impish. "It appears I have a gift that way."

Corin gave a vigorous nod until his pale hair flopped in his eyes. The tension in the air dissolved in gentle laughter. Men and women rose and began to leave after offering the regent their support, while he assured them of his protection.

Corin looked up at Celine. "I am sure you will bring them home. But that dagger you bear... it has an uncommon shape. Will you keep that close to? Have you ever killed anyone with it?"

"No."

"May I see it?"

The regent raised a brow. Celine blushed and glanced uncertainly at Berd.

"We have until the horses are ready," he said, amused.

She brought the falcon dagger out from hiding.

"Ahhh. May I?" At the regent's request, she laid it in his hand. "So, this is the sigil that brought Kyrin Cieri home." He examined it with wonder and handed it back. "May all who bear it do as well as she in the service of Britannia and her people."

Celine bowed her head. "My lord."

Corin peered at the falcon's deep, sparkling eyes in awe. "The falcon sees... far."

"Yes," Celine said. "Loyal and true hearts do." She looked at Berd.

# 10

# Armsman's Trust

*... a faithful messenger to those who send him. ~ Proverbs 25:13*

Before the inn stables, torches burned bright and wild against the dark night and the wind. Rain was coming. Berd mounted amid a whirl of preparation. Stable boys hurried up with saddlebags of provisions for the men, and another with his arms full of spears.

Darren's half squad armed themselves with a bow and quiver and two spears each, in addition to the blades they carried. He grinned when he noticed Berd's interest. "The Welsh on the other side of the mountains use longbows, like your Lord Dain, but we've taken to the easier pull of your lady's recurve design." He shook his head. "I'd hate to see what you can do with a bow. What you did at your trial was supernatural." He eyed Berd. "How you got close to that filth, and why, and how you tried to stop him, those are not things many men think of."

"But I didn't stop him, and you would be most disappointed by my aim with a shaft."

"You would have had him if Jorren hadn't tried to help you." Darren sighed. "He was a good man. He would have paid a season's coin to see you pull your bonds in front of you, and as for catching that sword," he shook his head. "Even more, your testing of your man will be the talk of the barracks this night. Respect and leadership are so earned." He smiled across Berd at Celine, who sat her horse impatiently, waiting for Henges. "Your Lady Celine's bow work is also unearthly, though you say your aim is poor. Are you sure you are quite of this world?"

"Quite," Berd said. "You would agree if you saw how we train. We aim for versatility in weapons, ability to fight over ground from mountain to moor, the art of surprise and the unexpected, as you saw. There is naught of the other world about it. It is practice, practice that challenges the mind as well as the body. Hope must also be instilled in those who fight, and determination to gain victory. Any man can learn these skills who is not ill. Women are fit in the same way, particularly for wielding the shorter swords and archery." He shrugged. "They have different gifts, but the same vigor of mind." Celine had gained the strength to give him the sword.

He glanced at her. If he did not divert the conversation, she might fire hot words at him or Darren. Besides, curiosity ate at him. "Why did you throw the sword to me?"

Her face sobered in the dancing light, for once without challenge. "When you saw it, your hand twitched that way you always do before a fight. I could tell you ached for it." She settled her mare's uneasy stamp, stroking her neck. "Most blades do not fit me, as you say." She gave a small shrug of one shoulder. "The Damascus steel fits you. You can wield it well, for you are an armsman who knows what he is about." She patted her bow with an arch look. "This fits my hand. I will spend long days with Kilden soon." She reached in a slit of her tunic and handed him the falcon blade. "This will fit Myrna better than I, if Kyrin sees fit. Will you give it to her for me? Oh, there is Henges. I need to ask him what mount to bring for Mary." She nudged the mare away.

Darren laughed. "That's a firebrand, that one, but she seems to suit you, eh?"

"Aye, she has a strength I've seldom seen."

"It's good you are both strong. You will need it. If Armsmaster Nith has trained any of my Lord Durand's men to be like you, he will be well pleased indeed. You are a dangerous man, Berd of Cieri."

Celine soon departed with Henges on Esther's trail, and the regent insisted in the end that ten men went with them immediately. Berd was glad. She and Henges seemed to have struck up a friendship over Mary.

Darren rode with Berd to be sure he kept his word to return to the regent, and to report on any other thing of interest he could discover. Berd did not care. The sword was regained for Cieri, and the rat was found to be not such a rat.

One life renewed made it worth his pain. The scratch that stung his neck and his throbbing forehead were negligible. Now there was Kyrin, her unborn child, and countless others they must save. If Cierheld fell, Britannia itself was in danger. His mouth hardened.

Thain and his mercenaries presented a task that would test everything he had. Nith would know where to place him to make best use of him. Cernalt would demand his report and approve the warning he'd requested the regent send immediately to Alkborough, Fenwrd, and Bolton Abbey.

He grinned wryly. If the riders used all haste, warning would reach the abbey then Alkborough before Vespers the next evening, and Fenwrd after the bell for Compline. He would not reach Cierheld until well after Lauds, or later if delayed by ambush. Scouts and spies would be mobilized, then the squads would take to the field. Still, he would reach Cierheld at least a day ahead of any possible support from Alkborough or Fenwrd.

They did not take the road for Cierheld, but the swiftest, little-used track he knew, and without torches. They kept the best pace the horses could sustain in the dark.

Darren sighed. "My lord regent bids us follow you, within the bonds of my oath."

Berd's smile was in his voice. "I give you both my thanks, as does my Lord Dain Cieri. He would not ask more."

"I am right glad your Celine saved the lad's life."

"So am I. She did well."

"Corin will also do well. He will be a good king; do you not agree?"

Berd grunted. "I'm beginning to think we do not look for an earthly king, but him who comes from above, who will rule this dust. He will make all things right. In that day, the earth will be green again, until he brings in the new heaven and a new earth."

"But will you not support any ruler until that day?"

"Of course; I will support any man who rules lawfully and well. But none of them are our final hope." Berd sighed. "No, you are right about Corin. Holding a place for the best ruler we can aligns with holding a place for the last king. We occupy for him. He approves of righteous rulers." Rolf dared a little more. "It is true, what I told the regent. Brother Rolf, Kilden and others of the abbey watch out for Corin. To protect him they will also seek out Thain, to destroy the brigand and his men, as I do."

"That is well."

They fell silent. They passed across grassy vales and streams, and Berd listened to the rustle of leaves overhead, the clip of hooves on packed earth, and the whispering rush of the storm as it swept down from the northwest mountains. He hoped it slowed Thain, but he doubted it. It could not slow him.

The drizzle stopped eventually. Swaying with weariness, damp linen and leather rubbing unpleasantly, they stopped to rest for a bell at midday in the higher hills to spare the horses. They ate and slept. Then they climbed into their saddles again. As was his habit, Darren sent one of his men to scout ahead, two to guard the flanks, and two to prevent surprise from behind.

Before they reached the pass into Cierheld the next night, Berd called Darren's men in so they would not be cut down as attackers. He knew where the first sentry would be stationed. They approached down the middle of the road in double file at a walk. "Ho, Cieri!" He called low.

"Who comes?" The voice was tense.

"Berd, first armsman of Kyrin Cieri, with Darren, first armsman to Regent Durand Tolman, and a half squad of good men."

"What is afoot?" The sentry's voice tightened further.

Berd swung down, and his legs shook. "Cid, you know me." He knew at least two others waited to attack them if they proved to be enemies. "Do not show a light. Lord Thain Mornoth and a large force are coming, not to mention his band of brigands. We will leave two men with you. If any pass, track their movements and send word."

"Has warning been sent to Alkborough and Fenwrd? Shall we send to Jornhold?"

Berd told him what had passed with the regent, omitting the charge standing against him, and told the sentry what forces he might expect. "Do send word to Jornhold, if you have a man to spare. I should have thought of that myself. Is all well at Cierheld?"

Berd thought the man sighed in the dark. "Sir, you are to go on to the hold. I may not say more." He gave them the watchword for the wall.

Cernalt tied his hands even in this. Berd gritted his jaw silently, and they rode on. At the gate of Cierheld stronghold, past the deepest hour of the night, Berd hailed the wall guard.

The small door in the gate opened. Berd entered alone as ordered, while the other three waited. The wood shut behind him with a thump.

Immediately, two men bore him back against the smooth oak and pinned his arms. They were nothing but dark shapes against the stars.

"What is the meaning of this?" Berd protested. "I gave the watchword."

"Silence." The strange, gruff voice and a sharp point at his side stopped Berd cold. Had Cierheld somehow been taken without a blow struck? The man ordered a torch brought, and did not call for Nith or Cernalt.

When the torch came at the head of another half squad, Berd sagged in relief. Nith's second led them. "Ives, where is Armsmaster Nith? You must get him at once!"

"He and Cernalt are out on patrol. Not to worry, we're only to hold you until Cernalt can speak with you."

"When will he be back, you fool?" That roar bought him a prick from one of the startled guards, and alert tension from Ives and the men behind him.

"Tomorrow."

"Too late," Berd groaned. They were not telling him everything. Of course, Cernalt would wish to speak with him before he went back on duty, if he cleared himself sufficiently of Cernalt's accusation. Doubtful, as he was under the regent's official judgment for a crime that tied into his supposed theft from Cierheld.

"What is going on, first armsman?" The question was respectful but firm.

"Who is in command?"

"I am."

Berd looked at Ives and the dark eyes of the men in the torchlight, three of whom were from his old squad. "There are dark deeds coming, armsmen. Thain Mornoth has betrayed us and attacked the regent's son. We have learned Thain is the brigand. There is more. He has hired men from across the mountains against us. One hundred swords, another hundred archers, five polearm squads, and another five of cavalry. Now, where is my first daughter?" His hands knotted.

Ives swallowed. "She would go for a last ride with the armsmaster before she was confined, to watch the maneuvers with Jornhold in the morn. We could not sway her from it."

Berd slowly straightened. He knew what must be done. "Ives, I must ask you to release me."

"No."

"For the first daughter of Cieri." The guards tightened their grip, and it took all Berd had not to rip free. "By the blade I bear, I will bide under guard as soon as our first armsmaster, Cernalt, and Lady Kyrin are safe in this hold with the rest of the men."

Their gazes flicked to the Damascus blade, and one man shifted uneasily.

"I have my orders," Ives said, a stubborn cast to his mouth.

Berd drew himself up, formal. "What will you do, then?"

"We will send out a messenger, bring everyone in behind the wall, and wait. Alkborough and Fenwrd will certainly send reinforcements."

"If they marched the moment they got word from the regent, none will reach us before the morrow. That's if they kill the horses and themselves to get here. Thain's mercenaries may come before the next bell. Do you know where they are? Who will you send to harry them before they reach us?" He kept unspoken the thought that Kyrin must be retrieved.

Sweat gleamed on Ives' cheek. He looked to the men holding Berd. "Take him to his quarters and guard him well."

Berd let them bring his hands behind him and made one last effort. "Don't do this, Ives."

"I am sorry, first armsman. I must."

"Have our people been warned?" Berd asked, then feinted toward the man on the right only to throw himself on top of the man least enamored with his work. Berd bore the guard to the ground and rolled off him, snatching a dagger from his sheath. Aric, Berd's old second, smiled.

Berd spun to his feet and reached Ives in two steps. He disarmed him as he attempted to draw his blade and struck him in the temple with his own hilt. Ives crumpled in his arms. Berd lowered him to the ground, leaning Nith's second back against his legs. He rapped, "Aric, tell your man to hold that torch high and steady. Everyone must see what happens here." The torch holder snapped straight. "Good man."

Berd eyed the guard he had winded on the ground. "Call out every man in the barracks."

"Yes, sir." He rolled to his feet, saluted, and went.

"Aric, how many men do we have in Cierheld?"

"Two tensquads, sir!"

"Very well. Send someone to alert the hall. Get someone to look at Ives. Put the best ten men we have on the wall. The stables are to prepare horses for the remaining tensquad. The kitchen will stock food, hot oil for gate rammers, and water buckets for fire arrows as needed against a siege, if it comes. The tensquad guarding the walls is to bring all our people and readily available stores inside the stronghold. You are with me."

"Yes, sir!" Aric gave quick commands, and in moments the yard was busy as an anthill.

The man in the barracks bellowed, "Night drill! Night drill!" at the top of his lungs. Men answered. A light lit in the hall, a dog barked, and a horse neighed, kicking its stall.

At the top of the hall steps, a woman gave orders to a servant. It was Myrna, clad in Subak training clothes. She ran down the steps toward Berd.

At attention, Aric looked at Berd sidelong.

Berd growled, "What I told Ives stands. We have much to do, first."

Aric grinned. "Certainly, sir. Let me open the gate for the regent's men, sir."

Berd braced his shaking legs. "Very well. I must speak with Lady Myrna." She would know more than Ives would tell. He wondered if the southlords were involved. Now they would see the fruit of Henges' work. He prayed it was not catastrophic.

"Myrna! Where is my lady?"

Myrna halted in front of him, breathing hard, and wasted no time on greetings. "I do not know. I would think they are on their way back from Jornhold. They were to take the vale road." Myrna glanced behind him at the regent's men. "Where is Celine?"

"We may have to guard against a force from Halwende." Berd told her what passed with the regent and Thain, and of Henges and Celine's task.

She stared at him, wide-eyed. "Then it seems we must stand as best we can."

"Yes. Celine and Henges mean to haste here after they release his family from Esther's grip. For now, you will have this." He laid the falcon dagger in her hand. "Hold it in trust. For Kyrin." He touched her shoulder gently. "Fear not for Celine. She knows her strength now, and Henges and a squad of the regent's men are with her. They will look after each other." If Henges did not, he would answer to him.

Berd did not know when he had come to love Celine. It had been a slow thing. How he hoped they would not lose each other.

He drew a choked breath. "Whatever servants can bear arms, send them to the wall."

"We will do what we can." She looked at him, a strangely piercing glance. "You are an honorable man. Celine is blessed, as am I, to know you." Her hand tightened on the falcon. He thought she was near tears.

"Thank you, Myrna. Do not discount yourself." He did not know what else to say. He inclined his head and turned away.

Aric suggested Berd, Darren, and his armsmen take rest during the bell it would take to prepare the stronghold and ready the tensquad. Berd did not think he could sleep but surprised himself. Before the bell rang for Prime, he woke to Aric's hand on his shoulder.

## 11

# Pierce and Protect

*From my deadly enemies, who surround me. ~ Psalms 17:9*

Thain Mornoth inspected the ranks drawn up before him with a wide smile. He had employed a host of seamstresses at Keffold, and each torch embroidered on a wood-brown tunic was a work of craft in a fiery flame that licked the night. The old would burn, the new be forged.

He had arrayed his longbow archers across from the river road along the ridge, just inside the edge of the forest where they would be protected and able to fire down on any Cierheldens below. He would keep to the high ground opposite and force them to cross the river after him. Concealed men waited there, too. He would guard the way to Keffold and his return in triumph.

The brigands would mop up any who strayed into the woods on the Jornhold side. Some forty more men had joined them, the discontented or outcasts of the south who streamed to his promise of plunder, bringing their number to seventy. He'd caught two of Cernalt's men trying to infiltrate among them. He scowled.

They were dead; Thorgil had dealt with them summarily. He hoped the cunning old armsman rode with Nith. He could cut down two problems at a stroke.

When he took Cierheld, he would remove any chance of an heir. Then they would hold it against Dain and Talik's forces. Better yet, he would destroy them separately as they rode for the hold while they were strung out along the road. De Re Militari would never be infernally joined with the defiant spirit and skill of Subak. Not in his kingdom. His teeth glinted. It would fade away as if it had never been.

A scout trotted up on his mount, one of the archers, armed with bow and sword. "My lord, they are about a mile down the road, coming in good order, but unaware. There is a woman with them, heavy with child. She rides well protected, with a silver-haired armsman beside her who carries the short sword and shield of the old Eagles."

Thain straightened in his saddle, excitement coursing through him. "It cannot be!"

The scout bowed his head. "She is the daughter of Lord Dain Cieri, my lord."

Thain grinned. "As Thorgil says, Odin smiles on us." He remembered Esther's kiss before their last parting. Her words had been sweet. *Be not long on the road, my love. I will meet you at Halwende.*

He would send a message of triumph before the day was out, with a note to take the head of Henges' brat. Evil deeds could not go unrewarded.

§

Berd led Aric and the tensquad within the edge of the oaks growing upon the hillside. The sun peeped over the ridge of the dale. Light filtered through the trees and across the track before them, warming their dawn-chilled faces. A green acorn plunked onto his saddle and rolled over the shield leaning against his knee. The scent of oak leaves swirled on the dawn wind under their horses' hooves. The grass whispered.

Peace was so elusive. But to keep it, there must be war. If he did nothing, mercy and justice would be gone. He wondered if his men were ready. Further up the hill, dew thick grass swished.

Berd threw up his hand. The squad stopped instantly. He glanced at Darren. The regent's armsman gave a signal and one of his men legged his horse along the hill in the opposite direction of the noise, while another slipped away to circle behind. The rest waited, hands on spear, sword, and bow. Berd checked the cap on the five javelins nestled in the hollow of his shield. It was ready for instant removal.

Nothing was visible but tree and grass swaying in the wind, under the call of crickets. They ceased. Berd held his breath.

The wren's scold for 'all clear' sounded. He remained alert, but soon the rider returned with another man mounted behind him. The Cierheld scout slid down and ran to Berd.

"Thain's men hold the river crossing and the road that turns for Bolton. They may let you into the trap, but not out of it." He reported no knowledge of Kyrin or Nith.

Berd grinned at him. "Do we wish to get out?" He turned to the men ranged behind. "Stay close on me! We must hasten, but attack as the field warrants. Of first importance is the safety of Lady Kyrin and our armsmaster. For the last hand of seasons, we have trained. We have been forged. Now comes our tempering. For Cieri!"

With an answering shout, they streamed down the hill after him. The ground flew away beneath thudding hooves. Staying off the road, they swung wide, out of hearing of the cavalry posted where the scout warned them. At last, they slowed. The dale split ahead, one arm of the vale swinging toward Bolton and the other, Jornhold. He wished for the men to warn Nith, but he could be anywhere. It was a small comfort that he never moved without scouts.

Dismounting, they left the horses below the crest of a rise. Berd, Aric, and Darren crawled to the top. Below them, the vale parted. Both ways were empty.

The dusty road for Bolton wound beside the water through stretches of grass and wood until the dale side rose in a wooded slope on their left. The same forested dale side rose opposite, flanking the rutted track to Jornhold.

Berd pointed ahead at the dividing ridge. "From that high point, we can move to the left or right from a place of strength."

Aric grunted. "We may also study the ground from outside their net, if it is not already occupied, and watch for movement the scout missed."

Berd nodded. "Nith may come on either road, depending on the distance their war games with Lord Jorn extended. It is strange we have seen no enemy scouts. I think we may be sure they are there. Yet Thain is ever confident of his superiority." He shrugged. "With his numbers. it is not unreasonable."

Darren looked at him. "Do you foresee defeat?"

"No. Only his mind. We must bring our small numbers to bear on his weakness. He has foolishly spread himself over three long fronts, setting his forces here at the parting ways instead of further up the vale, where he could bottle two ends easily, with men five deep. Still, it is not likely we will reach the ridge unchallenged."

The regent's first armsman frowned. "If they do see us, they will be loath to move and give away their positions."

Aric sighed. "They know we must fight them sooner or later."

"True." Berd grimaced. "Thain would not spring the trap early and warn off his prey. But we must be wary of squads like ours that may have changed position and be lying in wait. For us or Nith."

Swiftly, they rejoined the squad and Darren's men. Barely had they started across the vale when Aric lifted his spear. "There, sir! A flash of movement along the Jornhold track."

Berd stared. A flicker of black and a dot of blue and yellow. None other wore those colors. "It's Nith. Form up!" If they moved fast, they could reach the armsmaster and Kyrin, then take the higher, little-used path for Cierheld that diverged from the Jornhold road further south, and outrun Thain's men to the hold. Or turn for Jornhold.

He kicked his mount into a trot and removed the cap on his javelins, shoving the leather into the shield cavity beside them.

A faint shout on their left, and a distant line of swordsmen rose from concealment below the riverbank. Over a quarter mile away, they could not hope to engage before Berd's squad reached the woods ahead. Two polearm squads burst from a copse at the bottom of the ridge near the Jornhold road. Boots quick, they trotted at the double, weapon tips twinkling overhead. They would cut the squad off.

Berd pulled a wooden whistle from his tunic. The high scream of a falcon split the air twice. Nith would not miss that signal. Berd's men broke into a thundering run after him to crush the enemy squads who dared stand between them and Nith.

Blood rushed in Berd's ears as he leaned into the wind. He must engage the polearms before they reached Kyrin. She would be their first target. He desperately hoped Darren's men knew how to use their bows. He had instructed them to pick off archers or anyone closing with Kyrin. If only Celine was here. She would be a fiery force of protection at Kyrin's back.

Lean and straight, Nith raised his sword. He stood with the men to bolster their courage. Two of Cierheld's squads snapped into a double line, ten mounted men behind ten swordsmen, all shields out. The third squad faced the rear, ready.

Berd pressed his lips tighter. Sword against polearm was not the best tactic. Polearms had more than triple the reach of a blade. If one somehow managed to deflect the heavy weapon for a thrust, then, and only then, the advantage became the blade's. Attempting it was hazardous.

Kyrin kept to her black stallion, Cauldron, and Cernalt to his mount, doubtless ordered to be ready for any opening for escape. Kyrin straightened, lifting a bow across her swollen belly, her dark hair braided back, and adjusted a quiver at her knee.

Berd's heart leaped. She was not defenseless. *Lord, guard us and guide us, heart and hand.*

Nith warily backed the group into the tree cover, herding the horses before them as another layer of protection for the first daughter of Cieri.

Closer, closer. Berd could see the eyes of a helmed man ahead. Instead of rushing Nith's force, the polearm squad leader shouted, and the ten men facing Berd lowered arms, a phalanx of wicked spikes. The front squad did the same and advanced on Nith.

Aric raised his spear. "Cieri! Cieri!"

Darren was at his shoulder crying, "The regent! For Corin!" Two of his men loosed arrows.

"For Cierheld!" Berd lifted his spear, and they all roared the last cry. And closed.

Berd deflected a sharp polearm from his face with his shield. Instantly, he twisted aside to avoid one aimed at his chest. Then leaned across his horse's neck to strike down a third whistling for his mount's legs. He thrust his spear into a man who darted in to snag him from his seat like a hooked fish.

All was dust and movement, danger and focus. Then he was past the first rank and urging his mount to greater speed, gaining on the backs of the men between him and Kyrin. He slid the first javelin from his shield.

"Sir!" Aric bellowed.

Berd spared a glance back. Behind his second, more than two squads of mounted lancers galloped along the road. But he did not point behind, but ahead. Berd whipped back around.

Men marched half-seen through the trees beyond Nith. They cried, "Keffold! Keffold and Lord Thain!" The chant stopped, as the first of the brigands engaged Nith's left flank.

Cierheld's forces were surrounded. Yet Thain had more men unaccounted for. Tucking that in the back of his brain, Berd whirled his horse, its sides heaving.

Nith cried behind him, "Slings!"

"Form up!" Berd yelled. He must trust Kyrin and leave Nith for the moment. Aric made it to his left hand and Darren growled up on his right, cursing the bleeding cut over his brow. The others straggled up around them, minus three who had fallen. "Tighten rank!" Dirty and bloodied, they obeyed. He turned to Darren. "Wait and follow as you can." To his squad he called, "Veruta!" Those who had spears yet in their hands hastily cast them at the remainder of the polearm squad they had just overrun. They missed. Hoots rose from the polearms men as they hurried aside to make way for the charging cavalry.

Berd glanced along his line. All held the shorter javelin in hand. "Aim. Cast!"

Seven javelins arced through the air. All struck their targets, enemy shield or beast. A horse rolled, head over tail. Neither beast nor rider rose again.

"Aim. Cast!"

There was no hooting now. Men dropped shattered shields, each stuck with a heavy, unwieldy pole, and horses broke formation. Their attackers were too scattered for a third cast. Berd did a hasty reassessment. If he could apply the things they had learned, it might turn the tide.

The trap was sprung, only it had caught something larger than Thain knew.

"Combine tactics!" he called sharply and had the men's instant attention. "Spread!" At the riders' signal of hand and foot, each horse sidestepped, almost dancing. Their ranks opened. Darren watched with his mouth open. "Pick your opposite man!" Each tracked one opponent. Their mounts stood rock still, haunches bunched.

*"Se jok!"* Berd dropped his arm. The men each shot for their chosen enemy at a dead gallop. Guiding their mounts with legs alone, they lifted their javelins across their chests. They closed with a shock of passage.

No beast collided. No force was used against force. In silence, each warrior evaded his man's blow and unhorsed him by a strike to the back of the neck at the base of his helm as he passed; by flicking a leg free from a saddle; by a cross-body strike to the collarbone. Three men fell, each to a weakness in balance or position. Then the rest. All but one broke bones as they landed.

Berd hung back. Noting which man gave orders that turned the cavalry toward Nith's squads, he plucked a javelin and threw, and followed it in. The leader tumbled out of his saddle.

The few remaining horsemen converged on Berd. Darren charged the first that went for his flank with a yell, sword out. His men followed and acquitted themselves well. The rest of Thain's horsemen angled away from the skirmish.

Aric circled their squad after the fleeing horsemen. Berd and Darren came in with them on Nith's left. The squads merged as if they had never been apart. Thrusting swords in the air, they cried, "Cieri!" and gave a rousing cheer.

The woods' edge was littered with bodies. Many were Thain's, most without blood upon them. Protected behind the front line, his mount blowing, Darren looked at Berd. "Slings and lead shot," Cieri's first armsman said. "They are as good as bows at short range, and it is not apparent you have them."

The regent's first armsman chuckled and shook his head.

Nith strode through the press and reached up to grip Berd's hand. Berd bowed his head. "First armsmaster. Where are the brigands?"

"They have retreated, for the moment. You are well come. As are you, first armsman." Nith bowed to the regent's man.

Berd glanced over the grinning squads at Kyrin, who gave him a wan smile. She was pale but whole and rested one hand on her stomach. "He kicks, thanks to you."

"Where is Ives?" Cernalt stared up at him, arms crossed. "I ordered you detained."

Suddenly weary to his bones, Berd dismounted and handed his rein to Aric. He came to attention. "Sir, I took command and removed him to the care of the healer."

"Why?"

"There was need." His courage failed him. He dared not look at Nith.

"I ask again, why did you disobey your commanding officer?"

Cernalt meant to pin him down. With Thain coming there was no time.

Kyrin looked at him in alarm. But he had to stand on his own; she must trust him in this. Every man must face the consequences of his doing. His men must not be blamed. "Ives would keep all inside the hold and wait for reinforcements. This endangered our first daughter."

"So, you took command."

"Yes." Berd took his courage in both hands. He might never come before the regent's judgment. That thought must not be allowed to influence him.

"Your men followed your rash action."

"No. I commanded them. They obeyed."

Cernalt snorted. Aric cleared his throat, and Berd shot him a quelling glance.

Kyrin bit her lip, hands white on her rein. She looked between them and said nothing.

Berd was grateful and proud. Their first daughter showed great trust in him and Nith and Cernalt, in their judgment. His companions were worthy of her trust, as was every man here. They were proven. Unconsciously, his mouth tilted up.

Cernalt closed with him, nose to nose. "You dare smile?" The hawkmaster smelled of clean woods and sweat, and his grizzled chin and scarred cheek spoke of enduring loyalty.

Yet he could kill him in a blink, if Berd gave him cause. "I do not smile at what I did, sir." Berd stared back, not giving an inch, calm and quiet. He would wait one more moment, and then he would take himself out of the way. So they could deal with the problem at hand. The swordsmen were coming. And where were Thain and his remaining men? They had seen nary an archer.

Nith asked, "Would you do it again?"

Berd twitched. He did not take his eyes from Cernalt. "Yes, sir." The hawkmaster would have to accept that, or not.

Incredibly, Cernalt glanced up at Nith and nodded. Then grinned. "So is a new armsmaster tested. He flew true."

Nith smiled at Berd. "It seems answers have been found, and your mettle forged for the hour of our need. You have learned well."

Berd reddened, so angry with Cernalt and relieved by Nith that he shook.

Cernalt clapped him on the shoulder. "Come, our trial is not yet over."

"No, for a hundred swordsmen come on my tail," Berd said tightly.

"The scouts will sound the whistle before they reach range." Cernalt grinned, blue eyes dancing with delight.

"But there are another two squads at least of cavalry and polearms, with a hundred archers from over the mountains. Those are only the ones we know of. There may be more."

Nith's face tightened. He nudged his horse aside and directed five more men to spread out and search for the enemy, while Cernalt rapped at Berd, "Who told you this?"

"Henges."

"Ah. So, he took the sword, but did the right thing?"

"You knew he took it?" Berd gaped at him.

"The chimney was a logical hiding place. I suspected, and checked to confirm when the way was clear. I left it. We needed to know his allegiance."

"His heart is with you," Darren broke in crisply. Still mounted, he scanned the horizon. He looked down. "Not least because of this man's actions." He grinned at Berd. "Now Henges and your lady's young lass," he nodded to Kyrin, "pursue an errand on behalf of the regent." He told them the rest and looked like he wanted to spit when he spoke of Esther.

Cernalt eyed the regent's first armsman. "I think we will have an ale together when this is done."

"It would be my pleasure." Darren's gaze on each was sharp. "But on my lord regent's behalf, what do we face here?"

Nith said, "A man who would take the kingship and grind other men into the dust."

"We stand in his way." Kyrin sat on Cauldron's proud back, eyes afire. "My lord father declares the heirs of my line no threat to Regent Durand Tolman or Corin. We seek no kingship, but that each man should rule his heart under God and rightful authority."

"There are more in the north and south of Lord Thain and Lady Esther's mind than you think." There was a wry twist to Cernalt's mouth.

"It has always been so. Many men hunt for power and position." Berd shook his head. "Yet we hold hearts in a trust that must not be broken." His gaze reached for Kyrin. "Your heir will find me at his side, Master of the stars willing."

Kyrin smiled. "May it be so." Then she bent over with a small gasp, face tensing in pain.

12

# Treachery's Truth

*He is like a lion that is eager to tear. ~ Psalms 17:12*

"My lady!" The men gave way for him, and Berd touched her saddle. A wet stain spread upon it. There was helplessness and determination in her eyes. A pit opened in Berd's stomach. The heir was coming. They would both fight for him.

Nith saw what had happened at once. "Berd Stronghand, your first charge as first armsmaster of Alkborough, is to get Lady Kyrin Cieri back to Cierheld. If the regent's armsman wills it, he will go with you and the rest of your squad."

"Yes, armsmaster."

Across the road and two hundred yards off, the falcon's shrill call of warning rang out.

"One moment." Cernalt held out his hand. "My lady? Step down and give me your cloak. Quickly now, before they are in sight." He switched his cloak for hers, mounted Cauldron, and balled an extra tunic before him, pulling the cloak over the round bulge.

Berd helped Kyrin mount another horse, with a heartfelt nod for Cernalt's consideration, and bid one of the youths sit before her as if wounded, to conceal her condition. Shy, the boy said, "I am Hadwin, lady. Lean on me all you need."

From the ridge in front of them, another cry of the falcon rang down the wind.

Their enemies were close. Darren tied a rag about his head with swift fingers, and a couple other men bound small wounds, then Berd turned his horse's head east. When Darren raised a brow, Berd said, "We will cut behind them over the top of the ridge, go down, cross the river, and run parallel at their rear on the other side of the dale. Then travel up the vale until we reach Cierheld." There were no questions.

"Go now!" Nith cried. "May the Master of All go with you!" At that moment, with a shout, archers burst from the tree cover of the ridge above. Their ploy was too late. "Back! Back inside the line!"

Berd obeyed swiftly, Kyrin's rein in his hand. Immense tiredness crashed over him. It was hard to stand. He helped Hadwin and Kyrin dismount and leaned close. *"Pil sung,"* he whispered.

She translated Tae's tongue with a small smile. "Certain victory through courage, strength, and indomitable spirit."

"Do not lose heart. Be ready. Can you watch the horses? We may yet need them."

She sat on a mossy stump and nodded. "Watch your back."

"I have Aric for that." Berd smiled reassurance.

Aric grinned.

Kyrin wrapped the reins about her arm, opening her water flask for a wounded man on the ground beside her.

"Here, my lady." Darren knelt, taking the flask from her.

"Shields! Circle, circle!" Nith called.

Hadwin rejoined his squad, while Berd stayed by Kyrin, shield up.

"Arrows!"

Shield overlapped shield as the front row knelt, the second row crouched, and those in the middle stood around Berd as the center point. The arrows struck, rattling over them in a whistling wave. Most thunked into the ground on the far side like a hedgehog's back. A few men fell.

A cry rose on the south side of the circle. "Polearm squad!"

Nith roared, "Ready the *fragor!* Three!"

There was a hissing crackle and smell of burning rope.

Another hail of arrows.

"Slide shields! Throw!" Shields moved apart and together.

*Carump!*

Men screamed.

Darren's head jerked up. Two more explosions. Berd caught the scent of the horror he once faced at Cierheld's gate. This time, she would not fall.

"Ready *fragor!* Five!" called Nith.

Five more roars of noise and the sound of wounded men followed.

Arms cramping, Berd watched Kyrin look at Darren in the dimness under the shields, remembered fear in her face. "The black powder has great power. After Mornoth's attacks, our smith has been curious, I deem, and has fashioned a small device for use against our enemies." Her smile held a little of the solemn imp, then she curled around another pain. He reached for her, and she waved him off. "Old Margye swears the first babe takes its sweet time." There was sweat on her forehead.

"Slide shields! Throw!"

With every blast, the ground shook.

Up the ridge behind the archers came a wild hawk's cry. Another call from the woods, and then faint near the river. "Sorcery!" a man cried.

Kyrin's brow furrowed.

Others of the polearm squad and archers took up the call, "Witchery!"

"Cease!" Thain's voice rose over the din. "Are we women to fear sound and flame?"

Kyrin shook her head, and Darren returned her small smile. Berd's mouth quirked, shaking. They did not know his first daughter quailed at nothing.

"Archers, stand down!" Thain said, as if disgusted with the conflict. "Come out, Nith."

Nith signaled. Shields dropped into wall position with precise thumps. On the west side of the circle, some of the men with polearms jumped. Shield-arm down, staring through a crack in the shield wall, Berd had eyes for none but Thain.

Helm under his arm, the young lord impatiently elbowed aside the man who moved to his shoulder. The commander of the polearm squads bent over, wheezing.

Ignoring him, Thain spun his drawn sword and looked along the blade. "You are a worthy man, Nith. I did not expect to lead a merry chase after my prize around the dale." He sheathed his weapon. "Your skill is greater than I heard. Come, let us speak. I am a reasonable man."

Shield up, Nith stepped out of formation. The wall closed behind him. "I am here."

"Ah. We will speak face to face." Thain moved closer, arrogantly waving back the lead archer who moved to cover him. The man scowled, and Berd grinned.

Thain was three lengths from Nith. "I see two choices open to us. I may kill you all, or we may come to terms."

"And your terms?"

Thain rubbed his chin as if in thought. "If you yield to us Kyrin Cieri, we will wait until the heir is born. If it is a boy, he will die, and we will return your first daughter to you. If it is a daughter, both shall live." He shrugged.

A growl rose from the men, and Berd clenched his jaw. This man would die. He saw the same fire in Nith's eyes.

"Do you think us imbeciles?" Nith's voice was calm, almost curious.

Thain sighed. "I did not think you would take my first offer. Is your first daughter even with you?"

"She is."

"I would see proof. Or we may just keep shooting and pounding until you all feed the crows." He shrugged, and raised a hand, ready to signal his archers.

A falcon called overhead, brave and free against the sun.

Kyrin moved. "Help me up."

Berd opened his mouth, but her fierce glare made him close it. The regent's armsman gently helped her to her feet and kept her arm so she leaned against him. Anxiously, Berd stepped in front of her.

Her clear voice rose. "I am here, Thain Mornoth. The men of Britannia do not love oath breakers and murderers of women and children. You are not wise to be here."

"Ah, my lady. So kind of you to join our conversation." Thain smiled. "You may not stand in the way of the great reset. The new must rise, and the old die. It is the nature of things. A new tree must be set in fresh ground for it to grow well." He shrugged again. "A man must craft his destiny."

"I already stand in the way of this reset, as you name it. But what of your oath given?"

Thain paused. "No oath among men is worth an alliance that heralds betterment. I have outworn it. Against the mighty oak of a land remade, my oath is nothing."

"Your heart is revealed." Kyrin squeezed Darren's hand with a gasp, her eyes sliding shut.

"As is yours." Thain laughed. "But you cannot truly mean to throw your life away for these dogs."

She lifted her head. "That is where we differ, between those you name dogs and I name noble men." She nudged Berd forward and stepped up behind the ranks, laying her hand on a man's shield, asking him to lower it.

Berd said, "Don't do this, Kyrin."

She caught her breath, whispered, "We must force his hand. Give Nith an opening."

Berd's mouth set.

"Ah, there you are, my lady," Thain said softly.

Berd did not see his gesture that loosed the arrow. He was in front of Kyrin when it slammed into his shield, pushing him into her. Darren caught her under the arms.

Berd regained his feet, searching for Nith and Thain.

Cernalt bawled, "First line, swords! Second line, slings! Third line, reserve!"

Berd saw Nith's back as he rushed Thain. The traitor readied his dagger and whipped his arm down, aiming at Kyrin. Berd choked as he sprang to cover her.

Nith stepped into the weapon's path.

The blow shook him to his heels. He stumbled forward into Thain and bore him down. The first armsman's blade rose and fell once, twice, then he collapsed atop his enemy. Neither moved.

With a shout, the archers drew swords, lest they shoot their companions on the other side of the defending circle. The Cierheldens gave a wordless roar. The swordsmen from the river charged.

And then the wood came alive.

Cries of "A Jorn! A Jorn! Bolton and the abbey!" tore the air.

"The prince and the king to come!" a voice shouted, and five more squads carried the cry as they marched out of the trees.

On their flank, a rough crowd of men with scythes, pitchforks, cudgels, and staves surged for the line of swordsmen. Berd saw a man waving a smith's hammer thunder in, and another with a butcher knife.

Kyrin lifted her whistle to her lips, and the cry of the falcon soared over all. It was repeated on every side, and the bird above answered. Thain's forces drew into a great knot, finding themselves surrounded.

The nearest man glared at Berd, as his polearm commander snapped orders behind him. The man spat in the dust, eyes wild, ready to sell his life dear.

Berd tensed. "Hold! Men of Cieri, hold!"

Cernalt added his voice. "Hold, men! Look to the Lady Cieri!" That stopped the villagers' headlong rush as nothing else could.

In the hush, Kyrin groaned. "The babe comes. Get me home."

Berd stalked outside the shield wall and rested the point of the Damascus blade on the earth. His voice was formal as he addressed the commander. "My lady is to be gotten to safe haven no matter the coin we must spend. But it need not be your blood. You may take these men back where you came from. Or remain and pay the price. Any man who surrenders will have his life. The choice is yours."

A man with a bow over his shoulder said, "Even I, who shot at the lady?" He slowly laid his bow on the grass and went to his knees. His voice shook with shame. "I deserve death."

Kyrin stumbled out of the circle on Darren's arm. Wavering, she made her way to the man, Berd guarding her side. "Even you. You have my pardon." She looked at them all. "Which is it to be?"

Weapons tumbled to the ground.

Soon after, Berd leaned over his horse's neck, urging it to greater speed. Its mane stung his face. He left Cernalt to care for Nith's body, to relieve the captives of their weapons, and disperse the remaining men. Kyrin rode moaning behind him with an honor guard of five squads. Among them, Abbot Alton's ten-squad under Seldon, and one squad of Jorn's. It was the hour to uphold his oath. For Dain Cieri and the heir, for his Lord and land. He must get Kyrin to Margye.

§

It was a Seven-day after Thain's defeat. Myrna walked through the woods between Cierheld and Halwende. She was out of breath but smiling. Kyrin's twins were small but perfectly formed and healthy. This night saw their name day feast. She could hardly wait to hold them again.

Her smile faltered. Celine had asked her to watch Kyrin's back. She had been little enough use there.

Berd had returned with Kyrin after he led Cierheld to victory, and Margye delivered the heirs with paltry assistance from Myrna. Henges had retrieved his family with Celine's help, and the regent's men held her in immense respect. Myrna looked down at the falcon dagger that rested in her sash.

Berd had given it to her in trust. Waiting for Kyrin, waiting for the outcome of the battle, waiting for a force from Halwende that never came, waiting had used up her strength. This morn was the first she rose from her bed, to search out herbs for Kyrin's babes with Margye.

She was glad Celine had come into her own as an expert archer. Berd never had betrayed them; that was now clear. He would never hurt Celine as Esther had. Myrna sighed. She was happy for Celine, and she ought not to be the slightest bit jealous. He was a worthy man.

Cernalt had asked her, when the time came, to keep her eyes and ears open in Alkborough school, to find the worm in their apple. But what could she possibly hear, besides dreary gossip among those who sought her company for ends of their own, endless speculation about which lord thought what about the regent, or recipes for herbal remedies that never worked for her?

Myrna ran a thumb over the warm metal of the falcon. That was not quite true. Just days past, a wasp, the naughty jasper, flew in her window and stung her when someone outside disturbed its nest. She had been glad of her salve recipe, for it killed the pain more than ought else she'd tried, and quite reduced the swelling. And it had cured Gwenich, poor pup, when she nearly scratched her belly fur off. Myrna had simply not found the right herb for her consuming weakness. Though if she did not recover, that was also the mercy of him who knew all things.

Margye was a friend indeed. With her teaching, she could find much of use, to her and others. Myrna fought a sudden rush of tears. A looming sense of darkness and death stalked her, as it often did when she was weary.

Angrily, she wiped the tears away. She felt better today. It would not do to spoil another moment with maundering. She was outside, walking with Margye, and that was a blessing. She would get to see the meadow. They were not far from the hold.

Margye strode ahead, an iron kettle in her hand. The old woman looked a witch on her way to nefarious council about a night fire, though they were only after teasel as the shadows of afternoon drew down, broken by shafts of red gold between the thick trees.

The shadows were deep in the glen, but old Margye was fearless, chattering away. "Teasel be good against ailments of the stomach, ye know." She shook her head, sobering. "Little Ellen took the grippe, at Halwende. With the sweats and weakness and all. Celine told me this morn. Poor mite." Margye hiked the kettle higher. "It's well ye're wantin' to apprentice; the herblore is always needful. Tha's never enough of us."

Slowing to catch her breath, Myrna noted that teasel leaves formed a basin about the stem, collecting water to form Venus' bath, an invigorating drink.

The old woman went on, "The tea cleanses the bodily humours, and lessens the effect of fever and grippe tha' takes a child so easy."

Myrna nodded. The grippe could not come near the babies. Margye wandered ahead. Behind them a stick cracked, twice.

That was no falling branch. Myrna looked over her shoulder, wishing she had brought a staff. Nothing but the trunks of ash and alder. All she had besides the falcon blade was her eating dagger that doubled as an herb-digging tool. They were almost to the clearing that extended along both sides of the stream. She could smell the damp musk of it, the green of grass and meadow flowers, where the teasel grew thick. She walked faster.

The thud of feet hastened.

"Margye!" she called and broke into a run.

A man grabbed her from behind, his hand descending over her mouth. Myrna twisted, going for the falcon. His fingers closed over hers, and she dropped the dagger with a cry of pain.

She knew that hand, large as a bear's paw, the long pale hair, loose but braided back at the temples. Knew those broad shoulders as he jerked her around to face him. Thorgil.

"How dare you follow me, wench! This time yer' will not escape." Thorgil grinned. She would have screamed but could not. "There are other ships in the sea, other lords about the regent, and other ways to power. Lord Thain was ever a prancing cock, till he lost his head for overweening pride." He shook her, fingers digging in around her mouth, her head snapping back and forth. "Odin's breath, the hour of the brigand has come," he exulted. Blackness swirled. He slammed her up against a tree, teeth bared. "Cierheld is mine."

Her sleeve tore. His hand on her mouth slipped. But behind him stood a beast of darkness and flame.

Myrna knew it instantly. The tiger crouched, eyes locked on his back. It took the tiniest, silent step. She got out a scream.

Thorgil hit her so hard she sagged and would have fallen if he did not hold her up. Half senseless, she saw his leather boot toes dwarfing hers.

In scorn, he whispered, "I'll soon have another, more comely than ye. Any I want."

The falcon gleamed among the fallen leaves. The sun glinted across it. And Kyrin's verses fell bright in her mind. *A fall to worse than beast, where evils on us feast.*

There was a blur of motion. A thunk, the sound of a melon when it breaks, and Thorgil fell.

She slid down the trunk.

In a moment, old Margye leaned over her. "Look at me, lass. Are ye much hurt?" Her voice was anxious. "Yer' nose is bleedin' fierce."

Myrna found she could sit, swaying. "Thorgil," she gasped.

"Ah." Margye held her kettle ready and turned. Her shoulders straightened. "He will harm none again."

Putting her hand to her head, Myrna pulled herself up. The tiger looked at her, watching in endless hunger and hate. It licked its muzzle.

Then the beast turned and walked away. *Nor we, evil becoming, ever cease, where the tiger hides under fleece. Unless our hands take the blood of the least; revel in our Lord's sacrifice, joy, and love feast.* A shiver of horror ran over her. She was safe, but Thorgil had been taken.

Seemingly brought down by an old woman's kettle, he would go down in tales of ignominy about the winter fires. Her gaze caught on his feet. There was something about them she must remember.

The noise of approach brought her around too fast.

She clutched the tree, searching the woods. Margye grabbed the falcon and drew it along the edge of the pot, rasping with a sword's hiss of drawn steel. "Get ye gone, brigand! Here be one itching to try her steel on ye, trained by the first daughter of Cieri herself! Yer' companion is dead."

The footsteps paused, the man still out of sight. "Ha, witch! You but add bile to our wrath. Our hour is come."

Margye said loudly, "Myrna, shall his blood water the earth?"

Myrna sucked in a breath and spat red. *Fierce cry, in the sky, wild and high.* The falcon in Margye's hand called her to endurance. By the act was the fear broken.

She shouted in a voice stronger than she thought possible, "Armsmen, circle the oak! He must not get away! Swift!" She but guessed at the man's location. The oak was the only sizable tree near.

With a curse, the brigand crashed away. Myrna glimpsed his dark form disappearing through the trees toward the stream. It emptied into the river, where he surely had a boat. "He's making for a boat!" She wobbled forward.

"Wait!" Margye grabbed her elbow. "If Thorgil led the brigands, his second knows where his men are. They may be near. We must get ye back to Cierheld and warn Lady Kyrin, then see yer' head is not too rattled." She crossed her arms, forbidding Myrna to endanger herself, forgot she held the dagger and dropped it.

Myrna picked up the falcon. She stared after the fleeing man. A hunger for justice and immense sorrow filled her, and she came as close to cursing as she ever had.

# 13

# Breath and Bone

*Death and life are in the power of the tongue. ~ Proverbs 18:21*

When Myrna and Margye finally dashed through Cierheld's gate, they ran into Berd, leading out his mount.

Myrna gasped, "We found Ives on the way. He has taken the men to a pitched battle. He wants to catch the brigands at the river crossing. They are coming! Margye killed him."

"Margye killed who?" Berd gripped her arms. "Who's coming? What happened to your face? Who attacked you?"

Myrna winced, and he released her.

"Thorgil. He thought I followed him in the woods. He said the hour of the brigand was come. Something about other ships in the sea, other lords near the regent, and other ways to power." She grabbed his sleeve, gulping air. "There's—more. I remember. Brother Rolf mentioned the brigand. Thorgil—his feet were huge. Thain's weren't, at court."

Berd spun. "Get inside the hall!" He shouted up to the watch on the wall, "'Ware the gate!"

Within a half hour of pandemonium, Lord Dain, Bergrin Jorn, and Talik, led their squads to support Ives, leaving a goodly force behind under Cernalt. Thoroughly shaken from Thorgil's attack, Myrna answered a myriad questions from the servants to

Kyrin, and at last retired to a chair in Kyrin's room, before the oak at the window.

Evening approached. The servants had gone at last to help Cook with the coming feast. Margye bustled out, an object of their admiration. Myrna smiled wearily. She would have no lack of apprentices now.

Kyrin cradled her babes, one in each arm. They did not yet have a name. Myrna shivered.

Celine hovered near with a cup of water and a cool cloth for Myrna's face.

Nell sat on a nearby stool. She was large with child, her and Bergrin's first. Her brown hair becomingly framed her mis-matched eyes. Marriage agreed with her. Just now, her normal black eye and the bright blue that wandered aside were both wide. "Oh, Myrna, I'm so glad you were not hurt worse."

"I saw him, you know. The tiger."

Kyrin sat up. "Where? When?" One of the babes stirred, with a sleepy noise.

Celine was awed at what Myrna told, and Kyrin frowned. "We must be alert and ask the protection of our Father of all. If need be, we will put off the naming feast, though Talik is loath to do it."

Myrna prayed the men returned safely, and hoped it proved a slight skirmish. Nell stayed with Kyrin, while Celine helped Myrna downstairs after a while. Hungry at last after her ordeal, Myrna went to beg a morsel of Cook before the feast.

At the door of the kitchens, she stiffened. That was Lady Ynglida Govannan's voice.

"If you must know, Elinor, none bothered me on the road from Halwende. I am shocked to hear these marauders are at large again, but glad to say I saw none. Your sentries said naught of trouble."

The kitchen was full of the good smells of roasting meat, fruit sauces, bread, and stew. To one side were loaded tables, one with sweet puddings, pies, and other delicacies. The servants wove around the older lady with moonlight pale hair and a worn face seated by the main table, and Elinor's sturdy frame. The firelight brightened her wheat-brown hair with gold. Myrna slipped inside.

Elinor looked around. "Ah, Myrna, would you please put these with the sweets? Kyrin does love her apple tarts." She handed her a large basket covered with a white cloth.

Lady Ynglida smiled at her. It was a kind smile, though she was pale, doubtless from the heavy basket and the long ride. She also tended to illness. Myrna took it and moved toward the other table, where a servant sliced bread. The tarts held a hint of stringency and a fresh scent she had never smelled.

Ynglida said proudly, "Those are made with a sugar glaze and a fruit called lemon, all the way from Araby."

Myrna peeked under the cloth. There were ground bits of yellow-white scattered over the tart's shiny brown crusts. They were artfully decorated. She saw one with the first letter of her name, M. There was an E for Lady Elinor, D for Lord Dain, a B for Berd, K for Kyrin, and others, even down to C for Cernalt, and another M for Medaen. It was quite kind of Ynglida, seeing Esther was to be judged by the council soon, and likely to be condemned to be walled in, never to walk free again.

"Poor Esther." Her mother stared at her lap, and her mouth worked. "She cried when she gave them to me. She said, 'I can at least pass some sweetness to the world, to show my repentance.'" Her wrinkled hands twisted. "Do try that one, Elinor. It's an extra. Isn't the taste heavenly?"

Myrna's head jerked up, and she laid her tart back in the basket. They came from Esther? She had never been truly repentant for anything in her life. Myrna's gaze went to Ynglida. She really was quite pale, and her hands twisted again, gripping her stomach. Sweat dotted her brow. She smiled weakly.

Myrna tensed. Stomach grippe. Ellen died of it at Halwende. And wolfsbane, used for everything from unwanted rats in nun's cells to wolves that plagued the flocks. Her fingers tingled. She stared down at them in shock. And whirled.

"Stop!"

It was too late. Elinor swallowed her bite of tart and stared at her in surprise.

Myrna crossed the room in a moment, batting the rest from her hand. "No one move. No one touch that basket. If anyone else has a tart, drop it!" She swiped a wet cloth resting on the table and wiped her hands hard. She grabbed the nearest bowl and put it under Elinor's nose. "Stick your finger down your throat and get rid of it," she commanded. "Now!"

Elinor nodded, paling. Her hand went to her throat, fluttering helplessly, then she obeyed.

"But," Ynglida began, bewildered, and Myrna dropped to her knees beside her.

"Cook! We need some of that clay you wrap the hens and fish in for coal roasting. The purest and most fine that you have. Mix a quarter cup of the powder in water and give it to Lady Elinor. As quick as you can, now! Make another for Lady Ynglida."

"But what is it?" Cook asked.

"Wolfsbane."

The girl beside the basket dropped the bread knife with a clatter.

Cook looked at Elinor in horror, and her eyes pooled with tears. Then she ran for the storeroom.

Myrna laid a hand on Ynglida's. "How do you feel?"

Lady Govannon's mouth opened, but it took her several tries to speak. Horror darkened her eyes, a sickness deeper than any poison. "Are, are you sure?"

"Yes. Margye can confirm it. But that is not important now. How much did you eat?"

"Just one." She shivered. "Esther would not do this. She could not. How could she? And the babes, Kyrin... they would get it too, in her milk. Oh Lord God, I hope it kills me!" She sprang to her feet and collapsed.

Elinor sat on the floor and shoved Myrna aside. Gently, she gathered Ynglida in her arms. She looked at one of the girls. "You, get me a clean bowl. Molly, fetch Medaen and send for Cernalt."

Margye caught wind of the tumult. She helped Cook examine all the other food in the kitchen. There was no more poison. Thankfully, none other had eaten any of the tarts. Elinor was gotten to bed, and Ynglida. Margye gave her a dose of herbs to strengthen her erratic bloodbeat.

Margye gripped Myrna's arms. "Bless ye, lass! Thank God he brought you in tha' moment." She gave her a fierce hug.

A white-faced Cernalt sent a squad in full haste to the abbess, and messengers to Talik, Lord Dain, and the regent. Then there was nothing to do but wait.

At Elinor's bedside, Myrna swayed, blackness coming over her vision. Her nose was bleeding again. Clucking, Cook and Margye got her to bed in Meric's chamber. The fearless falcon she tucked under her blanket.

Myrna woke to the sound of the bell for Compline. By the feet on the stair at the end of the hall, and the voices below, the hold was wide awake. Beside her, Ynglida's breathing sounded stronger.

What torment would it be to know her daughter poisoned her, and in dishonor sought to kill them all? Elinor and Medaen had not left Ynglida's side until Margye gave her something for sleep. Esther deserved whatever the council decreed.

"Where is she? Is she well?" Lord Dain cried over a sudden babble below. He pounded up the stairs, going to his chambers, to Elinor.

Myrna sat gingerly and reached for her best kirtle. Esther had not won, nor Thorgil or his brigands. She would walk in courage.

Kyrin opened the door, lamplight streaming in.

Ynglida sat up in the shadows and reached for her, crying. "Kyrin, oh Kyrin. Can you ever forgive me?" Her sobs echoed, broken.

Kyrin entered with Celine. "Ynglida, Lady Govannon, this was no doing of yours. Whatever guilt you think you bear for not knowing of Esther's plans, I forgive it." She hugged her in the dimness and turned to Myrna. "Is that not so, Myrna?"

For a moment, the rage against Esther and all her unkindness over the years, culminating in this dastardly act, overflowed. Myrna wanted something to strike, preferably with the falcon's sharp edge. Her hand tightened on the weapon. But that would break its very being, what it meant. *Loyal to your Maker, to your created nature. Awe, to behold such stature.*

Loyal. The Master of the falcon called for justice and mercy. He would deal with Esther. Myrna released the falcon. "Yes," she said huskily.

"But it's my fault," wailed Ynglida. "I played the fool, as the last king's mistress. I wanted power and position and to be loved." She gulped. "You may not know Esther once pursued Lord Bergrin Jorn, until she discovered he was running out of coin. I used to do the same."

Myrna touched the falcon for strength. Her brother had spent coin as water for her medicine. Then Kyrin returned and opposed Lord Ludwin Mornoth. And Esther found new prey.

Ynglida went on. "She went after Lord Thain. As I did, they used each other to grasp for power and place."

Celine said out of the dark, "As a woman, who holds more power than a queen?"

"Yes," Ynglida whispered. "I know now it was the wrong way. I learned from my errors, Esther did not. I am sorry. Almost I would take my life, what little of it remains, but now I live for more than myself. I live for him who made me and—"

"And for your godchildren. You have much to teach them," Kyrin said firmly. "You are among the first to know their names. Gerit and Ellen will need your wisdom and your love."

Ynglida choked on a breath and broke into fresh sobs. But they were better tears, tears of grateful, gentler sorrow, and grief, rather than bitterness.

Soon they went down to the feast, for Margye brought good news. Elinor was recovering well and would join them. Margye was also astounded at Ynglida's state. She had expected her to be much worse. Instead, Ynglida declared it best that she face everyone at once and get it over.

At the long table before the great fireplace, all of Cierheld's friends had gathered. Brother Rolf turned to greet Margye and Myrna with open arms. "Here is the old mother who bested the brigand with a kettle, and here is the gentle woman who did what she could, and saved us all." He ushered them closer and raised a horn of honey mead.

"Hear, hear!" Smiling faces of those Myrna knew and loved stood around the great board. It groaned under a boar with an apple in its mouth, venison pie, fish, mutton, every vegetable under the sun, bread, cheeses, wine, ale, and mead. It was a feast fit for a king. Even the king to come. For Corin stood beside Celine and Berd, grinning, and eyeing his trencher hungrily.

Lord Dain sat down in his chair beside Elinor at the head of the board. Lord Bergrin, Lady Nell, and others on his left. Kyrin brought the babes in, one in each arm, and gave their son to Talik, who beamed with pride. They sat on Lord Dain's right, and Kyrin urged Ynglida to sit next to them. Lady Govannon did so and ignored the talk that sprang up at the two lower tables extending the length of the hall, where servants and armsmen sat.

Almost every seat at the three tables was filled. Henges and Mary took a place near Cook's, who would be the last seated. She had yet to bring in the sweets.

The great door of the hall groaned open. Cernalt entered, dripping, a leather-bound book held high in his hand. About to take her place between Ynglida and Celine, Myrna stared at him in surprise. A late summer storm lashed the steps outside. He said, "Before we name two new lives, let this be known." He looked at Ynglida, and there was sorrow in his face. "Lady, prepare yourself. Your daughter is dead by accident, by her own hand."

Lady Ynglida stood and braced herself against the table. "How?"

"This is her journal. I would not read it in your presence to spare you."

"Please, I should be the one to do so." Ynglida held out her hand.

Cernalt looked to Dain, who nodded. He walked up the room between the dead silent tables and gave her the book.

She opened it to the last page. "Thorgil has a good plan, since by perfidious means Kyrin was saved, and we may no longer plan accidents for our enemies at our leisure. The house of Mornoth and Govannon will be avenged. Thorgil will destroy them in the field, and I will destroy them in the hold.

"The juice of fresh monkshood has proven effective. Here I set down this poison, for I may have need of it again. Fresh pressed juice of aconite, strained. One lemon. Three cups of sugar. Cook it until it is clear and golden as honey. Pour it with a generous hand over..." Ynglida's voice quavered, and she put a hand to her mouth.

"That explains why ye are not dead." Margye stood, grim. "She cooked it long enough to remove some of its harmful potency. Yet she pressed the plant herself. The deadly fresh dose went through her skin. I expect she did na' know enough of its safe preparation. Or of how it is used for vermin."

Ynglida stood as if frozen.

Myrna swallowed. If she spoke of Ellen Aelwin's death now, it would not be Esther who fell under the blade, but Ynglida. *It is better to light a candle than curse the darkness.* She clasped Ynglida's fingers to steady her. "Let me." Ynglida relinquished the journal with a grateful look.

Myrna read, solemn and clear, "Who should die and who should live? Maybe I will take one, and not the other. So they may appreciate what I have felt, losing Thain. That is a sweet thought. What if I take Kyrin and leave Talik, if he does not fall in battle? Leave Dain and take Elinor. Meric will fall, and Corin, the twit, and Celine, Henges, and Myrna, trait – traitors. Berd and Cernalt will be left to live with their foolish pride that brought down all. The son of Aelwin and the children of Cieri will challenge me no more. The regent's line will end. I care not who takes up the kingship. I know now I will not be queen.

"I sorrow for mother, but they will get what they deserve. She will forgive me; I but end her pain. I ate the last tart, one without the glaze, and cried over her hands she stretched out to me through the pitiful slit in the door of my cell the abbess assigned.

"If the council condemns me, I will have this for comfort. The name of Esther of Halwende shall not die infamous. I shall be the greatest walled-in saint of the ages.

"Perhaps I shall finish tomorrow. It may be I am overwrought with – with delight." Myrna paused. "There is nothing more."

Dain rose. He looked around the hall, angry and sad, his brown eyes determined. "First, I thank you all for your dedicated service. Your strong hearts, from Dirk," he smiled at the stableboy seated near the door, "to Cook, to my sister Medean and my son Meric, have strengthened us every day, in so many ways. Well done. Elinor, you are ever faithful and true." He smiled at her softly, then at them all. "Every one of you fought for us, and I thank you."

Dain bowed to Cernalt. "A certain hawkmaster will now train a missive squad for the king to come. Once again, First Armsmaster Cernalt of this hold, we give you honor and thanks. To each of my armsmen goes all homage, who fought with the might of right. Still, there are those among you who deserve special honor." Dain paused.

"Rise, Berd Stronghand. You are to be first armsmaster of Alkborough in the days to come. There you will guard the heirs of Cieri with the sword you have won. Celine, who ably defended the king to come, you will train under Kilden."

They rose, with a curtsey and a bow, hand in hand.

Dain eyed them. "Perhaps you have news of further joy for us?"

Berd reddened, and Celine curtseyed again, with an impish smile. "We are friends at present, thank you, my lord."

"I don't believe it." Every head turned to Meric, fair like his mother, but slight. "Well, I don't," he said, defensive. Corin nodded in the solidarity of a budding friendship.

Celine glared at them. "You don't have to believe it. It is so—"

"Is it?" Berd turned her by the shoulders, looked long in her eyes, then leaned forward to kiss her soundly.

After a moment of stiff surprise, Celine kissed him back. Meric cheered loudest of all. Smiling and blushing, the couple took their ribbing from the surrounding crowd in good nature.

With a last chuckle and shake of his head, Dain continued. "Not least, we thank you, Lord Bergrin Jorn and your lady wife, for your help. Brother Rolf, you and the abbey also have our undying thanks. Corin Tolman, we thank you, your lord father Regent Durand Tolman, and his first armsman, who could not be here tonight, for your dedication to truth. There is no higher praise. We are honored to serve you."

"Margye, you have done us all great service, and have been named a friend of Cieri. You will always have a home in our holds, wherever you choose. Myrna Jorn, we love you. Faithful in the little things, you will now bear the falcon dagger at my daughter's back, to guard her from harm, so long as you desire."

He paused and cleared his throat. "Men and women of Cieri, there is much to think on. We are thankful for our lives this night. Thorgil and his band of brigands are no more. Let us also be mindful of the pain we wreak by evil, determine always to follow the right, and find mercy for one another in our hearts.

"We have lost those dear to us. Nith and others gave their lives that we might live. Give them honor. We nearly lost my Elinor, my Kyrin, and so many more, including this worthy woman." He lifted his cup of ale. "Ynglida Govannon, let this be known to you and to all. Kyrin Cieri, first daughter of Cierheld, names you godmother of the heirs of Cieri, of Gerit and Ellen. She has chosen well. We rejoice with you, and we sorrow with you." He drank deep, followed by every other in the hall. Everyone sat, Ynglida with tears streaming down her face. Kyrin laid Ellen in her arms.

Cernalt cleared his throat. "Sir, if I may."

"Certainly, my throat is parched." Dain gestured for him to proceed and lifted his ale to scattered laughter among the tables.

"How the falcon dagger first came to Cierheld is now known."

Kyrin stirred. Myrna held her breath.

"It appears from that journal, that Esther came by the knowledge Thorgil began his work as a brigand long ago. He struck a caravan of traveling strangers in this land and left none alive. My lord, you once said you discovered this dagger on one of a small band of strangers my squad found slain on the road. You thought it the work of a brigand who roamed then. You were right, though you did not know his name.

"Of all that the travelers had carried, the blade escaped, gripped in the hands of a young man who received his deathblow as he defended another. It lay hidden under him where he fell." Cernalt continued slowly, "You kept it after a year passed without word or knowledge of kin or friend and gave it to Lady Willa, of this stronghold. Then it passed to our first daughter, Kyrin, and brought great deeds. Now it returns to us from a far land to the hands of Lady Myrna, where it will continue its legacy." He nodded to her. "Will you bring it forth that all may see?"

Myrna rose and held the falcon dagger up by the sheath.

The bird's body was the haft, its etched wings extending down to brush the glittering blade. Tail and reaching talons formed the down-swept hand guard. She drew it, straight, sharp and clean. Beak open in a defiant scream, the falcon gazed over the hall, eyes glowing amber.

*Clear morn and bright, or dark as night, with the tiger we wrestle aright.*

With a strength she did not know she possessed, Myrna drove the falcon blade into the table. Her bones felt as ingots of lead, yet her heart was strangely light. Expectant quiet fell over the hall.

Myrna gestured. "Nith Nulduin will live on in our hearts, in our memories. He was as this blade, as the steel Berd carries. True to who we are made to be. First Armsmaster Nith has gone home in honor. His fight is over. Our fight is just begun. To live every moment true."

Berd's hand trembled on his hilt, and Celine's fingers closed over his. Brother Rolf got to his feet. "To live true!" The rest followed in a roar.

Then they sat down. Dain gave thanks, and they ate with a joy that was a kind of defiance. Of rejoicing in hope. The tarts were berry instead of apple, and delicious, leaving everyone with stained faces, but no one cared. Lady Ynglida even managed a bite.

The heirs were named and passed around the room again by Kyrin and Aunt Medaen, proud as a great aunt could be. Myrna held precious Gerit and little Ellen and kissed their soft faces. Northern blood had brought not a snow-haired child, but children. Children of Britannia.

Perched above the table, the watchful falcon mantled its wings, where it belonged. The tiger sought always to devour, but they had resisted him.

*Now warm arms cling tight where fear strolled,*
*our hearts richer by more than gold,*
*though unfinished in noble mold,*
*till we all grow old,*
*and pass beyond the wold,*
*to the last fold.*

Myrna smiled.

*But that is another tale to be unrolled.*

§

*Thus ends the Falcon Chronicle, though not the life of those therein. The story of men goes ever on until, as Kyrin says in the Ode, It is his ruling as prophet, king, and priest; Truth at last to kiss peace, in the East.*

*In my own words, I am most glad for my sister, and thankful to the Master of All who, as Berd says, rules this dust.*

*Of heaven and earth, my stronghold.*
*Two worlds mingling in one mold,*
*seamless when the last tale is told.*
*—Alaina Ilen, consort and scribe to Prince Faisal Ben Salin.*

# Cieri's Daughter~Rival

*The first tale of the Falcon Chronicle happened before my path crossed Kyrin Cieri's and we became sisters closer than blood.*

*By the grace of God, the first daughter of Cierheld stronghold was barely a stripling in the birthing time of Britannia. During dark days of uncertainty between the king, his stronghold lords, and the men and women whose destinies they forged between them, her soul rose, igniting the hearts of many as a flame. Here lie the roots of her story.*

At the gate, the sentry called a challenge. A voice answered outside, and the immense wood portal of Cierheld stronghold creaked open. Twenty-four riders swept into the courtyard.

Two ladies were in the lead, one with a pale gyrfalcon on her poised arm. Esther and her mother, Ynglida Govannon of Halwende, were early.

Kyrin scowled and stepped further into the stable between the wall and Alexander's warm side, hidden in the shadows. She rested her hand on the side of her father's warhorse to quiet her shiver.

Esther reined her mount to a stop beside Lady Ynglida, and their two ten-squads of armsmen drew up around them.

Many called Esther queenly and noble. Though her laugh tinkled lightly across the yard, the eyes of the first daughter of Halwende gleamed as she waited serenely for Cierheld stronghold to notice her arrival. Her rich blue tunic was delicately slashed over an under-tunic of the finest weave. The dress flowed over Esther's comely form and draped her side-saddle, the edges embroidered in green flowers with yellow centers. Cream sleeves slipped down to cradle her strong wrists. The sheerest linen hair wrap revealed golden hair pinned beneath, bound by elegant leather braided about her white brow. It was fitting for the daughter of so exalted a mother as the king's favorite.

Kyrin bit her lip. They were invited by Dain Cieri, her father and lord of Cierheld. Esther and her mother came to witness her twelfth name day. Alexander nibbled at Kyrin's hair. She pushed his nose away.

After dawn prayer with Uncle Ulf in his Benedictine guest cell, she'd gone for a quick foray in the woods. Back inside the gate, as old Medaen demanded, before the Terce bells rang the third hour, she was slipping by the hall toward the mews. Then the pounding of hooves outside made her duck into the stable.

Esther must *not* see her in a drab tunic any stronghold first daughter would scorn, let alone on her name day, though it was a tunic fit to gather flowers in. Kyrin had given a fragrant bunch of bluebells for her name day crown into the cook's hands and turned away, intent on her hunters of the air. The falcons always gave her courage. She would need every scrap, for her oath of heirship was to be held in the hall at the ringing of the midday Sext bell.

Alexander stamped and blew a horsey breath against Kyrin's neck. Esther turned to look at the stable, her blue gaze level, as if she spied them within. Kyrin buried her cold fingers in the horse's warm mane. Esther would not stop her. Not this day.

A footstep stirred the straw behind Kyrin, and she started. Berd moved into the light streaming through the stable door. The young armsman's dark eyes were unreadable. He let his gaze flicker past. A smile tugged at Kyrin's mouth. He would not give her away.

Berd strode outside, his gangly limbs for once somehow managing to be in the right place at the right time. He reached for Esther's hand to assist her from her mare.

"Ah, you anticipate my ardent wish!" Esther thrust out her white gyrfalcon, which flapped until its talons found Berd's arm.

It was no secret the first daughter of Halwende disliked all creatures of fur and feathers. The gyr was said to be a gift of the king to Lady Ynglida, who earned the king's favor. And Esther would use a rat if it bestowed honor on her in the eyes of others, then have it killed afterward. A flush crept up Kyrin's cheeks as Esther stared at Berd. Kyrin's mouth tightened. The armsman tensed, then held perfectly still.

Did Esther think all of Cierheld beneath her? Did she not see he had no hawking glove? Her father's youngest armsman was yet in training. Berd wordlessly bowed his head and stepped around the mare. He faced the stable, awaiting Esther's further pleasure, the mare's rein in one hand. Kyrin frowned. Nith would bellow at them all if the gyrfalcon bated and her talons damaged the weapon arm of one of his best armsmen-in-training. Drab tunic or no, she must help. She gathered the skirt of her tunic.

Cernalt, Lord Dain Cieri's first armsman, descended the stronghold steps in a clattering rush of boots.

Stocky and greying, his call was cheerful. "You honor stronghold Cieri, Lady Ynglida Govannon! My lord and lady of Cieri are within, in preparation. Those of Halwende are well come." His gaze left Lady Ynglida, drawn to Esther like a lodestone, and his sharp eye roved over the armsmen ranged behind them. Old though he was, Cernalt noted the unusually large escort. Kyrin grinned. The hawkmaster missed nothing.

Cernalt stepped to Esther's side and reached for her hand. With a gracious bow, she accepted and descended from her mount. Cernalt nodded Berd toward the stable. Courteously, Cernalt also assisted Lady Ynglida. As if their mistresses' descent were a signal, Halwende's armsmen swung down and started toward the stable in noisy disarray.

Without seeming to move faster, Berd got there first. He paused in the door with Esther's mare. The horse snorted and kicked, a hoof thudding into the doorpost as Berd blocked Kyrin from the sight of those in the yard. Mayhap he was not under Esther's spell as much as she thought.

One side of Berd's mouth turned up, and he spared Kyrin a grin as the gyr flapped and settled. "Quick, before the ladies of Halwende go in." He tilted his head toward the back door. "Your mother wishes your presence. But first—" He indicated a piece of straw caught in her honey-dark hair that straggled from its braid. Kyrin lifted her chin. It was sure that every strand had frizzed from her unintended dip in the stream after she tumbled down the bank, though her morning foray had been successful.

"My thanks, Berd." She inclined her head, batted the straw free, and ran to the dusty door to lift the bar. *Bless Father for insisting on a back door. Will I never reach the mews? I watch the falcons rise on the wind every morn. Every morn but this, the day I become the first daughter of Cierheld.*

But she was almost glad Esther was early. Whether or not Esther was to rise in rank, the gyr on Berd's arm was a queen among falcons, brave and wise. Her golden-dark gaze penetrated soul, earth, and flesh. If only Esther left her retinue, as usual. Kyrin shivered even as she escaped the stable and ran.

She might be able to visit the gyr, dare to fly her. But if Esther caught her before she was properly dressed... she'd rather face a bear. For the bear would attack, and then it would be over. Esther was a wolf with harrying nips that bled prey dry long before it fell.

§

"Kyrin! There you are."

As Kyrin slipped inside her chamber, her mother beckoned. Graceful in an embroidered blue and brown tunic, the snap of excitement warmed her grey eyes. "Come, quickly! We must get you out of that," Lady Willa Cieri looked her daughter over, and her mouth twitched with a suppressed laugh, "wet rag, and fit your robes. You must make your father proud. All of Cierheld will be watching our first daughter. From this day on, you are the heir." Her mouth turned impish. "Though the woods will still find us discovering their treasures. What was it this time?"

Kyrin drew in a breath and let it out in a rush. "Bluebells, for my name-day crown. They're perfect! All spicy and sweet. With mint to weave them with, they are better than roses. I gave them to the cook in the kitchen. But Mother, Esther is here."

Lady Willa waved her crooked left hand. "Fie! Young Esther and Lady Ynglida can wait a bit, king's favorite or no. I'll have Cook attend to them. You know Ynglida must always be consulted about her delicate stomach." With the ease of habit, she slid her black hair over her shoulder, her voice airy. "But you—this is *your* hour. You are my only daughter." She moved behind Kyrin and began to unlace her overtunic.

Kyrin submitted to the quick tugs, eying her disordered braid. Her hair refused to stay where it was bound. It seized every chance to fly about her head or slide loose in many tendrils she had to tuck behind her ears. Kyrin wound a bit of hair about her finger and pulled, frowning. It did seem mousy.

Esther's hair never disobeyed her. It didn't dare. But how much of their cook's pleasant prattle would Esther endure before she insisted she must greet the daughter of Cierheld? Kyrin grimaced. At least she would be out of the drab tunic, even if Esther Govannon always found a way to remind her of her less-than-desirable blood, of her conquered ancestors of the hills, of her unladylike ways. It would be a biting nip couched in courteous words. Kyrin sighed. First daughter Esther Govannon of Halwende was everything she was not.

If only Myrna Jorn would come soon, and Celine, who so often attended her. Gentle, dark-haired Myrna was adept at soothing Esther's ruffled moods, at engaging her regard. Her eyes, brilliant as grey-blue cornflowers, measured well in the sight of men beside Esther's sky blue gaze. Yet Myrna was a moon quietly willing to reflect Esther's bright rays of wit, basking in the warmth of approval she deigned to bestow on a lesser body in orbit.

Red-haired Celine was their companion, mostly Myrna's. In secret, she loved hawking and the mews. Even swimming, Kyrin knew. She grinned. Anything that promised to be slightly daring and matched the hue of Celine's fiery hair. She would have enjoyed falling in the stream, dashing through the first sunlight in delight to the patch of bluebells nodding on the grassy bank.

Kyrin let go of her braid. Celine could sit still for far less time than she. Sitting for the limning of her figure on wood a day past had been the worst. Forced to hold motionless with nothing but thoughts of her name day ceremony for company, she listened to the bells toll the slow hours. But Celine would want to see the gyr. She might even help them find a way to get to the mews before the feast. If they were careful, they might visit the falcons.

Quick steps pattered along the wood floor outside Kyrin's chamber. She glanced up in hope. Maybe Myrna and Celine came early. But it was Aunt Medaen who swept in.

Medium-boned and round in all the right places, her usually pleasant brow under her coiffed black hair pinched into a frown. "Look at you!" She seized the skirt of Kyrin's ankle-length tunic, where a dusty stripe across the linen skirt revealed her visit to Uncle Ulf's prayer cell, the stable given away by bits of straw sparking on her sleeve. Kyrin tucked her hands behind her. They were a little green from picking the stems of the bluebells. At least her tunic had partially dried from her morning dip, and she would soon be out of it.

It did not seem to hold weight with old Medaen. Dark eyes full of reproach, she threw up her hands. "What have you done? And you the first daughter of Cierheld this day? No one would believe it. Out in the woods *again,* I doubt not, though I did press your new tunic yestereve. At least you went to prayer first." She rapped Kyrin's head as she swept past her toward the clothes chest at the foot of the bed. "Be sure you keep the fealty oath Father Ulf taught you in that noggin' of yours. We must have you looking like the first daughter you are. Lord Bergrin Jorn and Lord Edsel are to attend, and all the lords and ladies of the largest strongholds from north to south in our fair Britannia."

Behind Kyrin, her mother squeezed her shoulders, and Kyrin bit back her words. *Not* so many lords. Ludwin Mornoth and Nidfael Keffer, and others of the more southern strongholds, were not coming. Father had not said why, but the southlords had come less often of late to the holds across the Humber river.

How could the other lords scorn her father so? Kyrin pursed her lips.

Did they envy him? Lord Cieri was not tall, with everyday brown hair and dark eyes, though he was strong. He had served Lord Edsel well, working his way up the ranks as one of his captains. He'd been given Cierheld in return for saving Lord Edsel's life. Now he looked to fortifying his hold.

Aunt Medaen always said her brother was a better armsman than any lord could ask. In her words, it was high past the hour Lord Dain Cieri should receive a stronghold of his own. It was his right.

No matter old Medaen's high dudgeon, no lord should object to a neighbor strengthening his walls, with greater ability to protect their people against lowlanders, robbers, and the dangers of the woods—especially such a far neighbor as Lord Ludwin Mornoth. But no southern lord would attend her name day feast, which pleased Kyrin. She stared down at the toes of her soft leather shoes with a slight curve of her mouth.

Lord Edsel was the best of the lords, grey-haired though he was. He treated his horses well, and did not fawn at other's heels to gain advantage. Kyrin sniffed. That was the old lords. The young lords were worse.

But she must make sure Aunt Medaen did not get the wrong idea about any lord who attended her heir ceremony. "Mother, you know Lord Edsel is only here because he wishes to speak with Father about Lord Fenwer's quarry and the stone for our wall. Like the sea, he is calm until stirred up, but ancient as—"

Old Medaen clicked her tongue. "He is not so old."

Lady Willa glanced aside at her sister-in-law, her lips tightening. "Medaen, remember what we spoke of—"

"Yes, yes, my lady. I know it is not her time to handfast. But," she shook her finger at Kyrin, "one must *always* prepare. There is more to Lord Edsel than steadiness and a mind for laying stone. One day you will see it. He is yet your father's benefactor, though Lord Dain has served his due. Keep *all* your prizes eating from your hand, child. Especially if you do not wish Esther Govannon to catch the one worthy of you." Her mouth thinned. "That one is a veritable stronghold daughter. She will go far. You must not let her gain on you."

Kyrin huffed out a breath. "Which prize does she wish, Aunt? Esther can have Lord Edsel or any of them. I care not."

"Nay, child, she does not sight Lord Edsel, though she might do worse. But the heir of Jornhold now, Bergrin Jorn..."

"Oh, Bergrin!" Kyrin shrugged. "Myrna's brother thinks too much of himself to cast his eye at any other." Though Esther might challenge any heir who noticed her.

Eyes full of laughter, her mother tugged off Kyrin's damp overtunic. "Hmm. Let us see." She tapped a finger against her chin. "Old Lord Jorn says his grandson must learn diplomacy before building walls. His daughter follows suit, and her husband prefers the peace of the scholar to warfare, within or without his solar. He avoids such arguments like the plague. I also hear Lady Ynglida believes every man should have a fair tongue, though I do not know if Esther perceives the lack, or anything beyond a pleasing figure. She believes Bergrin resembles a prince of the fae, with that ashy blonde hair."

Kyrin could not suppress her grin. It was just like Esther. She called her "sprite-get" often enough. Her smile dropped away.

Her mother and Aunt Medaen never heard Esther's taunts about her hill blood. They never saw the menial tasks the daughter of Halwende expected when they were alone, or the looks from under those long golden lashes. They never saw her knowing smiles to Myrna behind Kyrin's back or the beautiful tinkling laugh that stabbed Kyrin to the heart when she stumbled over a courtesy in conversation, dropped a bit of gravy on her dress, or tripped over nothing. Esther disdained those who did not fall in with her ideas of beauty, of use, and of place. If one was a stronghold first daughter, one was queen, a tyrannous queen.

Enough. Kyrin lifted her chin. She did not wish them to know Esther's taunts of her unworthiness. Her father, Lord Dain Cieri, waited in patience in the high hall for the first daughter of Cierheld. For him, she would hold herself this day as what she was. No matter what Esther said.

Kyrin held up her arms, and her mother and Aunt Medaen slid a thin linen tunic over her head, sheathing her in blue warmth, softer than the wool to go over it. Then the green outer tunic fell into graceful place atop the linen, embroidered with vines and white flowers about the neck, sleeves, and skirt. The blue linen peeped out beneath the wool. Her mother fastened a braided leather girdle about her waist to hold the pouch for her stronghold key.

Kyrin smoothed her new tunic around her hips, and fingered the pouch. The wool and soft linen gave her slender, boyish figure a bit of rounded substance. She tugged the leather tie from the end of her braid and shook out her hair, combing it into glossy softness past her shoulders. *Now* let Esther say she mistook her for Berd, which was as senseless as when she said it months ago. Her head did not come to Berd's chin. But she was glad old Medaen had made her wash her hair in lavender water. The scent remained, despite her wetting in the stream. Kyrin sniffed its sweet-sharp strength. Her mother nodded.

"Wait!" Aunt Medaen settled a twined knotwork circlet of bronze on Kyrin's hair, a cool clasp against her brow. "There." She stepped back, clapping her hands. "*Now* you are our stronghold daughter."

Kyrin hoped the wreath of bluebells the cook and her mother's hands fashioned for the ceremony would conceal the crown. She was not likely to rise to Esther's place, but the first daughter of Halwende would dig in her claws deeper to see her wear the mark of a high lady of the holds.

Lady Willa's eyes softened. She hugged Kyrin and whispered in her ear, "You have always been in my heart from the day you were born." She smelled of yeast and flour and the oats, nuts, and apples she had put in Kyrin's favorite tarts. Kyrin held her tight and then smiled back, a warmth flowering in her that drove off all thoughts of Esther. She even said to old Medaen, "My thanks, Aunt." Aunt Medaen had her moments.

§

Pungent cinnamon tickled Kyrin's nose. Beside her, Lord Dain Cieri sat straight and silent in his huge chair of polished oak, a thick ox hide beneath his dark-booted feet, his brown gaze benevolent as he gazed about his hall.

Firelight from the great hearth at the opposite end of the long room played over their murmuring guests, side-lighting faces, softening some smiles and hardening others. The shadows danced among the mingled lords, ladies, and servants but were never thick enough to hide Kyrin. None stared rudely, but she felt the pressing attention of their regard.

She looked carefully past them—Aunt Medaen's remembered words beating the red to her cheeks. "Of course they'll gaze, as they ought, if they've got eyes in their heads! You are a worthy first daughter, though you *do* burn the porridge. But Cierheld will make any man overlook *that.* With your father's wall to sweeten the dower and men to keep safe these lands, your place among them is assured." Kyrin was not so sure.

Quiet and motionless on the other side of Lord Dain's chair, his thick, capable arms crossed above a belt that bore a worn dagger and sword, Cernalt's gaze moved to Lady Ynglida and Esther near the fireplace, then in a circular fashion around the room among the other guests. He examined each person and weapon with a potential for trouble until his attention roved back to her father. Cernalt's gaze then rested on her, unreadable.

Kyrin drew a deep breath. Her father was generous with his armsmen, and held an honorable but strict rule in Cierheld. Many served him by choice, more than followed all but the most landed lords. She could hear some of Cierheld's armsmen, a rumble of conversation outside the great hall's door, doubtless trading jokes and news with some of the many other armsmen who escorted their lords to Cierheld stronghold to instate Lord Dain's heir.

Near two hands of northern stronghold lords were present in their persons or proxies, most with their own heirs. The only one of the absent southland lords she would miss was Lord Fenwer of Fenwrd stronghold. He quarried her father's stone near his hold on the cliffs above the ocean. She was curious about her godfather. Her mother said he kept falcons, but she had never met him.

Near the front of the crowd beside Myrna, Celine smiled at Kyrin, her green eyes bright with excitement. Kyrin smiled, then faltered at the wall of watchers behind her friend. Esther's arrival had left no time for the swift courage of her father's birds or the wise strength of the gyr. She resisted the urge to wrap a strand of hair around her finger and clenched her fist. A falcon would watch.

Several servants brought lamps from the kitchen, a building of stone adjacent to the hall's side door. The only natural light streamed through it and the great hall door at the far end of the room. No hall allowed large windows in the lower floor, which an enemy could turn to advantage.

Across the yard from the kitchen and the hall were the mews, part of the same long building that housed the stables and the smithy. Kyrin's other hand tightened on the arm of her father's chair. She must do the house of Cieri proud. Another servant scurried down the long room to poke the fire to a higher blaze.

There was a stir, and everyone straightened. Her mother, Lady of Cierheld, parted the guests as gracefully as an otter did a rill in a stream, clad in her swirling blue and brown tunic, a white hair wrap pristine against her black hair lying in waves down her back. Lord Dain stood to meet her. "My Lady Willa."

The lady of Cierheld lifted her arm. In her hand was a sizeable iron key. The key of Cierheld. Her gesture met Lord Dain's with a clink. Together, they twined the keys of Cierheld.

Lady Willa smiled at her lord. Her mother's crooked left hand curled against her skirt. It took nothing from the sweet straightness of her glance. Dain gave her a nod and a grin. Her gaze met his and spoke what only a bard could pen. There was a sudden sting in Kyrin's eyes. They loved each other well.

Lord Dain ushered his lady to her chair on his other side, then returned to his seat, lord of the hall. Her father's usually twinkling brown eyes became solemn. His silence gathered every gaze in the room. His seat was now a seat of judgment. Then he said quietly, "Step forward, Kyrin Cieri of Cierheld."

Kyrin's breath came short. She clutched her skirt, her heart stuttering, mouth dry. But Esther would never see her cower, a hare under the wolf's gaze—she would die first. She lifted her chin, and her feet found their place before him.

Lord Dain straightened, and his eyes leapt to the witnesses ranged about the hall. His strong voice carried to the least of them. "Behold our daughter of house Cieri, heir of our blood and bone." He examined her, brown eyes deep. "Kneel, Kyrin Cieri, first daughter and lady to come of this stronghold."

Kyrin stilled her trembling lips. She knelt and held her hands up as Uncle Ulf had instructed, as if in supplication.

Her father lifted the key, extending it above Kyrin. "Do you accept our charge?"

"I do." Her voice was loud and husky in her ears. The fire crackled and popped.

"With this key, I gift the heir of Cierheld." Her father laid the huge key, longer than her hands, inside her cold fingers. He pressed her palms around it with his warm, rough, callused grip. He stared down at her, his face strong and gentle as a king's. "So let it be!"

The guests broke into cheers and well-wishes. Young Lord Cor Gadral called, "Hail and well met, Lady Kyrin!" Myrna and Celine cried, "Kyrin of Cieri!"

But it was not over.

Kyrin swallowed.

Lord Dain lifted his hand, and quiet fell. "What will you swear?"

Uncle Ulf strode forward, inclined his head to Dain, and pivoted to face Kyrin, still on her knees. His priest's robe was dark, his grey hair clipped close. "My child, do you take this oath before God? Will you serve your stronghold and your people, to keep faith and do them good all the days of your life? To keep their honor as they serve you, and to obey both your earthly lord and he who rules this world and the next?"

Could she hold such a charge? To protect and provide for so many. Their obedience hinged on hers. It was a heavy weight. One face stood out among the others. Celine, eager and earnest.

Esther accepted Celine's presence only because of Myrna. Since Celine was not of Cierheld, and an orphan, in Esther's eyes, she had no place. Kyrin's hand closed tight, and the dark edges of the iron key bit hard. Celine would need her when she became Lady of Cierheld. Celine and others who were counted of little worth, ignored, or pushed aside. Yes, she could keep such an oath. It was her father's oath. The metal felt hot and heavy, it even smelled oddly of the furnace. But to help anyone outside her hold, she must first guard those within. For the first time, she felt to her depths why her father built the wall.

"I do, Uncle Ulf—I mean, Father Ulf. I give my oath. I will seek the meat and protection and honor of my people as my own." She turned her head to look her witnesses in the face and swallowed. Esther's gaze among the shadowed blur of guests was bright and burning, her smile welded on.

Turning back to the priest, Kyrin stilled her weak knees. "We are bound until death. To Cierheld and to—to the king!" She had practiced until she knew the words perfectly. Still, they stuttered in her throat. Esther was never less than well-spoken. Near the back of the hall, the daughter of Halwende's mouth curved, and she put her fingers together in a mocking, silent clap.

A falcon would gain height... Kyrin smiled. She would fly Esther's gyr later as the first daughter of Cierheld, an heir of the same standing. Let Esther chew on *that.*

"So let it be," Uncle Ulf intoned. He shot a warning glance at Kyrin. She pressed her mouth tight shut. He continued, "To prosperity, and the blessing of God on those who choose right. To hands strong in discernment, both in right and in might. And to our rightful King, long may you uphold him."

"To the king!"

"May you keep Cierheld long in wisdom under our Lord's eye. May his joy be yours on this day, your twelfth name day. May every blessing be yours, heir of Cierheld, first daughter of Cieri." Uncle Ulf set the crown of name-day flowers firmly on Kyrin's head, atop the circlet of woven bronze.

She stood and curtseyed to him with a broad smile, then turned.

Berd stood nearby, straight and proud as the spear in his hands, his dark eyes glinting. The rest of her people about the hall were no longer blurs. She knew every smile. Even old Medaen, who leaned to whisper in Lady Ynglida's ear, bore an expression of pure delight.

Kyrin surveyed them all. Her heart burned, a furnace of its own. Every man and woman of Cieri, from the cook to Nith, were worthy of her care. Someday, her father and mother would need her too. And Berd and the other men who would follow her, that was the burning within. Their need and hers. What did it mean? The house and hall of Cieri were what to her? The words she had sworn melted and swirled inside, ready to be cast forth.

Kyrin lifted her hand high, clenched about the key. She bit her lip, and the words welled, searing as hot gold. "*You* are Cierheld, and Cierheld is my life. So I do pledge you mine, my life." Her voice was young and clear and piercing.

Murmurs spread. A few guests shared glances. Kyrin lowered her hand. Was it not a fit oath? They had offered their lives to her.

It was Cernalt who moved first. He raised his sheathed dagger above his head, his leather and mail rustling. The muscles in his neck corded. "And we will answer the call!"

Every man and woman took up the words in a roar. Kyrin blushed. Their renewed obedience was not quite what she had meant, but maybe they understood. She curtseyed again and stepped back between her father and mother.

A chant rose from Nith and Berd and the other men and women of the hold who stood along the walls, joined by the armsmen on either side of the great hall door, hands on their sword hilts. "Cieri, Cieri!" Her mother rested her hand on Kyrin's shoulder, and her voice rose in counterpoint. "Hail! Lady Kyrin, Cieri's daughter! First heir of Cierheld!"

Echoing her people's salute, most of the other lords' voices and weapons rose. "First daughter of Cieri!" But Lord Edsel raised his horn of mead and frowned into it. Old Lord Jorn glanced from her to Father Ulf with an unreadable look under his white brows. Uncle Ulf's face was bland. His interlaced hands tightened across the front of his Benedictine robe. He had protested Kyrin's request for the bluebells. He and Esther thought alike in that.

Had she done so badly, did she shame her stronghold, did she dishonor the king with her last words? The awkward moment broke with a few laughs. One of them tinkled in light disdain. But Cernalt's eyes were on her, and there was no laughter there.

Uncertain, Kyrin looked up. There were tears in her mother's eyes, and her father gripped her shoulder fiercely. Her answering smile hurt. Her father did not look displeased. He leaned down to kiss her. Then her mother hugged her. "I'm so proud, Kyrin! Medaen is, too, though she may not say so. Oh, my precious first daughter!"

Kyrin's circlet slipped to one side, and she reached for it, then pulled her hand down and carefully held her head high. The double crown must not slide off, or someone would laugh, most assuredly Esther, but she would not care for that now. The freshness of mint brightened the air, lingering under the sweetness of the gingery bluebells. It was done.

It was done, and they were all smiling. Almost all. *First daughter.* Kyrin stuffed her key in her pouch. It felt surprisingly light.

Lord Dain spread his arms wide. "Now for the feast! The board is set. Come, greet our first daughter of Cieri with plenty of drink and ale for your thirsty throats, with every blessing of our stronghold, with all our goodwill, in the name of the king!"

Lords and ladies and their heirs stirred and lifted their drinking horns that the women of the kitchen hurried to supply. They tipped cups in eager hands to drink deep and seal her father's words of hospitality. The servants scrambled to the cook's flurry of orders, heard dimly without, bustling toward the tables inside and out, lading them with flagons of mead and ale, stoups of wine, and jars of milk.

Each long board soon creaked under steaming platters of hot bread and every kind of prepared vegetable, grain, and meat. There were carrots and peas in butter, spiced lentils and greens, barley rich with thyme and pepper, even boar in raspberry sauce. The herb salad was fresh with dandelion, watercress, basil, and nasturtium. There was lamb garnished with mint, mutton stew spicy with pepper and garlic, trout swimming in green sauce, and birds of every size crackling under a brilliant glaze of honey mustard. A haunch of venison had been roasted with ginger and fennel.

The heavier foods arrived in procession, led by the cook, one young kitchen boy struggling under a platter of an ox quarter near large as himself. Lively conversation and delighted laughter accompanied the parade when the boy proudly refused helping hands and safely landed his burden.

There were delectable lemon cakes, honey oat cakes spiced with nutmeg, clove, and honey, and Kyrin's best-loved nut and apple tarts with cinnamon. Cheeses of white and yellow topped the sweets. There were plenty of fresh apples and apples baked in wine to aid the digestion of those who sampled overmuch.

Kyrin sniffed in delight. Their dear cook had surpassed every feast she could remember.

Pickled roots were also set out in an enormous crock. She was glad Aunt Medaen relished the dish of her birthplace so much it was provided. She liked the beets too. No matter Esther said only the poor ate turnips and such, and turned up her nose. Scattered small crocks of butter, stewed fruits, and dishes of salt also spread along the board for all.

The guests eyed the groaning board. Lady Ynglida gave a short sniff at the baked apples but looked at the meat and cakes with longing. Old Lord Jorn shrugged, and his turkey throat bobbed, while Lord Edsel shot an amused glance at Kyrin. She grinned. Their trenchers were waiting.

Then she caught Father Ulf's glower. Kyrin flushed and looked aside. He did not understand. She *had* to open her heart at her oath-taking. It was the proper moment; it was her right to speak on her name day. She was almost sure. But few were looking at her now, besides those at the head of the line forming to greet her as first daughter. The rest were looking at the food, as she would be, in their place. Kyrin held back a smile and grabbed at her crown again as it slipped under the assault of her first well-wishers.

She returned their courtesies with grace. Lord Kem Landyl inclined his head to her, and his young lady wife embraced her, with enthusiastic blessings for Cierheld. Lord Lanner Fresen of Fresenheld towered over her and bowed, expressionless, while his short lady hugged her and complimented her on her key.

Now that she had a place among them, Kyrin could not withhold smiles from the other young heirs.

Cor Gadral of Gadrald stronghold was a rather thick-bodied boy. His broad grin reminded her of a frog's, not unpleasantly. She remembered his hail-and-well-met during the ceremony and offered him a willing curtsey. At the back of the waiting line, Esther's face was set. Kyrin grinned and gave an especially deep curtsey to young Bergrin Jorn, who stepped up after Cor. The heir of Jornhold was eying the boar and barley on the table. Kyrin wanted to giggle. Never mind Esther. It would be years before she must think of finding a lord to share her stronghold—this day, she was simply the first daughter of Cierheld. And she was hungry, too. She would eat, then find a way to leave without notice, for she must share her name day with the falcons.

Esther walked forward among the last to greet her, her teeth bared in a smile. The golden lamplight lay about her with heavy glints of yellow, light and shadow playing hide and seek in her hair as if in a game of life and death. She laid her hands lightly on Kyrin's shoulders and kissed her cheek.

"Daughter of Cieri," she murmured. The very sweetness of the words held threat.

"My thanks." Kyrin dipped a curtsey as Esther stepped back. The first daughter of Halwende did not name her *first* daughter of Cieri, as was courteous. Her cheeks heated, and Kyrin scowled and snorted at the honeysuckle and rose, cloying in her nose as Esther swirled away. She should not have felt surprised. But the daughter of Halwende was moving toward the tables as if she'd said nothing amiss, pulling every male glance after her.

Esther would not have the last word. Kyrin clenched her fists. She was also a first daughter this day, and she would not stamp her foot. The ceremony was finished, and even Aunt Medaen would say she had upheld the name of Cieri. Though it seemed they had not expected her last words. Kyrin sighed and rubbed at her itching nose. Uncle Ulf would call them unorthodox, which was what he named anything he disliked. But if he turned his attention to the feast, he would not keep her from the mews.

Then Myrna abruptly seized Kyrin's hands and swung her about, her eyes shining with happy tears. She stopped at last and squeezed Kyrin's fingers, then glanced at Kyrin's pouch bulging with her key and laughed and kissed her on each cheek. Kyrin smiled shyly back. Myrna, at least, wished her all joy.

Celine pounced, her coppery curls wild, and grabbed Kyrin's arm. "Come! It's your twelfth name day feast, you know! You ought to have the first trencher. I saw them putting the boar with the apple in its mouth on the third table outside. Come! Your mother made apple tarts, wonderfully sweet. You have to try them. I know where they are." She pulled Kyrin toward the door, gathering Myrna beside them as a lodestone pulls a needle. Kyrin walked with them. *Their* smiles did not harbor wolfish intent.

At the widest table, Kyrin more than made up for her missed morning meal with a helping of everything. With a last melting crumble of oat, walnut, and apple tart in her mouth, she brushed stray bits from her lap.

There were still so many people about. But even if it was Matins before the last guest departed, she would go to the hawks. She had need of their fearless bravery. Tomorrow, her true training to serve her people began. Did Esther yet lurk about? Maybe she would go to the stream instead—there would be moonlight on the water this night. There she could quiet her thoughts.

Why did Lord Edsel frown so and her people grow wary for a moment after her oath? She had meant every word. Might it have to do with the mercenaries her father had hired to guard the hold while he and Lord Edsel and Lord Fenwer began to rebuild Cierheld's wooden wall in the ancient Eagles' stone?

At their last gathering, Lord Edsel had bent seriously over her father's plans for the wall, as earnest as Uncle Ulf over his Psalms, his eyes intent. Excitement in his voice, he reached across the table to grip Dain's shoulder. "You are right; this is just the place. And see here, we could..." Some of the other lords standing close around the board were none too pleased, most notably Lords Mornoth and Keffer. Some, like old Lord Jorn, simply thought a stone wall foolish. Others, like tall, dark Lord Lanner Fresen of Fresenheld, approved.

But there could be no reasonable objection. Her father's wall would show them all his strength and wisdom in time. It was certainly not her father's fault that Lord Edsel's ancestor once fought beside the Roman Eagles and knew their lost arts of building. Though her father *had* been plain that he found much about their fighting methods admirable, the ancient Eagles no longer walked Britannia. But old Lord Jorn had looked at Uncle Ulf with such an indecipherable gaze. And Lord Edsel frowned. She must learn what it all meant. It felt dangerous.

# Cieri's Daughter~Revolt

Myrna and Celine, Lady Ynglida, and Esther were in her mother's chamber upstairs admiring Aunt Medaen's latest tunic of fine cloth. Lord Edsel was with her father somewhere. The other lords and their retinues had departed.

Cernalt and armsmaster Nith, his second, were gone to oversee the night guards at the wall and the gate, and to see that the remaining escort of the ladies of Halwende was well cared for. The guests had gone, but for a few.

Kyrin sighed and stretched out her chilled hands to the quietly hissing coals in the hearth. Berd said armsmaster Nith studied too many weapons to have time to be Lord Dain's first armsman, though he assisted Cernalt, who grew greyer every year. But at one's back, Nith was worth five men. So her father said. Berd had gone to sleep in the stable, as usual.

Kyrin threw a sturdy piece of oak on the fire. The falcons called to her, but her feet ached. Maybe the morn would be a better hour to seek the gyr; for now the birds slept, heads under wings. She could not stroke their soft feathers without disturbing them, or look into their far-seeing eyes, let alone follow their unhesitating strikes through the sky.

A cool nose nuzzled her skirt and ankle with a huffing snort. Kyrin regarded Berd's rangy young sight-hound and rubbed behind his ears. He whined and licked her fingers, snuffed eagerly around her feet, and came up with a bone. Ears pricked, the hound cocked his tan head. His eager eyes and laughing grin dared her. Kyrin caught the end of the mutton leg in a firm grip, and he sprang back, nearly pulling her over. She struggled for balance, laughing.

"The lady of her stronghold, sporting with a dog? If you play so at being first daughter of Cieri, be careful to keep your feet." Unsmiling, Esther glided out of the shadows, doubtless practicing her princess step. She had somehow come down the stairs without Kyrin's notice.

Kyrin edged back, still pulling on the bone. Play at being first daughter? Never. The greasy length slipped free of her grasp, and she straightened, suddenly bold. "Don't tell me you've never run with your dogs, Esther." She must have, surely with some of her attentive lords.

"I? As a child, of course. Now, there are higher aims, greater pleasures, larger purposes."

Kyrin's eyes narrowed. "Larger purposes, Lady Esther? Such as luring lords and their sons to your side? What about Myrna and Celine? Do they not deserve a lord as well as you?" As did she, but she did not care so much.

The hound crouched down around his bone. Kyrin shook her head as Esther's mouth tightened into a line. Must everyone look at her? "You don't care about your stronghold sisters, do you? You never have. It's always Lady Esther, like your mother, king's favorite. I wonder that Aunt Medaen can abide her."

Esther's gaze narrowed. "My mother is no business of yours, hill-brat!"

"No. Myrna and Celine are. And Cierheld." Kyrin glared, breathing hard. Esther could not see the worth of those who served her. Her eyes were elsewhere. But Mother would not be pleased. Best leave Esther to herself. "Forgive me. I must go." She turned toward the stair.

"Not yet, first daughter!" Esther grabbed the iron fire poker from beside the hearth to bar her way. "What *do* you mean, king's favorite?" Her teeth were bared.

Heat crept up Kyrin's neck. Strangely, she found she did not want to repeat the insult. "Surely you know, Esther, everyone does," she said, wearily. The hound whined and pushed between them. The bone in his mouth brushed the side of Esther's sky-blue tunic, leaving a smear of fat.

"Ughh, you ugly beast!" Esther swung the poker.

"Don't!" Kyrin grabbed at the bone in the dog's mouth to pull the animal from Esther's reach. The poker caught her arm with a thunk, she bent over with a gasp, and the poker slid forward to dig into her side. Pain flared.

She stared up at Esther, who looked back, torn somewhere between delight, uncertainty, and distaste. Kyrin took a step back and stumbled. The hound dropped the bone and darted in front of Kyrin, growling at Esther. She raised the poker like a spear, her mouth twisting. She wouldn't, she couldn't... not Berd's hound.

"No!" Kyrin fumbled for an abandoned mead cup left beside the hearth and flung the half-drunk contents into Esther's face. Esther cried out and lifted the poker over her head, mead dripping down her face and hair. The hound ran, brief defiance cowed.

Panting, Kyrin raised the cup in one hand and gripped the dog's bone in the other. Had the first daughter of Halwende meant her harm? She did not know. A cup and a bone might be enough to bat aside the poker. She daren't turn her back on her. She lifted her chin. "You have no right—"

Esther took a step forward, scornful. "You squawk of rights. First daughter, my faith! You're one of *those.* Heretics, I hear, by some accounts." Her blue eyes were watchful. She smiled the soft smile Kyrin hated and lowered the poker. Kyrin clenched the bone and gasped at the pain in her arm.

Esther stiffened and drew back, staring. "Bless me, it's true! Your priest was right. Look at your eyes—dark as the pit!" For a moment, she looked a little frightened, then she drew herself up. The poker in her hand became a scepter. Her voice full of poison and sweetness, she said softly, "Sorceress of the hills, when do you take on your beast skin? Shall I wait for Matins bell? Or is it wings you wear instead?"

Kyrin's anger flared white. She was no shape-changer, no sorceress. Her light brown eyes always darkened with pain or emotion. Her mother said it came from the blood of the hills—but it was not evil. Her breath came fast. Esther was a wolf indeed. She found herself poised to attack.

"My lady!"

Startled, Kyrin glanced over her shoulder. Berd strode through the great hall door, the hound at his heels. His swinging hand brushed his dagger hilt. "Did she touch you?"

Kyrin straightened and sighed. "It was the bone, really—she did not mean to hit me." Until guilt was certain, a first daughter must not accuse another. To be a first daughter meant above all to be a teller of truth.

Esther looked Berd up and down. "How dare you! I am a daughter of Halwende."

"And you bear a weapon before our first daughter." Berd stepped forward, his hand resting on his blade, his dark eyes hot. Kyrin opened her mouth but paused. He was her father's armsman, or near enough. And Esther challenged him. Uncertain, she said nothing.

"Give it to me." Berd reached for the poker.

"No." Esther moved back, then gave a soft gasp.

Reaching past Esther's shoulder from behind, Armsmaster Nith held the poker in a one-handed iron grip. After a first instinctive, futile tug, Esther unwrapped her hands from the handle and stepped away. Nith tossed the poker into the far end of the fire in a shower of sparks. He also laid his hand on his dagger, threat in every line of him.

"I did not—" Esther looked down, her face red, then white.

Kyrin set the mead cup down on the hearth carefully and rubbed at the pain in her elbow with a grimace. "She—she was angry at the hound. It dirtied her dress. Lady Esther was not trying to harm me."

"You are sure of this?" Armsmaster Nith exchanged a short glance with Berd. Punishment was severe for intentional harm to a first daughter or first son.

"Yes, armsmaster. She did not strike at me."

"Ah. And now she will not." Nith nodded, with a slight inclination of his body, a loosening of every alert muscle. He shot a look of chill warning at Esther.

Kyrin flushed. She could have held her own with the bone. That alone would have scared Esther off. "The iron did little damage." She shrugged.

"Did it, indeed?" Nith said, thoughtful. He glanced at Lady Esther again, his expression opaque, and Esther paled yet more.

"Kyrin!" Lord Dain called sternly and stepped from the stair at the end of the hall. He walked past the deserted tables to her side with a frown, his brown eyes sharp, glancing at them all. Lord Edsel strode just behind him, his face unreadable. Her father reached them and said, "Esther, Lady Ynglida wishes your presence."

"Yes, my lord." Esther curtseyed deeply and walked regally past him toward the stairs, her steps unhurried. Lord Edsel muttered something in Dain's ear and followed her.

At Dain's short nod, Nith and Berd left the hall also, Berd with a last look back at Kyrin. She smiled and laid a gentle hand on the hound's ears as it pattered after them. The dog licked her hand with a warm tongue. She released the bone into his care. His tail wagged. He was grateful, at least. Kyrin wiped away a sudden tear. Her elbow stung, and her side ached.

"What happened?" Lord Dain sat on the edge of the hearth, flames leaping from a disturbed, half-charred log, the light playing over his face. Kyrin leaned against the end of the table, wrapping her arms around herself.

"I—I played with Berd's hound, and his bone." She looked down. So she was an undignified first daughter, but it was not the pup's fault. "The hound got Esther's skirts dirty." She said softly, "We called each other names."

"I gather 'beast' is not a kind name for a dog."

Kyrin looked up in time to catch the twinkle in his eye. He had heard. She grinned briefly. "Not the way she said it." But it went further than any joke. King's favorite, heretic, sorceress. Kyrin wished for something to wipe her fingers on. A moment later, she twisted her hair around her finger, then remembered the mutton grease would make it smell. She dropped her hand, her face flaming. "My words did not befit a first daughter, but Esther tried to hit Berd's pup, so I threw the mead—"

Her father picked up the poker beside him and stirred the fire, which crackled hungrily. "I overheard somewhat."

Kyrin swallowed uneasily.

"Yes, I also heard her accusation of sorcery." Lord Dain laid the poker aside and nodded, his eyes warm. His voice was low and strong. "You must overcome evil with good, especially now that you are the first daughter of Cieri."

"Yes, Father, I—I know." But Esther was a veritable wolf, cunning and hard to catch in anything. Uncle Ulf would be very angry if he heard even a whisper of such paganism as Esther had cried down on her head. It had been many seasons since he took the priest's cell near Cierheld; some said to quiet the cry raised about Lord Cieri's heresy. She'd been too young to know what that was about, but she knew well Uncle Ulf's smile of triumph when he delivered any wrongdoer to penitence. Yet Esther hinted it was their priest who told her something ill of his first daughter. What had Father Ulf said?

Kyrin shivered. Nothing like Esther's suggestion of wings or skin had ever happened, though the wood's creatures did seem unafraid when she and her mother rode among the trees after herbs or flowers for the kitchen or the table. She loved the forest and the hawks. Sometimes she almost wished she *was* a falcon so she might fly away when she had need. But never did she seek other-worldly power or consort with spells or witches. Surely that old trouble would not be stirred up again against her father?

She did not relish the thought of endless dawns at Prime bell in Uncle Ulf's cell on her knees if he thought her in need of his counsel or repentance. He especially hated interruptions of any sort when he was scribing. His latest work was translating a journal from Latin to the common tongue for her father. Lord Edsel's ancestor had been a Roman Eagle conscript, and both Lord Edsel and her father wished to know if the journal held any secrets of warfare or Britannia's history.

"Come, sit." Lord Dain patted the stone hearth beside him. Kyrin sank down with a wince. Her father looked at her sharply. "You say she did not hurt you? Let me see." He examined her arm, where a dark bruise was forming, and bent her elbow this way and that. She hissed a little but did not mention her aching side, where there was likely another bruise across her ribs. He could not look at that in any case, and Aunt Medaen would make enough fuss for two when she saw it. It hurt little more than the fall she'd taken from her mare last moon.

Lord Dain grinned and folded her arm softly back against her side. "As you say, this wound will not drain your life away this night." Then he shook his head and wrapped an arm around her shoulders. "I am sorry, my daughter, for Esther's blow. More, I sorrow for her words, which probably struck deeper. Remember, once a daughter of Cierheld, always a daughter of Cierheld. Your mark of heirship is here." He touched her tunic over the heart.

Despite her hill blood, a first daughter would not forget. A tear trickled down Kyrin's face. She was so tired of watching against missteps. "When—when I gave Cierheld my oath, Lord Edsel frowned at me. He never frowns. I—I did not mean to bring trouble. Father, does Lord Edsel think ill of me? Did I say ought wrong?"

"No, my daughter." He wiped her cheek and held her close. "You are the heir twice over. It is witnessed by your oath to your people. This day you made that quite clear. Our Lord has given you charge of this place, these lives, and neither seas nor time nor any man can take them away. Not until he relieves you, through circumstance or dictum, or your knowledge of what is right." His voice rumbled in his chest.

So, her Lord made her heir of Cierheld, and gave her this charge as first daughter. Then might he help her be worthy? Kyrin scrubbed her face. There was yet a hot ball in her middle.

"Esther says I'm one of the heretics." It was all so confused. Even now, her anger fought with her fear and a bit of pity. She did not know which would take the day. "And Uncle Ulf seemed angry."

Her father lowered his voice. "Lord Edsel told me he approved your claim, and that you gave him considerable pleasure this day. Seldom has he heard such an honorable pledge from the lips of a stronghold lady, and one so young. His frown was doubtless for some other thought. As for Esther—" He sighed. "She plows a hard road with her mother. She dares not disagree with her over the king. Esther also believes my thoughts do not follow Father Ulf's, neither about the king nor other things of the church. And she is right."

Her father paused. "We must speak quietly, now. Though your Uncle Ulf is a worthy translator and scribe, his words are not God's. God's word is higher. Though it pains your mother to set aside her brother's wishes." He smiled, a wry twist of his mouth. "Your uncle is not as our Willa, except when circumstance and opportunity suit him. Then he can be agreeable. But your mother... she thinks of the right thing first, then of my benefit, and always of others. She is worth her weight in gold."

Kyrin nodded. Her mother's crooked hand, the gyr as gift of the king, the disapproval of Uncle Ulf, Esther's words, and old Lord Jorn's watchful gaze flitted through her mind. She did not know why, but she felt like a hawk rising high on an uncertain wind.

Lord Dain said slowly, "Not all kings are alike, but all die. Some would be pleased if our present king's life were shortened; one such is your uncle. Esther," he sighed again, "it is only clear she dislikes you. Yet, you are both first daughters. So, this is your first lesson as the heir of Cierheld." He stretched out a booted foot and rested it on the bench below the table. "What would *you* do to guard our neighbors' peace and ours?"

Kyrin's brow furrowed. She couldn't have Esther escorted from Cierheld, much as the thought made her smile inside. Her head ached. A momentary victory in the eyes of others mattered less, unexpectedly, than the well-being of Cierheld. She bit her lip, heart sinking.

They were first daughters, and for the good of all the northlords and their holds, Cierheld among them, they must find common ground. But how to do that with Esther, who hated all she did? She knew what Mother would say. Kyrin whispered, "I ought to make peace with Esther again. If Lady Ynglida is so unkind, it is not all Esther's fault. Yes, mayhap she may change her mind about me in time." As unlikely as that might be. Esther's constant undermining *was* a kind of treachery, even if she did not mean to hit her with the poker. Kyrin wished she had a falcon's vision. She would need it, if a falcon could see hearts, and let her see what might bring Esther to peace.

"The ladies of Halwende have watchers among the lords' wives."

"Watchers?" Kyrin stared at him in surprise. The fire behind them in the hearth whispered to itself. Berd slipped back inside the hall, a dark shape beside the great door, leaning on his spear, his hound at his feet. Her father paid him no heed. The stars shone outside, and though armsmaster Nith did not return, for the first time, Kyrin did not feel Esther's presence hovering at her back.

"Medaen, for one, and your mother."

*That* was the reason for her mother's increasing visits to Halwende, not that she particularly esteemed Lady Ynglida, though Aunt Medaen did. Kyrin smiled. So, the ladies of the strongholds watched those of Halwende. If Esther did more than shoot polite barbs at her, it would become known. But what would Halwende's enmity mean for Cierheld?

Kyrin scowled. "I must be true, and deal with Esther if I must." Despite the laughter, the needling remarks, the way Esther hunted her. The knowledge was gritty as bitter ash in Kyrin's mouth and hot as coals inside.

"True. But your mother will help you. The Lady of Halwende was once her worst nightmare. Now they can speak together civilly, if they are not exactly friends." Dain smiled. "As for your uncle—it is no crime to believe a king unfit." He chuckled. "I hold ideas quite contrary to your uncle and even to most of the church, myself."

Kyrin frowned. So, her mother had dealt with an enemy herself in Halwende. Surely it would not be so hard to set things to rights with Esther and her mother, proud as Lady Ynglida was. Of particular interest to her watchers would be any interactions with the king. But Uncle Ulf's words troubled her more. "Uncle spoke so fair of the king during my oath-taking... should not the king know his real thought of him?"

"Unless he uses words as a weapon against his life, there is nothing that might be judged against Father Ulf, among the lords." Lord Dain said softly, "Though a split tongue is one way to get close to an enemy, it is not good to have a double heart." His voice became brisker. "But I do not know the truth of the matter, my daughter, and you remind me of one creature with a loyal heart indeed. Come." He helped Kyrin to her feet and led her out past Berd, who touched the back of his hand to his mouth and brow and flicked his fingers out in salute to his lord, then to Kyrin, his face in shadow. She inclined her head, blushing, glad he would not see more than the fire glow brushing her cheeks.

Her father led her out past the oaken doorposts, down the wide steps, past the smithy, smelling of hot iron now cooling, past the stables with their smell of horse, to the silent mews.

Inside, the birds rustled sleepily in the light of the lantern her father took from beside the door and lit. Before the six usual open-spaced perches, there was a freshly carved perch of ash. Doubtless, Cernalt, who loved the hawks as much as she, had supplied it for the gyr. Kyrin smiled. She had called him 'Hawman' before she could speak in sentences.

But the gyr did not rest there. A young goshawk sat upon the pale ash, a male, its feathers sticking out here and there in bedraggled, awkward plumage. A male, and the females were the best hunters, being larger and able to bring down bigger prey. Why had Cernalt kept it?

Lord Dain cleared his throat. "One of the men found him, cast out of the nest, I believe. He is not a longwing, nor a gyr. Only a common falcon. I have seen your heart over them, my daughter. I fear Esther would be sorely disappointed if I offered it to her. Mayhap it is not a worthy enough bird?" His gaze was intent.

Kyrin's throat tightened. Esther could not have this falcon. "My father, it would die in her hands." Esther was not worthy; she would treat it ill. Since her mother's gyr gave her much more prestige among the ladies, if Esther must go hawking, she would give the goshawk to an underling to fly, or it would be injured, or she would confine it to its perch. Kyrin stretched out her hand toward the bird. No falcon should be robbed of its wings.

"Ah. It is our responsibility to guard all under our care, creatures and men alike. Some will always die. But best we make that number as small as we may, eh? The bird is yours."

Kyrin pulled her hand back from the falcon's soft head, wordless with surprise, a smile blooming.

"So, daughter. Name him well." Her father grinned and gently urged her forward.

Kyrin nodded and stepped closer. She stroked the goshawk's head, blinking hard. What a gift, and what a father she had. The goshawk peeped and ducked his head, aiming his beak defensively at her fingers. He was strong. "His name is Samson."

"A good name." Dain paused. "Do you remember the story of Samson's strength, daughter?"

"Yes." As she remembered his downfall. She would never be as weak, never give her secrets to one who had not earned the right to hold them, such as Esther, or a spoiled lordling. That, she swore.

Kyrin cocked her head. Her hawk cocked his and gazed back, eyes wide and wise, the pupil of his eye brightest black in a red-gold orb. They were two strong hearts beating as one. And standing in her Lord's favor, in her oath, surely all was well. She would not be weak.

Her father said, "It's a strange thing. The man Samson in the Word did not ken where his strength lay, so he did not guard his heart. Only when he fell did he learn where his heart had gone. His strength lay in his king, where his heart did not rest. And so, his strength departed from him."

Yes. That always made her sad and a little angry. So much good mixed with so much evil, and the weakness that could have been avoided. Her father's hand fell on her shoulder and gave her a little shake. "You will understand more of that story when you are Lady of Cierheld. For now, never forget. All power, truth, and loyalty lie in the one who governs our destinies. He is ever true, though we are unfaithful. We must always return to him who is the heart of our strength." He stroked the bird's breast. "This one has a loyal heart. When you win him, he will ever be true. May he prove to you his loyalty—and bring rich evidence to our stewpot, of course."

Kyrin laughed, he grinned, and the moment lightened. "Yes, Father." Samson was hers.

Esther would go in the morn, and though she had landed a blow, it was not to the heart. Though Esther had no father to teach her, it did not absolve her. She had been caught for once in her ill-wishing. Armsmaster Nith listened to Kyrin's word on the matter, as first daughter of Cierheld. And for certain, Berd and his hound could attest she was no quivering hare, for no hare could fly a falcon.

Uncle Ulf might break his fast at her father's table in the morn, if he did not depart at first light for his cell. Kyrin rather hoped he did. The quiet would be welcome. "Father, might we fly our birds in the morning? There is a spacious meadow near the stream, with flowers, and lots of squirrels and hares. I even saw a pheasant a seven-day ago."

"Hmm." Her father considered. "That would be an outing most welcome to your mother. But now she waits for us. We will ask her." He grinned at her and turned toward the door, about to blow out the lantern.

Kyrin could not repress a light step for joy. She must find time to feed Samson on her fist in the morn. A falcon's heart was not won in a day. Then her father's falcon and her mother's goshawk would enjoy the stream to bathe in before their hunt. Cernalt would surely give her permission. When she freed her mare from her stall, she would shake her mane and snort, ready to ford the nearest stream for a drink and then a gallop, while her first daughter looked to the sky. Their cook would have plentiful hare, red squirrel, and pheasant for the morrow's dinner and many after.

"But what of the gyr, Father?" She had near forgotten it. The white gyr sat in the corner beyond Samson like a motionless, muted candle on her perch, alone in her dark corner. Kyrin swallowed. Alone. Esther thought a goshawk beneath her, yet she had no father at all to show her better.

Kyrin's mouth firmed. The first daughter of Halwende had nothing for her but anger. And she could not forget the story of Samson, and how his weakness led to his downfall. No, she could not give in to the daughter of Halwende and her unceasing prying. But she could leave her gyr alone. Let it be her first offering of peace, though Esther knew it not.

Lord Dain watched her turn away and blew out the light. "I know you wished to fly the gyr. Your heart has found the right place, daughter." They stepped out of the mews, and he fastened the door. "Know that Cernalt and armsmaster Nith and your mother have things well in hand concerning Halwende. And you, my daughter, this day you hold a key like to your mother's." He stopped. "You wielded your place well, with Esther, but for the words about her mother. I am proud of you." He wrapped her in his arms. Kyrin laid her head against him. He was kind, and strong, and bravest of all. Her father was warm and solid, the smells of leather and cinnamon lurking about him.

Wrapped in that safety, she sensed every other heart also held possibilities of hurt and hope both within and without. Her key of cast iron *could* break. The ladies of Halwende *could* cause trouble, as could Uncle Ulf, but she would follow a falcon's courage and loyal heart, however she stuttered or stumbled. She could always get up again. If Esther would accept it, she would ask her to join her, Myrna, and Celine at needlework when she could, under her mother's watchful eye.

Kyrin leaned back against her father and hugged his arm to her chest. "Samson will be great, Father. I'm sure he will." With his clear sight, they would hunt far, dive swift, and climb the wind. They flew within their Lord's regard. He would keep them all.

Kyrin's lips twitched. One day she would be keeper of the keys. How Berd would laugh, watching her fold house linens, as Lord Cieri's daughter, who loved horse and hawk and falcon.

But as first daughter, she could go more often to the forest. When learning all the endless tasks of her stronghold at Medaen's heels grew harder than she could bear, she could pick flowers and hunt. No embroidery would keep her still too long. In any case, she would far rather hunt hares than lords.

She remembered Samson's feathers, soft on the edges, but with a ridge of living strength down the middle. She must fly true. For her people, for Father and Mother, for the Lord of this world and the next. And there was always Berd's pup to chase. *Daughter of Cieri.* Her hand closed on her key.

§

*Kyrin's deeds after this tale I tell in Falcon Chronicle I, Falcon Heart. Where the murder of her mother and the mysteries hidden in the falcon dagger rip Kyrin from Britannia and lead her to Araby. There, she is pitted against slavers, desert raiders, and treacherous lords deep in the intrigue of the Caliph's court.*

*In Chronicle II, Falcon Flight, instead of escaping to Britannia, Kyrin accepts the wazir's charge to return to her land and seek his lost relative, on pain of the death and the torment of myself and another, whom she loved as a second father. That is just the beginning.*

*During the threads of her journeys, a few good men and women have always walked at her back. I was privileged to ride there for a time and defend her life as my own.*

*But I weary your ears, though I am a teacher and a mother of princes. This is but one tale of Lady Kyrin, first daughter of Cieri. Now I set quill to parchment lest the deeds done, good and ill, be lost to the mists of time. Was she worthy of her name? Were those who followed her worthy of theirs? Read on and see. –Alaina Ilen Late 900s Araby*

PATH OF THE WARRIOR PART I

# The Warrior - 1

*We wrestle with memories to find meaning.*
*Without knowledge, we live in emptiness, for without truth, life and death have no purpose.*
*Memories give sight through the mists of time.*
*Where do I come from and where am I going?*
*The watermarked parchment rustles.*
*I read words written in quill and ink and a man's soul.*

The night was dark and warm as blood. Unseasonably warm, as the maples had not leafed in the courtyard. On nights such as these, the tiger walked unheard.

Tae-shin rolled the silk-smooth paper in his hands and tucked it into the message case. He took the lamp from his table and handed it to his messenger. He did not fear darkness and silence, not when he had his sword, and his hands and feet. "Ha-nuel, run fast, and we may yet preserve our people."

His student bowed, thin face sober, and ducked out into the driving rain. The white band tied about his head bore the black characters of official sanction.

*Hwarang* Master Ryu Tae-shin rested his hand on his sword, the long hilt familiar under his fingers, and watched the light disappear into the dark.

It would be a simple thing to follow to ensure loyalty. There lay the danger. Now he must fight with his heart, mayhap every drop of his blood, against enemies within and without.

But he had known before he wrote the message to Jeong Jinho, rebel *kuksun* of the five thousand soldiers massed outside his kuksun's gate, that one hwarang with a false tongue walked among his two hundred. One of his students reported to hwarang Master Cho Seung. No one but Master Cho or Kuksun Kim Paekche would dare stop a hwarang messenger.

Tae-shin's heart beat heavily in his chest. With the dawn, he would be his kuksun's most esteemed hwarang—or he would be dead.

Every *Choson* hwarang fought with sword and bow, hand and foot, with a prowess that even the Mongols heard of on their far steppes beyond the great northern wall of China and respected. To his people of Choson, in the Land of the Morning Calm, the tiger symbolized strength and protection. His brothers of the hwarang, the flowering warriors of his people, worshipped the tiger spirit.

The punches of the most adept cracked ribs like dry pine, could crush an attacker's throat, or shock the heart so it ceased to beat. Their open-hand strikes could knock a man senseless, disrupting the nervous system in precise combination.

His two-hundred students had followed his every hand strike and sword blow as he led them in honored techniques of *Subak* and *Kum-sool* as the sun rose over the rim of the world, glinting flame on the water of the river they practiced beside. Their feet flashed high in jumping kicks and sent their mounted opponents' hats of horsehair spinning to the ground.

Tae-shin clenched his fingers around the hilt of his blade. His students had grown strong, from *rangdo* to hwarang.

Surely his most trusted messenger was true. Ha-nuel would carry his offer to Kuksun Jeong Jin-ho of the five thousand with courage. Or, yearning for advancement, would he take the missive to Kuksun Kim Paekche? Did he believe his kuksun, that it was an honorable path to fight to the last child? He might even follow Master Cho.

Tae-shin resisted the urge to draw his weapon. Nearly two hundred of his hwarang sought to serve as faithfully as he, who held the heart and hand of their kuksun's daughter, Kim Jin-dae.

Tae-shin's breath stopped for a moment. Beautiful, she was. As Paekche's son-in-law, he had been favored.

He took much pleasure in Jin-dae's cooking, or his Huen, as he so often called her in his heart and whispered in her ear. He had not tasted the hot bite of her fermented cabbage and spice for days. The village had little food left, bottled behind the ramparts as they were, with many hwarang who ate much.

Carefully, Tae-shin wrapped his sword-hilt for a solid grip against the wet. None knew the undercurrents between the villages better than the hwarang and the supporting warriors from the lower bone ranks. The rebel would need them to peacefully oversee his new land and people. So Kuksun Kim Paekche and his daughter, Kim Jin-dae, might live. And his brothers, from *chin-gol* to the lowest bone rank.

Satisfaction tugged at Tae-shin's mouth. Life, and his Huen's smile. He would see her live if it meant his own death. His mouth tightened. He had a task to finish.

Tae-shin stepped out into the thundering dark and shut the door. Rain misted against his face as he slipped away. The budding maples smelled sweet.

Moving through the courtyard garden toward hwarang Master Cho's ceramic-tiled roof, Tae-shin kept to the shadows. His breath came faster. No spark of quicksilver ran along his bare, blackened blade in the light of the lamps from his old master's open door—which yet quivered on its hinges. Cho Seung also hunted this night.

Ryu Tae-shin listened warily. There was no going back.

No one stirred behind the carved porch pillars, no voice or clatter of dish came from within the house. Then Master Cho stood in the garden archway, a dark shape against the square of light. It was as if the hwarang master manifested there in his leather and cane armor for one of their practice bouts. Then he turned his head in a sneer, and his teeth glinted. Sliding his sword from its sheath, he stepped down to meet Tae-shin. He was as sure-footed as a cat in the dripping grass.

Tae-shin retreated into the dark. The light must not blind him. His weight even, he did not lift his feet despite the mud beneath his boots. He must feel his way along the earth and avoid the stray branch, the tuft of grass, the rock that would turn.

Master Cho shifted his heavy frame as a feather, circling Tae-shin, a blot of darkness in the night. Noiseless, his old master lifted his blade and sliced up and across Tae-shin's body in an adder-swift strike. But Tae-shin was not there to be gutted.

Hwarang Master Cho rained down heavy blows, precise and swift with hate. Steel grated on steel and sparked in the black. Tae-shin's steel gave before his—deflect, attack, deflect. He stumbled.

Master Cho hissed and extended his arm in a slashing lunge with all his weight behind it. Tae-shin struck. Master Cho's weapon flew from his hand and thudded to the earth. Before it hit, Tae-shin spun to grab his opponent's arm. With a quick blow of his hilt to the neck and a heave over his hip, he bore him heavily to the ground. Dropping astride him and locking his legs about Master Cho tighter than a strangle-vine, Tae-shin rested his blade against his throat. His old master did not dare try to throw him but struggled to speak. Tae-shin lifted the silvery edge a finger span.

"We could uproot the house of Kim and plant the house of Ryu and the house of Cho in its place. Together we could rise far." Kimchi and fish mingled sour and warm on the hwarang master's whistling breath.

Tae-shin's last doubt died under a storm of fury and sorrow. He gripped him harder. He was the only one with the authority and knowledge to judge him, and there was no more time. Master Cho plotted to kill his Huen and his brothers. His throat felt suddenly thick. Not for him, the mountain-cat playing with the mouse.

He forced out a hoarse, "I am sorry." He slammed his hand down, and hot wet flooded his fingers. The struggling body beneath him went limp. After a moment, his stomach roiling, Tae-shin got to his feet.

When he returned to his command post, the rain had washed the blood from his hands and the tears from his face. He stood outside, letting the rain patter around him with his thoughts. He could not let the traitor live. A hwarang who betrayed his oath would betray again. Tae-shin swallowed hard. The same might soon be said of him.

Dawn was near, and they could not find him with Jin-dae. She could not be accused of conspiring with him against her father's house. A faint smile lightened him, despite the chill that spread over him with the coming light.

When he first saw his Huen, he had been a student of Master Cho. That long ago morning, he was ordered to display the way of the sword with one of his brothers, to show their martial skill before the kuksun's daughter, who walked through the courtyard.

She had been such a bright spirit, her cheeks soft as a slender peach, her form and deep brown eyes reminding him of a graceful water deer. Her low words to her maid as she watched them begin the dance of the blade were as swift as the red that crept up her neck, a rosy blush on her golden skin.

With a feint and a rush, Tae-shin disarmed his brother in a moment. The surprised hwarang stared in disbelief at his empty hand where his weapon had been. Jin-dae laughed in equally surprised delight, then brought her hand to her mouth in dismay.

Red-faced, Master Cho sharply ordered Tae-shin to strike his brother with the flat of his sword. He stopped after three blows. Master Cho yelled at him to continue.

Tae-shin bowed, reversed his blade, and offered the hilt to his master. "I did not teach my brother the sword aright." Then he bent across his brother's back and took the rest of his master's bitter instruction.

After the lesson, as Tae-shin returned from washing his bloody back, he contrived to pass near Jin-dae, who lingered in the garden nearby. He overheard her quiet aside to her maid. "That hwarang has a spirit about him—a tiger's strength—yet with the gentleness of the deer." She said it thoughtfully, words that would be cause for blood coming from any other mouth. He thought her rather perceptive. He had bowed deeply, straightened, and met the sardonic gaze of his kuksun, who stood just beyond his daughter.

From the beginning, Master Cho Seung had sought to protect his place as the most respected hwarang Master, driving the hwarang under him mercilessly, without care for life, limb, or purpose. No warrior among them attracted Kuksun Kim Paekche's notice without paying a price. So hwarang Ryu Tae-shin soon performed his master's toughest tasks.

Tae-shin traced the rough wood of his command post door and bowed his head. He still did not lift his sword without reason and held it until he completed his task.

Master Cho had sought to kill those hwarang of rank around him and sell his people to rebel Jeong Jin-ho. To gain a new kuksun who would place him at his side, as Kuksun Kim Paekche had not. Those who had reached enlightenment would call Master Cho demonic, one who walked in greed and hate. What could he have been if he had kept his oath?

Tae-shin stepped inside the command post, wiped his sword, and slid it slowly back into its wooden sheath. His own journey to become hwarang had not begun in truth.

Before his test to become a hwarang master he traveled to the Chinese mainland to study scribing and medicine, as well as their arts of war. He had so many questions.

He yearned, but nothing he attained filled his longing. He pursued higher rank for his father's sake, as did many others among the hwarang. But why did one succeed and another not? Why did he feel every time he gained a step in life, or drew closer to his desire, that something or someone knocked him back? The earth was chokingly full of injustice. It reigned under Master Cho. Life felt broken.

In China, he found answers. A man, shunned by the rest, showed him a bit of a book by a man named John. In it, he spoke of another, Yeshua, who was more than a man. And Tae-shin discovered the power of truth.

Inside his command post, Tae-shin settled himself against the wall and laid his sheathed sword before his feet.

Zen, or *Seon,* as his people put it, had given him power. Seon gave inhuman strength to both flesh and spirit but never the power to dispel his darkness. That grew ever heavier. He felt its hunger but could not name what devoured him.

Ryu Tae-shin smiled wryly. Strange that one could seek enlightenment, the end of delusion, and still be so deluded, caught in the darkness of hate and wrong, where there was no light to see. The book was different.

Its light reflected the ugliness of Master Cho, but also his own hate. But the book haunted him, and its words would not leave. Turning his face toward the Buddha, drinking the power of Zen, had changed little within him.

Tae-shin caught back a soft laugh. Though he had beaten the man who showed the book to him, who asked why a hwarang warrior feared the truth, soon after, Tae-shin could no longer petition the spirits of river and hill, or follow the way of Seon. The looming meaning of the book and its purpose kept him unsettled in spirit until he found a copy of the entire Book of the I Am, and read further.

He discovered the Master of the stars gave the path of meaning to all things he created. That path was not easy, for the Master of All did not look at things as men looked at them. Tae-shin's throat closed.

He knew soon after he met Jin-dae that he could never attain rightness as the Master of the stars was righteous in all things. Compassionate, just, pure, strong, existing in himself, the Father of all was good. But Tae-shin knew his own hatred too well and could name other slithering things within.

He also knew swords. And the Book's edge was keen; it divided the pure from the impure. He could never be worthy of the touch of the Master of the stars. But then he learned something else. Unlike any weapon, the Book also brought healing.

The Master, in love for him, had paid his debt with a blood-soaked price. If he would accept it, the Master of All expunged his darkness and made him a new creation, sending him on to live, to love, to grow in joy. The pieces of the universe slid into place. Injustice had an end.

Tae-shin had asked pardon of the man who showed him the book of John, and they parted as brothers. Then he became a hwarang master.

Tae-shin tipped his head back against the wall. He took truth and left the power of Seon, the Zen.

It was not so comfortable, dividing intentions, hearts, and men. But the Master of All cared for him and taught him to wield the blade in both worlds, the realm of spirit and flesh. Though life held much suffering, his father, master, and brother had overcome it. He shut his eyes. His fate lay in the strong hands of another.

§

The thin cane door of the command post bent under heavy blows. "Open, in the Kuksun's name!"

Ryu Tae-shin lifted his head from his knees. The door burst open. He did not move.

They took his sword and seized him, two men for each arm. Six guards marched him between them into his kuksun's presence.

Tae-shin knelt one moment before the guards forced him down. He would die with few faces to witness his dishonor—Kuksun Kim Paekche gave him that. He raised his head.

Paekche's mouth was flat, his black eyes hard. A frown wrinkled his wide brow beneath his black hair in its simple warrior's knot, bound by a green silk band stitched with the *sigil* of the house of Kim.

Had Jin-dae fashioned that dignified band with pride and joy? Tonight it would bring her sorrow. His kuksun had never fully trusted him. Tae-shin let out his breath. If he were of the house of Kim, however distant, or born chin-gol, it would be easier to convince his kuksun of the truth. But for that, there was no remedy.

"My kuksun." He leaned forward whether Kuksun Kim Paekche raised his keen edge above him or not, baring his neck in trust.

"Why?" Paekche growled. The stinging blow of his hand numbed Tae-shin's cheek and rocked him back on his heels. The carefully shaven lines of his beard framed his square chin, working with rage. "How could you give us to Jeong Jin-ho! The tiger is dead in you. The master of my hwarang has turned his back to his enemies!"

Word had gotten out. Had they taken Ha-nuel on his way or returning? "I do not give our people to Kuksun Jeong Jin-ho. I give them life." Tae-shin's jaw hardened. "I seek to master the tiger before he devours us all. Then, I serve the Master of the stars, who bids us not to kill without rightful need. As for my enemy, I have faced him."

"So, you lift your name beside the tiger. Do you also seek my seat?" Kuksun Kim Paekche glared at him.

"No, most honorable kuksun. I fight for our land and for the house of Kim. That both may endure." Tae-shin bowed his forehead to the floor.

His kuksun paced back and forth on the dais. His silk slippers whispered over the polished wood, and his robes loosed the scent of cloves, star-anise, and musk.

"Did not your Master of All die without lifting a hand for *his* kingdom?" Paekche's voice was harsh.

Tae-shin could not keep from stiffening and sat back on his heels. The wary guards pressed down on his shoulders but let him gain his knees. "He died for *us,* honorable kuksun, and as such is one of the greatest hwarang who ever lived. He rose from death to build his lawful kingdom in our hearts—in any who wish for purity and strength." Tae-shin's eyes stung abruptly. "He holds my heart in his hand."

"As I, your kuksun, hold your body."

"Yes." Tae-shin lifted his gaze. "As does lady Jin-dae. My Huen also holds my heart. My kuksun—I seek rebel Jeong Jin-ho's face that you and Jin-dae may live, and the house of Kim. There are five thousand outside. It is death to fight them with but five hundred." He strove to keep the heat from his voice. If it would place his weapon between Jin-dae and suspicion and ambition and fear, he would beg indeed.

"The houses of Kim Paekche and Jeong Jin-ho both lay claim to the same burial land. Each claims it stolen. Our ancestors remain in our memory, but bones cannot speak, or touch, or laugh. Though that earth is sacred, their dust sleeps. Would they not rather we walk in life than for our blood to water the ground where none can ever touch them?

"My kuksun, the rebel will need you. Our new king may rise for a day, and the next he may fall. There is no need for more blood if our hearts remain true to him and our people. The ministers are not settled at court. Yield for a moment, and carry the battle." Tae-shin swallowed the knot in his throat.

Kuksun Kim Paekche lifted his hand.

The men holding Tae-shin's arms tensed, their fingers binding as steel. The sixth guard stepped forward, a moon-blade halberd in his hands.

It was his answer. Tae-shin bowed his head. He had one thing left to lose.

If only he could know Ha-nuel got through. *Master of lights, my Father with whom there is no shifting shadow. Give me your tiger's heart, the hwarang heart of your son.* "So I will not shame you." It was a whisper.

"Speak, if you wish me to hear!" Paekche stroked the medallion that rested against his silk-clad chest, and his mouth twisted.

"Your pardon, honorable Kuksun. I asked a hwarang heart from the Father of all. I would not shame him."

His kuksun snorted.

Tae-shin's chest tightened, and his breath came short. "My kuksun, do not listen to crooked tongues who seek their own power. I have silenced hwarang Master Cho Seung. He would have opened the gate to the rebel. There are others who followed him. Some would see the house of Kim fall and take your place. I do not know their names."

Kim Paekche's mouth twitched, and his hand tightened on the medallion. "A treacherous murderer speaks wisdom. Your words I will heed." He gestured. With a rustle of the guard's robe, the moon-blade loomed above Tae-shin's head.

*If my kuksun were not blind—but he may yet see—when it is too late. My Father, Master of the stars, have mercy on us. Huen.* "My kuksun," he choked out, "give my lady Kim my sword and my mother's land." If he could be calm, there would be time for Paekche to think again after his death.

Tae-shin found his hands shook and straightened his arms, pushing against the hard hold of Paekche's men on either side for steadiness. They braced.

He could escape. It would be quick. One twist left, a spin and a kick to the knee—a blow with the bright iron taken from the guard on his left who kept licking his lips—then he would be free. Every hwarang master knew the touch of death. His executioner would fall in his own blood, and the moon-blade would be in his hands.

Every muscle rigid, Tae-shin leaned forward, exposing his neck. They were only loyal.

Kuksun Kim Paekche did not mean to surrender. He would need every man to hold the wall.

# The Path - 2

*May the moon prosper us!* Kuksun Kim Paekche frowned and flicked his fingers. His guard's weapon paused, and he rested the haft of the moon-blade on his shoulder. Paekche fingered his chin and turned away from Tae-shin, whose gaze followed him.

His hwarang approached the rebel kuksun only to keep his rank and Jin-dae. A true hwarang would keep his oath and give everything for honor and his kuksun. The hwarangdo did not give way before flood, fire, or threat of death. Paekche smiled grimly.

Now his hwarang waited. That silent, expressive mouth had spoken of his kuksun's life and Jin-dae's. One guard slammed his head against the floor for his insolence, to stare so at his kuksun.

It must be that god of his which made him trample the fragile blossom of Jin-dae's heart in such a way that he so little regarded an honorable death. A heart of water polluted other hearts, especially among those who led. His hwarang brought shame and dishonor to the matter of Master Cho Seung. Paekche paused. As a wise kuksun, he had pondered Ryu Tae-shin's offered terms to their enemy. He had time. But so had Tae-shin.

Why had he not run? Or gone to inspect his hwarang along the river? Put himself in a position of strength to bargain with his kuksun, or even with the rebel Jeong Jin-ho? Paekche turned sharply. "I have your message. Why did you wait?" he barked.

"Honorable Kuksun?" His hwarang's voice was suddenly husky.

Let him fear. The guards had brought his student to him, caught as he sought to slip back through the gate. When a guard read the contents of his message aloud, Ha-nuel's horrified face had gone white, streaked with tears, though for the honor of his kuksun or his treacherous hwarang master was uncertain. Paekche frowned. He flicked a hand to indicate his men. "Why did you wait for them?"

Tae-shin swallowed, but his gaze did not waver. "I did not... I would not leave my kuksun and lady Jin-dae to believe—"

"What your traitorous offer to our enemy has proven."

Tae-shin's mouth flattened. He drew a breath. "None other knew the message."

"Your hwarang had no part in your treachery?" Paekche smiled. His hwarang master would not argue with him again.

"I presented my offer. Your hwarang who carried it knew nothing." Tae-shin's eyes pleaded as he looked up from his awkward position, the white lock in his hair about his ear straggling among the black. Jin-dae often pushed that white lock back. It was white from an old wound. A wound gained in true-bone service to his kuksun. He would plead for his student, but not for himself.

Rage welled higher in Paekche. After this night, would Jin-dae ever smile at him again? His son-in-law betrayed them all, and he awaited his fate no less implacably than Jeong Jin-ho awaited their defeat outside the gate. Kuksun Kim Paekche's brows snapped together, and he spat on Tae-shin.

His guard raised the moon-blade as Paekche lifted his hand, staring down at their betrayer. But need he send their enemy a message with Tae-shin's head? Might the gods of Heaven smile on a deceived one for reasons of their own?

The signal for his hwarang's execution turned into a disgusted gesture, and Paekche snapped, "Put him outside the gate, tied in a sack. Let us see if Kuksun Jeong Jin-ho has our people in his heart, as he claims. Let the gods sentence the traitor and have mercy on my Jin-dae."

His hwarang wisely put his forehead to the floor. His guards bowed swift and deep, avoiding his glare.

None of his men wished to be part of the death of the hwarang who fought off fifteen of the mountain people with his sword and, when he lost it, tore away a length of green bamboo that splintered in his hands. Tae-shin had wrapped it in a bit of his robe and fought on to victory. Those hands had scarred remarkably little for a warrior past his first score years.

But how could his hwarang force him to this? Paekche circled his hwarang master thoughtfully, hands behind his back. "A hwarang must fight for his kuksun. If Jin-ho does not mount your head on a spear for your ill offer, and you live. Even so, I will not see your face again." It was a fitting sentence of death or exile. The gods would decide. Mostly. As his men lifted Tae-shin to his feet, Paekche reached out and twisted the silk tunic at his throat until his face went purple. "Hear me, water-heart, if Jin-ho breaches my walls with martial skill born of your knowledge, my Jin-dae will be the first to fall. By my blade. I will not have her bow before a rebel."

Tae-shin stared at him, and Paekche loosed his hold. There, that shook his hwarang.

Tae-shin gasped, "Give... give me a knife, a small one—in the sack."

His kuksun grinned, a baring of teeth. "No. Let the spirit of the tiger and Seon and the gods take revenge for your disloyalty—or your god uphold your tongue and your offer, son of mine."

His men turned Tae-shin and bound his hands at his back. The guard with the halberd looked at him in question, and Paekche lifted his chin. His guard kicked Tae-shin behind the knees and watched him fall.

He assured himself that his guards had fastened his hwarang's hands tight behind him to his bound ankles. They contained Tae-shin as a murderer. Paekche scowled. This unpropitious hour robbed him of two hwarang masters.

Ryu Tae-shin lay on his side quietly, limbs bent back. They fastened the last cord around his neck, with slack to breathe only if he did not struggle. They slid the rough sack that one guard brought up around his knees, over his bound ankles and hands, and up toward his neck, carefully not looking at his face.

"Honored one." Tae-shin's voice was low but strong, and the men paused. "Tell my hwarang—remember your oath."

The guard with the moon-blade glanced at his kuksun. Paekche snorted a bitter laugh. "He swore them to 'Follow the good, follow the light, for wife and son, for kuksun and king. For Silla.' And then he betrays us. He is dead."

His guards looked at one another. Those words would get to Tae-shin's hwarang faster than they cast him outside the gate. Paekche's hand constricted, the medallion cold to his fingers.

His son-in-law closed his eyes. The sack slid over his head and was stitched with thick cord. The sacking against Tae-shin's face fluttered evenly, but Paekche smelled sweat. He shrugged, though his shoulders felt a burden of bronze.

The rebel Jin-ho knew well the craft of a thousand cuts. Small cuts, given with a sharp edge, cuts that bled slowly, with much pain. Yet the wounds could heal and the questioning go on for days, seasons, even years at the skilled torturer's desire, until he gained the desired end. Paekche sighed soundlessly and stroked his chin. Should he thrust a blade through the sack? No, he shook his head. He had spoken.

Only one so skilled could fall so far. Though treacherous, Tae-shin had trained his hwarangdo well. With the two traitors gone from their midst and none to lead them into further dishonor, he would not punish the rest of the hwarang. There was a chance Ryu Tae-shin might succeed in his fall. Kuksun Kim Paekche gripped his medallion until it pained his bones. His voice carried the cold of first snow. "Even in death, a hwarang should fight for his kuksun and his land." Perhaps he and Jin-dae and the house of Kim would survive their loss of face.

It remained to be seen if Kuksun Jeong Jin-ho would take the bait.

§

Tae-shin forced himself to keep his breath long, to slow his pounding heart. He would need his strength if he made it to the gate, past his men who would seek to save him from dishonor with a quick strike. All things were possible with the Master of the stars. There was fear, despair, and death to fight—and many ways to fight them—with breath and blade, heart and hope. He was never alone. He drew it to him.

Life was the aim of the arrow, not death, though the path of a warrior was never certain. Was that not what every hwarang fought for, the life of others? Jin-dae would understand. *My Huen, you know my heart.* His people were worth his death and his life.

If his message reached Jeong Jin-ho, if he proved the kuksun he thought him, then his arrival would seal his offer. If Jin-ho took it, he would seek the city the Master of the stars walked in his mortal form before those of the Roman Eagles killed him.

§

They dropped Tae-shin over the wall. He fell, tried to curl his body within the ropes to roll, and hit hard. His shoulder and hip ached savagely, but after a moment, nothing felt broken. The chuckling rush of the rill beside him told him the woods lay a few bow shots distant, where he knew lace-leafed maples and oaks clothed the hills that rose toward the piney mountains. A bird twittered.

The rebel kuksun's men would be before the trees as they had been when the sun set, tents and flags bright, men eating and laughing around their fires, pausing to jeer at the hungry watchers on the wall, their wagons of spears and scaling ladders drawn up behind the orderly horse lines, all waiting.

Tae-shin rolled over.

There was a shout above him and raised voices. He shivered, suddenly cold. One of his hwarang had seen him taken, or a guard had given them his last message. He hoped so. The strength of his offer lay in the hearts of his hwarang, in the truth of their oaths.

"Here is a gift for the Kuksun Jeong Jin-ho!" The shout rang out above him.

Silence. At last, feet pounded close. Someone grabbed the end of the sack beyond his bent knees. The wall above was quiet. There was a tug, and then he was moving.

Blind, Tae-shin slid rapidly backward over stones and earth on his stomach. An unexpected stick could stab through the sack and gut him, tied as he was. He twisted swiftly. Facing up, all his weight on his legs and bound elbows under him, he grunted, half strangled by the neck rope as they pulled him over a wet log. The wood scraped his ankles, then caught the back of his head as he thumped down.

He had to protect his head, though it meant he stayed on the edge of choking. He curled upward against the steady pull of the sack, despite the pain of his bound limbs. There was a roar of voices ahead, growing above the din from the wall behind.

The panting men who dragged him changed direction several times as they ran, likely to evade arrows. Tae-shin struggled for balance and for air. He did not know if his hwarang were shooting, for he heard nothing over the sound of running feet, the swish of grass, and the blood thundering in his ears.

An interminable age later, the pull on his sack abruptly ceased. His knees slammed to earth, caught, and he rocked forward to his belly, choking helplessly against the rope around his neck until he could get his head up. He gasped for air, which sucked the rough sacking against his mouth. Fire smoke was thick in his nose, voices called, and many feet drew near. He tried to relax his limbs where he could and reached out with every sense.

Against the glow of dawn sifting through the woven sack, the shadow of a hand closed on it near his face and jerked up, lifting him tight against his bonds yet again. He struggled to stay on his knees and tipped his head back as far as possible, arching his spine.

A blade thrust through the cloth near his throat and ripped downward, a line of fire where the point nicked his chest. He sucked in his stomach instantly but knew the steel was slicing down toward his thighs. Shoving hard against the earth, Tae-shin threw himself forward, twisting his shoulder into the dagger-wielder's arm. There was a sharp exclamation, the arm caught beneath him, then the blade jerked as it dug into the dirt, and the man holding it pulled free.

Tae-shin rolled over twice and stopped, again arching his head back. He could not feel the cord at his throat, only a mass of burning pressure. Too little air made it past his swelling neck. He was a trussed chicken.

But that knife had not been meant to kill. The one holding it was only careless. But he did wish for children, and so did Jin-dae. Tae-shin opened his mouth wider but felt himself sag, then his whole body convulsing after air. Many hands were on him now. Several cut the sack away.

He was able to draw a breath and blinked at a circle of curious faces and warriors' knots. He caught the plumed crest of a hwarang master's helm. He stared at the man, determined not to break his gaze, but his sight was dimming. The man reached behind Tae-shin's head with his dagger. There was a tug, and Tae-shin's throat bond was gone. He breathed deep, twice, his throat burning, and shakily looked up at the hwarang.

Without taking his sharp scrutiny from Tae-shin, the hwarang master ordered, "Young-sool, ask our honored Kuksun Jeong Jin-ho if he wishes to inspect a gift from Kuksun Kim Paekche."

"Yes, Master Choi." Young-sool bowed and dashed away.

His lined face stern, the hwarang master beckoned. "You, bring the archers."

"Who is he?" asked another young hwarang beside Master Choi. He held a dagger at his side, bits of earth still clinging to it.

Tae-shin said nothing, unsure if he could speak, but Master Choi plucked the dagger from the hwarang and pushed him away. "Do you not see he is a master hwarang? Other men cannot bend their bodies to save themselves so tied that way. If you are careless again, your blade will be his."

Tae-shin inclined his head, and a wry smile tugged at his lips. He could like this man.

Master Choi nodded to him. "I would cut the ropes, but I am not sure of *them.*" He jerked his head to indicate the wall. Tae-shin saw that the men who dragged him from the base of the gate had stopped short of the rebel's camp, just at the edge of a long bow shot. Someone still breathed hard behind him. Tae-shin refrained from turning his head; he would not have them think him uncertain or fearful. But now he could watch his brothers.

Hwarang and other men and women lined Kim Paekche's wall, heads and shoulders visible, shielding their eyes against the early sun under the flapping pennants. The tip of a bow moved beside one head, and there were other archers behind him.

Tae-shin stiffened. His hwarang were not there with bows to cut down the rebel kuksun's man who brought him to his master, but to assure his sentence if Master Choi did not take his offer. If he failed, he was twice dead.

"Kuksun Kim Paekche tests us." The hwarang master's voice was soft, his dark gaze certain as he watched Tae-shin.

"Yes, he tests us. Guard your kuksun, Master Choi."

The hwarang's jaw tightened, and his hand rested on his sword. "My kuksun guards his own choices."

Did Paekche think of bringing his enemy down with a long shot? But hwarang Master Choi must guard against that; he'd warned him. Blood could only be avoided if they kept their hearts strong against fear. And if one kuksun of the two yielded to the right.

The dizziness was passing, and his limbs seemed to have survived the headlong course away from his kuksun's gate, though he ached in every muscle. Tae-shin gritted his teeth. If he convinced Jeong Jin-ho to honor his word that any who surrendered would go free, would Paekche let him go into exile without an arrow through him? His breath caught, then he stiffened at the thud of quick steps behind him. But Master Choi took no undue notice, so Tae-shin relaxed as the hwarang gave a hand signal to a bowman, out of breath, who slid around Tae-shin to bow respect to his master hwarang.

The archers formed a straight line, but not between Tae-shin and the wall. They purposefully left him open to fire from both sides.

"Honorable Kuksun!" came the call. Silence fell, except for a muffled, steady shout from the wall. Tae-shin repressed a wild grin and rocked up to a strange position, balanced on his knee-caps, his shoulders pulling painfully against his bonds. He would not grovel unless forced. Master Choi let him rise as he could, a hand still on his blade.

The lines of hwarang, servants, and lesser soldiers gathered between the tents bowed like a swathe of wheat, arms and armor reflecting the dawn-streaked, golden sky.

Kuksun Jeong Jin-ho walked between them, robed in pale blue, cream, and silver, regal and graceful as a crane. His long face held more of a scholar's thoughtfulness than a warrior's hard strength. He stopped, shielded by a half circle of his archers, and stared down at Tae-shin. Unlike a scholar, his eyes were hot and brown and sharp. His mouth was a flat, thin line.

Master Choi stepped behind Tae-shin, his dagger in his hand.

Tae-shin froze. He would not flatter or beg. He inclined his head, his voice rasping. "Kuksun Jeong Jin-ho." He dared no more.

There were enough weapons out among the men around him. He was too dangerous for them not to be ready. He clenched his hands in his bonds. He knew ways to kill with more than a hundred weapons, with anything that came to hand, or with nothing.

The kuksun looked over Tae-shin's head and nodded. Master Choi gripped Tae-shin's shoulder from behind. They might execute him. Tae-shin's neck tingled. It was their right. But he could not waver. He stared straight at Jin-ho. He had chosen. He was hwarang.

"Is it Master Cho or Master Ryu I speak with?"

Tae-shin almost choked. Fool! Of course, the kuksun did not know him from Master Cho, with his dishonorable offer of advantage. It was a precarious position, being sent to an enemy as a criminal and an ambassador with a lesser offer. He inclined his head, careful of his balance. His knees hurt. "Honorable Kuksun, I am hwarang Master Ryu Tae-shin, as you say."

There was a pressure against his wrists. His bonds parted. His shoulders rolled forward, and his feet thumped to the earth. Tae-shin drew a deep, free breath, lifted his hands slowly to rest on his knees, then sat back on his heels and bowed.

Jeong Jin-ho's mouth pursed. "I am glad you are not Master Cho. I do not approve of traitors." He grinned suddenly. "Hwarang Master Ryu Tae-shin, I find myself curious. You sent me such well-ordered terms of surrender. Is it not so? You spoke of an offer, an offer that will avoid wasting the blood of men, to encourage the spirit of generosity, which you say will honor the life of our land and our ancestors' memory." The rebel kuksun cocked his head.

Ha-nuel's message had reached him. Tae-shin's heart eased. He did not think Paekche had killed his student, or he would have twisted that knife. He bowed his head, giving full respect. "Yes, Kuksun Jeong Jin-ho."

"Yet, you arrive bound as a murderer." Jin-ho watched him with suspicion. He was no fool.

Holding his gaze, Tae-shin rose, conscious of Master Choi at his back. On his feet, he said, "Master Cho sought to unlawfully take the lives of those he swore to protect. I killed him. My kuksun did not believe my offer to you honorable. He sent me as one dead to him."

"Ah." The early morning wind stirred the grass. "Do you now come to cut the head from the snake and regain your place with honor?"

"To speak with a crooked tongue is not honor. I await your answer on your terms that you will free any man who surrenders."

"You trust my straight tongue?"

He could protest it was so or speak of advantages. But it was enough. "I am hwarang." Tae-shin looked at his brothers on the wall, then back at Jin-ho. "It would be needless blood, shed for nothing."

"I see. They will not open the gate unless I accept your bloodless surrender." The kuksun frowned.

Tae-shin bowed again. "We humbly wait for your decree. As for the gate, I could not let Master Cho destroy us and you. My hwarang do not give way easily. Many of your men would fall."

He fought back a cough. Now was the time to gather words of advantage beyond his pain. "Kuksun Jeong Jin-ho, there is another way I did not speak of. Seek the king for your stolen lands. My hwarang will work hard at your command under an edict from the king. All men now find you wise and generous. My kuksun cannot deny it. I do not wish to deny it. If you honor your word, they will call you prosperous. For you will gift the king's people with life and nourish the generosity of peace. My—kuksun will be grateful not to take his daughter's life, in fear of her dishonor." Tae-shin's sweat dripped down his face. "There can be life instead of death."

Jin-ho's face hardened. "So your kuksun finds you without value and gifts you to me, a traitor who follows the wind of advantage. Where is his honor? Where is yours?"

The rebel also believed him ambitious. Tae-shin swallowed back the sudden anger and sorrow that rose to choke him. He clenched his hands. "My kuksun's honor is his own. I chose life for my people instead of my kuksun's command, instead of honorable death." His crime hung in the air. It took him a moment to get out his next words. "In his eyes, my offer of surrender without battle is treason, given by a hwarang without honor. I may not return to them."

"So, you will not be there to assure they keep the peace." Jeong Jin-ho stared at him for a moment. "Should not each man have what is his? The burial ground has been in the care of the house of Jeong since my grandfather's father. Is it not just that it is returned to us without appeal to the new king for what is rightfully ours?"

"Just, it may be. Merciful, it would not be. Better our rich goods and crops that we make go to you, who are generous, than to pay lord death with every life within our walls."

Jin-ho said, slow and studied, "You have not yet told me where your honor lies, and your student let slip something of a Master of the stars you follow. Do you not forge your destiny?" It was warning, question, and challenge, with more curiosity behind it than he had shown before.

Hot blood rose in Tae-shin, and gave him grace to go on. "Our creator, who forbids murder, gives me my honor and bids me to defend the defenseless. In him is no dishonor. He holds my destiny."

Jin-ho lifted his brow. "This changes our agreement." He waited, silent.

Tae-shin looked at him. "What do you wish?"

"I have not yet decided. It depends on you."

He was down again to his life, with nothing else to give. *I am hwarang.* He grasped for breath to speak. "All that is honorable,

I will do. But if you mean to refuse my offer, I ask one thing. Do not let me go. Kill me here. You do not wish to try to hold me, and another's life rests on my sentence if you release me and still attack." Out of breath and words, he did not say it was a thin chance his Huen would see another sunrise. He did not say he would prevent all questions from the knife one way or the other. "You may tell them I asked it. I would count it your greatest mercy." *Huen, may you not be on the wall.*

"Do you give up so easily?"

"No. I aim for life. It would please me if no blood were spilled this morn." He paused. "What may I do for you?"

Jin-ho looked at him without expression. He turned his back and walked to his lead archer, who stood a little apart, beckoning Master Choi to follow.

With a sharp look for Tae-shin and a motion to the archers to cover him, the hwarang master left him and approached his kuksun. Their words were indistinguishable.

Tae-shin trembled as he waited. He had tried to be honest, to speak the best he could. He must trust the Master of the stars now.

A respectful distance from his kuksun, Young-sool led up a mount with a deep red coat, a black mane and tail, and a solid build. A good horse for an archer, it was saddled and armed with a sword and bow. Tae-shin looked it over. The beast was well-cared for and gleamed in the sun.

Jeong Jin-ho turned to look at the wall while the lead archer bowed at a soft command from his kuksun and spun to speak rapid words to his second. The council was over.

Tae-shin's gaze snapped back to the rebel's face. There was one thing he had forgotten. "If I must, and our honor is not satisfied otherwise, you will find me between you and the wall."

Jeong Jin-ho blinked, then tipped back his head and laughed in pure delight. "Ah, a man who is true chin-gol, translucent as the rarest jade. I do wonder, does your kuksun know what he has lost?" He stepped close, abruptly earnest. "Will you serve me?"

Tae-shin shut his eyes. It was the one thing he could not do. He shoved back his anger. "I sorrow," he said, with a small bow. "I may not. I became hwarang of the bone ranks when my father was elevated from head-rank five to true-bone. I must follow in his steps as chin-gol, for my hwarang follow me. I cannot divide their hearts from their kuksun." He did not wish to offer again to do something else, not for this kuksun.

Jin-ho smiled, and it was an open smile at last. He nodded with satisfaction. "Let this man who serves our people go free, and take our request to our king."

It was Tae-shin's turn to blink. It had been a test. Inside, he reeled as if from a blow. When he overcame the surprise, his mouth turned up on one side. Jin-ho neatly ambushed him with a distraction. He freed him in one breath, only to take his message to the king in the next. Tae-shin inclined his head. It was well.

Master Choi glanced at the departing archer, just mounting the red horse, and moved toward Tae-shin with a smile. Two steps from him, he sprang, his dagger driving straight for Tae-shin's belly.

Tae-shin's hands came up on instinct. He swept aside the blow and grabbed the man's arm to break it. Master Choi dropped his blade and countered the grab. It gave him a small opening he was slow to take advantage of.

Tae-shin was not.

In an instant, he was at the hwarang master's back, securing a chokehold that cut off blood and breath, keeping Master Choi's body between him and the archers. The man's entire body was tense, but he did not resist. His knees weakened almost at once. Tae-shin hesitated. It seemed almost purposeful.

Jeong Jin-ho threw up his arm. "Cease!"

Every man around them lowered their weapons. Tae-shin loosened his grip the barest bit.

Master Choi coughed. Under his breath, he said, "My kuksun agrees to your offer. Take the horse; go to the king." Before Tae-shin could think of an answer, the master hwarang sagged, slipping down through Tae-shin's hold. He came up lightning quick with a flat-palmed blow to Tae-shin's chest and a kick to his stomach that pushed them fiercely apart. They were solid blows expertly applied without harm. A wild joy and fear rose in Tae-shin.

This man would keep his kuksun's word. He fought him in full view of the wall so they would witness his dislike of his kuksun's decision to let the house of Kim surrender peacefully. Life was in sight.

Jin-ho's yelling archers had half-drawn their bows, confused, for Master Choi was in the way, protecting his kuksun. Tae-shin was already moving between him and Kuksun Jeong Jin-ho. He looked deep into Master Choi's eyes as he passed and bowed his head. Here was a man he would not mind calling brother if things had been different. He gave Kuksun Jeong Jin-ho a hwarang salute. The kuksun returned it.

Young-sool lunged at him, and Tae-shin knocked the dagger from his hand. He cuffed his head to teach him wisdom and caution, careful not to strike too hard. Master Choi stepped a beat behind Tae-shin and also cuffed Young-sool. Then the horse was before Tae-shin. The lead archer lifted his bow.

Ryu Tae-shin gathered every muscle. With a spinning leap, arms up to protect his head, he swept the bow aside with one forearm, momentum never slowing, and kicked the archer from his seat. Then Tae-shin sprawled across the horse's saddle, fumbling for a stirrup.

One foot was solid, then the other. He heard the slap of a blow on its rump, and the horse threw up its head and sprang into a gallop.

An arrow whistled past. Tae-shin leaned forward, urging the beast on. The stream was ahead. He glanced back under his arm.

"Hold! Do not stain my honor!" Their kuksun's bellowed command was sure to be heard clearly on the other side of the wall. Men milled about rebel Jeong Jin-ho, who stood tall and still, a protective hand on his hwarang master's shoulder, his lead archer on his other side, his bow resting upright before him. Just so, a kuksun made it clear he could have killed him, but did not.

Hwarang Ryu Tae-shin rode parallel to the wall. As his mount pounded past, Paekche's guards had their weapons ready, arrows on the string. None fired. Some hwarang pointed, others called to each other. A chant rose. "Ryu Tae-shin! Ryu Tae-shin! Kuksun Kim Paekche and Kuksun Jeong Jin-ho!" It was his two hundred, yelling in unison, lifting their bows in triumph.

His hwarangdo served Kuksun Kim Paekche and his family. They would protect and watch over their people. They would find the traitor among them. It was their answer. Tae-shin raised his arm. One kuksun cast him out, and another kept his word. Trust was forged. It was a beginning.

A moment more, and Tae-shin threaded his horse through the maples. Using all his craft, he rode into the damp forest, then higher into the clean-smelling pines. At last, far out of hearing of any who might follow, he wended just below the crest of a mountain ridge, down through a valley, then across a cold, fast river. The horse stumbled, and Tae-shin gripped hastily at the saddle. His hand closed on a message case.

At the nearest quiet messenger post he judged safe, Tae-shin left the lathered horse in the trees. Dismounting, he tucked the message case into his tunic over his heart. He stripped the saddle, with the bow, quiver, and sword from the beast, along with its bridle and a forgotten bag of rice cakes.

The first horse that strayed near the back of the red-roofed messenger post where he concealed himself was his. He walked it into the cover of the trees. None saw him.

Far enough away that a gallop would not be heard, he swung up, the bow across his back. The bundle of war arrows he bound near his knee. His neck ached, as did the rest of him. It was nothing to the pain within.

Tae-shin nudged the fresh horse on. He would petition the king with Kuksun Jeong Jin-ho's request and return with the king's answer. Then, after he gained the shores of the Yellow Sea, he would hire passage with those of Araby for the desert lands, half a world away. Many men surely had need of a warrior, a healer, even a scribe. They would pay him well on his way to Jerusalem.

Kuksun Kim Paekche would honor the terms he had fashioned, with loyalty to the king the binding glue between him and Jeong Jin-ho. Jeong Jin-ho would be a rebel no longer when Tae-shin returned with the word of their king.

His brothers could still break the fragile peace and make an end in fire and arrows, blades and blood. But this day, his Master of the stars divided hearts and men and found him worthy to stand in the gap for his people. Tae-shin's heart beat hard and fast. He was near to tears.

To seek to go back would be to drive his own weapon through his heart. The sword he prayed Jin-dae now held. He would miss that keen edge and willing balance. He rubbed his face, casting his anxiety on the Master of All. He was weary to his bones.

Surely Jin-dae would not curse his name. He could not know if he'd left her with a child. She loved his sister's daughter and son. The pain was swallowing him, inside and out.

He looked up into the blue sky between the trees ahead. *Be with her, Master of All. Give her a son, or a daughter. Let her not forget me.*

He let the pain roll over him, breathing through it. The unseasonable clouds of the night were retreating into the east after the warm rain where the tiger walked. Already the frost closed in, riming his hair. Behind him, within the wall, every house would have its fire.

Jin-dae would order the furnace under the floor stoked for the evening hour. He would not feel that warmth radiate through his feet, her soft arms slide around him, or smell the peony oil in her long black hair. He could not watch her smile creep across her face, teasing him for training late. Tae-shin gripped the missive under his tunic.

The aim of the arrow. They would live. His path was uncertain. He was an exile. And he was hwarang. *My Huen, wait for me. I will return.*

§

*His memories held darkness and light, despair and courage.*

*The aim of the arrow led him far into the mists of Britannia.*

*There three souls were by fire, murder, and love bound.*

*There the tiger chased one 'round, till a falcon's courage rode the beast to ground.*

*In truth, meaning was found, and memory came round.*

*So life does astound, for their tale with endless purpose was wound.*

*-Kyrin Cieri first daughter of Cierheld 900s Britannia*

# Other Books 1

**First daughter. First enemy. First escape.**

Noblebright YA Fantasy
Strong heroes and heroines
Adventure in far lands
Stories you don't want to end

In Falcon Chronicle 1, slavers seize Kyrin from the coast of Britannia and sail for Araby. With a dagger from her murdered mother's hand, an exiled warrior from the East, and a peasant closer than a sister by blood, Kyrin is determined to overcome her fear of the blade and escape. But the falcon dagger is at the root of intrigue, martial skill, and danger within the caliph's court. It haunts her through dreams of a stalking tiger, love, and battle in the Araby sands.

To defeat her treacherous master and defend those she loves, Kyrin must face the blade that killed her mother. Dagger against sword, love against hate, can she find the courage to overcome?

Falcon Heart is the first Noblebright epic adventure in a teen and young adult fantasy series with threads of medieval mystery, martial art, and multicultural conflict.

# Other Books 2

**One disguise. One usurper. One defense.**

In Falcon Chronicle 2, Kyrin, the long lost first daughter of her stronghold, returns to Britannia from slavery in Araby. But the wazir seeks the power of the death touch at any cost, and Kyrin's adopted father refuses to give him the deadly knowledge. When the wazir takes him hostage, Kyrin and her sister rescue him and flee into the desert. Then Kyrin departs for Britannia alone to lift the price from their heads.

Yet ambitious lords and the intrigue she left behind in Araby engulf her stronghold. Torn between a lord's son she has sworn never to hand-fast, a rival, and her father's life, Kyrin struggles to save her people and Britannia. Only to discover the falcon dagger is the key to life, death, and a traitor deeper yet. If she does not become who she was born to be, all will end in ash.

Falcon Flight is the second Noblebright YA fantasy adventure in the Falcon Chronicle series, with threads of the supernatural. Love, loyalty, and power collide, marking a clash of cultures.

#Noblebright #Fantasy #Novel #ComingofAge #Fiction #Clean #Christian #YA #nonmagical #Series #YAFantasy #MartialArt #Medieval #Historicalfantasy #Multicultural #Story #TaeKwonDoBooks #FalconChronicleSeries #AzaleaDabill.

# Other Books 2.5

**One refuge. One love. One choice.**

In Falcon Chronicle 2.5, Alaina flees the Caliph's rose perfume and court gardens to seek refuge with a prince of the sands.

Disguised as an apprentice healer to an exiled warrior, Alaina tends an ailing sheik. But the prince pierces her deception and soon has her scribing for him. Struggling to be worthy of his grandfather's seat, Prince Faisal has enemies Alaina would gladly shield him from.

But she must keep her identity hidden, even as she faces Faisal's rival. Falling in love with a prince she is not worthy of, Alaina falls yet again to his rival's cunning schemes. For a traitor lurks in the Oasis of Oaths.

When enemies converge, Alaina must break the webs of deceit. Can she put down her quill and healer's bag to take up the staff of war before it is too late? Will the girl who desired a scribe's cushion in the caliph's court find richer things than rosewater and immortal poetry in the sands? Lance and Quill is a young adult Noblebright fantasy with threads of sweet romance and mystery. Here cultures clash and teens come of age in an epic adventure featuring martial arts and a lady of battle.

# Falcon's Ode

**Fierce cry, in the sky, wild and high. Echo my heart's cry.**

An epic poem in the medieval style, Falcon's Ode journeys from capture and the depths of slavery to heights of freedom through a grand adventure. This poetry companion book to the Falcon Chronicle can be read as a stand-alone or with the Noblebright young adult fantasy series it depicts in epic verse.

Far must we hie, to seek the land without a sigh.
There curse of evil eye
and black ring of slavery in my ear will die.
The wazir's Hand pursues us across Araby sand and sky,
for the touch of death, my sister and I,
hunts my second father, who keeps the secret close by.

Fierce cry, in the sky, wild and high, echo my heart's cry.

# Fantastic Journey

**The best gems lie hidden.**

The secret soul of imaginative fiction broadens our horizons and enthralls our hearts with enchanting beauties on a voyage through a perilous realm.

Fantasy adventure benefits us in three areas: The spiritual arena, the wide world of ideas, and the sphere we breathe in.

The soul of imaginative fiction conveys secrets deeper than sand and sea. It breathes into being lands nearer than we know. It shows us the adventure of love in all its facets, and carries truth from mere thought and experience to our heart's grasp.

*Fantastic Journey – The Soul of Speculative Fiction and Fantasy Adventure* is a non-fiction guide to the ocean of fantasy.

Vast lands of mystery and danger await every adventurer seeking riches, yearning for jewels of strong and precious story. Dive for treasures untold for yourself, your family, and your friends.

When the dive is done, what precious things from the deeps will you bring to light? The best gems lie hidden.

Will you find that which is the wealth of souls?

# Story Chat

*If you have read other Falcon Chronicle books, how did this book's look into the deeper intrigue around the Damascus blade and the falcon dagger influence how you see people and their choices? How do you think of facing conflicting choices in your life?

*At first, brother Rolf does not want to face what he thinks of himself. How do you know this? What does Father Ulf do that affects brother Rolf? How does Rolf overcome what both he and Father Ulf think of him? How does their relationship change throughout the story?

*What does Rolf do that makes Seldon see him differently? How is their relationship better from the beginning than Rolf's with Father Ulf?

*After Berd leaves Cierheld, he and Celine encounter many adversaries. Who? What does each enemy teach them? How do they grow closer, and know they love each other? Have you ever had an adversary who taught you something? Or a friend? What was it?

*Does this book make you want to learn martial art yourself? What do you want to see in a good teacher of martial art or anything else? Can a person learn while they teach another? Do you want to teach something? If so, what?

*Have you ever been assigned to something that led to something else, and neither ended how you thought it would? What is Kyrin's goal in the book, and what did her patient perseverance lead to, though she did not have a starring role?

*One theme in this story is about pursuing a good place in life. How does Henges find his "good place"? Does it change? What makes his ending place good? What is good about your present place? Think of three things you can do in your place to make it better, and help others live in their "good place".

*Another thread of the story is leadership. In his story at the end of the book, how does Tae lead, despite being a captive? How do you feel about leading? Have you ever had to lead when you didn't want to? Can you think of some good ways you can lead others, and help them make good choices?

*Different beliefs about who God is and who we are, become apparent in *Falcon Dagger.* In the story, who is God to us, and who are we to Him?

*There is also a thread of poetry throughout the Falcon Chronicle series. Does the free flight of the falcon and its wild cry carry meaning? What does it stand for, fly for, and rise for? Hint: Read Falcon's Ode. Can you think of two meanings the falcon holds?

Ever since I was a girl I have loved the call of hawks, so wild, pure, and beautiful. Pure in the sense that they never pretend to be something they are not. This adds to their strength and

beauty. I hope you grow up into the same freedom.

# Readers

My dear reader,
What adventure will you find in your life?
What will you dare to overcome?
What truth will you hold to?

Join me. Find what lasts, and never let go.

Whoever believes in Him will not be disappointed.
—Romans 10:11

Thank you for reading this book. I am excited and so blessed to have a reader like you!

If you enjoyed this book or another in the Falcon Chronicle series, would you be willing to share your honest opinion with other readers? Leaving a short review at your retailer or on your favorite book platform can make the difference between success and failure for an independent author.

I'm present on all the most common platforms. Not named here for fear of treading on the giant's toes.

We appreciate your support! Reviews are such an important part of the publishing process. This author couldn't do it without you!

Thank you,
Azalea Dabill
Crossover – Find the Eternal, the Adventure.

# Glossary

* These terms and names span the world of the Chronicle. Not every book will have every word. Mispronunciations and mistakes are my own. For easier pronunciation I have reduced some words to phonetic spelling. May contain slight spoilers. Enjoy the adventure!

**Britannia:**

*Armsman*—"Arms-mun" a lord's sworn man who protects the lord's person and stronghold

*Bells*—Lauds "Lawds" (just before dawn), Prime (just after daybreak), Terce "Terse" (third hour), Sext (sixth hour), Nones "Nons" (ninth hour), Vespers (eleventh hour), Matins (just after midnight)

*Britannia*—"Bri-tan-ee-uh" ancient name for Britain

*Brooch*—"Broach" a pin often worn in pairs, used for cloaks

*Death touch*—Possible with a strong man trained in Subak—a death thought to be brought by a single blow. Most often the culmination of several deadly nerve points or blows

*Eagles*—"E-gulls" an ancient name for Romans

*Evil eye*—Ali believes Kyrin can bring evil with her dark stare and brands her with a jet earring in her ear, besides his bronze ring of ownership in her other ear

*Eyas*—"Ee-ass" a young falcon in the nest

*Eyrie*—"Ear-ee" a falcon's nest high on a cliff

*Falcon, Peregrine*—"Pear-uh-grin" the bird Kyrin loves, which draws her to follow the Master of the stars

*Falcon dagger*—a mysterious dagger shaped like a falcon that Kyrin finds hidden in a cloak on her murdered mother's breast

*Girdle*—"Gir-dul" a kind of belt for women, often braided of leather or linen

*Hose*—like leggings but for men, usually fastened by cross garters attached to leather shoes

*Mantle*—"Man-tul" a woman's wrap, with a central hole for the head, like a poncho

*Stronghold key*—a large key that signifies authority over a stronghold. Women often wore them on their girdles

*Tunic*—"Tune-ick" a medieval shirt-like or robe-like garment worn by men and women, worn over an under-garment or shirt, often of linen, flowing to the knee for men and the feet for women

**Names of important characters:**

*Aart*—"A-art" Kyrin's horse, means like an eagle

*Alaina Ilen*—"A-lay-nuh I-len" Kyrin's peasant sister, closer than blood, means one who harmonizes, noble, stone

*Aunt Medaen*—"Ma-day-en" her father's tart-tongued sister, who Kyrin hears in her head more than she'd like

*Father Annis*—"Ann-iss" an important monk who opposes Kyrin

*Brother Rolf*—"Rawl-f" a sympathetic monk who plays a part in Cierheld's fate

*Father Ulf*—Kyrin's uncle, pivotal to events in Falcon Flight

Berd—a young armsman in training who becomes Kyrin's armsman

*Celine Loring*—"Suh-lean Lore-ing" a childhood friend who antagonizes Kyrin. I liked the name for a red-haired girl

*Etain*—"E-tain" Alaina's mare in Araby, means fairy

Esther—a stronghold daughter, and Kyrin's beautiful rival

*Cernalt*—“Sir-nalt” an old armsman and hawkmaster to Lord Dain Cieri

*Dain Cieri*—“Dane Si-eery” Kyrin’s father. His name fit the time and place, to my mind

*Willa*—“Will-a” Kyrin’s mother. The connotations of the name fit her gentle strength

*Elinor*—Kyrin’s stepmother in honor of Sam’s Elinore in LOTR. It sounded right

*Gwenich*—“Gwen-itch” the saluki pup that Alaina gives Kyrin, means blessed

*Hal Loring*—Celine’s father and Kyrin’s first student in Britannia

*Kyrin Cieri*—“Kai-rin Si-eery” I liked the sound, the name reminds me of dark hills, Celtic times, and Elizabeth Moon’s Paksenarrion

*Lord Bergrin Jorn*—“Bur-grin Jorn” Myrna’s brother, who holds Kyrin captive for a time, and is an ally in war

*Lord Ludwin Mornoth*—“Lud-win More-noth” who is Cierheld and the strongholds’ nemesis

*Lord Nidfael Keffer*—“Nid-fi-el Keff-er” Mornoth’s second in command, and Kyrin’s nemesis

*Meric*—“Mare-ick” Kyrin’s stepbrother. His name fits his scholarly bent and nature

*Myrna Jorn*—“Mur-nuh” Kyrin’s friend, means tender

*Nell Trinley*—a girl with mismatched eyes that Kyrin rescues, who becomes a healer

*Nith Nulduin*—an armsmaster, first in command of Cierheld in Falcon Flight

*Ragad*—“Ra-gad” shipmaster of the Howler, Sirius Abdasir’s ship that brings Kyrin on her task to find Hamal

*Seliam*—“See-li-am” the wazir’s slave, an askar who threatens everyone Kyrin loves in Falcon Heart

*Sirius Abdasir*—“Sear-ee-us Ab-duh-sir” wazir to the caliph, who holds the secret of the falcon dagger and threatens to destroy Kyrin and all of Cierheld

*Talik*—“Tal-ick” a messenger between the strongholds who rescues Kyrin, loves and quarrels with her

*The Master of the stars*—the meaning of this name is for you to discover

*Wolf-ship warrior*—another name for a Viking

*White Christer*—a Viking’s name for one who follows Christ

§

**Araby/Arabia:**

*Aba*—“Ab-uh” an Arabian women’s cloak

*Aneza*—“A-nez-uh” a tribe of Araby people in Kyrin’s world

*Askar*—“Ass-car” means fighter, warrior

*Bisht*—“Bi-shit” an Arabian men’s cloak

*Bedu/Bedouin*—“Bed-du” or “Bed-o-in” a name for those who live in the desert

*Caliph*—“Kal-iph” Araby ruler in Baghdad

*Dalil*—“Dal-lil” a caravan guide, often across the desert

*Djinn*—“Jin” jinn, genie, jinni

*Empty Quarter*—Al Ramlah, the ocean of sand south and inland of the coastal mountains

*Hattah*—“Hat-tah” the desert women’s light head covering. Not a veil, though it can be used to cover the face

*Kaffiyeh*—“Ca-fi-yuh” Araby men’s head covering

*Mahr*—“Marr” a desert maiden’s dowry, often precious metal anklets, bracelets, and coins sewn into a bridal headpiece or veil

*Nargeela*—“Nar-gee-la” a water pipe

*Nasrany*—“Nas-rany” an infidel unbeliever

***Nur-ed-Dam***—"Nur-ed-dom" oath of the Light of Blood, or blood-feud oath

***Reem***—the black-horned gazelle and others of its kind

***Shaheen***—"Sha-heen" Arabic for a falcon, also the name given to Kyrin

***Sheyk***—"Shay-ick" a desert leader of a tribe, such as Gershem Ben Salin of the Twilkets

***Souk***—"Sook" an Araby market

***Thawb***—"Thaw-ub" an Araby tunic

***Twilkets***—"Twil-kets" an enemy tribe until events bring unforeseen secrets to light

***Umar's Hand***—"Oo-mar's Hand" Umar's pack of salukis he trained against their gentle nature to hunt men

***Wadi***—"Wad-ee" a watercourse, usually dry except during the rainy season

***Wazir***—"Wah-zeer" the advisor to the caliph

**Names of important characters:**

*Ali Ben Aidon*—"Ali-ben A-don" Araby slaver, a common Arabic name

***Basimah***—"Bass-i-mah" means one who smiles

***Cicero***—"Siss-er-o" Kyrin and Alaina's saluki, named after a wise man

***Faisal***—"Fie-sel" desert prince of the Twilkets, loves both Kyrin and Alaina. Means a wise, just judge

***Farook***—"Fa-ruke" the wazir's slave forced to betray Alaina, means one who discerns right and wrong

***Gershem Ben Salin***—"Ger-shem Ben Sa-lin" Twilket sheyk and Faisal's grandfather. I liked the name

***Hafiz***—"Ha-feez" first warrior, and Alaina's opponent in Lance and Quill. Means the guardian

***Hala***—"Hall-uh" Sirius Abdasir's daughter, means halo around the moon

***Hamal***—"Ha-mall" the wazir's lost traveler, means gentle as a lamb

***Jachin***—"Ja-chin" Ali's bodyguard and Tae's friend. I liked the sound for a friendly Nubian

***Kentar***—"Ken-tar" caravan guide and Tae's eyes and ears. I liked the name from The Blue Sword

***Mey***—"May" Shahin's wife and Rashid's mother. I liked the sound of the name

***Nara***—"Nar-uh" Umar's Egyptian mother, Ali's cook, and Kyrin's friend in Ali's house, meaning unknown

***Nimah***—"Nim-uh" first to welcome Kyrin and Alaina to Ali's house, means blessing

***Neddra***—"Ned-druh" an Aneza girl who admired Kyrin's falcon dagger, the sound drew me

***Qadira***—"Ka-deer-uh" head concubine in Ali's house, means powerful one

***Rashid***—"Ra-shid" the young sheyk's son, means the well guided

***Sahar***—"Sa-har" Faisal's red saluki, means the dawn

***Sarni***—"Sar-nee" the name a desert prince gives Alaina, means the elevated one

***Shahin***—"Sha-hin" sheyk of the Aneza, shelters Kyrin during the desert war for saving his son, Rashid

***Truthseeker***—the falcon eyas the Aneza tribe gives Kyrin

***Umar***—"Oo-mar" Ali's treacherous and unacknowledged son, means flourishing, long-lived

***Zahir***—"Za-heer" Faisal's stallion, means shining, radiant

***Zoltan***—"Zol-tan" Nimah's brother, means a ruler

§

**Land of the Morning Calm/Korea:**

*Ap bal Chagi*—"Op-ball-chagi" front-kick—a snapping kick that best attacks the groin or stomach

*Barow*—"Ba-row" means return to starting position

*Chin-gol*—"Chin-goal" means true bone. It was one of the highest military ranks after head-rank five.

*Choson*—A name for the early Korean culture, specifically applied in my books to the Silla dynasty.

*Death touch*—death thought to be brought by a single blow. Possible with a strong man trained in Subak, but more often the culmination of several deadly nerve points or blows

*Dwi Chagi*—"Dwee-chagi" a back-kick. The strongest kick, this one stops an attacker like a stone wall

*Hwarang*—"Huh-waa-rang" flowering warrior or leader of 500 to 5,000 hwarangdo—one trained in martial arts, literature, the arts, sciences, and one hundred and eight different weapons

*Jun be*—"June-bee" stance ready for attack. There are several variations

*Kum-sool*—"Come-sool" means sword skill

*Kuksun*—"Kook-sun" a commander or general, a lord who led by example

*Naryu Chagi*—"Nari-yu-chagi" an axe-kick or spinning kick often used to attack enemies on horseback

*Open hand*—attack with the fingers, palm, or knife-edge of the hand to the eyes, temples, neck, etc.

*Pil Sung*—certain victory through courage, strength, and indomitable spirit

*Poomse*—"Poom-say" a sequence of training techniques done in flowing order, often with multiple techniques hidden within

*Hwarangdo*—"Huh-waa-rang-doh" or "Rang-do" a martial art student who learned under a hwarang master and followed Sesokokye

***Seajok***—"Say-jock" a command to begin (the fight, etc.)

***Seon***—"Say-on" Tae-shin or Tae Chisun, after his name was changed—left Seon to follow the Master of the stars, means the way of Zen

***Sesokokye***—"See-sok-o-kye" be loyal to your country, honor your parents, be faithful to your friends, never retreat in battle, use good judgment before killing any living thing.

***Silla***—A dynasty spanning the first century B.C. to 935 A.D. Our story happens around 830 or 840 A.D.

***Subak***—"Soo-bok" a component of Tae-shin's way of the warrior, means hand technique

***Tiger***—a beast of terrible power that haunts Kyrin's dreams

***Yeop Chagi***—"Yee-op chagi" side-kick. This can cripple, used against the knee at an angle

**Names of important characters:**

*Cho Seung*—Tae-shin's treacherous hwarang master, means candle, beginning, or second, and rise or achieve

*Jeong Jin-ho*—"Jee-ong Jin-ho" the rebel kuksun who honors Tae-shin when he is cast outside his clan as a traitor. Means quiet or loyal, and great, brave, heroic, or chivalrous.

*Ha-nuel*—Tae-shin's brave student who carried an essential message for the life of his people, means sky

*Kim Jin-dae*—"Jin-day" the name of Tae-shin/Tae Chisun's wife, means truth, or jewel, and greatness. "Hu-en" (pet name) may be associated with judgement. "Kim" means gold. I liked the sounds of these names

*Kim Paekche*—"Kim Pack-chi" is Tae-shin's father-in-law who exiled him. "Kim" means gold, "Paekche" is thought to mean one hundred crossings

*Ryu Tae-shin*—"Rue Tie-shin" where "Ryu" means willow tree, "Tae-shin" means great, and belief, faith, or trust. He came to be named Tae Chisun "Tie Chee-sun" by his captor, in his exile. Tae (great) is the first name of a grandmaster, Tae Hong Choi. I also liked the sound for a hero's name. Choi, as in Master Choi in Path of the Warrior, means governor of the land and the mountain, or high, superior, lofty

***Young-sool***—means dragon or valiant one, and martial art technique

# About the Author

A reader of epic fantasy and new worlds, Azalea Dabill loves grand adventure and a satisfying, happy ending. Noblebright characters, the fate of the world, and story tension fascinates her. She explores how to shape words so they wield meaning. Every word holds the force of an arrow, shot either for good or ill. A well-placed bolt can protect, defend, and encourage. Every day is a good day to fight for the kingdom!

Her debut Noblebright fantasy novel was released in 2015. When she isn't writing her next magic free series you can find her growing things, raiding bookstores, or hiking the wild.

Her website is the hub for all her books, news, and reader resources. You can get your personalized, signed books from the store and support my writing directly at https://azaleadabill.com/store/

Or find my books at your favorite retailer pretty much wherever books are sold.

You can find me on:

GoodReads: https://www.goodreads.com/azaleadabill

Facebook: https://www.facebook.com/azalea.dabill

Instagram: https://www.instagram.com/azaleadabillauthor/

BookBub: https://partners.bookbub.com/my_books

Twitter: https://x.com/AzaleaDabill

Happy reading!

Azalea

Crossover ~ Find the Eternal, the Adventure

# Acknowledgements

So many wonderful people have assisted me on this writing journey to finish out the series.

First of all, I thank the Lord from Whom all good things flow.

A huge thank you to my family for their support in so many ways.

I also deeply appreciate the early critique and editing advice and encouragement that Mary Buckham gave me on the story Kingdom's Fall, as well as so many others for their teaching, encouragement, and advice at pivotal points.

I could never get far without my Advance Review Author Collaboration group. You know who you are!

I also thank you, my reader, from the bottom of my heart.

*Another magic free series with dragons is in the works. Sign up for my newsletter to keep up to date.

Click here: www.azaleadabill.com if you are reading the ebook, or Google www.azaleadabill.com if you have the print book.

Happy reading!

Azalea

Crossover: Find the Eternal, the Adventure

www.ingramcontent.com/pod-product-compliance
Lightning Source LLC
Chambersburg PA
CBHW020716310726
48979CB00004B/941